SECRETS OF TANORIA: THE CRYSTAL WARRIOR

SECRETS OF TANORIA: THE CRYSTAL WARRIOR

Lori Hyrup

TABLE OF CONTENTS

1

NEW FACES

As Aria walked with long, purposeful strides, her eyes scanned everything. She sensed the beast. A half dozen more steps and she heard the faint but unmistakable ting of crystal. Her lips turned up at the corners.

Aria took three additional strides, and with no further warning, the glimmer worm launched itself from the shadows. A shimmering, liquid-like substance erupted from the small crystal shard at the base of Aria's thumb and instantly solidified into a chiseled crystalline bastard sword. In the same motion, she grasped the weapon and arced her arm around, slicing the vermin in half. The two sections of the creature shattered as they hit the ground.

Aria held her long krusword for a moment longer, relishing the power pulsing from within. Glowing like effulgent lichen found deep in caves, the soft, radiant intensity of the blue-green crystalline blade ebbed and flowed in time with Aria's heartbeat. With reluctance she retracted the weapon, and the sweet sense of its aura dissipated. She frowned at the remains of the worm. How such a tiny thing caused so much trouble was beyond her. Glimmer worms were only a nuisance, but if reports were correct, this one small critter no bigger than a cattle dog, had destroyed three homes, a barn, and several outbuildings and devoured thirty head of prized livestock.

Shrugging to herself, Aria collected all the larger worm fragments. Sane people feared shard beasts and steered clear of them, but they also understood the value of the crystal. Most people who commissioned a kruusta to get rid of shard beasts paid a bit extra to acquire the shards as well. Fragments provided a variety of uses, from jewelry and window glass to fine-edged medical blades. Those who learned to work crystal made a decent living.

Satisfied she had picked up most of the fragments, Aria headed back to where she had tethered Xierex. He always got skittish around the worms, so she had left him behind. The zegu faced down shard drakes without flinching, but these little things made him panic.

Xierex nickered a greeting as Aria approached. She held her hand up to him, allowing him to nudge it affectionately. The distraction failed. His eyes grew wide when he spied the bag, and he snorted in annoyance.

Aria chuckled and shook her head. "Don't worry, the worm is dead." Zegus were intelligent creatures. Some people considered them shard beasts because the development of the species had long ago been influenced by the crystals, but they were still mammals. Despite the crystalline plates of armor that grew along their chest and neck and the sharded horns that decorated their heads, they were warm-blooded, air-breathing, young-nursing mammals. They hated shard beasts just as much as humans did, but not everyone believed in the distinction, not even all the kruustas. Between that, the zegus' intelligence, and their tendency to range in remote regions, few people used them as mounts; horses required less hassle to acquire. Aria alone among the kruustas rode a zegu—one of the things that set her apart from others in her line of work.

Aria fastened the sack containing the worm fragments to the rear of her saddle and climbed up on her loyal companion. With a gentle tap of her boots, they headed back toward Murali, the community that had requested aid to deal with their problem. In her sixty-seven years as a kruusta, Aria had only been called to Murali three times to deal with shard beasts, but as it was on the main road between the coastal city of Summerton and the inner towns and villages within the province of Aelland, she had become well acquainted with the agrarian community.

Kelmer and Wei lingered high in the sky by the time she reached the small village, and the two opposing moons cast irregular shadows on the village's buildings. Aria headed to the Golden Rose to collect her payment from the mayor; he also happened to be the innkeeper.

Voices grew hushed when she entered Murali's largest establishment. As she scanned the packed room, searching for Talmani Domnur, she noticed the people who hid their eyes or faces behind mugs of ale, beneath their hats, or under the hoods of their cloaks. Even after her many years as a kruusta, she still grew annoyed by people's reaction to her. They feared making contact with her luminescent green eyes, a side effect of being a kruusta for so long, as if she would see into their souls and reveal something they did not wish to be known. Aria caught a glimpse of three priests from the Order of the Heart. Each of them wore their telltale yellow-trimmed maroon robes. They were engrossed in conversation and were the only ones who did not duck as her gaze swept across them.

With an inaudible sigh, Aria continued her scan of the room. A series of lanterns set in a wrought iron chandelier hanging from the ceiling and iron-cupped sconces along the red-brushed walls illuminated the common room. Different types of tables divided the space. A stone hearth for keeping the entire place warm in the winter months occupied the right wall. On the far side, opposite the entrance, a well-sanded bar lined with seven different small-sized wooden kegs kept the flow of drink coming to the customers.

Aria located the mayor moving in and out of the kitchen through the door behind the bar. He was a man of average height with wide shoulders, a roundness to his belly, and curly brown hair cut close to his head. He caught her eyes and nodded. The place was bustling with business, so she would need to wait for a while before he could get to her. Aria maneuvered her way toward the only empty table in the establishment, one of the rectangular ones in the far back corner. People sitting at nearby tables shifted uneasily as she lowered herself onto her seat, but at least the volume of the room picked up once again as the customers resumed their previous conversations.

A young girl with large freckles and mousy curls, no more than ten years old, approached her. "Hel-Hello, miss. My fa-father said you are to have whatever you wish."

Aria gave the girl a gentle smile, but that only seemed to make her more nervous. "A light ale, please. What's the main dish tonight?"

"Jurassis swine, spiced taro, and millet, miss."

"I'll have the swine, then."

The girl bowed her head and shuffled off to the kitchen.

Before the serving girl returned with the food, Mayor Domnur stopped by her table. He placed a small leather pouch in front of her and eyed her possessions. "Where are they?" he asked in a low voice.

"Outside on my zegu," Aria said as she opened the pouch and counted the coins within. Satisfied, she looked up at the mayor. "They still need to be cleaned. I didn't think your customers would be appreciative if I brought fresh glimmer worm bits inside while they ate."

"Of course. You're right." The mayor turned away briefly. "Torga!" he bellowed over the din of the tavern chatter.

A scrawny youth with pale blond hair poked his head through the kitchen doorway. "Yes, Father?"

"Go retrieve the shards from the kruusta's zegu."

"Right away, Father."

The boy moved to leave, but Aria jumped to her feet and cleared the room in four strides to intercept him. Her quick movement startled the boy, causing him to stumble backward as she cut him off.

Aria turned to the father. "I should be the one to retrieve them." She peered down at the wide-eyed boy. "You're welcome to come with me. My zegu doesn't know you, and as much as he hates the worm, he may give you a fight if you try to take the sack." The boy nodded.

Aria led the lad out to the stable where the zegu was waiting patiently. Xierex bobbed his head when Aria appeared, but his eyes focused on the boy. Aria untied the brown doeskin sack from the saddle and handed it to the boy. He accepted the bag but so intent was he on staring at Xierex that he almost dropped what he had come to retrieve.

"Do you want to pet him?" Aria asked.

The youth looked both terrified and intrigued. "Will he bite me?"

Aria smiled. "Not with me here, no."

The boy glanced at Aria and then back at Xierex. Childhood curiosity won out, and the youth reached a timid hand out toward Xierex. The zegu leaned his head down to sniff the boy's hand. Xierex snorted and then nudged him with his velvety blue nose.

The boy's eyes grew wide. "He's soft and warm!" he gasped as he scratched gently around Xierex's muzzle.

"Yes, he is."

"Wow, thank you, miss! My friends are not going to believe this!"

"You're welcome. Now, why don't you take those shards to your father?"

"I will. Thank you again!" The boy hefted the sack over his shoulder and sprinted out through the back entrance of the stables.

Aria returned to her table in the inn, pleased to find that her ale had arrived, if not the food. People no longer stared at her from under their hats and hands. In fact everyone seemed to be acting normal, as if she was just another villager. She wondered if the mayor had said something to them.

Aria sipped at her ale, savoring the light lingering tang of lemon— unmistakably, Ralo Swiftwater Ale. The village of Ralo always made excellent ale. Aria closed her eyes and allowed the din of the common room chatter to wash over her. As she did, individual conversations resolved into focus.

"That's such a shame about Niradan's shipment," said a voice, older and masculine. "His entire harvest, all that fine silken wool, lost."

"Lost?" asked another voice, also masculine but younger and with a nasally quality. "What happened? He had a huge harvest."

"Storm," said the older masculine voice. "Out o' nowhere, they say. Blew the entire fleet save two ships right into the gray mist."

An older but gruff woman's voice retorted, "Serves them right if they are going to try and ride the quicker currents so close to the edge of the world."

"That's jus' the thing," said the older man. "According to the survivors, they were hugging the coastline. They said winds kicked up out of nowhere and pulled them out while rounding the narrows."

The woman simply grunted.

Aria tuned the conversation out of her head as the little serving girl arrived with her meal. She thanked the girl and focused on her food. She had only taken a couple bites from her dinner when two people, a man and a woman, entered the common room. The man was incredibly tall with long, straight white hair tied back loosely with a black band. His hair framed a handsome, youthful face with a strong jawline. His blue eyes absorbed every single detail, and when they made contact with Aria's, she felt as if they bore down into her soul. In that moment Aria felt exposed and vulnerable. Was this the sensation others experienced upon meeting her eyes? His brown cloak, his long tan tunic, and his loose-fitting gray breeches obscured his lean frame. He was no local.

The man's companion, an unassuming young woman of short stature with dark-brown hair and equally dark-brown eyes wearing a forest-green tunic and black leggings, scanned the area and pointed to Aria's table. The man nodded, and the two made their way across the common room, unaware of the stares they attracted.

As they approached the table, the young woman asked, "Are these seats taken?"

Aria swallowed her mouthful of food. "No, go right ahead."

The woman smiled at her. "Thank you." She sat beside Aria, and the man took a seat on the bench across from her. Aria tried not to stare.

The young serving girl returned to ask the newcomers what they wanted to eat. The white-haired man responded, "What is your name?"

The girl blinked, not used to people inquiring about her identity. "Yuli, sir," she replied. "My name is Yuli."

"Well, Yuli, we will have what she's having." He nodded his head toward Aria. The man's voice was soft yet powerful. The girl bobbed a curtsy and retreated to the kitchen.

The man looked across the table at Aria. "Hello, I'm Zephyron." He extended his hand in the common greeting. Even though Aria was not from this region, everyone in Tanoria knew what a kruusta was and could identify them on sight, so she was somewhat stunned at the casual introduction from these strangers. Aria wiped off her hand on her napkin and grasped his in return. As their skin touched, a surge of energy flowed from his hand to hers. While not an unpleasant sensation, the reaction caught her by surprise. Her first instinct was to pull away, but she held firm instead.

"Aria," she responded with a nod as she glanced at the crystal on her hand, noting the soft blue pulse. Blue was usually the color it took on when she summoned her krusword. Aria found it odd her crystal would react to this man at all. What did it mean? He was not a kruusta. He was not a shard beast. So what was he?

"And this is Kharra," he said.

Aria released Zephyron's hand and grasped Kharra's outstretched one. Aria had considered the woman unspectacular, but with sudden realization, she knew she had been a poor judge of character. If she thought Zephyron's eyes could see into her soul, then this woman could not only see into it but knew it as well. Unlike with Zephyron, however, Aria's crystal did not react to Kharra's touch.

Aria withdrew her hand. She then realized she had been holding her breath and forced herself to exhale. Who were these people? Aria turned her attention back to her meal.

Yuli returned with two plates of food and two mugs of ale. Zephyron smiled at the girl. "This looks and smells wonderful, Miss Yuli." The man reached into his pocket and pulled out a small carved wooden figurine. He handed it to the girl. "Miss Yuli, I would like you to have this for your wonderful service."

The small girl's eyes opened wide as she extended her hands and gingerly accepted the offering. She held up the fine carving, revealing the shape of some type of feline creature. The amount of detail on such a small object was amazing. "What is it?" the girl asked.

"He is a tigron. He still needs a proper name, though, if you can think of one."

Yuli met Zephyron's eyes, her beaming smile broadcasting her joy.

"Do you think you can keep him safe for me?"

The girl nodded with enthusiasm, her pale-brown ringlets bouncing about her face. "Thank you, thank you." The girl launched her arms around Zephyron's chest.

Zephyron chuckled and said, "You're quite welcome."

Just shy of squealing, Yuli turned and ran back to the kitchen.

Meanwhile, Kharra laughed, shaking her head. Tilting an eyebrow, she glanced at Aria and said, "He has too much charisma for his own good, and he has a weakness for children."

"I don't recall you complaining back when you received those gifts," the man said in a playful tone.

Kharra laughed louder. "Who said I was complaining?"

With that, Kharra and Zephyron began eating.

Uncertain what to make of the strangers, Aria focused on her own meal and contemplated where she needed to head next. She noted the others in the common room had returned to their meals.

"What is that?" Zephyron asked. "On your hand."

Aria's eyes came up and then glanced at the hand she was using to eat. "The crystal?"

Zephyron nodded.

"You're not from around here, are you?"

Zephyron shook his head.

Aria did not think anyone in all of Tanoria, except maybe a young child, would not know what her crystal meant. "I am a kruusta."

Zephyron frowned.

"What's wrong?" asked Kharra.

"The word is an old dialect, I think," he responded. "I believe the word means…" His eyes grew distant. "Crystal warrior."

Aria nodded.

Zephyron asked, "And the crystal is part of your flesh?"

Aria took another bite of her meal and nodded again.

"How does that happen?"

Aria pursed her lips and furrowed her brow. No one had ever asked her that before. "We have a tradition called the Ritual of Sharding when one is chosen to be a kruusta."

Both Zephyron and Kharra gave her blank looks.

"I belong to the Order of the Shard. The priests of my order commune with the Prime Shard. They receive revelations, which direct them to select children who have been chosen by the Prime Shard to become kruustas. When a child is chosen, they are taken from their family to be raised by the order."

At the alarm on Kharra's face, Aria added, "Being chosen is considered an honor. The family is treated well if their child is selected. When we're taken by the order, we're given an education and trained in combat. On our fifteenth naming day, we are embedded with a sliver of the Prime Shard." Zephyron's eyebrows rose at that, but he remained silent. "For three more years we train and learn the Way of the Krusword. On our eighteenth naming day, we're tested for our readiness. If we are deemed ready, we earn the title 'kruusta.' If we're not ready, we continue training until we are."

"What's the purpose of the kruustas?" Zephyron asked.

"We hunt down and eradicate shard beasts. Our embedded crystals provide us with a special sensitivity to them as well as grant us enhanced strength and speed and the ability to bring forth our krusword."

Zephyron bit off a piece of his meat, looking thoughtful for a moment. "Interesting. There are no ill effects from this?"

Aria met his eyes but did not answer. Who was this man? Aria swallowed the last bite of meat and washed it down with a long sip of her ale. Wiping her mouth, she said, "Enough about me. What about you two? Where are you from?"

Kharra frowned and swirled her drink around in her mug. Zephyron began scooping taro into his mouth.

After a few silent moments of eating, Zephyron answered, "Far away."

Aria frowned. "What brings you to Murali?"

It was Kharra, rather than Zephyron, who responded. "We're just passing through. As you can tell, we're not familiar with the area. In fact we're looking for a guide. We asked a few of the townsfolk in the village, and several of them gave us your description. Would you be interested?"

"Hm," was all Aria said.

"We'll pay you well," Kharra added.

"I'm not worried about the compensation. I just don't think I'd be appropriate for the task. Why do you need a guide?"

This time Zephyron replied. "We search for a place called Ei'ars'anu."

Aria froze, her mug poised for another sip. Instead of taking a drink, she set the mug down. She looked from Zephyron to Kharra and back to Zephyron. She leaned over the table toward the white-haired man and said in a low voice, "Do not say that name too loud. You may find a knife in your back for it. You should return to your home and forget you ever heard the name you spoke."

"I'm sorry," Zephyron said, his face serious, "but that's not possible. We've come a long way, and we cannot return until we have completed our mission."

"I hope your quest is worth your lives because there is a good chance both of you will die in that place. We now call the entire region Death's Pillar."

"We understand the danger," said Kharra, careful to keep her voice low, "but as Zephyron mentioned, we can't return home until we've completed our mission. We must get there. I don't blame you for not wanting to go. If you are unable to guide us, could you point us to someone who can?"

Aria grabbed her mug, tilted her head back, and swallowed its remaining contents. She replied, "There is no one else capable of guiding you. Just to reach the mountain, you need to travel through Wilderland, which is dangerous to anyone who is not a kruusta. Only a handful of sparsely populated villages are located even near that region, and their citizens keep to themselves. They would not help strangers, especially those who wish to climb the pillar."

Kharra stood. Zephyron finished his ale and did the same. Kharra turned to her and extended her hand once again. Aria took it with a measure of uncertainty. "Thank you for your time and the information. It will be helpful." Kharra released her hand, pulled up her cloak, and headed for the door.

Zephyron gave her a tight but respectful nod. Then he placed a handful of coins on the table and followed his companion. Yuli, the mousy serving girl, rushed out from the kitchen and wrapped Zephyron's waist in a hug. "Thank you again! Let me give you this."

Zephyron knelt down so he could be at eye level with the girl. With meticulous care, Yuli strung a blue bead onto his tunic. "This is for luck, so the Guardians will know to protect you."

"Is that so?" he responded with a chuckle.

The girl nodded.

"Well, then, I will wear it always. Thank you. Goodbye now."

The girl released him and waved.

Zephyron stood and headed to the door. Mayor Domnur watched from the window that separated the kitchen from the common room and nodded a silent thanks to the white-haired stranger as he disappeared through the front door.

Aria stared at the spot where Zephyron had sat just moments before. It was unfortunate those two were set on their quest for fools. She liked them.

Kharra stared downward through the darkness of the evening's shadows. Her eyes barely acknowledged the area though as her mind searched for answers. She bit her lip and furrowed her brow. As she and Zephyron reached the edge of the village's torchlight, she paused and looked back at the inn.

"Are you sure she was the one?" Zephyron asked, his warm voice low and subdued.

Kharra's furrowed brow transformed into a confused scowl. "I'm certain of it." She sighed in frustration. "We didn't come halfway around the world for me to be wrong. There's too much at stake."

"Could you have misinterpreted?" he asked.

Kharra looked at him. "The dream?"

Zephyron nodded. "Your mother was right most of the time as well, but sometimes she misunderstood the message."

"I suppose anything is possible, but I saw that woman's face as clear as I see yours now," Kharra said as she pointed toward the inn. "I mean, exact. It was not a figment of my imagination or some old dredged-up memory. And the tugging that brought me to this remote village...I still feel it. She's the one I needed to find."

"And you still don't have any additional insight as to why we would need her?"

Kharra's shoulders drooped as she shook her head. "No. It was your idea to ask her to be our guide."

Zephyron gave a half chuckle and a grin. That grin almost always defused any of her negative feelings. "Well, we still need to get to Ei'ars'anu, and we don't exactly know our way around this land. She is an experienced fighter and traveler. It's not out of place for us to ask someone with those skills to be a guide. We would probably scare her away if we led with, 'Hey, my friend here had a prophetic dream about you...'"

Kharra smirked and smacked his arm playfully. "Let's camp nearby. I'm sure we'll find some opportunity to interact with her again."

Despite the momentary mirth, Kharra grew quiet again as they picked their trail through the lightly forested hills. So many things tugged at her mind, all vying for attention, and each brought with it its own magnitude of worry.

"You're doing it again," she vaguely heard Zephyron say. "Did you hear anything I just said?"

Kharra blinked at the change of Zephyron's tone and looked up at her tall companion. "What?"

"That would be a no," he responded. Despite the levity in his voice, there was an undercurrent of concern. "What's wrong?"

Kharra sighed. "Have I done the right thing by coming here? What if the dream was just a dream? That could be a costly mistake."

Zephyron studied her. "That's not like you to question yourself."

"I know. It's just that if this is just a wild chase and we end up wasting months in this land while—"

Zephyron stopped and put a hand on her shoulder, interrupting her in the process. "Kharra, they are going to be fine."

"But what—"

"Hey, they are building, not pressing a fight. Aerous is a big place, and Xareen doesn't know where they are. Between your sister and Brii, that group of rabble will be in fighting condition by the time we return. You just focus on what we need to do here."

Kharra sighed. "You're right," she said with a nod as she started to walk again. Jayde, she thought, please be safe. Though the worry for her sister lingered, she suppressed it as well as she could and forced herself to focus on her more immediate concerns.

Kharra did not often experience prophetic dreams, but when they occurred, she never confused them for regular dreams. Her mind somehow distinguished the difference. The one that compelled her to travel to Tanoria included the place called Ei'ars'anu, something called the Heart of the Sauru, and Aria. Prophetic dreams, though, proved difficult to decipher, so how everything fit together remained a mystery.

Having met Aria in person, Kharra had found a tangible thread to follow but no answers as to how the kruusta fit into the bigger picture. They needed to learn more about Tanoria, its people, the shards, and Aria.

2

A SHARD IN PAIN

Aria left the Golden Rose and headed across the village green. Dozens of songbirds flitted about the small fruit trees that lined the grass-covered town center, singing their morning serenade beneath the sun of the early day. Aria inhaled deeply, letting the crisp spring air fill her lungs and the sounds of the village wash over her. Saws and hammers echoed off the circle of buildings surrounding the area. A horse snorted impatiently as its cart was loaded. A pair of small dogs yipped at a passing cat. She found all of the sounds around her to be soothing.

Aria took a well-worn path on the opposite side of the green. It wound beneath a series of large oaks and up a steep incline. Thick vine-like plants followed along the dirt-packed trail, meandering up and over rocks and fallen trees. A twig snapped to the left. Instinct compelled her to call forth her weapon, but it was only a young meadow deer pulling on low-hanging foliage. She clenched her fist and scolded herself for being jumpy. Even here, in this quaint little town, Aria found it difficult to relax. From her brief conversation with the Order of the Heart priests the night before, she had learned that four kruustas had died over the past two weeks. Danger defined a kruusta's job, and occasional injury, sometimes serious, resulted from their work. On rare occasions one even died. But four deaths in such a short period of time never happened.

The temple's chiseled stone steps came into view. On either side of the steps, massive granite statues depicted giant serpentine creatures. Dragons, the priests called them. According to the legends of old, dragons had once been the "Guardians" of the shards, though no one knew for sure what that meant. The dragons had disappeared from Tanoria a long time ago, but many pieces of art and architecture around the world still preserved their image.

A low wall circled the temple, its sides carved in a complicated and intricate relief pattern. Aria climbed the first ten steps, which were cut into the relief-carved wall. She came to an open area about three paces wide that followed along the top of the wall's circumference. The area transitioned into a short path lined on either side by a series of thick round pillars holding up a heavy stone overhang.

Down the path and up the next four steps, Aria continued on through the temple's open door. The small antechamber gave way to a vaulted ceiling that rose to dizzying heights. Even though she had been in and out of shard temples all her life, their architecture never ceased to amaze her.

A handful of worshippers dotted the pews, each kneeling and holding their steepled hands against their foreheads. The Order of the Shard held group services twice a week, but individuals often visited on their own to seek additional wisdom or courage, or some other form of enlightenment. An intake of breath from one of the worshippers brought up the heads of the others. Though none said a word, one by one, each person vacated the hall until no one but Aria remained.

Soft footsteps announced the arrival of the resident priest. "Ah," said a familiar voice. "Aria, I received word that a kruusta had come to deal with the glimmer worm, but I did not expect to see you. You look well, the same as ever."

Aria turned to the white-haired man. His face bore wrinkles around his eyes, cheeks, and forehead. A full head shorter than her, the priest wore a floor-length blue robe, a long golden chain about his neck, and a bracelet of crystal on his wrist. Priests wore the robe and chain as part of their normal outfit, but the bracelet was something new. She had seen three other priests with them during her travels over the past season; it must be some new fashion.

"Priest Malechi," she said, "a pleasure to see you again." He had just become an acolyte when she had been brought to the order to become a kruusta. In a way, the two had grown up together. Though never close, they had always been friendly as acquaintances. A kruusta's lack of aging disturbed the average person but not the priests of the order. They understood the nature of the calling. "Though I have to say, a single glimmer worm is hardly worth the time of bringing in a kruusta."

"True, but the people in this village are not fighters. They are simple farmers. They fear shard beasts of any type. I'm certain you are aware of the destruction the critter caused."

"Yeah, I heard. I am a little concerned about that, but I'm surprised some of the local hunters failed to eliminate it."

He studied her. "Have you come for your next assignment?"

Aria thought for a moment. "Yes and no. I'm here to commune."

The priest raised an eyebrow. In general practice, the priests communed on behalf of the kruustas. While kruustas were not forbidden to commune, the practice was uncommon. "Is something bothering you?" he asked.

"Actually, yes. Last night I met a pair of travelers, strangers who didn't know a thing about kruustas or the order. They wanted me to guide them to Death's Pillar."

"By the shard, you can't be serious. You warned them of the dangers, right?" Malechi asked in earnest.

"Of course."

"And you didn't agree to take them, correct?"

"I turned them down, and they've already gone."

"Then why do you need to commune? You did as you should have done."

Aria shrugged. "Peace of mind, maybe. Direction. I'm not sure."

"Why don't I commune for you?" he insisted. "Remember, I trained for this. I will let you know what the Prime Shard desires."

"I appreciate the offer, but I feel the need to do this myself."

The priest's lips grew taut. "Very well. I will leave you be."

"Thank you," Aria said as the priest departed through a side door. Once he disappeared, she moved through the central chamber toward the dais. The metal tips and heels of her boots clinked against the polished gray tiles. She studied the grand, ornate windows lining the tops of the walls, taking comfort from the lively cacophony of color sparkling from their murals of stained glass.

Aria arrived at the dais and pulled aside a velvet curtain, revealing the brilliant white-and-violet-streaked shard. Its pearlescent sheen brought a smile to her face. A golden filigree frame outlined where the base of the shard came up through the floor. For as long as anyone could remember, it had been considered a grave offense to sever and move a shard. Because of their immobility, ancient people long ago built shard temples around the crystalline formations. Over time, town centers grew around most of those temples. That had happened a long time ago.

In the centuries since those ancient days, human populations had continued to grow and expand, and over time people left the villages and cities with shard temples to establish new communities until only a fraction of the total villages and towns possessed temples. As a result, many people started traveling for leagues to visit them in order to have their prayers heard.

With each shard connected to the Prime Shard in the holy city of Aloazai and the Prime Shard serving as the physical conduit for the Great Consciousness, the priests could commune with their local shards in order to interpret the will of the Prime Shard and respond to those prayers.

Aria pulled back her tan doeskin cloak and knelt down on the curved hassock. She closed her eyes, lifted her hands, and placed them against the shard's smooth surface. She steeled herself for the flood of energy and emotion she had experienced the only other time she had communed. Nothing. Aria concentrated harder, hoping maybe she was just out of practice. Still, nothing happened.

Concerned, Aria released the tip of her krusword from her hand, allowing it to make contact with the shard. Using her own crystal as a conduit, she allowed her consciousness to follow down through her sword and delve deeper into the shard's consciousness. At first, only darkness filled her mind's eye, and only her own distant thoughts tumbled in the background. But then at last she detected something. A slow, rhythmic pulse beat weakly. The pulse climbed sluggishly up through her sword and tugged at her crystal. Her mind, now able to see the blue nimbus of energy, followed where the shard's energy finally met up with her own. It lunged at her spark of life and clung to it like one who came upon a river after days in the desert.

The pulse she sensed was slow and laborious, not unlike the faltering heartbeat of an animal on the verge of death. Her stomach grew cold. The shard reached into her heart. Sadness filled her. Since time immemorial there had been trust, cooperation, love, and communication. Now fire and agony flayed the exposed nerves of her spine, and sorrow with the weight of a mountain pressed down on her. Aria's chest and throat constricted, aching physically as she shared in the shard's suffering. Every emotional conduit of her body and mind swam with anguish.

At last Aria retracted her sword and released the shard. Tears bubbled along her closed eyelids. She took several long breaths, and the feeling of despair reluctantly loosened its grip on her chest. Aria opened her eyes and was startled to find the temple dark. Isor, the sun, had long since set, and the only illumination in the room came from the candles lining the spacious hall.

Aria looked around the room, wincing at the stiffness in her hips as she stood. She stretched her legs, unsure why a few hours in commune would leave her feeling rigid. As she turned to leave, her boots scuffed lightly against the tile, but the ting that reverberated across the room may as well have been a roar. Priest Malechi appeared from the side door.

"At last you finish your commune. I could have done it much faster for you, had you let me."

"Faster? How long was I in the trance?"

"You began your commune two mornings ago."

"Two days? I thought I was there for just a few minutes."

The priest nodded. "It is easy for one to get lost in prayer. Did you find the enlightenment you sought?"

Aria frowned. "I'm not certain."

"Don't fret. You would not be the first one to walk away without a response. That's why the priests are needed."

"No, I got a response. I think."

Both of Malechi's eyebrows rose.

"The shard is dying. It's in pain. Priest Malechi, why is it in this state?"

Priest Malechi's lips drew tight, and his brow lowered. "That is unfortunate."

Aria's sorrow turned to simmering anger. "What is? Priest Malechi, why is the shard dying?" Aria stared at him. "Priest Malechi, answer—" Before Aria could finish her sentence, the crystal on her hand flared to life with energy, and she was overcome with an all-too-familiar sensation, a mixture of pain and exultation. "Priest Malechi, get to safety," she commanded as she pointed toward the back entrance of the temple. "I sense a large and powerful shard beast heading right for us. You escape while I deal with the creature."

"How can it even enter?" Priest Malechi asked cryptically. The man smiled, but no hint of kindness touched his face. Aria caught a glimpse of the bracelet on the priest's arm. It was glowing softly. She glanced at the priest, at the bracelet, and back at the priest. Aria's eyes narrowed at the observation.

In addition to the shard beast she sensed heading toward the temple, Aria now sensed at least two others moving toward the village with incredible speed. Cursing under her breath, she turned and bolted out the door.

Aria sprinted down the hillside path as fast as her legs would carry her, much faster than any normal human. As she reached the village green, a massive shard drake crashed through the tree line on the north. Sword in hand, she continued sprinting toward the beast. A second shard drake burst through the path she had just vacated and pursued her. Flames erupted to the south as the third shard drake demolished the village's only forge. Three? These were solitary creatures. Why were they attacking together? Later, she said to herself. Focus on the task at hand.

The first shard drake saw her and let out a piercing screech. The creature's elongated neck undulated back and forth. Its sharded, crystalline head, jagged and cracked at irregular intervals, moved side to side. Tiny black eyes sat high on its forehead, and a long, wide, crooked mouth displayed teeth as long as daggers. Craggy plates of crystalline armor covered its entire body, neck, legs, back, and tail. Its body swirled in an ebb and flow of colors covering the entire spectrum.

Aria reached the shard drake at a full run, slashing at its snapping jaws. Unused to its prey retaliating, the creature jerked its head away from the blade. Normal swords would have trouble piercing a shard drake's armor, but not a krusword. Aria swung around just in time to slash the second shard drake on the side of the head as it attempted to catch her off guard.

Led by Mayor Domnur, villagers poured out from the Golden Rose to investigate the commotion. Others from nearby homes joined them. The third shard drake, still on the opposite side of the green, spotted one unfortunate villager who stumbled out onto its path. Before Aria managed to shout at him, the creature lunged at the man and snapped him between its jaws. The mayor issued commands to the people around him. Each armed with some type of implement—swords, pitchforks, shovels, even brooms—they attacked the beast in an attempt to free the man. The sound of the man's screams cut off abruptly. The creature flung the man aside and swiped at its attackers.

Parrying the first and second drakes, Aria moved to intercept the third. Before she got there, the drake sliced the mayor's arm with its serrated claws. The people of Murali stood no chance against these things. Whenever a shard drake was the intended target for a hunt, two or three kruustas worked together to deal with the menace. Three shard drakes at once was beyond a nightmare even for a kruusta fighting force. I need to get these things away from the village, she thought. Even if she did not have a chance at defeating the creatures, she knew she had to get them far enough away from the village to avoid further casualties.

Aria caught up to the third drake and slashed its shoulder as she ran by. The beast howled and turned its attention away from the villagers and over toward her. The clang and ting of crystal sword on crystal armor made for an almost melodic rhythm as Aria continued to parry the creatures as fast as her arm would move. They would soon wear her down, so she needed to get away while she still could.

Out of the corner of her eye, Aria spotted the mayor's son, the same boy who had retrieved the sack full of glimmer worm fragments two days before. He watched her with frightened intensity. "Torga! Release my zegu." His eyes grew wide, but he nodded and sprinted toward the stables. Within moments, Xierex charged up beside her. Though smaller than them, the zegu's rearing hooves gave the drakes pause, buying enough time for Aria to get mounted.

Aria continued to slash and thrust at the beasts, making sure their ferocity remained focused on her. With a simple nudge of her knees, Xierex took off down the eastern road. Enraged by the fleeing prey, the drakes pursued. Their eerie bugling screeches carried through the dark forest. Any creature with any amount of intelligence would know to stay hidden this night.

Aria drove Xierex hard. At times she slowed or even circled about so she could get a few slashes in on the shard drakes to be certain they remained interested in their quarry rather than break off and return to the village.

After what seemed like several hours later, when Aria deemed they had distanced themselves far enough from the village, she reined in her zegu and decided to make her stand. Xierex's blue coat glistened with lather. His muscles quivered at the exertion, but he was just as ready as her to face their foe.

The shard drakes, their sides also heaving after the chase, snarled and growled in fury. Their mouths frothed with excitement, knowing their target was near its end. Xierex stomped and snorted, rearing and kicking any time the drakes drew too close. While he fended off one from the front, Aria slashed at the two coming from the sides. Sweat dripped into her eyes, but she ignored the stinging. She had no time for discomfort.

Each drake bore wounds from the zegu and rider but none were life-threatening. Xierex's breathing became labored. While he had much more stamina than any horse, he still had his limits, and those had long ago been exceeded. Aria jumped down from his back, tucked and rolled on her landing, and came up under one of the drakes. Surprised by the change of tactics, the drake attempted to leap away. Its reaction was too slow, and Aria's upward thrust drove through its underside armor and pierced its heart.

The drake's ear-piercing wail caused Aria to wince despite being ready for it. The beast staggered backward, tripped over its own feet, and fell to the ground. It thrashed around, writhing in pain, and finally fell silent and still. The other drake she had been fighting wasted no time and leaped over Xierex to get to her, taking advantage of Aria's vulnerable position. She rolled out of the way, but its claw connected solidly along her ribs. Her momentum carried her beyond its reach as she clutched her bleeding side.

A shrill scream from Xierex caused Aria to spare him a glance. He stumbled and fell as the other drake overwhelmed him. Cursing herself, she scrambled away from her drake toward the fallen zegu. From his side, he glanced at her with wide eyes. He was still alive, but he had nothing left to give. Aria positioned herself between the zegu and the two drakes. She knew it was pointless, but she was not just going to lay down her sword and give up. If she was lucky, perhaps she could take one, or even both, with her before the end.

One of the drakes attacked low. The wound on her side prevented her from parrying the strike cleanly. The attack connected with her calf, and her leg buckled immediately. The other drake, attempting to take advantage of her vulnerability, lunged at her. With a twisting thrust of her sword, she drove the blade through the roof of the creature's mouth and into its brain, killing it instantly, but the drake's momentum caused its corpse to crash down upon her before she could roll away.

Hopelessly pinned, her back against the ground, Aria lay vulnerable. In order to pull the crystalline weapon free from the drake's mouth, she retracted her blade, allowing the weapon to soften and loosen its form as the crystal on her hand reabsorbed it. The other drake was on her then, its sharded jaws snapping at her face. Instinctively, she brought up her free arm to protect her face. She closed her eyes and anticipated the snap of her bones, but nothing happened.

Daring to open her eyes, she caught sight of something white streaking across her field of vision. The white blur disappeared as quickly as she had seen it. Pinned as she was, she could not tell what the blur was or where it went. The drake's angry trumpet bellowed, followed by sounds she was unable to identify. Something sizzled and hissed behind her. Aria growled at her inability to see what was going on around her. She heard a series of footsteps. She strained to twist around, but the pain on her side made her wish she had not. She closed her eyes to let the pain wash over her.

"Hold still," said a gentle, somewhat familiar voice.

Aria opened her eyes and focused on the face that was just a few inches away from hers. "Kharra?" she said, not quite believing what she was seeing.

"Yes. Don't move. I'll have you out of here in just a moment."

"Wait, there's another drake."

"Don't worry, Zephyron's taking care of it."

"No, get him away. He'll be killed."

The weight pinning her down disappeared as the drake's corpse lifted from her and moved a short distance away. Unable to comprehend what had caused it to move and simply thankful it had, Aria was finally able to twist around. Worried that she would be too late to help Zephyron before the drake killed him, she started to rise, but before she fully gained her footing, she stopped, lowered herself back down, and stared at the scene before her.

Not only was Zephyron unharmed, he was overpowering the drake. In his hand, he held some type of blade Aria had never seen before. Crackling vibrant blue energy conformed to the shape of a sword; the weapon sliced through the shard drake's crystalline armor as if it were no more than skin. With each strike to the drake's crystalline armor, the blade hissed. Zephyron moved fluidly and effortlessly. With each strike from the beast, Zephyron dodged and sliced, which only served to enrage the drake more. Light bluish-purple fluid oozed from dozens of wounds across its face, neck, and body.

Watching Zephyron's body sway, weave, spin, and turn was like watching an elaborate dance. Aria could almost hear the Battle of Tazah Overture playing along with him. Mesmerized by the spectacle, the kruusta almost forgot her own pain. At last the shard drake stumbled forward and fell on its chin. Its sides heaved laboriously, and saliva dripped from its jaw. The drake looked up at Zephyron, seeming to know it had been beaten, and then it closed its eyes. With one final, long sigh, the beast stopped moving.

Zephyron's blade disappeared as he left the beast and came to Aria's side. He must have seen the confusion on her face, for he winked at her as he approached. "I hope you don't mind our assistance," he said cheerfully.

Aria found herself smiling, if weakly. "Not at all. I'm just not used to it. Assistance, that is. Those drakes can tear a person apart with little effort, so people's desire to assist tends to turn into a liability." She studied him for a moment. "But you're not a normal person, are you?"

It was his turn to study her. "Observant. What gave it away?"

With a shake of her head, Aria chuckled half-heartedly in response. The chuckle caused her to wince in pain. Once the pain cleared, she shook her head again. "All that matters is that you saved my life, and I am in your debt."

With a start, Aria remembered Xierex had fallen. Her moment of panic passed when she saw him standing a short distance away. Kharra stood with him, petting him along his chin. Aria's stunned expression must have been obvious. Xierex never let anyone touch him without her being present, and he was especially sensitive to having his face petted.

Kharra smiled as she walked back to Aria and Zephyron with Xierex moving alongside her. "He was worried about you. He said you saved him from the drake that had you pinned."

Aria realized she was gawking and clamped her mouth shut. "He said that?"

Kharra nodded as she drew closer. Xierex lowered his head and nuzzled Aria's face. She smiled and scratched his chin. "I'm okay," she said with a chuckle. The zegu snorted.

Zephyron knelt beside her, his face suddenly concerned. "Mind if I lift your shirt so I can get a better look?"

"No, go ahead." Aria had never been bothered by modesty. No kruusta was.

Zephyron lifted her shirt and frowned. "This gash on your side is pretty bad." He leaned back and glanced at her leg. "And the one on your calf is not much better. We need to get them both cleaned out."

"With a little rest, I'm sure I'll be fine."

Kharra tilted her head slightly as if listening to something. "There's a creek farther along to the southeast," she said. Zephyron nodded, scooped Aria up in his arms before she could protest, and set off through the trees in the direction of the water source. Xierex and Kharra followed right behind.

No one ever mistook Aria for a small woman, but Zephyron carried her, in full armor, with ease. Neither of the travelers spoke, so

Aria's mind turned inward as she reflected on the fight and the events that had led up to it. Zephyron's heart thudded in her ears like a war drum, giving a cadence to her thoughts. By any logic Aria knew she should be dead. No one fought a solitary shard drake alone, let alone three, and expected to survive. Yet here she was, accompanied by two strangers who had risked their lives to save hers. She had a lot to process.

3

THE FATE OF A KRUUSTA

The two travelers had come prepared for emergencies. With gentle hands Kharra cleaned and bound both of Aria's wounds. The kruusta sensed the crystal in her system already at work, mending the torn areas of her skin and muscles. She would not need to keep the bandage on for more than a day or two.

With darkness full upon them, Aria's new acquaintances decided to make camp a short distance away from the creek where they had treated her wounds. Kharra pulled out a number of provisions from their packs while Zephyron started a fire. He then disappeared, only to return a half hour later with three large whitegill, already cleaned and ready for cooking. He skewered each fish with a stick and set them to cook over the crackling flames.

Kharra unfolded a small pan on her lap, opened a tiny paper bag, and scooped out a handful of mushrooms. With dexterous fingers she cut them into fine slices and dropped them into the pan. From a second, wax-wrapped package, Kharra sliced off a wedge of cheese and added it into the pan with the mushrooms. Zephyron reached into his pocket and pulled out two eggs.

Kharra beamed. "You found some!"

"You didn't think I'd forget, did you?"

Kharra took her prize from Zephyron's hands, broke them, and poured the yolks into the pan. With a spoon she stirred up the contents and placed the pan over the fire beside the fish. Zephyron grinned as he grabbed a piece of wood from a pile beside him and unsheathed a small knife at his belt. He turned his attention to the wood, and with swift, deft hands, he began whittling.

Aria sat in silence as the two, demonstrating familiarity with traveling and sleeping beneath the stars, went about their routine. They knew how to provide for themselves and how to fight.

Kharra looked over at her. "What were those creatures you fought?"

"Shard drakes," Aria responded.

"And your job is to hunt them?"

Aria nodded. "Those and other shard beasts like them."

"Sounds like a rough job."

"It's not so bad most of the time. Shard drakes are among the most powerful of the shard beasts. They're solitary creatures by nature. Under normal circumstances two or three kruustas are called in to handle one to be safe. I don't know of any instance prior to this event where someone fought multiple shard drakes."

Zephyron set his project aside, pulled the fish off the fire, and asked, "What changed?"

Anger welled up in Aria as she recalled the events that transpired in the village. She ground her teeth and forced the anger down. "I-I'm not entirely certain," she answered as she continued to replay the scene in her head.

Zephyron placed each fish on a metal plate and handed them one at a time to Kharra. His eyes met Aria's. Though she could not quite read them, within them, she found confidence. A whispering sense deep within her told her these two travelers were trustworthy; it was a sensation to which she was unaccustomed. Her mind of reason warred with her gut of intuition.

Kharra divided the omelet into three parts, scooped each part onto a separate plate, and served two of the plates to Aria and Zephyron. Aria accepted and offered her thanks. Her stomach rumbled in anticipation as she took the first bite of her meal. She recalled that it had been two days since she had last eaten. The cheese was sharp but not bad, and an unfamiliar spice accentuated the flavor.

As she ate, reason lost its battle, and Aria soon found herself reciting her experience in Murali. The two companions listened quietly and attentively as Aria explained her meeting with Priest Malechi, her two-day commune (including the pain she had sensed in the shard), the priest's odd behavior after her commune, and the subsequent attack by the shard drakes.

"Back up a minute," said Kharra. "You mentioned a glowing bracelet. Made of crystal? Are you certain?"

Aria nodded. "Is that significant?"

Kharra looked at Zephyron. "Is it possible?"

Zephyron shrugged and then nodded. "Anything's possible."

"What am I missing?" Aria inquired.

"Long ago," Kharra began, "there used to be people who could make devices out of crystal, devices with unique properties. As far as I know, those people no longer exist, but we encountered some of their devices a few years ago."

"What was special about them?" Aria pressed.

"The devices we encountered were paired bracelets and necklaces. The wearer of the bracelet could control the wearer of the necklace."

Aria leaned back and wrinkled her nose. "Are you serious? One person could control another?"

Kharra tapped her chin with the handle of her fork. "Not completely control, no, but the wearer of the bracelet was aware of the wearer of the necklace and could cause them pain just by thinking it. Some people used those devices to train other people to be obedient slaves."

"What does that have to do with my situation?" Aria asked with a raised eyebrow.

"What if this bracelet you saw was similar but different?"

Aria shook her head. "I don't follow."

"What if this bracelet worked differently? Instead of controlling people, it allowed the wearer to control these shard beasts."

Aria stared at Kharra. She slowly finished chewing the food in her mouth and swallowed. "No one controls shard beasts."

Zephyron swallowed his own food, a thoughtful expression spawning on his face. He began nodding. He held up a finger toward Aria and said, "For the sake of this discussion, let us say someone did have the ability to control them. Then that person could send them after a target, say a kruusta. Should the kruusta die, people would think they did so in the line of doing their job. Would that be safe to assume?"

Aria frowned but nodded. "And if for some reason the attack failed," she added, "then no one would be the wiser. It would just seem like another shard beast attack." She studied Zephyron's face. "Are you suggesting Priest Malechi tried to kill me?"

Sympathy filled Zephyron's eyes, and he shook his head. "I'm not suggesting anything. I'm merely theorizing based on the pieces displayed before me. I mean no offense."

Aria pursed her lips. "No offense taken. Your theory may be correct, though I still don't see how someone can control shard beasts."

Zephyron's eyebrows scrunched in disbelief. He had not expected her to agree. "Why would this priest want to kill you?"

Aria furrowed her brow and stared into the fire. "I think I stumbled onto something I shouldn't have."

"Like what?"

Aria collected her thoughts, and then for the next hour, she recited the history and doctrine of the order, information that every trainee and acolyte knew by heart before they graduated to become full-fledged kruustas or priests.

Long ago, in the early days of man's life in Tanoria, a young man by the name of Therian Graymist awoke in the night to a dream so profound he could not shake it from his mind. Each night the dream returned. He grew more and more distracted, unable to complete even the simplest of chores. When asked by friends and family why he was in such a state, he answered, "It calls me." When asked to clarify, he would simply repeat, "It calls me."

Concerned that their beloved son and brother had succumbed to an illness of the mind, the Graymist family sent for a doctor. When the doctor arrived, Therian was nowhere to be found.

Unknown to the family, Therian had followed the call he alone could hear. Pausing only to catch brief moments of rest, the young man traveled through the wilds and eventually climbed the treacherous slopes of Mount Eishar. At a point where even he began to question his sanity, he came upon a vast cavern with walls and a ceiling rising some hundred feet overhead, blanketed with veins of crystal of all colors. From the middle of the cavern rose the most magnificent crystalline structure. Over thirty feet in height at its apex and nearly as wide around the base, the pyramid-shaped structure contained millions of sparkling facets. Natural skylights in the ceiling of the cavern caught the rays of Isor at all hours of the day and delivered the sun's brilliant light to the giant shard below. The resulting meeting of light to crystal created a visual cacophony that radiated every color of the spectrum.

That was the Dragon Shard.

Spent physically, emotionally, and mentally, when his eyes at last came to rest on the Dragon Shard, Therian fell to his knees and wept. The weeping did not last, for a great surge of strength and energy flooded into the young man, and with it came understanding. This magnificent shard was a nexus point for the Great Consciousness, the mind of the world of Tanoria.

Therian become the first oracle of the Dragon Shard. Eventually word spread of this discovery, and others came to him. Acting as the voice of the Great Consciousness for those who could not hear it, he told the visitors about smaller shards spread across the land; they were giant crystals connected to the Dragon Shard and the Great Consciousness over vast distances.

Oracle Therian explained to his visitors, these pilgrims, that the shards were sacred but vulnerable—accessible and exposed for anyone to touch. In order to protect the shards, Oracle Therian asked these pilgrims to go find the shards and build around them protective structures. He told them that people should be able to visit and share in the splendor of the Great Consciousness, but he did not want human ignorance to bring the shards harm.

The pilgrims dispersed and found the shards. Around the shards people built temples, some grand and others small and humble. Some people demonstrated the potential to learn how to commune with the Great Consciousness using those shards. Thus formed the Order of the Shard and those people became the first priests of the order. Using the connection to the priests through the shards, the Great Consciousness conveyed its desires to the general populace.

Aria wet her throat with water and continued, "Over time, many people came to live near the temples. While some of those areas remain as tiny villages, other places have become large cities with populations in the multiple thousands. The village we met in, Murali, has a shard temple.

"A kruusta such as myself can commune with the shard on their own, but because that is not what we are trained to do, the communion is more difficult and less clear than for a priest. That is why we tend to leave the communing to them. Like kruustas, the priests are selected and taught from a young age. Their focus is communicating with the shards and interpreting the will and desires of the Great Consciousness so that other people can understand what is expected of them or receive answers to their prayers. Kruustas tend to get their assignments from a priest after their communion."

Aria frowned. "After meeting you two and declining to act as your guide, I started second-guessing my decision."

Zephyron raised an eyebrow.

The corner of Aria's lips turned upward. She nodded. "Yes, I was having doubts.

"In any case, Priest Malechi pushed for me to allow him to do the communion for me, but I needed to commune on my own for personal clarity rather than just to receive an assignment."

Aria looked Zephyron in the eyes, their blue depths threatening to swallow her.

"What I found disturbed me," she said.

"What did you find?" Zephyron asked.

"The shard is in terrible pain, and it's dying." Her voice sounded strained to her own ears.

Zephyron held her eyes and said something she had not expected to hear. "I know."

Aria blinked at him. "How?"

"In a moment. Finish your story first."

Aria nodded. She finished her meal while she recounted the dialogue she had with Priest Malechi, the subsequent attack on the village, and her harrowing race to lure the drakes away.

Zephyron smiled at her. "That was an amazing feat you performed. You not only got them so far away that they would never be able to backtrack to Murali on their own, but you managed to kill two of them by yourself."

Aria shrugged. "That's my job."

"From what you described, your performance seems a little beyond the normal job description. You said two or three kruustas are called to fight one drake, yet you took out two by yourself."

Aria smiled, still unused to having such a casual, friendly conversation with anyone. "The same goes for you. Had you not come when you did, I would be dead right now. Xierex as well."

"You can thank Kharra," he said, gesturing with his head to the young woman. Caught at an awkward moment because she was taking a large bite of her fish, Kharra's eyes went wide. Zephyron watched Aria as if he was performing some sort of assessment. At last he continued, "She has the ability to sense things. She sensed your distress, so we came back as fast as we could. She was worried I wouldn't get there in time." He made the last statement seem as if they were sharing a private joke.

"Hey," Kharra said, trying to cover her mouth, "that's not fair."

"I expected you two to be much farther away. You had a significant head start."

Zephyron finished off his meal. "We were."

Aria narrowed her eyes. "I know there are things you're not telling me."

Zephyron set his plate aside. Instead of responding to her statement, he said, "We still need a guide if you're interested."

With a sigh Aria pushed her blond hair back behind her ear. Too many moons had passed since she had last cut it. "I'm not certain I can, not now anyway. I need to return and find out what's going on with the shard in Murali and how Priest Malechi is involved."

"Understandable," Zephyron responded. He sat there for a moment and then said, "Do you know if he has used shard beasts to attack the villagers before?"

"If that is what he is doing, I don't think so. I only came out here to deal with a glimmer worm, which was just a minor annoyance that managed to cause a lot of destruction. No people were hurt. Someone would have mentioned anything larger attacking or if anyone had been injured."

Rubbing his chin, Zephyron continued with his line of thought. "If he is the one controlling the shard beasts, then whatever is going on, his objective doesn't seem to be targeted at the local people. He didn't send those creatures after you until you found out something was wrong with the shard. I can sense the shard." Zephyron paused.

Aria blinked at him a couple of times as she let his words sink in.

Zephyron continued. "In fact I can sense most of the shards in your land. Some areas have grown dim and others dark. To me, those two things say there is probably something larger going on. The situation will likely require a detailed investigation.

"Regardless of the objective, the villagers do not appear to be in any immediate danger, and since he sent three shard drakes after you, it's safe to assume that if you do not return immediately, he will think they killed you."

"If he was the one who summoned them," said Aria.

"If he is the one who summoned them," Zephyron conceded. "Our mission is vitally important not just for our people but likely for yours as well. If you help us with this, we promise to assist you here however we can to uncover what is going on with your shards."

Aria picked up a twig from the ground, stood, and stretched out her legs. She winced at the pain in both her side and calf. She walked over to the edge of the firelight, twisting the tiny piece of wood between her fingers as she went. Her anger still simmered. She placed her hand over her bandaged side. The wound throbbed, partly in response to her anger and partly in response to the healing. While her crystal allowed her to heal fast, the process was always painful. The bigger the injury, the greater the pain.

As much as she wanted to deny it, Aria suspected that the assessment of Priest Malechi was accurate, that he had summoned the shard drakes to attack her. She wanted to do nothing more than confront the priest and show him the type of wrath only a kruusta could bring, to teach him why people feared her kind. Her rational side, however, agreed with Zephyron. Her gut told her something bigger was going on. She needed to get more information and a better perspective.

Turning to face the pair of travelers, Aria said, "Ei'ars'anu, the place you seek, is on the pinnacle of Mount Eishar, the very place that is home to the Dragon Shard. The place is dangerous. From what I was taught, something tragic happened there about a century ago. The Dragon Shard somehow became tainted and twisted. When it first happened, some people in the area were killed. Some transformed. Others were consumed. When the event was over, the area for leagues in every direction was overrun with all manner of shard beasts, some of which do not exist elsewhere.

"Today, no one journeys to Death's Pillar, not even kruustas. To do so is suicide. Most of the shard beasts created during the event, as well as any spawn of that ilk, stay on the mountain. If any do come down, then people call for us to destroy them, but we don't go into their lair to provoke the swarm."

Aria studied first Zephyron and then Kharra to gauge their reactions, but neither face revealed what might lie beneath.

"Thank you for the information," said Kharra. "What we seek is more valuable than either of our lives."

Aria weighed the woman's words and what she had observed about the two of them so far. Their attitudes and demeanor were not those of glory seekers or treasure hunters. They did not behave nor were they outfitted like mercenaries. At the same time, their cause was great enough for them to risk their lives.

With a mental nod to herself, Aria said, "I'll guide you, but I have one condition. Four other kruustas have died in the past two weeks. With the exception of the Battle of Death's Pillar, there has not been a time when so many died in such a short period. I'm afraid you may be right. Something bigger is at work here. I don't know what, but I intend to find out. On our way we'll pass through a number of other villages and cities with shard temples. I wish to investigate them as we travel."

Both Zephyron and Kharra smiled and agreed to her condition. They happily welcomed her, a kruusta, into their company. They even expressed concern for her situation. These people fascinated her.

"It seems you were right," Zephyron said over their small campfire.

Kharra nodded. She looked over toward the sleeping woman and frowned. "This isn't exactly what I had expected when I said I thought we'd cross paths with her again." She returned her attention to Zephyron and noticed he was studying Aria as if trying to solve a puzzle. Kharra's mouth twitched up at the right corner, but she only waited silently.

The white-haired man looked up at his companion. "What?" he asked.

Kharra smiled and shook her head. "Nothing."

He raised an eyebrow at her. "I know that look and that tone. What is it?"

"What are you trying to figure out?" she asked.

"Figure out? Nothing. I just find these kruustas fascinating."

Kharra nodded and did not pry further. Kharra had seen Aria's reaction when she and Zephyron had first clasped hands. The kruusta had sensed something from Kharra's companion, and Kharra suspected Zephyron had sensed it as well.

Kharra stared into the fire and bit at her lip. She did not yet know why she was drawn to Aria, but she knew that her own fate somehow intertwined with that of the kruusta.

When Aria awoke the next morning, Kharra and Zephyron were up and packed for travel. They sat a short distance away, chatting casually. The dew had already burned off. Aria glanced up through the trees, but they obscured the sun. Kharra moved toward her.

"How are you feeling?"

Aria winced as she sat up. Her side burned. "Sore," she said. She licked her lips. "And thirsty."

Zephyron joined Kharra and handed Aria a canteen. She accepted the offering and took several long swallows.

"Sorry, I don't usually sleep so late. Why didn't you wake me sooner?"

Kharra's expression grew concerned. "You were feverish. I hoped the additional sleep would help fight it off."

Aria frowned. Feverish? Kruustas never got fevers.

"Do those shard drakes possess any type of venom or toxin? Like the prism wraiths?" Zephyron asked.

Aria shook her head. "No."

Kharra frowned. "Your body is reacting to something," she said. "The fever broke a little while ago, so I think the worst of the reaction is over. Would you mind me checking your wound before we leave?"

Aria shook her head again. She turned to her side and lifted her shirt. Kharra carefully unwrapped the bandage. Her sharp intake of breath startled Aria. Zephyron moved closer and knelt beside her, his face appearing intense.

"What is it?" Aria asked as she stretched her neck to see. Her own breath caught. The wound had not only healed, but the area where it had been had crystallized.

Kharra reached out and touched the spot. "Hard, just like crystal. Can you feel me touching it?"

Aria nodded.

"Does this hurt you?" Kharra asked.

"It did last night but not now."

Aria's new companions stood, grabbed their packs, and waited, neither saying anything nor giving anything away in their expressions. Aria followed suit, gathering her own gear and packing it onto Xierex's saddle. She offered to do the same for them. Once everything was secured, they headed out. Since neither of the other travelers possessed a mount, she decided to walk along with them. Aria made it a point to remind herself to purchase some horses at the next village; otherwise, their trek could be very long.

After a time Zephyron said, "The crystallization, that is a side effect of the crystal embedded into your hand?"

"Yes," Aria answered.

Looking forward, Zephyron nodded. "If I had to hazard a guess, I would say that the longer one has been a kruusta, the farther it spreads. It probably also ties in to how much power the kruusta draws from it. Am I correct?"

Over Kharra's head, Aria studied the taller traveler out of the corner of her eye. Who was this man? Aria walked in silence for several moments, staring downward, though at nothing in particular. "Yeah," she answered, her voice a whisper.

Kharra turned her head to regard Aria. "How far does it spread?"

Aria sighed and pursed her lips downward. "Eventually a kruusta is consumed by the crystal."

Kharra simply watched her as if she knew Aria had omitted details.

Aria gave herself a mental shrug. It was not like the rest of Tanoria did not already know. After all it was the main reason why people feared kruustas. The only person not of the order to have ever truly treated her like a normal person was her brother, Delf, but he had died over two decades before. "When a kruusta is consumed, the person becomes what we call a krumetus, a monster that is no longer human. We call the process 'conversion.'"

Aria peered down into Kharra's eyes. The depth of emotion they held was beyond anything Aria had ever seen. With mere eye contact, the other woman seemed to sense Aria's pain and anguish, dreading what she was destined to become. "Most kruustas can serve for at least three or four decades before needing to worry about conversion."

Kharra disengaged her eyes from Aria's and scanned the trail before them. "Does it always end that way?"

Aria nodded. "As far as I know."

"Aria," said Zephyron, "how long have you been a kruusta?"

Aria almost stumbled on a root at the question but corrected herself in time to avoid embarrassment. She walked along quietly for several minutes. At last she answered. "I was eighteen when I earned my title, and it has been sixty-seven years since."

Kharra's eyes widened, but Zephyron just nodded.

After a time Zephyron asked her, "Are there any kruustas who are longer-lived than you?"

Aria thought for a moment. "I don't think so," she answered. "There was one who was two years younger than me, but he was one of those who died last week. Other longer-lived kruustas I knew were consumed by the crystal a decade or more ago."

"Can I examine your hand?" he asked as he exchanged places with Kharra.

Aria tilted her head and glanced at him dubiously.

Zephyron chuckled. "I'm not flirting with you. Kharra would probably smack me if I was. I just want to see something."

Aria held her hand out for Zephyron to hold. As before, her skin tingled with a rush of energy from him when they touched. They walked on with her hand in his. He stared out at the trail ahead of them but did not look at anything in specific. "Impressive."

Aria looked at him sideways. "What is?"

"Your body is harmonizing with the crystal within you. You have an immense reservoir of untapped power, but I suspect you don't release it often. That's how you have been able to go so long without being consumed as you say. With your injury yesterday, however, you released a huge amount of that reservoir."

"I didn't do anything," Aria said hastily, pulling her hand away.

"Maybe not on purpose but your body made the decision for you. The crystal helps you heal faster. It mended the wounds but with its own substance rather than with your flesh. My guess, you've never been injured to this extent before, so you may not have been aware of the process before."

Aria sighed. "I try not to draw any more power than I need. I have no idea how much time is left before the crystal consumes me."

Aria eyed a gershawk as it circled above the trees, screeching in protest as dozens of smaller birds assaulted it. The bird dived and circled a number of times, trying to brush off its harassers. After a time the smaller birds gave up, allowing the bird of prey to alight on a nearby tree. Several tiny, high-pitched cries welcomed the bird back to its nest.

At last Zephyron said, "I am not certain the phenomenon is as black and white as you think it is."

Aria continued to watch the bird. "I witnessed the transformation once," she replied. "The kruusta's name was Charold. The moment it began, he screamed about being on fire. He was in agony. He asked me to kill him, but I froze. Because of my inability to act, he went through the entire process. When the metamorphosis ended, he was no longer the same. He didn't recognize me, and I saw nothing in his eyes that I recognized as human. It seemed very black and white to me."

"Did you kill him afterward?" Zephyron inquired.

"No, I couldn't. I tried, but he was too powerful. I was young at the time, so I did the only thing I could think to do. I fled and reported his whereabouts. A group of four much more experienced kruustas returned to destroy him, but he ended up killing two of them and wounding the other two. The krumetus he had become disappeared and was never located. To this day my inability to eliminate Charold when he asked still haunts me. Those kruustas would not have died, and who knows who else has been hurt by him?"

Zephyron started to say something, but Aria cut him off. "Don't worry, I'm not feeling sorry for myself. It happened, and I learned from the experience. I know that I don't want to become that monster. You would kill me if I asked, right? If I reached my limit?"

Zephyron glanced at her. "If I deemed it necessary."

"Don't hesitate like I did." Aria held few convictions stronger than that. She had spent her entire life fighting shard beasts so that others in Tanoria could remain safe. The thought of transforming into the very thing she fought against and endangering those she had sworn to protect terrified her.

4

PRISM WRAITHS

All three moons—blue Kelmer, orange Wei, and white Aery—hung high in the sky on the evening of their third night together, providing almost as much light as Isor in the day. Aria found comfort in the celestial trio's watchful vigilance. She and they were old companions.

Living the life of a kruusta for as long as she had, traveling from place to place, Aria thought she had been to every major village and city in Tanoria. Yet her companions continued to mystify her. They both used phrases such as "from far away" and "your land." They came across as intelligent and capable, and Zephyron possessed a deep understanding of the crystals and shards—not of the kruustas and the order but of the shards themselves.

Was it possible there were lands of which she had no knowledge? Tanoria was a big place, taking several months to travel from one end to the other if one was swift and direct. Being a kruusta for many decades, however, she had circumnavigated its coastline and zigzagged across its interior many times. She also had detailed maps drafted by some of the most respected cartographers in Aloazai, the capital city. A thought struck her. Was there more beyond the gray mist perhaps? That possibility boggled her mind. She had never had any reason to consider that before, but what if? She found the idea both fascinating and daunting.

Aria caught sight of a familiar pillar of rocks. The supporting base of the pillar was made up of dark gray sediment called mudstone and shaped in the form of a pyramid. The actual pillar itself began at the top of the pyramid. From that point the pillar rose into the sky, towering over all of the surrounding trees. Years of wind and rain had worn bits of it away, making the top much wider than the foot. According to scholars, the formation had stood in that spot for thousands of years. How such a thing could remain standing at all baffled many. The locals called the pillar the Arm of the Guardian, though no one living knew who or what the Guardian was.

"We'll be in White Bluff within the hour," said Aria. "They have a few decent inns for us to choose from, and we can get you two some horses."

"We need horses?" Kharra inquired.

Aria gave her a quizzical look. "If we want to reach Death's Pillar sometime this year, then we need to move a bit faster. Xierex can't carry all of us."

Kharra glanced at Zephyron. He shook his head in return. Aria was unsure what to make of the exchange but said nothing.

Kharra paused and held up her hand, listening to something in the distance. A moment later Aria felt a faint rumbling of the ground. The sound grew more intense and evolved into the distinct sound of pounding hooves. From a dark cloud of dust, several horses emerged into view, heading straight for them. Aria, Kharra, and Zephyron stepped to the side of the road. Xierex snorted in protest at having to shuffle sideways. Moments later the riderless horses sped past the group without slowing.

"They were frantic," said Kharra.

Aria's crystal began to pulse, and a gaping pit of dread formed in her stomach. "Shard beasts," she announced to the others.

Kharra looked at her white-haired companion, worry etched into her eyes. "Zephyron, the people, we need to get there fast."

Zephyron spared a glance at Aria. With a resigned sigh, he nodded at Kharra. Zephyron fell forward onto all fours. Before her eyes, his limbs grew longer, and from his body grew pure white fur. His face changed shape, widening and thickening. The most gigantic feline-looking creature Aria had ever seen stood where a man had been just moments before. When the transformation was complete, he looked her in the eyes, bearing the same intense blue as before. Those eyes definitely belonged to Zephyron. Kharra wasted no time and vaulted onto his back.

Xierex shrieked and reared, just about tearing away from Aria's grasp. With gentle yet firm force, Aria quelled his rearing, but his eyes remained wide and his nostrils flared.

Seeing Aria had Xierex under control, and without giving the kruusta time for questions, Kharra said, "Let's go!" The feline creature launched itself into a full sprint and disappeared up the road, leaving Aria and her zegu behind.

Both stunned and pumped with adrenaline, Aria leaped onto Xierex and urged him to follow. The zegu shook his head but complied with the request of his trusted rider.

Aria arrived just behind her companions and joined them at the edge of the town to survey the scene. Dozens of shimmering white creatures drifted in and out of the buildings, up and over rooftops. Beneath their drifting forms, on the streets, across the square, along the planters, bodies littered the area.

"Prism wraiths," said Zephyron, not caring to hide his disdain. Aria cast a wary glance down at him from the corner of her eye, noting he had taken on a human form once again. What in Tanoria had she witnessed? Needing to focus on the problem at hand, she forced her kruusta discipline upon her mind.

Aria said, "I've never seen so many of them in one place before."

"Do you sense anything?" Zephyron asked Kharra.

Kharra nodded. "There are still a few who live. The closest are there, in the second inn. I sense five." She pointed to the Raven's Roost.

"And the others?" he asked.

"One is in the stables of the same inn. There are three more in the home beside the general store."

"Okay, inn first," he said.

The energy blade Aria had seen before suddenly flared to life in Zephyron's hand. In some ways the weapon reminded her of her krusword; she called forth her own blade. Resembling white quicksilver, liquid-like crystal poured out of the exposed facets of the shard on her hand, rolled down over her fingers, and quickly spun together, hardening, crystalizing. In less than a second, she held her weapon firmly. It was a large sword with an edge sharper than any steel. Back when she had first begun her training with her sword, it had often taken several hours to call it forth. More often than not, even with a successful attempt, the crystal would not harden, and she would be left with a goopy, shiny mess. Many years had passed since those days of training.

Kharra, armed with a crossbow, had been watching Aria as she summoned her krusword. She smiled, her lips tight, when Aria caught her eyes. Aria gave her a nod, and they followed after Zephyron.

The three of them skirted along the gravel-packed road leading into the village, avoiding attracting the attention of the prism wraiths by staying close to the buildings. They arrived at the Raven's Roost undetected. Zephyron stood guard while Aria attempted to enter the establishment. The door was barricaded from the other side. Not wanting to make any more noise than necessary, Aria looked in through one of the front windows, but a table pressed against it blocked the view to the interior.

Aria went back to the door and tried to force it open with her shoulder. Even with her kruusta-enhanced strength, the door refused to budge. After Aria's third failed attempt, Kharra grabbed her wrist and met her eyes. Aria heard, "Let me," though she never saw Kharra's lips move. Aria took a step back, and Kharra placed her hand on the door. With a gentle shove, it swung open, pushing aside the tables, chairs, and other debris that had barred the way.

Zephyron waited outside while the women stepped into the establishment and over the pile of obstacles. Terrified eyes peered at them from behind the bar. Aria approached and in hushed tones said, "Come, we're here to get you out." Each of the five faces recognized her as a kruusta. Under normal circumstances they would have regarded her with trepidation. In this situation there was none of that. They saw their salvation.

"Thank the shard!" said one of the two women in the group.

"Get us out of here," begged one of the men, his hair hanging limp across his face.

"We are going to get everyone to safety," said Aria in a calm, firm voice, "but I need for all of you to be absolutely quiet. Prism wraiths aren't smart, but they'll come if they hear us."

Eyes wide, the five of them nodded.

Aria led the nervous bunch out the door and back the way they came. Kharra waited, helping each person climb over the remains of the barrier. When the dark-haired young woman exited the tavern, Aria caught a glimpse of her nodding to Zephyron. The man left his post and dashed off toward the stables. Aria considered calling out to him but stopped herself. Staring after him as he disappeared into the building, Aria ushered the villagers along quietly. At last they arrived on the outskirts of the village where Aria had left Xierex.

To Kharra, Aria said, "Stay here with these people, please. I'm going to get the three out of the house."

Aria half expected a protest, but none came. Xierex, on the other hand, stomped his clawed hoof. Aria chuckled in spite of herself. She patted the zegu on the neck and said, "You stay here and protect them."

Sword in hand, Aria sprinted along the opposite side of the street, scanning the area as she went. This is going to be tricky, she thought. The house was on the far end of the town square, and the wraiths milled about in all directions. There would be no skirting anything to get near undetected. She paused to wait for some of the vile creatures to meander out of the way. The fewer she had to fight, the better.

Seeing her opening, she took a deep breath and ran as fast as she dared straight through the center of the square, hurdling hedges and low decorative walls in the process. Before she was halfway across, three wraiths saw her and turned to intercept. They were quick and closed in on her from either side. Not wanting to stop and allow them to surround her, Aria slashed at the one closest to her, shattering its spindly arm as she went. The blow would not halt the creature, but with one claw removed, the wraith became much less dangerous.

Two other wraiths joined the first three before she reached the house. Positioning her back to the front of the home, Aria steadied herself. Within seconds the shimmering shard beasts were on her. A long time ago, their pupilless eyes disturbed her, but not anymore. She gave the eyes little thought in fact and instead focused on their arms and crystal-sharded claws.

With a hiss the wraith in front of her attacked, clawing at her face. Aria brought her sword up to parry the attack and then flung the creature to the side, into one of the others. The pair on her right launched at her together. Aria ran the first one through and kicked the second. The shard beast on her blade continued to claw at her. She twisted the weapon, shattering the thing. The one on her left tried to sneak up while she was dealing with the other two, but Aria knew it was there. She raised the sword back over her shoulder and swung outward, blocking its strike and beheading the wraith in the same move. Moving with quick efficiency, she dispatched the three she had knocked off balance before they had a chance to recover.

As soon as the final wraith fell, the front door to the house inched open and revealed the face of a young man. "Are you here to save us?" he asked in earnest.

"Yes," Aria responded. "Come quick. We won't have much time."

Aria stood guard as the man opened the door farther. Despite his youth he appeared worn and haggard. Behind him came a woman no more than twenty years old, her eyes red and puffy. In her arms she carried a small toddler.

"Let's go," was all Aria said as she guided the family back across the square.

The young woman, running between Aria and the man, clutched the child to her chest. The man's panicked eyes darted from side to side. A solitary wraith pursued them, and Aria turned to engage it. Not wanting to move too far away from her charges, she allowed the shard beast to draw closer. When it came within reach, Aria used a backhanded slice to cleave the creature in two. The wraith fell to the ground and shattered.

"Keep moving," Aria whispered as she pushed the woman along.

Another single wraith moved into the square but did not see them right away. Aria crossed over to the other side of the couple and swung at the wraith, removing its head cleanly from its body. As she turned, yet another wraith came upon them, this time from the front. The young woman yelped in surprise just as Aria spun around and decapitated the shard beast.

The woman's noise brought the attention of several more of the vile creatures. As a unit the wraiths turned toward the group and moved to intercept them. The woman panicked and started to run ahead, ignoring the dangers around them. Aria tried to grab her but missed. The woman stumbled and fell. With her hands full, she landed sharply on her elbows. The woman yelped, and the child began to scream. Every remaining wraith, several dozens of them, responded.

Aria scooped up the screaming child under her left arm. With the fingers of her sword hand, she plucked the woman's sleeve and lifted her upward. Aria pushed the woman toward the man. "Get her out of here," she ordered.

The man tried to do as he was told, but the woman twisted out of his grasp, shrieking frantically for her child. The first wraith came in from the right, and Aria backhanded it with her pommel. The man reclaimed the woman's left hand, but she attempted to grab at her child with her right. Aria grunted in frustration when she realized the woman was not going to be pulled away while her child was in danger. With the child held protectively under her arm, Aria said, "I'll keep him safe. You two stay close."

Though it was clear the woman still desperately wanted to be the one holding the child, the compromise became enough for her as the man wrapped his arms around hers. But during the exchange, they lost precious moments, and the wraiths closed in on them. Aria danced her way around to either side of the couple, swinging, spinning, twisting, and dodging her way through an increasing number of wraiths. Before long a wall of the creatures drifted into place between her and the couple. "Keep moving," she ordered. "I'm right behind you." Despite her efforts, Aria lost ground, but that did not matter as long as she kept the child safe.

Movements turned into a rhythmic dance as Aria continued to push her way across the square, careful to keep the wraiths from getting too near the youngster. Even a small drop of their toxin would be lethal to one so young. Her arm moved faster and faster until her blade became a whirl of prismatic colors under the moonlight. This was her element, her time. Several of the shard beasts went down beneath the tempest that was Aria. Faster and faster the krusword spun, causing the crystal to sing as it cut through the air. She glanced ahead, noting she was close to breaking free of their blockade.

The young couple reached their destination and waited in the distance, beyond the edge of the town and out of the range of the wraiths. Realizing sound attracted the wraiths, they kept quiet. The man though gestured for her to hurry, and the woman wrung her hands nervously. Aria barely spared a thought for them except to note that they were out of harm's way.

With each wraith she slew, two more seemed to take its place. Why were there so many? Spin, slash, whirl, slash, twist, slash, dodge, slash. Only a small part of her brain acknowledged that she still held the child, so focused was she on destroying her targets. She became the wind dancing to the song of the sword. Despite the dire circumstances, it had never sounded so beautiful. Time lost all dimension. There was only Aria, her blade, and the wraiths that shattered in a shower of stars.

Suddenly Aria's arm stopped moving, and the song ended. Why had she stopped? She looked up at a white-haired man holding her wrist. Aria blinked as recollection returned to her. "Zephyron?" she asked.

"The fighting is over," he said as he gently pulled the toddler from her arms. The young mother rushed up to reclaim her child.

"Thank you, Kruusta. Thank you." The woman met Aria's eyes and backed away into the safety of her husband's arm. The two of them distanced themselves even farther.

Aria scanned the village. Nothing but white shards covered the area between the house and the edge of the town. Fortunately prism wraiths did not bleed, or the ground would have been saturated with blood. She eyed Zephyron, hoping to find an explanation.

"That was all you," he said in an incredulous tone. "As far as I can tell, every one of them is gone."

Kharra and the other people who had been rescued returned, each one of them wearing the same stunned expression as they looked out over the carnage. In ones and twos, the villagers broke off to investigate the damage. Zephyron did as well.

A burning sensation ignited across Aria's shoulder, forcing her to her knees. Kharra rushed to her side. "Aria! Are you okay? Did one of them scratch you?"

Aria remained where she was for a moment. The pain pulsed and ebbed with the beat of her heart, but after a few moments, it subsided. "I don't know," she said at last, her breath short in coming. "My shoulder's on fire."

Kharra's deft hands removed Aria's shoulder pad and pulled back her light mail shirt. "I don't think this is a scratch from the wraiths," Kharra assessed, her voice laced with the faint sound of sorrow.

Aria sighed. No, it was not a scratch from the wraith. On her shoulder grew four perfectly formed crystalline shards, the largest of which was at least the length of a finger. She recalled how Kruusta Charold, the one she had failed to end before his transformation, had screamed about being on fire as he went through his conversion. Aria's body was finally turning against her.

Aria planted her sword tip into the ground and hoisted herself up. "The pain has gone. I'm fine now." She readjusted her shirt and allowed the crystal in her hand to reclaim her weapon, its solid form taking on its quicksilver-like quality once again before disappearing.

Kharra regarded Aria with an unreadable mask.

It was both good and bad that the other woman did not seem fearful of these early signs of Aria's transformation. Aria said, "I don't know if you overheard what I said to Zephyron before. If during our trek I come to the point where I am no longer me, I have asked him to release me."

"Aria," Kharra replied at last, "I won't let it come to that."

"I appreciate your concern for my well-being, but I'm a kruusta. This is something we all know will happen, some sooner than others. I will help you both for as long as I am able, and maybe I will be lucky enough to last beyond your mission. But I don't wish to become a threat to people. If I start to lose myself, I would like someone to kill me before I hurt someone else."

"Don't worry," Kharra said solemnly. "We won't let you hurt anyone."

"Thank you." Aria gave the young woman a tight smile.

Zephyron returned a short while later, his face a dark thundercloud on the verge of bursting.

"What's wrong?" Kharra asked.

"I went to the local shard temple. The entire shard…it's gone, destroyed."

"That explains why there were so many wraiths," Kharra said, her face still unreadable.

A fount of emotions boiled up through Aria. "Destroyed? How does one destroy a shard?" she demanded.

Zephyron shook his head. "I don't know, and it's really too late for us to investigate tonight. I say we get some rest and come back tomorrow to take a closer look."

The two women agreed. While Aria was fairly certain that all of the wraiths had been eliminated, she was too exhausted to double-check.

On her recommendation the villagers gathered some of their belongings and joined the three travelers in camping a short distance away from the village. She reassured them that they could return the next day to do a thorough sweep of the area.

5

THE TRUTH

"Are you coming?" Zephyron asked as the villagers shuffled away.

Kharra shook her head. "No, I'm going to wait here until she wakes."

Zephyron nodded. He did not seem to be looking at her but rather through her.

"What's wrong?" Kharra asked.

"Ah, nothing. I'm just processing all of this."

"The shard?" she asked.

"The shard—or shards for that matter. Aria. Our mission. I don't think it was a coincidence that our mission brought us to this place, not just to Aria but to whatever is going on with the crystal in this land at this point in time." His brow furrowed, and his jaw became stiff.

"You're angry," Kharra said pointedly.

Zephyron rocked his head forward and back subtly.

"Because of the shards?"

"Well, some of that, yeah, but also the stuff that's happening to her," he said as he jutted his chin in the direction of Aria's bedroll. "She's a fascinating woman—skilled, intelligent, and open-minded. It's horrible that she has to endure this conversion process. I don't get it. The crystals don't behave that way. There's something else that's causing this reaction she and the other kruustas have. I know it. And whatever that something is, it's been going on for roughly a century." He regained his focus, his face set with resolve. "We won't let her fall to this. We will find out how to stop it. There's got to be something that can be done. If we had a Sauru singer, we probably would have figured this out already."

"But the Sauru are extinct," Kharra interjected.

Zephyron sighed. "I know, but there's got to be a way."

"Well, you're the next best thing to a Sauru," Kharra said encouragingly. "You have sensitivity to Mattekan and the crystal veins that others don't. I'm sure something will occur to you."

Zephyron nodded. "I hope so."

"You wouldn't kill her, would you?" Kharra asked.

"What? No," Zephyron said with an emphatic shake of his head.

"You don't think she'll turn into this krumetus monster?"

Zephyron shrugged. "I don't know, but I think if we can keep her focused on this mission, keep her from giving up, we can probably delay it until we find a cure."

Kharra nodded. "And if that isn't enough? What if she does transform?"

"I don't know. I really don't want to think about that. Maybe we could restrain her until we find the cure."

Kharra refrained from voicing her doubts. If an entire land could not find a cure over the course of a hundred years, what chance did they have of finding one in a matter of weeks? Kharra studied Zephyron briefly. To any other observer, he likely looked composed and in control, but Kharra could tell that this situation had rattled him. He was determined to do whatever was necessary to save Aria.

Aria woke to a blast of sunlight breaking through the tall cinnabar trees standing at attention over their camp. The light fell on her face, blinding her for a moment when she opened her eyes. As she allowed them to adjust, the shards on her shoulder pulsed gently in rhythm with her heartbeat. She wanted nothing more than to cut them off, but she knew they would just grow back. They were as much a part of her body now as her hair or skin. For some reason not being able to wear her left shoulder pad annoyed her even more than having shards protruding from her shoulder.

Aria sat up. Kharra poked at the fire, but the rest of the camp was empty.

"The villagers returned to the village to begin cleaning up," Kharra announced without looking at her. "They also sent a messenger to deliver word to the other nearby villages announcing that the menace has passed and requesting people return home. Zephyron wants us to meet him at the shard temple as soon as you're ready."

Her energy drained despite the sleep, Aria forced herself up and followed Kharra's lead. She rubbed her fingers through her hair as images from the previous night drifted back to her. She had lost herself in the crystal, even if for just a moment. That had never happened before, and it frightened her. How long before she lost herself forever?

The two women passed through the town on the way to the shard temple. Dozens of villagers milled about already hard at work repairing the damage from the night before. Bodies of the deceased, wrapped in white linen, lined the town square.

A man working on a door to one of the houses looked up to wipe his brow. As soon as he saw Aria, his expressionless face broke into a bright smile. He waved. Aria's lips turned upward at the edges, and she nodded to him in return. Three other people they passed did the same.

Unlike Murali, where the shard temple had been set back away from the town, here in White Bluff, the temple sat right beside the other major buildings lining the square though obscured from the road by a dozen blossoming fruit trees. Aria caught the sweet, slightly tart scent of apple blossoms as she and Kharra walked up the footpath toward the temple's front entrance. Aria frowned at seeing so many of the blossoms on the ground.

Kharra stopped. Aria looked up and scowled at the scene. Of the temple, only the doorway and the lower portion of the front wall remained standing. The rest of the building lay scattered in thousands of pieces. Kharra continued forward, picking her steps through the shredded debris. Aria followed. Bits of wood, stone, glass, and metalwork littered the area. Mixed in with the wreckage, Aria spotted small fragments of crystal, most no bigger than her finger.

Zephyron, who had arrived some time earlier, was sifting through what should have been the shard's dais. Both women joined him, trying to be careful of where they stepped. A twinge of sadness panged in Aria's heart as shard pieces crunched beneath her foot.

"This exploded outward," Zephyron announced as they arrived. "The force of the blast demolished the temple and killed the priest. His remains are over there in what was once another room. I haven't seen destruction like this since the war."

Aria peered into the crater. The ground sank down to the height of a man. The only thing left of the shard was the frayed edges of its root, blackened and dead. Kharra placed a hand on her arm. It was at that point she realized she had been shaking with anger. The crystal in her hand pulsed in response to her emotion. She closed her eyes, took several deep breaths, and composed herself. She could not afford to allow it to spread further.

"This confirms what I said last night, why so many wraiths swarmed the town," Kharra added. "Aria, have you ever seen anything like this before?"

Aria shook her head. "Never." She found herself pushing down her anger once again. "But I intend to find out who caused this and why. This is too much to be a coincidence between here and Murali." Her companions both agreed. Her gut told her something else as well. She stared at the crater and poked at random pieces of debris with her toe.

"I'll be honest though," she said at last, the sound of her voice constricted even to her own ears. "These things are happening just as you two arrive in our lands."

Kharra's head whipped around to look at Aria, her expression stunned. "You don't think we have anything to do with this, do you?" Zephyron stood and crossed his arms, his expression wary.

"I don't know. Not directly, no, but you both possess a lot of information about the shards. You come from a strange land and know nothing of our ways, yet you want to go to Ei'ars'anu, the site of the most powerful shard ever known. At the same time, other shards are dying or are being destroyed, something that has never happened in my entire service as a kruusta. Burn me if the two aren't related."

Aria regarded the two calmly, weighing her next words carefully. "You both withhold details from me, and I am certain your reasons are good for doing so. I was fine with you keeping your personal business to yourselves, and I had no plans on prying. But my understanding of the circumstances has changed. If I am going to continue to help you, then I need to understand everything. Who you are. What you are." She stared at Zephyron to emphasize the what. She continued. "Where you are from. Why you are here. What you are after." There. She had said it all.

Zephyron studied her, his blue eyes piercing and intense. Kharra eyed her passively, the woman's face not betraying her emotions. Both of them stood silently for many moments. The silence unnerved her, but Aria refused to move, not even to shift her weight.

At last Zephyron said, "Let us get food, and we can talk."

The three of them picked their way carefully back through the door and out toward the town square. There were even more people moving around than before: some carrying supplies, others hammering or sawing at various pieces of construction, and some loading the bodies into wagons.

A woman with long, rich brown hair ran up to them from one of the buildings. A man, sawdust covering his pants, followed her. The woman stopped just in front of them and held her hands together.

At first Aria thought something else had happened, but the woman beaming from ear to ear caused her to dismiss the notion. She looked Aria in the eye. "Thank you, Kruusta, so much for coming to rescue my husband and the others. I don't know what I would have done had I lost him."

The man beside her dwarfed her frame with his wide shoulders and broad chest. Aria recognized him as one of the people they had rescued from the Raven's Roost. "Yes, thank you. My name is Ian. You were exhausted when you returned last night, so I didn't want to bother you, but I did not get the chance to thank you properly." He extended his hand, and Aria took it. "The Raven's Roost is my establishment. We've gotten the place cleaned up, and the fires are going, so the least I can do is offer you all a meal and somewhere to rest."

"That is generous of you," Aria said in response.

A scruffy youth with reddish-brown hair, somewhere between a boy and a man, ran up to the group as well. He took Zephyron's hand in both of his and shook it. "Thank you, Zephyron, for getting me out of the stables." The boy glanced at Aria and said, "After I released the horses, I got trapped and couldn't get back."

Zephyron smiled. "My pleasure, Adarn. You were pretty heroic yourself, thinking of the horses like you did."

"I just did what I could, sir. Everyone was so panicked about getting out of the village, many of the extra horses were left behind. They couldn't get away, what with being locked up in their stalls and all."

More people joined them out in the square, wanting to either shake their hands, give them thanks, or both. One little girl with golden hair and bright-green eyes wove her way through the crowd and hugged Aria's leg. Aria placed her hand on the girl's head and smiled. Despite losing a number of people from their village, they were grateful help had come and appreciative that others had been saved.

In all her years as a kruusta, Aria had never before been the center of such positive attention. For the first time ever, her actions felt like more than just a job, and seeing so many happy faces affected her in ways she never thought possible. Having helped these people, positive emotions threatened to overwhelm her. Yes, she would find out who was behind the problems with the shards and who was responsible for the massacre here.

At last Ian held up his hands. "Okay, folks, let them get something to eat. Dara, take them inside, will you?"

The woman with the long brown hair hugged her husband and then beckoned the village saviors to follow her into the Raven's Roost. She told them to sit anywhere they wanted while she went to fetch them their meals.

The inn had indeed been cleaned up as Ian said—debris cleared away, tables and chairs righted, floors swept and mopped, and counters wiped clean. Only two other tables held occupants, people who had come in from working to take a break; Ian and his wife had opened up their kitchen to offer a meal to any of those who helped with the rebuilding.

Zephyron led the way to a table in the far back. The other customers smiled and nodded their heads to them as they passed. Dara returned moments later with three plates heaping with meat, bread, vegetables, and even fresh scoops of butter. She had offered them ale, but none of them wanted to imbibe alcohol. Instead she brought them large mugs of fresh-brewed tea sweetened with a few drops of honey. Aria's stomach growled as soon as the food appeared in front of her. Zephyron raised an eyebrow and grinned.

Aria took her first bite of the thin slice of roast and savored its salty, juicy flavor. She did not recall anything tasting so good. Her body craved more, and she gave in to its desires. Aria spread the butter on her bread and dipped it into the juice of her roast. She sank her teeth into the bread, allowing the juice and butter to mingle on her tongue. Every bite she took exploded with sensation.

Kharra watched her. It was not exactly unnerving, but the woman seemed observant about everything.

"That was an amazing display last night," Zephyron said, bringing Aria's thoughts away from the food. "I've been a fighter for a long time, and I don't think I've ever seen anyone move as fast as you did."

Aria finished her bite and swallowed. "I've had many years of practice."

"So have I."

Aria stopped her hand before the fork reached her mouth and looked at him. The undercurrent of his tone conveyed something she could not quite place. She continued with her bite.

Zephyron continued. "You wish to know about us, and rightly so. I believe your instincts are correct. Our mission may be related to what is going on here, though I do not think we specifically are bringing the problem to you. It would have arisen whether we showed up or not.

"What and who we are is a bit complicated."

Aria gave him a level look and, with her kruusta-disciplined voice, said, "Complicated or not, I need to know."

Zephyron nodded. "Kharra is confident we can trust you, but you need to be careful with the information we give you. Based on my observations, I'm not certain other people in your land are ready to accept what I am about to tell you. We are also not without enemies, some of whom may be in this land. If they are here, we don't want to alert them to our presence."

Aria nodded.

"Good. I'm going to have to jump around a bit in order to convey the more important bits; otherwise, we could be here for weeks giving you a history lesson. Tell me if I lose you.

"First off, the thing you refer to as the gray mist is a barrier of sorts created by powerful mystical energy. The barrier surrounds Tanoria. Tanoria, however, is actually just one land mass in a much more massive world. There is so much more beyond the gray mist."

Aria could not help but ogle at him. Theorizing fantastical possibilities was one thing. Having them expressed as fact was quite another. "How is that even possible?"

Zephyron shook his head. "As to the how, all I know is that it was created by a very powerful being using rare mystical powers. Your land has been isolated and hidden from other lands for centuries. The people of this land have never been able to leave not because someone forced them to remain but because that is what they were taught. The Guardians contributed to the myth long ago. Over the centuries, some people have left, but once they moved outside the boundary, they found themselves unable to return. That only served to reinforce the myth."

Aria's eyebrow twitched. Using Guardians, a religious reference, as part of the story lost some of the credibility in her eyes. Still, the idea of other lands beyond the gray mist intrigued her. Aria nodded again. "Leave where? How?"

"Across the ocean, by ship."

"Interesting," she said. "We were always taught that the ocean made a ring about Tanoria. There are various myths about what happens to the people who sail into the gray mist. The most prevailing of those myths are that people sail off the edge of the world, are taken to the land of the dead, or are stuck in the mist for eternity in a state of limbo. Only a handful of my missions have ever required me to be on a ship, so thoughts of the gray mist rarely cross my mind."

"Well, there is no edge to the world," Kharra said as she held up both hands facing one another, fingers and thumbs curved as if she held a large round fruit. "The world is round, a giant sphere filled with many oceans and land masses."

"So," said Aria with more than a hint of skepticism creeping into her voice, "what is the name of this bigger world?"

"Mattekan," both Kharra and Zephyron responded at the same time.

Aria's lips twitched upward. Though part of her wanted to dispute their story, the other part of her saw how these two acted, how they fought, and how they talked. They came from no place she had ever known. As someone who knew Tanoria better than almost anyone else still living, Aria did not doubt they came from somewhere else, perhaps another land as they said. Just the possibility of the existence of places beyond Tanoria fascinated the kruusta.

Zephyron washed down his food with his tea and continued. "Mattekan is not just the world. It is also a living entity, what I believe you call the Great Consciousness. It is more ancient than anything else in this world, possibly in any world. It may even be older than Isor, but our records don't go back far enough to know for certain. Our information comes from impressions left to us by Mattekan.

"Now, the soil we stand on is not living but rather a protective layer Mattekan built up over billions of years. Beneath the ground crystal veins crisscross the entire world, some thick and strong, some fine and fragile. They are all connected. What you call shards are physical parts of that network, of Mattekan.

"Mattekan has neither eyes nor ears nor a mouth like you and me, but it can see and feel and communicate. Many species of animals instinctively react to Mattekan's needs, but this is not so with humans. Only a small fraction of humans have been born with the ability to hear Mattekan. Fewer still can understand it. As a result of their inability to understand, humans sometimes bring harm to the entity without realizing they do so."

Kharra finished the last of her meal and continued the story. "For example, the land I grew up in, Marimon, is a place where people mine the crystal veins because they discovered the crystals to be an effective power source. Even if the vein it came from has been completely severed from the rest of Mattekan's structure, the crystal pieces will still provide power."

"You can't be serious," Aria said, louder than she intended. She glanced around the room but relaxed when she realized they were the only ones still there. "Cutting a shard that deep is a grave offense here. The only thing resembling an exception is when a kruusta receives his or her crystal, which is done with the blessing of the Great Consciousness." She glanced around to be certain no one was staring. The bubble of anger returned.

Kharra nodded in understanding. "The people there couldn't hear Mattekan even though it tried to get them to stop. To protect itself, Mattekan created an impassible mountain range out at the sea, cutting Marimon off from the rest of the world so those people could not spread their practice elsewhere. Within the entire Marimon region, Mattekan is dead. Still, the people there happily mine the massive amount of remaining crystal."

Zephyron continued. "Though Kharra grew up in Marimon, she and I are both from a different land called Aerous. I am a Guardian, and part of my responsibility is to keep such a thing from happening elsewhere."

Aria nearly choked on her vegetables. She forced herself to swallow and looked up. "You're a what?"

"A Guardian. Do your people know of Guardians?"

Aria raised both eyebrows. "Guardian? As in one of the gods of old?"

Zephyron chuckled. "Hardly a god but, yes, I am a Guardian. I was once human like you or Kharra, but I was called by Mattekan to be one of its protectors. That is how Guardians come to be."

Aria took her last bite and scrunched her brow in thought. She believed in the Great Consciousness and the shards because both were tangible to her, but not Guardians. She had never believed in them. The only information anyone had about them came from children's bedtime stories and myths passed down through the generations intended to teach people about the morality of life.

At last Aria said, "Forgive me if I have a little difficulty believing you're a Guardian." She emptied her mug of tea and wiped her mouth.

"Understandable," Zephyron replied.

With everyone finished eating, all three of them stood. Dara hurried over to ask if they wanted anything else. Aria declined and informed their host that now that the village was safe, they needed to be on their way. They still had a lot of ground to cover before they reached their destination. The woman asked for them to wait.

She disappeared and returned a moment later with a large pack in her hands filled with a variety of foodstuffs—meats, cheeses, breads, even packets of tea leaves so they could brew more tea along the way. All three thanked Dara and headed out.

Aria shaded her eyes as they exited from the Raven's Roost. Isor's radiant light smiled down from the sun's zenith, and the cloudless sky and light breeze indicated a warm and pleasant day, a wonderful day for traveling. The villagers worked hard at repairing their homes and businesses, yet each of them stopped to wave as the three travelers departed. Aria bid farewell to Ian and thanked him for their meal. He in turn gave her an open invitation to return any time. This had been a different experience in her dealings with people, and Aria appreciated the offer.

At their camp Xierex snorted and stomped, a display of annoyance at being left behind, but it was all a show. By the look of the nearby vegetation, he had enjoyed spending the morning browsing on the flowering trees of the surrounding area. Aria smiled and gave him an affectionate rub. His crystalline horns spun and swirled with colors as the light filtered through them. She pulled a biscuit from the pack given to her by Dara and handed it to the zegu. He accepted the peace offering and quieted, earning a laugh from both Kharra and Zephyron.

Aria took extra time to strap down their gear on the back of Xierex's saddle, half distracted by all the questions popping into her head. The massive bluish zegu stood with patience but attempted to play with her hair each time she walked past him. She scratched his chin in response. Over her shoulder she caught Zephyron's gaze with one eye and asked, "So last night, the cat, what was that? I mean, that was you, right? I wasn't imagining it?"

"Yes, that was me," he said with a grin. He grinned a lot Aria noted.

"Is that a Guardian thing? Assuming I believe what you say about being a Guardian." Aria tied down the last of the gear and turned to face her two companions. They were ready to go as well. Aria took the lead and picked the direction. The other two followed.

Zephyron shook his head. "Actually, no. That was one of two abilities I had prior to being called."

Aria responded, "I've never known of people having such abilities."

"Not surprising. As I mentioned earlier, there are only a small percentage of humans who can hear Mattekan. Those people are imbued with tiny amounts of its immense power, which manifests into different abilities. The types of abilities vary, with similar abilities tending to run in family lines.

"For thousands of years, people of Aerous embraced those with abilities. We call the power used to draw on those abilities leyoen. Those without abilities we call couren, meaning deaf: deaf to Mattekan's voice. Over time, different leyoen families went their separate ways, forming numerous tribes. The tribes became known for the type of leyoen they wielded. The Alaswani, for example, were the People of Fire, and their dominant leyoen abilities were fire-related. Not everyone born to those families was born with leyoen. In fact most born were couren, but still, the people of the tribes embraced and honored those who manifested leyoen even if their abilities were weak and seemingly insignificant.

"My people were the Duani, the People of the Twin Souls. When young people of the Duani come of age, they seek the wilds and sit in prayer. They open themselves up so their twin soul, if they have one, may find them. The twin soul is an animal spirit that seeks to be joined for a higher purpose. If a person is chosen by a twin soul, the spirit of the person and the spirit of the animal become one. From that point on, they may take on the form of either the person or the animal. Those who are chosen are called saoul.

"Most, but not all, twin souls are wolves. I was different. Not only was I fortunate enough to have been chosen, but I was chosen by a tigron, the cat form you saw. Tigron are rare, mystical creatures."

"Hm," Aria said, digesting the information. "Can you change your form at any time?" she asked.

"I can," he said in response.

"And you can carry a rider?"

"Yes."

Aria thought for a moment. "I understand now why you didn't need horses. So then why are we walking? We would make much better time if we rode."

"We could, though conversing would be more difficult, at least initially," he explained.

Aria nodded in understanding. While he could follow a conversation in his tigron form, he would not be able to speak.

Zephyron added, "Kharra has the ability to facilitate that, though I'm not certain you're ready just yet."

"Ready for what?" Aria asked, glancing at Kharra, who walked on the opposite side of Zephyron.

"She'll be fine," Kharra said, "but I think I'll explain it to her first."

The conversation continued as they traveled, and Aria repeatedly found herself amazed by what she learned. Kharra's people had been called the Zumai, the People of the Spirit. According to Kharra, the Zumai had the widest variety of abilities of any of the tribes. Born with several of her tribe's abilities, Kharra considered herself both fortunate and unusual. One of her abilities she called mind seeking, the ability to both know the thoughts of another and to project her thoughts to that person. With sudden realization Aria recalled witnessing Kharra use the ability the night before, when they tried to get into the Raven's Roost. Aria had heard Kharra ask to be allowed to open the door, but Kharra's lips had not moved. Zephyron also had mind seeking, but according to him, the ability was weak compared to Kharra's. He explained that it was his main mode of communication while in his tigron form.

With the mind-seeking explanation out of the way, Zephyron transformed. It happened so fast Aria just had time to register that it had occurred before she was greeted by the grinning face of a massive white cat. His lips did not move, yet when he looked at her, she knew he was grinning. Xierex's eyes went wide, and he tried to rear. Aria held his reins steady, but he continued to tug away.

Kharra approached the zegu. Aria warned her to stay back, but she insisted she would be fine. Kharra placed one hand on his nose and another on his chin. He flinched once and then calmed, lowering his head until it was eye level with the dark-haired woman.

"He's okay," Kharra announced. "He thought the cat ate Zephyron and wanted to eat us. He now understands the tigron is also Zephyron."

"He understood all that?"

Kharra nodded. "He is very intelligent, much smarter than a horse."

With Xierex calmed, Aria looked at Zephyron. He stood as tall as Xierex, who himself was taller than a draft horse. Zephyron's feline form had a sleek, muscular body with thick, strong legs. His fur was a brilliant white with a thick snowy mane crowning his head and neck. Aria realized she was staring and shook herself. "My mind is having trouble seeing that as you. It just doesn't seem possible."

6

PEOPLE OF THE CRYSTAL

Both Aria and Kharra mounted up, and Aria allowed Xierex to set the pace. He was eager to run, and Zephyron had no issues keeping up. While riding, Kharra introduced Aria to mind seeking.

As you can see, mind seeking can be advantageous while on the move, said Kharra's "voice." The kruusta found the sensation a little disconcerting at first, hearing a voice in her head as clear as if someone was talking to her.

"Are you able to read my thoughts?" Aria asked over the thudding of Xierex's hooves.

I can if I choose, but out of principle, I don't go into a person's mind without good reason. However, I can receive thoughts that are projected at me without reading thoughts that may be more personal.

"I assume that requires another person who has your ability?" Aria asked with a glance out of the corner of her eye.

She caught Kharra's shake of the head. *Not at all. Anyone who can think can learn to project thoughts. The only thing that's a little different is that you have to open up your mind so that the thoughts are released. Those who don't have the ability tend to close their minds if their voices aren't involved.*

"I see." In some ways, the concept reminded Aria of how she communed with the shards. She thought of what she would say next but did not voice it. *Are you able to receive this?*

Kharra's eyes widened in surprise, and she nodded with a smile. *I did. You're a natural. I know others who spent weeks before they were able to do it reliably without using their voices.*

Aria allowed herself a faint smile. *What about Zephyron? Is he hearing this conversation?*

Kharra shook her head. *Not yet. His strongest talents are not in mind seeking. He does have the ability, and he could send thoughts to you with it. However, it's not strong enough to receive thoughts from those without any ability at all. Mind seeking is one of my stronger talents. Not only can I receive thoughts from those without the ability, but I can act as a conduit between people of different levels of talent.*

Aha! came a distinctly masculine voice in Aria's head. *At least you did not scare her away.*

Oh hush, you! said Kharra as she swatted at the top of his head.

Zephyron's mental voice made a distinct chuckle.

Aria appraised their banter. Part of her longed to have had even one individual in her life with whom she could have been so casual.

Time passed swiftly as the trio carried on their mental conversation. Aria assaulted her companions with a barrage of questions as she fought to understand the foreign concepts they introduced. To their credit they answered everything with patience and understanding. If she was going to be with them for several weeks and facing dangers she knew they did not fully appreciate, then she wanted to know as much about them as possible.

Kharra admitted to possessing two other abilities. The first was empathy, which allowed her to sense the emotions of those around her. She explained that while she did not try to read another person's thoughts with mind seeking, her empathy was automatic, and it was sometimes difficult for her to block out really strong emotions.

As Kharra explained the workings of empathy, Aria reflected on the time she had spent with the two travelers. Aria noted several occasions during which her emotions, most notably anger, had threatened to overwhelm her. Kharra must have sensed that. On each occasion Kharra had touched her, usually on her arm or shoulder. Now that

Aria thought about it, she realized those moments of contact had had an immediate calming effect.

Aria knew she was only just beginning to grasp what these abilities could do, but she surmised that Kharra had also been able to use them on Xierex. It explained how a woman the zegu did not know was able to calm him and even get him to understand abstract concepts, such as Zephyron's transformation.

The conversation shifted from the discussion of empathy to one about her last ability—mind moving. Kharra could cause objects to move, apply force to something, and even create invisible but tangible barriers with just a thought. Through their discussion, Aria realized that Kharra had used the ability to open the blockaded door in White Bluff. The nature of this ability boggled Aria's mind most of all, but still, the logical side of her brain worked through all the practical applications such an ability could afford. Aria pressed Kharra with questions about mind moving, but the other woman often evaded or redirected them to something else. Aria relented, sensing Kharra's reluctance to discuss it further.

Aria's mind wandered from the conversation as she slowed Xierex to a cooldown walk. She patted the zegu and scanned the sky through the trees but said nothing. Zephyron slowed beside her.

You've gone silent, came a much softer thought from Kharra. *I hope this is not overwhelming you.*

"Not at all," she said. Now that they were walking, she thought it appropriate to use her voice again.

You are taking all of this very well, Aria, said Zephyron.

"I take it my reaction isn't typical?"

Unfortunately, Zephyron responded, the tone of his mind voice solemn. *Wars have been fought because some feared these abilities.*

Aria fell into a quiet cadence as she rode. Her mind swam with an abundance of information to process. Her two companions grew silent as well.

They rode for several more hours with no new words or thoughts exchanged, at least not with Aria. Her mind had wandered back to her own immediate concerns involving the shards. A sense of anxiety festered at the bottom of her stomach, but she ignored it the best she could. At last she located the small trail she sought. Leading with Xierex, she guided their group off the main road and up a narrow game trail. After climbing steadily for another two hours, Aria called a halt near a small lake.

Aria dismounted and walked to the lake's edge, stretching her legs as she went. Kharra followed. Aria stood in silence as she stared out across the water. No more than one hundred feet across and two hundred feet wide, the lake was dominated by a pair of waterfalls that fell from vastly different heights but mingled together partway down, giving the main waterfall the appearance of having two colors—one of beautiful cold blue water and the other, warmer, a translucent white. The waters fell against a backdrop of vibrant mossy-green cliffs, and Aria closed her eyes as the spray washed over her face.

"Aria, this is beautiful," whispered Kharra beside her.

Aria nodded. She loved many places across Tanoria, but this was one of her favorites. "I come here every time I pass through this region. When I leave, I always feel revitalized."

"There is a shallow vein beneath us," said Zephyron from behind them, clothed and kneeling with one hand on the ground.

Aria frowned. She had not heard his approach. "I never gave much thought to veins as you call them," she admitted.

Zephyron nodded. "In fact," he said as he pulled off his tunic, "I believe there is a shard beneath those falls there." He continued to strip. Aria crossed her arms and raised an eyebrow but said nothing. Kharra blushed, but a small smile twitched at the edge of her lips.

The man rippled with lines of muscles, and the handful of scars across his torso and back only gave them more definition. He dived out toward the center of the lake, swimming with long, powerful strokes. Even in the water, he moved with majestic grace; the water barely stirred with his passing. Aria gave herself a shake as Zephyron's head disappeared beneath the surface.

Several minutes passed, and he had not yet surfaced. "Don't worry. He can hold his breath for a long time," Kharra said without turning her head.

Aria regarded the younger woman.

Kharra's head turned to meet her eyes. "You gave nothing away. In fact you are very adept at controlling your outward appearance, but..." She tapped her head. "Empathy."

Aria frowned. "That must be a burden, to always sense those around you."

"It used to be, before I learned to shield myself from the outside. In the village where I grew up, any time a child scraped their knee, I burst into tears. When siblings argued, I'd snap at anyone who spoke to me. There was a father who used to beat his wife and children. It got so bad at one point that it left me almost comatose. Thankfully my father and other villagers learned of the abuse. They intervened and put an end to it. That was the first time I'd used my gift to help someone, and afterward I was able to help the children through their trauma.

"Nowadays only the strongest emotions have a chance of getting through my shield. It's fatiguing but necessary; I've built up quite the endurance. That's why, though, around those I trust, I lessen my shield. Around friends and family, it's not a burden."

"How do you know you can trust me?" Aria asked. "You don't know me. From what little I know about your situation, you've taken a significant risk sharing your information with me."

Kharra nodded. "I have good instincts about people."

A splash from the lake diverted their conversation. Zephyron's full height emerged from beneath the water near the shore. Water ran down the length of his body, outlining his lean muscles. Aria realized she was staring and chided herself. She had seen plenty of men and been with a number of them, but she had never found herself appraising them as she was with Zephyron.

"Did you find anything interesting?" Kharra asked.

"Actually, I did," he replied with a broad smile across his face.

Aria glanced out at the churning water and frowned. "You were under for quite a long time." She turned back, and he was clothed again and wringing out his hair. "What did you find?"

With an almost childlike level of excitement, Zephyron explained. "Not only is there a shard beneath those falls but ruins as well. It looks like there was once a cave system farther below, but the force of the waterfall eventually bore through it. The ruins and the shard are farther back within the cave beneath, away from the direct force of the water. They are fairly well preserved and quite ancient. In fact I believe the building was constructed before the waterfall came to be here; well, the waterfall was probably already here, but it probably did not fall in the exact same location. It looks like there may have been some sort of earthquake that caused the ground there to collapse and sink. At least that is my guess. It's hard to be certain though. Mezon would be able to say for sure."

"Mezon?" Aria asked.

"Oh, sorry," Zephyron said with an upheld hand. "He's a...well, he's another Guardian, and he originated from the Vaeton tribe— People of the Earth. He's an expert on anything to do with earth-quakes or fault lines."

"I see," Aria responded. She was still not sure she bought into the whole Guardian bit, but she found herself becoming more open-minded at the prospect. Refocusing her attention, she asked, "How could you tell their age?"

"There were glyphs, runes, and script still visible in various places. Of most, I was not familiar, but the script is similar to something we have in Xi'ari'asi, an older dialect."

Aria puckered her lips to the side. "But according to you, some of our language here in Tanoria is also an older dialect compared to what you are used to."

"True, but what is written down there is even older. *I* didn't study those ancient scripts much, so I had trouble making out a lot of the writing. Parts though were close enough to words I know that I could decipher the meaning."

"Which is?" Kharra asked.

"Not only is this a shard but it's also a moonpath." Kharra's eyebrows rose in surprise. Zephyron must have seen the lack of recognition in Aria's eyes. To Aria, he said, "A moonpath is a means to travel vast differences in a short amount of time. They are only accessible to Guardians and, rarely, special leyoen users."

He ran his fingers back through his hair. "I don't ever recall seeing this one. In fact there are no known moonpaths connecting Tanoria to the rest of the world."

"This is a significant discovery then," Aria said.

Zephyron nodded. "Indeed, it is. I'll have to remember this location." He cocked his head to the side. "Do you have any idea how many people know about this place?"

"I don't think many do," Aria responded. "This region is not unknown to roaming shard beasts, so even the most adventurous people tend to avoid it. This particular location is also a considerable distance away from roads or well-traveled paths, so it doesn't make a convenient stopover. I'm a little more inquisitive than my fellow kruustas, so I've done a considerable amount of exploration over the years. I found this place only because I trailed a herd of zegu for a week and they stopped here to water. I felt an immediate connection to this area, and I always feel at home each time I return."

Zephyron studied Aria. His piercing blue gaze held an unfathomable intensity that made Aria's breath catch. The kruusta, who had never in all her life lacked self-confidence, felt unsteady beneath the Guardian's scrutiny. Goose bumps ran up her spine, but Aria did her best to ignore them. Why did he have this effect on her?

Kharra broke the silence. "Are we setting up camp here, or are we moving on? It is still a little early."

"My plan was to stop here for a short break and then head east. We'll skirt along these hills for the rest of this afternoon, and then we'll reconnect with a real road near Braylore, which is the next village with a shard."

Zephyron rubbed his chin and looked up at the sky through the tree cover. "We only have a few hours of daylight left. Is it safe to travel through this at night?" His hand swept across the area to indicate both the terrain and the undergrowth.

"We'll be going over rugged land. There's a good chance we'll encounter shard beasts, but this will shave at least three days off our travel. If we had horses with us, I probably wouldn't suggest it. They would likely break a leg; not to mention, they spook around shard beasts." She looked to Kharra and then back at Zephyron. "Am I correct to assume that you are comfortable traveling at night? I mean, in your other form? I figured that since cats have an uncanny ability to find their way through the dark that you might share that characteristic. Besides, we'll have all three moons tonight."

"No, you're correct. I can see fine in the dark."

Aria nodded. "Xierex can as well. As for shard beasts, I figured between the three of us, the chances of us coming across something we can't handle is slim."

"I'm all for shaving time off our journey," Kharra added.

Zephyron grunted in agreement and said, "Well, you are the guide. You'd know best, and we do appreciate time savings where we can get it."

The three of them each sat on rocky protrusions overlooking the water as they picked through their meat buns, light pastries wrapped around jurassis swine. The buns were just one of the many provisions provided to them by Dara at the Raven's Roost. Xierex browsed on nearby bushes, stripping them of their sweet leaves in places.

"These are really good," Zephyron said, breaking the silence that had fallen over the group.

Aria nodded, hearing his comment but not really paying attention. Her mind was in another place, partially entranced by the falling water and by the calming effect of the entire area. A small iridis quadwing alighted on a rock beside the waterfall. It fanned all four of its multicolored wings and danced beneath the spray of water, creating a mesmerizing kaleidoscope of peach, pink, and teal. Done with

SECRETS OF TANORIA: THE CRYSTAL WARRIOR

its bath, it hopped to the only dry protrusion on the rock, fanned off the water, and began meticulously preening its feathers.

Aria inhaled, savoring the moment, but then her mind pulled her back to the present and her companions. "I know that you are searching for something in Death's Pillar," she said softly, "but how did circumstances bring you to this point?"

Zephyron pushed the last of his bun into his mouth, stood, and brushed off his hands and clothing. "If you two are done, let us start moving, and we can discuss it along the way."

Aria nodded in agreement and finished the last of her meat bun. After collecting Xierex, the three travelers departed on foot. The game trail provided enough clearing for them to walk comfortably. Aria knew the trail narrowed, but that would not be for a while.

"Our homeland, Aerous, is a vast place several times the size of Tanoria," Zephyron began. Aria raised an eyebrow skeptically but said nothing. "One hundred thirty-one years ago a war began, and it ended only eighteen years ago. The conflict was initiated by a different land called Kelan, a kingdom whose citizens feared those with leyoen abilities." Zephyron described the escalation of the war with terrifying detail.

"You sound as if you were there at the beginning."

Zephyron turned his head slightly, meeting her eyes. "I was."

Aria's gait faltered. "Exactly how old are you?" she asked.

Zephyron's lips twitched upward at her reaction. "I turned one hundred sixty-one just before we left on our journey here."

Aria stopped and stared at him. Xierex whinnied at the abrupt change. She shifted her gaze to Kharra. The shorter woman nodded. "And you?" she asked Kharra. "I don't mean to be rude. I'm just curious."

Kharra looked startled at the question. "Oh, me? I'm only twenty-two."

Aria began walking again. To Zephyron, she said, "You make my many decades of fighting shard beasts seem insignificant by comparison."

Zephyron shrugged. "Seems neither of us are strangers to fighting. Just our circumstances vary. In any case I was thirty when the war began and had not yet been called as a Guardian."

"I can't even fathom a conflict so great that it would last for so long," Aria admitted.

Zephyron nodded. "I couldn't either when it started. As I mentioned, Aerous is a massive continent. The Kelani became fixated not just on conquest but on extermination and enslavement as well. Aerous had been home to many different people, including the Zumai and Sauru tribes. I mentioned before that the Zumai were the People of the Spirit. They had been acknowledged as the tribe that presided over the other tribes. Their system kept the different groups civil with each other and helped avoid conflicts, including those with couren. The Sauru were the People of the Crystal."

Aria kept walking over the rocky terrain but turned her head to catch Zephyron's eye. He smiled. "I thought that would interest you. In any case, though each tribe was left to manage its own affairs, the other tribes considered the Zumai their overarching rulers. So if the Zumai were the rulers, then the Sauru, specifically the Sauru swordsaints, were their knights. They served as enforcers, an elite fighting force with the ability to manipulate crystal. While not feared outright by the people, their strength and battle prowess earned them respect. Even the couren among the Sauru tribe were considered to be some of the most skilled fighters in the land.

"Just over twenty years into the war, something happened to the Sauru. They went mad and turned on those they were sworn to protect, killing many in the process. Unable to find a cure for the madness, the Aerans were forced to destroy all of them. People who had once been their friends and protectors had to be eliminated, and the effort required a large force of the combined tribes to do so."

Aria's stomach grew cold.

"Are you okay?" Kharra asked suddenly. "You look ill."

Aria had forgotten about the woman's empathy. "Your description of the Sauru madness," she forced herself to say, "it hits very close to home. Could that incident be related to what happened on Death's Pillar and the event that created the krumetus?"

Zephyron took on a thoughtful look. "I don't have firsthand knowledge of what happened here, but I suppose that is possible. The timing and location seem to be oddly coincidental."

As they continued on their trek, Zephyron continued his tale. "The war ran deeper than we realized."

"How so?" Aria asked.

Zephyron frowned and stared out at the path before him. "I discovered something that shook the core of everything I believed."

Aria raised an eyebrow but said nothing.

Zephyron exhaled. "The war...it was orchestrated by those who at the time were Guardians." Zephyron's eyebrows drew together. "We discovered nineteen of them who had betrayed their calling and were actively working against the will of Mattekan. We call them the Betrayers." The Guardian sighed. "I was so naive back then. Our connection to this world runs so deep, I'd never even contemplated that one of us could ignore Mattekan and stray from our calling."

"Why start a war?" asked Aria. "If I understand your tale, they are more closely related to leyoen users than couren. So why turn couren against them? What was their agenda?"

"I...don't know definitively," said Zephyron. "The few I encountered face-to-face tried to kill me, so we only exchanged the briefest of dialogues. I threw the question at them, of course, but they never gave me a clear answer. Kharra has a pretty solid theory though."

"Oh?" asked Aria, shifting her gaze back to the young woman.

Kharra nodded. "I've had encounters with their leader, Xareen, and a few others who worked with her. As former Guardians—they all still have their Guardian powers—they're more difficult to read than humans, but I was still able to pick fragments from their minds."

"And that gave you enough for a theory?"

"I think so. As Zephyron pointed out, despite what the stories say, Guardians are not gods. Mattekan, for all its power, is a being of harmony. The Guardians were meant to be a conduit between Mattekan and those who live upon its surface, but many Guardians come from humanity. Much of that humanity remains with them even after they are called."

"Oh…" said Aria, "I think I see where this is going. They weren't gods, but they wanted to be?"

Kharra smiled. "That's my theory. They didn't want to serve. They wanted to be worshipped."

"Seems like they had a population of couren to worship them. Why would they bother starting a war?"

It was Zephyron who responded. "Because a large population of leyoen users could challenge them and because new Guardians are called from those with leyoen. If the Betrayers eliminated or controlled that population, then no one could stop them."

"They almost succeeded in wiping us out," said Kharra, her voice tinged with sorrow. "I think Mattekan has some awareness of that, but its way of thinking is so foreign to our own that I can't be certain. Still, I received a vision in a dream, one I believe to be prophetic."

"And that's what brought you here to Tanoria?" asked Aria.

"Yes," Kharra replied. "I needed Zephyron's help decoding it, but we determined that I needed to travel to Ei'ars'anu and retrieve something called the Heart of the Sauru. Whatever it is, it will prove instrumental to the future of the world."

"That's a lot of pressure for one so young."

Kharra shrugged. "I don't see it that way. I have friends and family who help me shoulder the burden."

"You know, you're very wise for one so young," said Aria.

Zephyron chuckled, his usual mirth restored. "That's just one of the reasons she's the leader and why the people of Aerous still have a chance." As the group continued on the path to Braylore, talk of war and betrayal waned to be replaced with topics of a more casual nature.

7

THE SHARD'S EMBRACE

Aria and her two companions arrived in Braylore shortly before dusk two days after leaving White Bluff. Their trip through the Byannu Hills was almost uneventful save for a small run-in with a nest of young glimmer worms. Aria and Zephyron dispatched the entire group of them within minutes while Kharra merely remained watchful from the side of the trail. The creatures never stood a chance; Aria almost felt bad for them. Almost. The rest of the trip afforded Aria the time to become better acquainted with both Kharra and Zephyron. For reasons she could not explain, she felt more comfortable around them than she had around anyone, even other kruustas. It was not just that they accepted what she was and would become nor was it the lack of fear from either of them; it went deeper, something she could not quite pinpoint.

Entering Braylore shattered Aria's comfort. At the sight of her, people of the town ushered their children indoors and averted their eyes. If it was not the crystal in her hand, then it was her eyes that always gave her away. They were still the green color she had been born with, but as part of becoming a kruusta, they had gained a luminescent quality others found unsettling. The longer one was a kruusta, the more profound the effect became. Aria sighed. She caught sight of Kharra watching with a thinly veiled look of sympathy. Aria gave her a tight appreciative smile.

Five times the size of White Bluff, Braylore boasted several inns. Aria skipped the first one, the Angry Ale Inn. She had stayed there twice before, but the inn's name seemed to attract loud, rowdy clientele. The innkeeper did not care so long as someone paid for the drinks—not the type of relaxing atmosphere Aria desired. Instead Aria chose to continue on through the town to the Laughing Owl.

Only two small groups of patrons and two additional individuals occupied the main floor of the Laughing Owl. Every one of them stopped talking or eating to watch the three new arrivals. Their faces boasted a mix of apprehension and curiosity. Even though Aria avoided meeting anyone's eyes, the crystal visible on her hand caught the light streaming in from the door, making it impossible for anyone to miss. It was the appearance of her companions, though, that overrode the apprehension of some. Zephyron cut a striking image in any environment, and Kharra, small with her warm smile, could never be mistaken for anything but a kind soul. The three of them together were the cause of the curiosity.

Aria's gaze swept around the room, noting every detail. Zephyron did the same. Kharra, on the other hand, walked out in front of them to meet a woman who rushed out to greet the group.

The woman, seeing the kruusta, almost overlooked Kharra. Her eyes focused on Aria. While many people preferred to avoid kruustas, most innkeepers appreciated their patronage. They always paid their tab, never created a mess, and always provided respectable gratuity. On top of that, with the exception of the Angry Ale Inn and other poorly run establishments like it, the presence of a kruusta usually kept troublemakers away.

Kharra stepped in front of the woman and said, "Excuse me."

Startled, the woman looked at Kharra, then Aria, and then back to Kharra. "Sorry, yes. What did you need?" the woman asked, flustered in front of the kruusta.

"My companions and I," Kharra began, nodding to Aria and Zephyron, "would like to get three rooms for this evening."

Both of Aria's eyebrows climbed high, but she said nothing.

"Oh, you're together," she said in surprise. "I'm so sorry." She looked up at Aria and then back at Kharra, "I just assumed..." The woman threw up her hands and gave her complete attention to Kharra. "My name is Vera. I'm the innkeeper here. Three rooms, you said?" Kharra and the woman moved off to the side to negotiate the arrangements while Aria went back outside to retrieve their gear from Xierex. Zephyron joined her.

"Once we get settled, I'm going to visit the shard temple," she told him as she unstrapped his pack and handed it to him.

Zephyron took his pack from her. "Thank you," he said. "I'd like to join you, if you don't mind."

Aria looked up from the second pack she was working to remove. "If you're concerned for my safety, I'm sure I'll be fine."

Zephyron displayed his signature grin. "I'm certain you can handle yourself. I'm still curious about your land and these shards." Aria found his grin infectious, and she smiled in return. How could this same man have such a startling effect on her when he pierced her with his serious gaze?

"Oh, sure," she found herself saying. "You're welcome to come along."

"Thanks," he said with the briefest of nods. Aria handed him the second pack and nodded in return.

Aria and Zephyron returned to the common room of the Laughing Owl and found the woman and Kharra shaking hands.

"Enjoy your stay," the woman said.

"We will. Thank you."

With a gesture of her head, Kharra led the way up the stairs, around two left turns of the hallway, and to the last three doors on the floor. Kharra opened the doors for them so they could drop their packs. Zephyron disappeared into the second of the three rooms, allowing Aria to stop at the first.

The rooms were much nicer than Aria would have selected, and her wide eyes betrayed her surprise. "Don't worry," Kharra said. "I got these for a good price."

"Good price or not, these rooms can't be cheap. Where in the world are you getting your money?"

"We bartered quite a few goods when we first arrived in Summerton," Kharra answered, "including several of Zephyron's carvings. We have enough money to last a while."

Aria gave her a doubtful look. If any merchant realized a pair of foreigners had a lot of loose coin, that surplus would soon disappear. "I get a regular stipend that covers my expenses," Aria said as she looked about the room, "but I'm used to being much more frugal."

"Considering how many times we've been and will be sleeping in a bedroll on the ground, I consider an occasional room at an inn to be money well spent."

Aria hefted her pack onto the polished wooden stand against the far wall and raised an eyebrow in Kharra's direction. Zephyron returned from dropping off their packs. "She's a skilled negotiator," he said, leaning against the doorway behind Kharra.

"Is that like your other skills?" Aria wanted to know.

"Not directly, no," Kharra responded. "However, it does help me to interpret a person's comfort level. If they feel really strongly about something though, I can't help but pick up on that as well."

"Handy," was all Aria could think to say in response.

"Kharra," Zephyron said, "Aria and I are going to head up to the shard temple."

"Okay, I'll stick around here."

Zephyron looked at Aria. "Are you ready to go now, or did you need some food and rest first?"

"I would prefer to go now while it's still light." With that the two of them bid Kharra goodbye and made their way to the shard temple.

The shard temple was south on the outskirts of the village. Sitting by itself atop a lonely hill, it looked like a weathered sentinel who had refused to give up his post. Though easily seen from a long ways off, the walk to reach it took ten minutes. A sea of tall green grass to either side of the trail rippled beneath the gentle winds sweeping through the area. Aria inhaled but did not speak. Neither did Zephyron. In fact when she glanced his way, she found the Guardian walking with his eyes closed and his head tilted back. He breathed slowly, appearing relaxed. Aria smiled to herself and turned her attention back to the temple ahead.

As they drew closer to the hill, grass gave way to dozens of fine-limbed trees standing five times her height. The pink tips of the cherry blossom buds dotted the otherwise green trees. They would bloom very soon, and the entire area would transform into a weeping pink cloud of beauty and tranquility. People from the surrounding villages would journey to Braylore for the Cherry Blossom Carnival where they could enjoy the festivities—music, exotic foods, competitions, acrobatics, menageries, even fireworks—and visit the temple, finding inspiration in sight of the cherry blossom grove. Other places had cherry blossom trees, but none had a grove such as the one that grew here.

Aria sighed. Her life had a singular purpose—the destruction of shard beasts. She believed it a noble purpose; she performed a service for Tanoria so that others could enjoy life without the fear of monsters. Now that she knew she was near the end of her days, she felt a pang of regret at missing simple pleasures such as festivals dedicated to blooming trees.

What would it feel like to be able to live openly in a small town or village? Would she own a small cottage? Raise chickens? Maybe knit blankets that she could then sell at the local market? She chuckled internally as images of her chasing chickens flitted through her head.

Other kruustas, on occasion, tried to integrate themselves into normal society, but such interaction was fleeting at best. Even in the rare instances in which a kruusta had become accepted, it only took the whiff of a rumor that another village had been attacked by a krumetus to remind the people of the danger of associating with a kruusta. After all, who knew when this one might go through conversion and attack their children? It was only when a shard beast was already present and threatening a village or city that someone called in a kruusta to eradicate the problem.

"Are you okay?" Zephyron asked, his voice gentle.

Aria looked at him. He was watching her with one eye, the other closed against the glare of the sun. "Of course. Why?"

"You look a bit down."

"Just...reflecting," she answered.

Zephyron pursed his lips but continued to watch her. "Nature has that type of power over us," he said with a gesture toward the trees above them. "I do the same from time to time. Sometimes I wonder how my life would have been had I been born at a different time or if my options had been different."

Aria studied the tall Guardian. "You've had to bear a lot of burdens over the years. Does it ever become too much?"

Surprising Aria, the Guardian nodded. "There were times when I thought it would swallow me."

"How do you not just give up?"

"I've been close. Then I remind myself that there are people who care about me and whom I care about in return. I know that if I did give up, they'd be hurt, and that is something my heart can't tolerate. I will continue to bear these burdens for as long as I have the ability to do so. However, it doesn't mean that I don't take the time to appreciate the beauty of life.

"You and I, we're not all that different."

Aria averted her eyes from the Guardian and looked up at the tree branches. True, their burdens were similar, if hers not quite as extensive as his, but it was the other side of the equation she was missing—the balance. It was only her sense of duty that kept her grounded. Was that why others went through conversion earlier than she? Because they gave up?

"Different enough. I have no relatives and few friends. I doubt anyone would miss me if I died tomorrow."

"That is where you and I would have to agree to disagree."

Aria's head whipped in his direction. "You know nothing of my personal life," she said, harsher than she intended. "You've not been in Tanoria long enough to grasp what I am. People are afraid of me.

They think I'll eat their children, and I don't really blame them. The monsters that we inevitably become might not stop at the children. Trust me, no one would miss me except as a tool that would need to be replaced."

Zephyron's eyebrows creased, and his face darkened. Oddly though he said nothing. Was he angry with her?

The kruusta and the Guardian walked the rest of the distance to the temple in silence. The path veered west. Zephyron's reaction continued to weigh on her mind until the rising walls of the temple buildings came into view. Here, the packed dirt path and cherry blossom trees both ended at a courtyard-like area of low-cut grass and square stone slabs.

No two shard temples were the same. Braylore's temple was several thousand years old, consisting of five orange-tinted brick towers on a common terrace. Facing east and surrounded by a small moat of gurgling water, this particular temple was well-known for its striking lines and symmetry. The middle tower stood higher than the rest and featured diminishing tiers carved to mimic the look of a cascading waterfall.

Aria continued walking through the courtyard toward the central tower. The interior of the building revealed several large bas-relief depictions of a particular dragon the priests called Krushnu. The images were carved into the walls of orange brick, which were connected by a compound made of vegetable matter.

In one relief Krushnu sat amid hundreds of crystal shards with his head pulled back and raised high as if looking off into the distance. The theme of a second image showed Krushnu and several smaller dragons fighting against humans: some armed with weapons, some with water, some with fire, and others with weapons Aria could not identify. In a third image, hundreds of humans huddled behind Krushnu, who was shown with a raised talon from which radiated a hemispherical shield. The shield appeared to hold off hordes of grotesque creatures and one giant serpentlike creature that drove them forward. Broken crystal shards surrounded their feet. In a final image, Krushnu lay lifeless on a pyre, with humans on their knees weeping around him. One particular human, called Daruuk by the priests, was surrounded by what looked like a radiating glow. His eyes were closed, and his hand rested on Krushnu's head.

Not even the priests knew the original story of Krushnu or why the images were carved, but many temples had them, no two alike, and the priests taught their own interpretations as to what they meant.

Zephyron paused at the fourth image. His face betrayed nothing, but with his finger, he traced the lines of Krushnu's fallen form. He then closed his eyes and lowered his head, though his hand continued to rest on the image.

"Please," a voice called from the far end of the chamber, "don't touch that." The elderly priest scurried up the aisle that split a dozen rows of polished rosewood benches. Aria recognized Priest Gavron from her previous stops in the village.

Without raising his head, Zephyron opened his eyes and rotated his view to watch the approach of the slight man in his blue robes. When the priest gazed upon Zephyron's intense visage, the man stopped midstride.

The man's face paled. He licked his lips and swallowed. "I-I'm sorry, sir. I did not mean to come off as rude." The priest looked at Aria and then back to Zephyron. One corner of Aria's lips twitched as she tried not to smile. She had been on the receiving end of that gaze, so she understood what the poor priest felt. "It is just that the oils on people's fingers, over time, cause the images to wear down. We are making efforts to better preserve them, particularly these of Krushnu and Daruuk. There are not many of these left in such good condition."

Suddenly, Zephyron smiled. "No offense taken, good priest. It is good that you care so much for such treasures. Who did you say these were?"

The priest, appearing more comfortable under Zephyron's smile, walked up to stand beside Aria's tall, white-haired companion. Short for a man, the top of the priest's head did not even reach Zephyron's shoulder. "The dragon here is the god Krushnu, and the man next to him is his follower, Daruuk. These images come from a time when dragons and demons fought to claim the souls of man. In the end Krushnu gave his life to protect Daruuk's soul, who would in turn lead humanity into the light of the First Shard."

Zephyron rubbed his chin. "Interesting. Where I come from, the dragon is called Lothtoru and the man is Brashuun."

The priest eyed Zephyron. "I don't know what village you are from, my boy, but I have never heard those names. Are you a man of the shard?"

Zephyron looked to Aria for assistance.

Aria said, "Zephyron here is a traveler. He is more of a man of… nature than of worship." Zephyron raised an eyebrow at her. "He is not very familiar with the teachings of the Order of the Shard."

"I see. Well, my boy, you and I should have a sit. You have an eye for artistic quality. I would love to have a chance to provide you with any information you may be lacking."

"Priest Gavron," Aria interrupted, "we are only passing through Braylore on a mission. I came here to commune with the shard, if that is okay."

"Oh, I'm sorry. Of course, Kruusta…"

"Aria," Aria filled in at his hesitation.

"Of course, Kruusta Aria. Forgive my fading memory. I know we've met before, but my recollection of names and faces is fading."

"That's quite all right." Even when the priest was younger, his ability to recall names of people had been flimsy at best. His memory regarding any fact about the shards or their history, however, was unmarred.

"Did you need me to commune for you?"

"No, thank you. I would prefer to do it myself, if that is okay."

"Absolutely. We do not have worship today, so you shouldn't be interrupted. I will be in my study if you should need anything." With a shallow bow of his head, the priest returned down the aisle and disappeared into a door at the side of the chamber.

Aria kept her eyes on the door where the man had disappeared and said, "I get the feeling you know more about these images. Would you care to enlighten a curious kruusta?"

"Lothtoru was the first Guardian," he answered, his voice somber. "Obviously, he was a dragon."

Aria turned to face Zephyron. "I always thought dragons were just myths," she said.

Zephyron shook his head. "They were real. In fact they were Mattekan's most advanced race for thousands of years."

"So what happened?"

Zephyron frowned. "Humans happened. Do you remember when Kharra and I told you about how Mattekan created an impassible mountain range out of the sea, cutting Marimon off from the rest of the world so those people could not spread their practice of mining crystal to other places?"

Aria nodded.

Zephyron explained that at the same time Marimon was being cut off from the rest of the world, Mattekan—the entity that was also their world—called its first Guardian as an additional measure of protection. Because most humans could not hear Mattekan, the Guardians were to become its means to communicate on a more direct level. The first Guardians came from Mattekan's most advanced, intelligent, and connected race: the dragons.

A handful of individuals from the newer generations of humans had eventually developed a connection with Mattekan and manifested leyoen, but they had failed to get the couren to stop their mining practices. In fact only the leyoen users believed in what was happening off the shores to the north as the Serpent Spine Mountains rose from the sea. They gave up trying to convince the others and fled north before the mountain range could cut them off from the rest of the world. They settled on the southern tip of what would become Aerous and over time spread out.

During their expansion of Aerous, humans encountered and fought against all manner of nightmarish beasts. When the humans encountered the dragons for the first time, they only saw them as more monsters. With their fully developed leyoen abilities and greater numbers, humans attacked the dragons. The fighting was brutal and lasted several years.

Some of the humans began to see the difference between dragons and the other creatures they fought, but they had trouble making their leadership believe them. Wyverns, winged reptilians that were intelligent and malicious enemies of the dragons, were among those other creatures. After the wyvern Malicolc and its minions overran Sadon, the humans' oldest and most important city, and threatened to destroy all of the humans who had left Marimon, a young human named Brashuun sought out the aid of the dragon Lothtoru against the wishes of his elders.

As the humans made their last stand, Brashuun returned, riding on the back of Lothtoru. With the powers of the Guardian, they turned back Malicolc and his minions, and the humans prevailed. But Lothtoru was mortally wounded by Malicolc during the encounter. Having witnessed the Guardian's aid and sacrifice, the humans finally realized their grievous error.

On the evening of Lothtoru's last breath, Brashuun, an empath, placed his hand on the Guardian dragon's head. Witnesses claimed to see a nimbus of light surround both dragon and human.

Zephyron turned to the last relief, the one he had traced with his finger. "It was at that moment that Mattekan truly recognized humanity, and through Lothtoru's fading spirit, the first human Guardian was called."

"So Brashuun was the first human Guardian?"

Zephyron nodded.

Aria eyed the Guardian—she had actually come to believe his claim of this status—for several long moments and decided she believed his tale. "As I said, I'd always thought dragons were just myths, legends created by artists, sculptors, and storytellers."

"You thought the same of Guardians."

"True. So what happened to the dragons?"

Zephyron shrugged. "I don't know. No one that I know has ever seen one. My fellow Guardians believe them to be extinct, but there are no definitive records about what may have happened to them."

Aria nodded. "And the wyverns?"

"Oh, they're still around." Zephyron scowled. "Kelan used them against Aerous during the war. They are vain, temperamental creatures, and the Kelani leadership learned how to use that to their advantage. Those creatures were responsible for the deaths of many of my friends."

"I'm sorry. I didn't mean to dredge up painful memories."

"It's okay. I don't mind. I just hate wyverns."

"Well, your story was very enlightening. Thank you for sharing."

Zephyron's scowl softened to a smiled, though a hint of sadness ringed his eyes. "You are welcome, Kruusta."

"Please, just call me Aria."

Zephyron's smile widened, and his eyes lit up. "Of course. I understand how daunting formality can be."

"Thanks. Now let us check out the shard."

Aria closed her eyes and touched the shard delicately, afraid of what she might sense. Within moments of placing her hand on the warm crystalline structure, a sense of euphoric exultation swallowed her, flooding every fiber of her being. Anticipation, excitement, welcome, and embrace—these were sentiments a corner of Aria's mind understood. That was the reception she felt from the shard. It was not just the shard, though, but rather something deeper and more profound. Tender emotions stirred from within the kruusta that she never realized she possessed, and a longing resonated from the depths of Aria's soul. Why either became evident, she could not determine.

Awareness engulfed Aria's mind in a way that she had never before experienced in all her eighty-five years. She could sense every living thing—plant, beast, animal, human, and even Guardian—for miles around. The near-budding cherry blossoms sang like a symphony reaching for its crescendo. Hundreds of birds flittered about the trees, settled on rooftops, and fed their young. A family of mice living beneath the foundation of the temple gathered about a wedge of stolen bread; unlike other mice, these ate well. A falcon passed swiftly over the grassy fields between Braylore and the temple.

Aria sensed Zephyron beside her. Though her eyes were closed, she could see him in her mind as a beacon of white light, tendrils of which connected him to both the shard and the network of veins below the surface. He radiated curiosity and what she could only describe as acknowledgment. She sensed Priest Gavron in his study, reading and oblivious to those outside. Though he radiated no light, a very thin white tendril connected him to the shard. Aria followed her awareness farther outward toward Braylore. Large groups of people traveled into, out of, and through the town.

Kharra broke the second carrot in half and held it up to Xierex. He took it from her fingers and bobbed his head appreciatively, his eyes lively as he enjoyed his snack. A tingling sensation tickled the edge of Kharra's mind. Survival instincts kicking in, all of her senses immediately came alert, and she tightened her mental shields. Still, the sensation remained. On instinct Kharra threw her consciousness outward to sense for the intruder, systematically scanning the surrounding area. At last she encountered something. It was a consciousness and an awareness but not a mind, not really. The consciousness carried with it a familiarity.

Aria? Kharra sent out. No response came, and the consciousness faded from her detection. She was so in control of her abilities that Xierex never became aware of Kharra's momentary alarm. He simply nudged her hand until she gave up the second half of the carrot.

Kharra frowned. How had Aria touched her mind? She knew the consciousness had sensed her, which was a cause of concern. No one, not even her sister, could use their minds to detect Kharra unless she gave them permission.

With the alarm passed, Kharra stifled a yawn and meandered her way to her room.

Despite the quantity of people, Aria sought out and located Kharra's presence at the Laughing Owl. She knew the young woman was feeding carrots to Xierex. In an instant Kharra's mind suddenly grew alarmed. Was Kharra in danger? No, the woman relaxed almost as soon as her alarmed state had triggered. Like Zephyron, Kharra's being was accompanied by the beacon of white light. A surprise to Aria though was that where Zephyron had dozens of tendrils connecting him to both the vein and the shard, Kharra was connected by hundreds. What that meant Aria could not quite understand.

Aria? Aria heard Kharra's mind voice as clearly as if the woman was standing beside her and had said it aloud.

A warm hand on Aria's shoulder drew her out of her trance and away from the voice. Almost regretfully she allowed herself to withdraw from the shard's embrace. Aria took several deep breaths before she opened her eyes. Her mind still buzzed with activity, and her body felt more energized than ever. She thought herself observant before, but she now understood how limited her own perceptions of the world around her were.

"Are you okay?" Zephyron asked.

"Absolutely," she said. "The reaction from this shard was different from anything I've ever experienced before. Through it I sensed everything—every person, every animal, every being—for miles around. I have never felt so alive."

"Mattekan can have that effect to those who can tap into it," Zephyron responded.

"Did you, by any chance, sense me?"

"I did," Zephyron answered with a nod. "Guardians can always sense Mattekan's structure, be they veins beneath the ground or shards protruding above. I can sense its power and strength or if it has been injured. It's also from Mattekan that we Guardians get our power. We don't, however, have the type of experience that you just described. You somehow became part of the network.

"I believe you've been given a great gift. You've essentially seen through the eyes of our world. Is that how your priests commune?"

"I don't think so," Aria answered with uncertainty. "At least it doesn't match any of the descriptions they've given. The way they describe it, they pray to the shard, and eventually they receive an answer."

"Maybe your connection has grown deeper over the years," Zephyron offered.

"Perhaps."

"What impressions did you glean?" he asked.

"From what I can tell, this shard is very healthy."

Zephyron nodded as he scrutinized her. "Quite interesting."

"It also seemed like it was waiting for me, expecting me. I know that sounds weird."

"Not at all. The shard is an extension of Mattekan, and Mattekan is a sentient being. Its thoughts and behaviors may be foreign and hard to interpret for those of us who walk its surface, but it does have sentiments and desires. Your commune back in Murali may have made it aware of you or opened something within yourself that you could not access before."

Aria nodded, her mind lost in thought. She had a lot of information to process. Together Aria and Zephyron returned to Braylore, and Aria attempted to describe to the Guardian some details of what she had experienced. As she walked, her eyes scanned every inch of the world around her, confirming everything her mind had sensed.

"That was you that I sensed last night, right?" Kharra asked as they broke their fast the following morning. She had fallen asleep by the time Aria and Zephyron had returned to Braylore.

Aria nodded. "I'm sorry if I scared you," she said. "I didn't know that was going to happen."

Aria recited her experience from the night before and how she was able to sense the world around her. Somehow she had been able to recognize Kharra. Having been with Kharra and Zephyron for multiple days and introduced to their method of speaking from mind to mind, Aria was aware of that particular sensation. When she had connected with Kharra through the shard though, it had felt different; it was as if it was coming through her bones rather than a tickle from someone's mind.

Zephyron's head came up and his eyebrows rose. "Wait. You actually sensed Kharra?" he asked, his eyes momentarily shifting to Kharra and then back to Aria.

Aria bit into her slice of apple and nodded.

Kharra smiled at the Guardian. "It's okay, Zephyron. I don't think this was normal, except for maybe Aria somehow."

Aria put up her hands in defense, scowling at no one in particular. "None of this is normal for me. As I told Zephyron last night, I've never had that type of experience before." She let out an exasperated breath, composing herself. "It was as if my mind was part of the shard's network. I could sense and feel every living being, you included. Is something wrong with that?"

Zephyron frowned. "Normally no one can sense Kharra—not Guardians, not leyoen users, no one. If you were able to do it last night, it is possible that someone else may be able to as well."

Aria finished her apple. "I can see how that might be a cause of concern, particularly if you rely on that ability to bypass enemies."

"As I said," Kharra repeated, "I don't think that was normal."

"I don't want to risk your safety any more than necessary," Zephyron said, his voice sounding very much like the Guardian he was. Kharra though was apparently immune to his piercing gaze.

Aria cleared her throat. Both Kharra and Zephyron turned their attention to her. "Some risk may be unavoidable. The best we can do is be prepared for those times. When I sensed Kharra through the shard, she became aware of me. I imagine that she would be able to do the same with anyone else. So in the event that someone else is able to detect her through that method, we would have at least some warning. The three of us should be able to react quickly to something like that."

Zephyron rubbed his forehead and exhaled. "You're right."

"Let's get going," Aria suggested. No one disagreed.

Aria's thoughts wandered as they packed up their gear and headed out, and she barely heard the playful banter between her two companions. She did not remember climbing into her saddle as her mind continued to process all the details it had experienced the night before, and questions to which she had no answers continued to assault her. Neither Kharra nor Zephyron bothered her as she sorted through her internal chaos. At last, as they passed by the last building of the village, she shook her head clear and focused on the road ahead.

8

MIGHT OF THE TIGRON

Aria dismounted and joined Kharra and Zephyron along the edge of the vista. She caught the scent of the animals long before they came into view. As far as her eyes could see, the seething mass of animal life flowed like a network of rivers and lakes. From the current vantage point, Aria could not yet make out the details of specific species, but she estimated several thousand animals were there.

Zephyron studied the scene below with arms folded across his chest. "I've never seen so many animals in once place. Is this normal?" he asked.

With hands on her hips, Aria shifted her weight to her right foot. Her eyebrows came together slightly. "Each spring many types of animals migrate from the higher altitudes to these warmer regions to give birth to their offspring, but this is by far the biggest migration I've ever seen." She ran her hand through her hair. "There is no going around this without losing at least two weeks of travel time."

Zephyron and Kharra exchanged a look. "Through it," Kharra said.

"Then we may as well get started," Aria said. "It's going to be slow."

Zephyron grunted in agreement. "The last thing we need is a stampede," he added.

Unsure of how the animals would react to Zephyron's tigron form, they decided to make the trek on foot. As they made their way down the easy switchback road toward the wide green valley below, it became easier to distinguish individual animals. What baffled Aria the most, beyond just the quantity of wildlife that filled the area, was the huge mixture of different species.

The first Aria recognized was the unmistakable bulk of the kougan, large black-and-white-furred omnivores that usually lived together in small family groups deep in the lowland forests. Though shorter than zegus, their dense musculature made them twice as wide, and their rounded heads, small ears, thick necks, and powerful claws allowed them to both thrive in the dense forest environment and defend against any shard beasts they encountered.

There were also the graceful, long-legged faselles with their sleek tan hides and flicking white tails; the large striped canine-like creatures called derringers; thousands of clover-hooves with their long, sharp horns; several packs of well-fed vohlk and their yipping pups; and families of massive slohn, each led by an aging gray matriarch. Even more surprising was the presence of the much more elusive creatures—the beautiful red unihorns; the solitary, knuckle-walking black kong; and even a few herds of zegu. The multispecies congregation of animals left Aria bewildered.

The road leveled out, and the hills gave way to rolling grasslands of greenery—now thoroughly trampled. A small aftsah, with its curly brown coat and bleating voice, stepped in front of Xierex, oblivious to the massive zegu. Xierex stopped and snorted. He lowered his head toward the small creature and sniffed. The aftsah bleated in the zegu's face, causing him to snort.

"Aw, I think it likes you," said Aria.

Zephyron chuckled. "Looking for mama, it seems." An answering call came from the other side of the road. The small aftsah dashed off to join the other. "There she is."

Aria patted Xierex on the neck and smiled. The aftsah were among the normal migratory animals Aria was accustomed to seeing during her frequent cross-country treks; their herds regularly numbered in the thousands. Individuals always looked the same to her, but the parents and offspring always managed to keep track of each other.

Hours passed as the travelers made their way along the road, meandering in and out of the sea of animals. As the shadows of the afternoon sun began to lengthen, Aria spied something different. Kharra and Zephyron also saw it.

"It looks like a large wagon of some sort," Kharra announced.

"Doesn't look like it's moving though," Zephyron added.

Aria vaulted onto the zegu's back, startling the nearby clover-hooves. The animals scattered a short distance before settling down when they realized nothing was pursuing them. "I'm going to ride ahead."

"Kharra," Zephyron said, "you go with her. I'll catch up."

Aria nodded. The kruusta clasped Kharra's hand and hoisted the girl up behind her. With a slight nudge of her knees, Aria urged Xierex forward into a slow trot, faster than they had been traveling but not so fast as to scare the animals that surrounded them.

As they neared their destination, the wagon's dilemma soon became evident. The large vehicle's back axle was broken, and beyond that the entire wagon was surrounded by a large pride, maybe two prides, of grass cats. The sleek, tawny beasts bellowed and growled as they paced around the wreckage. The other herds of wildlife were wisely keeping their distance.

"There are people inside," Kharra said softly.

Aria nodded, her own suspicions confirmed. "Stay here," she said to her companion as she jumped down from her saddle. On instinct she summoned her krusword and advanced toward the wagon.

"Hello?" Aria called as she approached. The grass cats immediately between her and the wagon turned their heads toward her, crouched low, and growled in unison.

No one answered.

"I am Kruusta Aria. My companions and I are here to help. Are you able to answer?"

A man's head poked out through one of the windows toward the front of the wagon. His fine brown hair clung to his head. "Kruusta, please, we need your help. We were on our way to Braylore, but we broke an axle when our horses spooked and sent us running out of control. We've been trapped here for two days. The excitement has sent my wife into early labor. No one else has passed this way, and I can't leave to get help for fear of these grass cats and other predators that have been coming at night."

"Just relax, sir. We'll get you out of there."

"Please hurry," he pleaded and then ducked his head back inside the wagon.

Other grass cats, noticing Aria approach, turned their attention from the wagon and focused it on her. She counted twenty-seven cats in total. Aria waved her krusword at those that approached too close, but it was to little avail. She soon found herself surrounded by the waist-high carnivores.

A single cat in front of Aria launched itself at her. She spun around in response and kicked it along the side of its head as it passed. The cat stumbled as it landed but soon found its footing and moved around behind its companions. They were testing her defenses. Two other cats rushed her. One came in low, clawing at her legs. She danced backward and slashed out with her blade. The second ran straight at her and launched itself toward her head just as she fended off the first. Aria pulled her krusword up just in time to pierce the soaring animal through the chest. She twisted and allowed the animal's momentum to carry its bulk past her, pulling her weapon free as it did so. The animal remained where it fell.

Aria crouched lower, making herself a smaller target. She kept her right arm and krusword raised out in front of her and kept her left arm poised behind her. She twisted her torso slowly back and forth, trying to keep her eyes on as many of the cats as possible. Four different cats, each from a different direction, lunged in and batted at her in rapid succession. She danced out of the way of two of them and kicked the third hard enough to make it withdraw. The fourth managed to hook its razor-sharp claws into her leather boot and pull her off her feet. Knowing it had the advantage, the cat pounced at her. She rolled away, but the cat pounced again without pause. Before it landed, however, a shadow passed over her eyes, and a massive white blur intercepted the cat midair and threw it back into the other cats that paced just out of reach.

The giant white tigron, four times larger than the largest grass cat, spared a glance at Aria before bellowing a deep-chested roar that rippled across the grassland. Several of the cats dashed a short distance away, but others were not to be deterred. They snarled and growled in response to Zephyron's challenge. One male animal, the largest of the grass cats, stepped forward and began circling the bigger white cat with a slow, menacing gait. It threw its head back and roared in response to the challenger.

With Zephyron's appearance Aria and the wagon were completely forgotten. Aria climbed to her feet but remained ready to fight. She caught Kharra out of the corner of her eye climbing down off of Xierex's back and then disappearing into the wagon. Aria focused her attention back on the cats.

The grass cat launched itself at the tigron. What it lacked in size, it made up in ferocity. Zephyron reared up to intercept the attack and throw the cat aside, but the animal clung to the Guardian's white fur and twisted with all its weight and momentum, forcing Zephyron into a roll. On his back, Zephyron used his large claws to push the cat's face away from his neck and down toward the ground. The grass cat twisted away and bit down on Zephyron's front leg.

With a snarl of pain, Zephyron used his back legs to kick the cat off him and righted himself to a crouch. The grass cat came at him again, but Zephyron was ready. With his powerful legs, he pushed himself out of the way from the other's attack. As the cat moved past him, Zephyron grabbed it around the neck with both of his paws and flung the animal to the ground. The move forced the grass cat onto his back. Before the animal could recover, Zephyron twisted his body around and seized the cat's neck with his teeth. The cat thrashed, kicking Zephyron with its back legs, but the Guardian only tightened his hold. Using his greater weight to his advantage, Zephyron pressed down on the grass cat until the thrashing stopped, replaced by only occasional twitches.

Though Aria was ready for additional attacks, no other cats moved in. After many agonizingly long minutes beneath the afternoon sun, Zephyron released the other cat. Aria expected to see blood coating the Guardian's face, but there was very little. Additionally the cat she had assumed to be dead bounced up and bounded away from the tigron. It stopped, looked back at the Guardian, and then let out a throaty roar. It then turned and trotted away. The other cats withdrew from the area and followed the defeated male.

Aria retracted her krusword and walked up to the fur-covered Guardian. "You're going to have to tell me how you did that."

Zephyron regarded her with his unblinking blue eyes.

Aria knelt down beside him to look at his leg, the blood from the wound visible. "We're going to need to take care of that."

Zephyron snorted and headbutted her on her shoulder.

"Okay," she said with a chuckle as she stood. Without realizing what she was doing, she absently ran her fingers along the fur of his head as she stared off in the direction in which the grass cats had left. The familiar surge of energy she had come to know from touching him danced up her fingers. The sensation was not unpleasant. "Thank you for saving me once again."

Again Zephyron snorted.

Pulling her hand away, Aria moved in the direction of the wagon. "I'm going to check on Kharra and the couple."

The scene within the wagon was bloodier than anything that had happened with the cats, though everyone's faces gleamed with smiles. A sweat- and blood-covered woman rested against two leather packs, and in her arm was a small sleeping newborn. Even more impressive was that a second newborn slept quietly in Kharra's arms. The young woman looked almost as haggard as the new mother.

The father was sleeping beside the mother with one hand draped around her.

At Aria's arrival, Kharra held a finger to her lips. She swaddled the newborn in a small blanket and placed it in a basket beside the father before climbing out of the wagon. She and Aria stepped a short distance away as Zephyron, human once again, joined them.

Aria said, "I don't have a whole lot of experience with newborns, but with what little I do remember, I seem to recall them screaming loudly. How did you get them to keep so quiet? I didn't even hear the mother call out while she was in labor."

Kharra spared a glance at the quiet wagon. "Apparently being an empath helps with childbirth," she answered. Kharra's face became pensive, and her mouth tightened.

"What's wrong?" asked Zephyron.

"We can't leave them," Kharra said.

"She's right," Aria said, rocking her head forward and back. "Their wagon's busted. Their horses are dead. They're hungry, scared, and exhausted. They won't be able to get out of this valley alive without our help."

"What do you suggest?" asked Zephyron.

"This isn't the greatest location, but the three of us can defend it. So let's set up camp here. In the morning we can help them fix their wagon."

Zephyron nodded. "After that?"

Aria's frown deepened. "Xierex can pull the wagon. That's not an issue. But there are no towns for several days in the direction we travel. Braylore is much closer. We'd need to backtrack…"

Kharra said nothing and stepped away. Arms crossed in front of her, she stared out over the pink-hued horizon as the sun dipped below the distant hills.

"Excuse me a moment," said Zephyron as he joined his companion.

Though Aria heard no words exchanged, Kharra's head nodded from time to time. After several silent minutes, they returned to Aria.

"This land is far bigger than I originally thought," said Kharra.

"How so?" asked Aria.

"Honestly I thought it was a large island with some sort of mountain in the middle. I figured we'd be to our destination and back in a week or two."

Aria's eyebrows rose.

Kharra shrugged. "We didn't have a lot of information about this land, and what we did have was pretty old. I underestimated."

"We both did," Zephyron added. "I should have done more research."

Kharra shook her head. "I was in a hurry."

"And now?" asked Aria.

Kharra's eyes locked on Aria's. "We need to complete our mission, but I realize now that it isn't going to be done as fast as I'd thought." She nodded her head toward the wagon. "The well-being of these people is more important. So we go back."

The ride back to Braylore the following day was slow but quiet and uneventful. With Xierex harnessed, Aria drove the wagon while the family cared for their infants in the back, out of the heat of the sun. Kharra and Zephyron sat with her on the wooden bench, but they said little. Perhaps they sensed Aria's mood, which was not one for chatting. Her behavior the day before had disturbed her.

Aria had long ago accepted her fate; the thought of her eventual death had never bothered her. It came with the territory of her calling. Living the life of a kruusta, any day could be her last. Because of that lifestyle, she had long ago decided she would never have children. She shared her bed with an occasional lover, but there had never been an emotional attachment. So why were her emotions stirring now?

Before she met the two foreigners, Aria had never contemplated that her life could have been more than just duty. Had she lived these eighty-five years serving Tanoria night and day only to have life pass her by? She had never thought of herself as lonely. She interacted with priests of the shard, other kruustas, members from the other orders, people who commissioned her services to eradicate shard beast threats, innkeepers, and others who sometimes needed her assistance. She also had Xierex and other mounts before him. They were always constant companions.

But now that Aria had spent time with Kharra and Zephyron, something from deep within her core was seeping out, something buried so long ago, she had failed to recognize it right away. Was this the feeling of friendship, true friendship? Whatever it was, her heart had latched on to it ferociously and did not want to let go. In both Kharra and Zephyron, Aria found kindred spirits, a sentiment she had never before experienced, not even with other kruustas. If she had met these two when she was younger, would she have so readily accepted her current fate? Was this feeling the cause of her recent turmoil?

Realizing her white-knuckled grasp on the reins and the tension throughout her body, Aria forced herself to relax and breathe. It mattered not what she felt now. Her body had already begun the slow process of conversion, and despite her desires, her remaining time in this life grew short. She just hoped that she could fulfill her promise to her new friends before that time ran out.

After two cautious days of travel, stopping often to see that the young mother was fed, hydrated, and in good health, the wagon and its passengers arrived back in Braylore.

As Aria unhitched the wagon from Xierex, shuffling feet drew her attention. She turned to see the young father approach. "Kru-Kruusta, ma'am."

Aria smiled. "Call me Aria."

The man nodded. "Kruusta Aria, ma'am. My wife, she wants to see you before you depart."

"Everything okay?"

"Oh, yes. Everything is perfect because of you. She wants to thank you."

"Okay, just let me finish here, and I'll stop by." The man smiled and retreated, not a bit of fear in him.

Aria finished settling Xierex and then left to visit the woman. She located the new mother in the largest suite in the inn, courtesy of the innkeeper. Aria knocked on the door.

"Come," said the voice from within.

Aria opened the door and leaned in. "You wanted to see me?"

The woman, nursing one of the babies—the little girl, nodded. "Yes, please. Come in." The baby boy slept in a basket at the foot of the bed.

Aria entered and approached the woman, suddenly feeling out of place. The little girl, with a head of dark hair, suckled with her eyes closed. The sight defused the tension Aria held.

"What can I do for you?" asked Aria.

The woman reached out with her one free hand and grabbed Aria's hand, the one embedded with her crystal shard. The woman gently rubbed the shard with her thumb. She looked up and smiled. "You've done more than enough for me, Kruusta. You saved my family."

"I'm just glad you're okay," said Aria.

The woman released Aria's hand. "I don't care what people say about kruustas," she said. "You're a hero. We all would've died if you hadn't arrived. We don't have much to give in thanks, so I'd like your permission to name my little girl after you."

Aria stared at the woman. Every thought in her head froze.

"Is that okay?" asked the woman. "Is something wrong?"

Aria shook herself. "No, nothing's wrong. Nothing at all. That..." Her throat constricted. "Yes, of course you can name her after me."

The woman beamed at her and then looked down at her baby girl. "Aria," she whispered. Looking back up at the kruusta, she said, "It's a beautiful name. We're honored."

"No, it is you who honor me." Aria knelt down to get a closer look at the baby. She put her finger in its hand, and the tiny fingers closed around it. "Hello, Aria," she whispered.

"Do you want to hold her?" the woman asked as she held the baby out toward Aria.

The kruusta's eyebrows rose in alarm. "I don't—" she started.

The mother cut her off as she carefully slipped the baby into Aria's arms. "Just hold her like this, and make sure you hold up her head like this."

Gingerly, Aria cradled the baby in the crook of her arm. With her dangerous, solitary lifestyle, Aria rarely interacted with children. On only a handful of occasions had she even seen a newborn, and she had certainly never before held any type of infant. She looked down at the tiny human sleeping peacefully in her arm. With her right hand, she traced the contours of the baby's soft cheeks. So peaceful she looked.

Despite the joyous occasion, Aria's heart weighed heavily. Motherhood was something she would never be able to experience, and it was one of the few things she regretted about her life as a kruusta. Her sight blurred, and she closed her eyes to keep the forming tears at bay. She continued to brush her finger along the baby's soft cheek and slowed her breathing. She pursed her lips and clenched her eyes tighter, but the quiet tears still found their way to the surface.

A gentle touch on her hand caught her attention. Aria opened her eyes and looked into Kharra's. She had not heard the young woman approach, but her eyes were filled with sympathy and understanding. Without a word Kharra lifted the infant from Aria's arm. Once Kharra held the baby firmly in her arms, Aria thanked the woman again for the honor and excused herself.

Aria found herself outside on the back porch of the inn. She stared out at the surrounding woodlands but did not really look at anything in particular. Slow, silent tears continued to form. One rolled down her right cheek. What might her life have been like had circumstances been different? What if she had never been selected to become a kruusta? Would she have married and had children? What legacy would she have left behind? Would it have been better to live a short life filled with the love of children over a life of unending battle, both with the monsters of her world and with the monster within herself? These questions she had never before considered, but they now filled her head. She realized that in all her years of service, she had never even thought about her own desires or needs.

A warm hand rested on Aria's shoulder. "Are you okay?" asked Zephyron, his voice soft and comforting.

"I don't know why this is affecting me like this," she said, her voice tight to her ears. "I don't even understand what it is I'm feeling. I've never had problems with my emotions getting out of hand before."

"Aria, this is not out of hand. This is normal human emotion. We're all subject to them. Even me. And there is nothing wrong with expressing them."

"Still, for me, something like seeing a sleeping baby shouldn't make me cry. It's not the first one I've ever seen. I don't know what's changed with me, why I'm reacting like this."

"White Bluff," said a female voice. Aria turned to see Kharra joining them. Kharra had her thumb over her lip, her mind working something out.

The discussion distracted Aria enough that she was able to will the tears to stop. With her thumb, she wiped away the one drying on her cheek. "What do you mean?" Aria asked.

"You asked what's changed with you," Kharra replied. "One was White Bluff, after the fighting. It was there you said that you expected your conversion to happen soon, and you asked Zephyron to kill you before it happened."

Stunned, Aria stared at Kharra. Regret. Longing. Missing. With clarity the answer to her own question formed in her mind. Kharra and Zephyron had told her of lands, people, cultures, experiences, and ways of life beyond what she had known in Tanoria. She had believed she had seen everything there was to see in this world, but now she knew that she had seen and experienced very little of it. Beyond all that Kharra and Zephyron loved life, and that love of life had proved infectious. They fought for it and lived for it. They enjoyed what life had to offer, even if that was sometimes hard or unpleasant. Throughout her eighty-five years, Aria had been a willing disciple of her inevitable fate, and because of that she had never truly learned to appreciate living. Because these two people had opened her eyes, there were so many more things she now wanted to experience.

Aria turned to go back in. "Give me a few minutes. Then we can be off."

"We'll be out front."

Aria smiled and nodded, her emotional pain from earlier embraced and tucked away in the back of her mind. She returned to the family's suite and spent a little more time with the exhausted mother and babies before bidding them a proper farewell. Outside the door to the suite, Aria stopped, took a deep breath, and collected herself. She wiped her eyes to make sure no more tears had escaped, and with a small smile, she made her way back to her companions.

9

CROWN PRINCE KIEM

T he second-largest city in Aelland, Valmont, boasted a population of almost fifty thousand. From sunup to sundown, industrious energy filled its busy cobblestone streets—mule-drawn carts conveying cargo across town, women in groups traveling to one of the many nearby marketplaces, soldiers from the local garrison patrolling, farmers in wagons delivering their harvest. It was a stark contrast to the hilly countryside that made up most of the northeastern section of the province. Shard beasts and other dangers remained a constant threat across the countryside, but within the protective boundaries of the city's walls, people worried about the prices of eggs and milk more than perils such as shard beasts.

The people of Valmont worked hard, conveying pride in both their goods and in their culture. Every marketplace, each located in a circular stone-worked convergence of streets, overflowed with people—buying, selling, and even just perusing. Most of the population originated from the more remote towns and villages of Aelland, places like Braylore, Murali, Summerton, White Bluff, Farcroft, and North Bank. According to the younger generation, Valmont was where the edge of civilization began. Young people often left their villages to explore life in that civilization. Most of them never went any farther.

Aria brought Xierex to a halt in front of the Wild Mercer, the inn she had chosen to stay at while in the city. Kharra and Zephyron already had their rooms, but Aria had taken a detour alone to visit the city's shard temple. The temple's priest had been unavailable for an audience, but one of his assistants had been more than happy to answer her questions and allow her to commune. She had been pleased to find nothing amiss.

A clattering of hooves on cobblestone captured Aria's attention as she dismounted from her zegu. She turned and watched the procession, which came to a halt almost in front of her at the large white stone building trimmed in gold across the wide street. The procession consisted of three dozen riders who rode six abreast and six deep. They wore gleaming white tabards over polished mail shirts, and a large gold star encircled by red roses decorated the upper-left quadrant of each tabard. One of the riders dismounted and strode briskly into the white building known as the Golden Horseman.

The Golden Horseman, boasting three stories, offered the most luxurious—and most expensive—lodging in Valmont. Only wealthy merchants, visiting or traveling provincial dignitaries, and nobility could afford their rates. However, because of its spacious ballroom, it was sometimes rented out by families for special events, such as weddings, engagements, and birthdays.

"Is everything okay?" Kharra asked as she exited the Wild Mercer and stepped up beside Aria.

"I'm not certain," Aria replied as she dismounted and led Xierex to the stables beside the inn, all the while keeping her attention focused on the men and women across the street.

"Who are they?" Kharra asked.

Aria led Xierex into his stall and unstrapped her pack. "They're called the Order of the Rose," she answered as she slung her pack over her shoulder. "They're a knighthood in service to the emperor. They don't often leave Aloazai except with the emperor himself or one of his family members. Aloazai is on the other side of Tanoria, so I'm a little bit curious as to what might have brought them here."

The rider who had entered the establishment returned, followed by more than a dozen attendants. The dismounted rider shouted quick orders to the other riders, each of whom parted to let the attendants reach the center of their formation. Another rider in the center dismounted, but between the other riders and the growing audience on the street, Aria could not get a clear view of the person's face.

"I'm heading to my room," the kruusta said, having seen enough. "I'm sure the rumors will spread to our inn before the night is out."

When Aria returned to the common room three hours later after a bath and a much-needed nap, the entire place was bustling with activity. Neither Kharra nor Zephyron had been in their rooms, and neither was visible in the crowd. Aria maneuvered her way to a seat in the corner and caught the attention of one of the servers.

"Hello…" the server began as she glanced down at the crystal on Aria's hand. "Kruusta," she finished in a much lower voice. "What could I do you for?"

"Your special will be fine…" Aria said, leaving her statement open-ended for a name.

"Gwin," the server said with a startled smile. "I'll return with your meal in a moment." Aria expected the woman to turn and leave, but she hesitated. Visibly working up the nerve to say more, the woman cleared her throat. She leaned down closer. "You are a kruusta. You might know more. Would you happen to know why a prince of the empire would come to our city?" The woman shifted with nervous energy, but Aria did not think it was because of her nature as a kruusta.

Aria gave the question thought and then shook her head. "No, sorry. There could be any number of reasons, I suppose. Seeing the people, searching for a bride, getting to know the governors?" She shrugged. "I'm not really a good source for current events. My work keeps me away from sources of information for long stretches of time, so your guess is as good as mine." She sometimes received updates on current events when she visited the shard temples, but those were often weeks after the fact. Nothing she had heard more recently had mentioned anything about the prince or the imperial family.

The woman stood up, pushed a lock of brown hair from her eyes, and smiled. "I'll go get your food."

Aria gave her a tight smile and nodded. While she waited for her meal to arrive, she allowed the ambient chatter of the room to wash over her. Several times she caught the words "emperor" or "prince." Sometimes they were intertwined with grumblings about taxes. Other times they were accompanied by laughs.

A few minutes later, the brown-haired server returned with Aria's meal. The braised beef, spiced pears, and fire mead smelled wonderful, and Aria's ravenous stomach growled in anticipation. The kruusta pressed a large silver coin into the woman's hand and offered her thanks. The woman peered into her hand and gasped. She started to say something, but Aria winked at her. Startled at first by such an exchange from a kruusta, the woman soon understood and beamed a smile. "Thank you very much!"

Aria smiled at the woman's enthusiasm. "You're welcome," she responded. The woman did not realize that taverns and inns were a much more reliable source of information for Aria than her infrequent updates from the shard temples. Even though innkeepers, barkeeps, and tavern maids feared those of her profession, they dealt with kruustas enough to know them to be a reliable source of honest income, and most of them made efforts to at least be professional toward their kruusta patrons. For Aria, chatting with them had become her primary source of social interaction.

As the woman departed, Aria dove into her meal. Despite eating a sizable breakfast of rabbit and eggs before they had left their last camp, Aria's stomach was behaving as if she had not eaten in several days. Her hunger plagued her often of late; she suspected it to be another symptom of her conversion process. With the edge to her hunger finally abating, she scanned the common room again. Still she saw no sign of either Kharra or Zephyron.

Aria caught Gwin's eye from across the room. Within moments the woman stepped up beside her. "Did you need something more?" she asked.

"I am staying here with two associates. One is a young woman with dark-brown hair about this high," Aria said, using her hand to denote Kharra's height. "The other is a tall, young-looking, very handsome gentleman with long white hair."

"Oh, you can't mistake that one!" replied the woman with bubbly glee in her voice. "They both left about an hour before you came down."

"Did they have their packs with them?" Aria asked.

"Oh, no, they said they were just going out to explore the city, but they were both dressed up far too nicely for exploring, if you ask me."

Aria exhaled. "Thank you," she said.

Taking her leave from the din of the Wild Mercer, Aria stretched her legs along the stone walkway that lined the cobblestone street. She started toward the stables to check on Xierex, but a familiar mental voice entered her mind. *Aria, we are across the street if you wish to join us.*

The kruusta chuckled out loud, earning herself a concerned glance from a passerby. The man recognized what she was and walked faster. *I was just wondering where you two had run off to,* she said as she turned her attention to the Golden Horseman. *How'd you guys get in there without an invitation? They have to be guarding the door with such important guests staying there.*

Oh, you heard that the crown prince was here?

I heard that a prince was there but not the crown prince.

When Zephyron realized there were important officials here, he couldn't resist the opportunity to mingle. To answer your question, Zephyron charmed a group of them as they headed into the Golden Horsemen, and the guards assumed we were part of the entourage. I left information with the guards at the door to keep their eyes open for you.

Aria groaned to herself and shook her head. In all her years of service, she had only been to about a dozen major social gatherings, and each time she had felt out of place. *I'll be there in a moment.* Aria looked down at her standard kruusta clothing and sighed.

As if anticipating her thought, Kharra's mind voice added, *Check the wardrobe in your room.*

Aria cocked her head and returned to the inn. She opened the wardrobe, and sure enough there hung a long gown the color of blue ice. *When did you have a chance—*

You nap; I shop, Kharra replied. *Hurry, come join us.*

Aria chuckled. *The energy of youth,* she thought to herself as she pulled the gorgeous gown from the wardrobe and held it up in front of her. It had been years since she had last worn a dress. Without delay, she stripped out of her kruusta gear and stepped into the gown. It was designed to look like two layered pieces, but in fact, it was a single piece. The gown was made from soft, flowing ice-blue velvet with a darker blue-on-blue, leaf-patterned silken center. The top portion of the overdress laced up in the front just under her bosom. The long sleeves opened wide at the cuffs with a trailing edge dangling beyond the reach of her hands. The inserts of the cuffs were also in the same deep-blue color and material as the dress's center. The left shoulder had a slit and some sort of flower-looking decoration. Aria realized it would accommodate and camouflage the crystal protrusions on her shoulder.

Once dressed, Aria looked back in the wardrobe and found a pair of matching blue slippers. She groaned a little bit to herself as she tried to put them on. Possessed of feet a bit larger than the average woman, she had to work to make them fit. Kharra's guess at her foot size was close but not perfect; Aria's feet were going to be sore afterward.

The small mirror in her room was insufficient for a full-length view of herself, but at least she was able to take a glance at the top half of herself. "What am I doing?" she said lightheartedly. Satisfied, she grabbed her kruusta medallion from her normal gear, tucked it under the laces of her bodice, and headed out the door.

At the bottom of the stairs, the serving girl Gwin caught her eye. The young woman's eyebrows shot up, but then she smiled broadly. She gave Aria a nod of approval. With an indifferent shrug, Aria left the Wild Mercer and strode across the street to the Golden Horseman.

The soft material of Aria's slippers made no sound as she approached the expansive pillar-lined porch of the expensive establishment; it was quite different from the metal clink of her boots to which she was accustomed. The doorman and accompanying guards waited silently.

"Name?" the doorman asked.

"Kruusta Aria," she responded neutrally.

The doorman pursed his lips doubtfully, the dress throwing him off.

Aria showed him a fox-like smile as she pulled her small silver-and-gold medallion from her bodice and flashed it in the torchlight.

For extra confirmation the man glanced at the hand that produced the medallion. He recognized the large crystal embedded there and cleared his throat nervously. Without glancing at the scroll in his hands, the man nodded. One of the guards opened the door for her. "Enjoy your evening," said the doorman.

Aria stepped into the foyer, and no less than a dozen people turned to look at her, some less obvious than others. As she passed by attendees, whispers of "kruusta" began bouncing around the vaulted domed room. Keeping her face neutral despite her annoyance, Aria scanned the area for her companions. The space was wide and circular, supported by six carved inner pillars and eight similarly carved outer pillars. A domed ceiling vaulted a second story above the floor. The artwork on the dome was divided into six segments with each segment delineated by a differently themed seam. Each segment itself revealed a mural of a forest skyline and mountains as if the dome were windows looking out into a vast wilderness. Circling the lower portion of the dome was a series of leaf-shaped windows. Below the windows circled another mural, this one resembling vines crawling along a trellis. Near each pillar sat a pair of small trees in giant carved stone pots. People wove in and out of the pillars, making it difficult to keep sight of any one person for long.

Word of the crown prince's arrival had certainly spread. Merchants, politicians, and even a number of guild masters and journeymen from every craft in the city, all in their best finery, gathered around in groups both large and small. Each held a drink—some two—in their hands and seemed to be enjoying everything such a rare gathering offered.

Aria, come through the foyer. We're in the room beyond.

Thank you, she thought in return as she wove her way between clusters of attendees.

The room beyond the foyer was the great hall. A rectangular room, the great hall had two large white stone hearths in either of the far corners of the room. A series of large, multipaned windows lined the wall between the two hearths, and long white drapes, pulled back and bound with golden ropes, hung around each window. Gold metalwork trimmed the panels of each wall, and golden multitiered candelabras danced up the walls at regular intervals, all out of reach of any of the attendees. Carvings and decorations, also in gold, filled up every inch of space on the walls.

A troupe of musicians—two drummers, a guitarist, two flutists, a zitherist, and a fiddler—had arranged themselves in front of the windowed wall and were playing a lively tune to which most of the occupants of the room were dancing. Aria skirted along the outside of the partygoers, hoping to spot her companions and using her height to peek over most other heads. At last the familiar richness of Zephyron's laugh filled her ears, drawing her to the far right side of the large room. Then she spotted his unmistakable head of white hair. Sitting on a high-backed white sofa, his eyes acknowledged her immediately, but he continued his conversation with the man sitting in the elaborately carved chair to his right.

Kharra sat to his left, listening to the conversation with a polite smile on her face. The young woman wore a simple green gown trimmed with gold, which brought out the warmth of her brown eyes.

"Ah, here she is," said Zephyron as he stood and extended an arm toward her.

Zephyron's appearance shocked Aria though she did her best to conceal it. He wore a long white tunic that she almost mistook for a robe. It had a tight neckline and a short collar, and it buttoned down the right side of his torso. The material glimmered in the light, as did the silver that lined the collar, cuffs, and trim. A pair of silver serpentine creatures Aria failed to recognize meandered down either side of his abdomen. Beneath the tunic he wore loose-fitting pants of the same material. His white hair, shimmering almost as much as his clothing, hung unbound down his back. Had she not known him, she might have mistaken him for the crown prince rather than the man with whom he sat.

The blond-haired prince himself wore a decorative red sleeveless robe over a black silk suit, both trimmed in a golden weave. A gold chain hung down around his neck, and on his feet he had simple black slippers.

"Kruusta Aria," said Crown Prince Kiem with an edge of excitement in his voice. The prince stood to extend a hand toward her. "I am such a big fan of yours. You look amazing."

Shocked by his use of a common greeting, she clasped his hand in return. "Crown Prince Kiem," she said. "Thank you. I have not yet had the pleasure to make your acquaintance."

"Even before Master Zephyron told me of your most recent exploits, I was a longtime follower of your career." Aria released his hand and cocked her head to the side. He could not have been more than eighteen years old, and she had never seen him before. So how he knew anything about her or why he would be interested in her career confounded her.

Kiem returned to his chair. "Please, sit and join us," he said, gesturing to the empty chair to his right.

Aria eyed the bodyguards around the seating area, each bearing the insignia of the Order of the Rose, and eased into the chair. She crossed her legs but fought against her impulse to fidget with her gown. "I didn't realize one such as myself would attract attention. I am just another kruusta doing my job."

Kiem flashed her a white-toothed smile. "I find your modesty charming. As you know, each of you kruustas report your activities to nearby shard temples. The priests also submit reports. In addition to the well-being of their local communities, they submit reports of both the shard beast and kruusta activity in their respective areas. Those reports eventually reach the Minister of the Orders. Each of the other orders submit similar reports." He shrugged. "If I am to be emperor one day, I want to know all there is to know about the land I live in and the people in it. I find you kruustas most fascinating, and your career in particular I find inspiring. You are quite different even from other kruustas.

"Let's see. Some call you Aria Moonblade because of your preference for traveling and fighting at night. Most others, even kruustas, don't like fighting at night. You are currently the oldest living kruusta and have also destroyed more shard beasts than any other. They say your ability to detect and defeat them exceeds all others. You adopted, raised, and trained a wild zegu, and you prefer to ride it rather than a horse.

"Hmm, oh, you often befriend the local innkeepers and their staff; they speak highly of you. Also, I have seen a few kruustas fight. I find that most of them lack finesse and rely mostly on brute strength. However, those who've witnessed you fight say you move both with efficiency and grace. I believe 'flowing' is a term often used. Does that sound right, Zephyron?" The prince turned his head toward the Guardian.

"It does, indeed, Your Grace," Zephyron responded with a stately tone. Nodding toward Aria, he added, "You have yourself a fan."

Aria raised an eyebrow at Zephyron but said nothing.

"I do wish I could travel and fight as you do," said the prince. "It must be a great life to have such adventure and freedom rather than be confined to a single city most of the time, surrounded by guards at all hours and having to attend boring meetings and social gatherings."

Aria suspected that the prince's trip to Valmont was the first time he had even been more than a few miles away from Aloazai. She worked to find the appropriate words to respond but kept finding herself treading down paths of mental negativity. At last she said, "A kruusta's life is one of duty, as is yours, and we each have our parts to play."

The music changed to something of a medium tempo. "Oh, I love this tune," said Kiem, his previous conversation already forgotten. He looked beyond Zephyron and said to the still-silent Kharra. "Would you honor me with this dance, Lady Kharra?"

Aria narrowed her eyes at Zephyron. His lips twitched.

Kharra flashed a brilliant smile at the prince. "I would love to." In her mind, Aria heard, *I'll make you pay for this.*

Aria did her best to suppress a smile. She knew Kharra had directed the comment at Zephyron, but her inclusion of Aria indicated it was a friendly jest.

Zephyron stood, and then to Aria's surprise bowed to her over one arm. "Would you care to dance, my lady?"

Aria's eyes went wide with terror. "I don't think—"

Before another word escaped her mouth, Zephyron grabbed her hand and pulled her toward the dance floor. As before when they touched, the crystal in her hand flared to life as soon as their skin made contact, pulsing a soft blue, and energy surged from his hand to hers. She had been ready for it this time, and it invigorated her. With graceful skill Zephyron pulled her right arm outward. To avoid tripping, she had no choice but to allow her body to follow the motion and spin into his arm. He spun her back until his other hand was placed firmly against the small of her back. With his large, powerful left hand, he made minute changes to their movement, and his extended right arm steered her in the direction of his choosing. Though she had never danced before in her life, the activity shared enough similar motion with her combat footwork that her muscles reacted to his lead.

With her face near Zephyron's ear, she said in a whisper, "I feel out of place. These dresses intimidate me more than a horde of shard beasts."

Zephyron smiled as he twirled her around. "You don't give yourself enough credit. You look stunning."

Aria's cheeks grew warm, unaccustomed as she was to compliments about her appearance. "Speaking of which, where did you get that outfit?" she asked the Guardian as a means of deflecting attention away from herself.

"Oh, you like it?"

Aria smirked. "I think you know exactly how you look. I've never seen that type of clothing design or material before. Did you find that in Tanoria?"

Zephyron shook his head slightly as he led her into a series of steps that took her to the opposite side of the room. "No. I've had this outfit for years. I keep it around for occasions such as this."

"You carry that in your pack?" she asked.

Zephyron nodded. "It's made from shardsilk, so it doesn't wrinkle. It's actually pretty durable in battle as well."

Aria cocked her head. "Shardsilk? Never heard of it."

"You wouldn't have. It comes from the Xi'ari silkmoth, which is only found in Xi'ari'asi."

"Ah, I see. That's the home of the Guardians, so it's a Guardian-only resource."

Zephyron smiled and nodded as he spun her about again. Then he frowned. "Unfortunately I don't think there's anyone left who knows how to work or even harvest the material."

"So I have to know," she said, changing the subject again. "How in the world did you get an audience with the crown prince?"

"Funny you should ask," he began. "Kharra and I just happened to start a conversation about current events with a group of wealthy merchants who were on their way to the Golden Horseman."

"Just happened…" Aria inserted.

Zephyron's mouth twitched as he continued. "The merchants became so enthralled with the conversation that when we all arrived at the front door, one well-known merchant spoke up on behalf of the entire group for entrance and included us as part of their group.

"With so much going on, once we were inside, it took little effort on our part to break away and mingle. As for getting an audience with the prince, that was a combination of Kharra and you."

"Me?" Aria asked incredulously.

Zephyron smiled. "Kharra played coy, smiling at him whenever she caught him looking her way. Meanwhile, we began a conversation about our travels with a particularly skilled kruusta. As you saw, Kiem's quite a fan of yours. Once he overheard the conversation, he escaped from the stuffier crowd that lingered about him and bounded to our side."

Aria narrowed her eyes at him. "How did you know he was a fan of mine?"

Zephyron ignored her question and instead spun her about again. "Honestly, I think he's actually more of a fan of Kharra's than of you, but he used our conversation about you to get close to us."

Aria glanced about the room and located their other companion. Kiem was talking to her. *He has not stopped talking since we started,* came the voice in Aria's head.

Zephyron laughed quietly. "I believe she's captured his heart," he said to Aria, though she was certain Kharra was listening as well.

Aria's lips curved upward even as she shook her head.

Zephyron danced with superb skill, able to keep her from ever fumbling, but Aria was thankful when the song finally ended. Together they stepped off to the side of the room toward a table of refreshments. Zephyron grabbed two glasses of wine and handed one to Aria. She took it with a thanks.

Aria swirled the wine on her tongue, enjoying the faint peach flavor. She eyed the dance floor. Kharra had not managed to escape as easily as they had; Kiem kept her on the floor for another song.

"So what have we learned?" Aria asked Zephyron over her glass of wine as they found seats at a small, somewhat secluded table on the far side of the dance floor.

"According to your crown prince, he and five hundred troops are passing through the Valmont area on their way to a place called Haan. His troops are camped a few miles outside of the city. This event you see here was a rather impromptu gathering; Kiem wanted to visit the city. I suspect there's more going on here than just a stately visit."

Aria stared into her wine before taking another sip. "Haan," she said. "That's a province within the Temple Peak Mountain Range southwest of us. Why would he be traveling there with so many troops?"

Zephyron gave her a tight smile rather than his customary grin. "According to him, Haan has gone silent. Over a year ago, rumors reached Aloazai that fighting and unrest had spread across the province. Kiem said that his younger brother and sister—whom he referred to as the twins—were sent to Haan several months ago with some trusted advisors and a handful of Knights of the Rose to both investigate the rumors and help resolve any issues that might arise.

"They've not returned nor has anyone sent word of their status. There could have been some travel delays due to weather, especially in the higher altitudes, but Kiem is very worried. On top of that, all trade and travel between Haan and the other provinces has stopped. Those who journey there haven't returned, and no one from Haan has come out."

Aria frowned at her wine, her taste for it suddenly soured. "It would not be the first time a province rebelled or a provincial leader was overthrown." She nibbled at the inside of her lip. "Valmont is the last major community in Aelland before heading into Haan. He probably came into the city to get information, but I don't think he realized how much of a local commotion the arrival of the crown prince would cause."

"Will our path take us into this Haan region?" Zephyron asked.

Aria studied the Guardian, more of his puzzle falling into place. "No, sorry. Our travels won't take us in that direction."

Zephyron nodded, but disappointment crawled across his face.

Aria reached out and placed her hand on top of his. A tingle of energy rushed through her fingertips and up her arm. She savored the sensation. "Remember, these are not your people," she said, watching both him and the people mingling nearby. "You and Kharra both already carry many great burdens. You have enough on your plate without worrying about this land."

The Guardian sighed. For the first time since she had met him, Zephyron's eyes bore the weariness of the years he had lived and the events he had witnessed. "My concerns span much farther than any single land; my concerns are for the world as a whole. Kharra has a dream of reuniting the world and rebuilding the realms that were shattered by our great wars. I share that dream.

"But a darkness grows. I can't place it yet, but I feel it as surely as I feel my heart beating. Kharra feels it as well. She has nightmares about it, and they terrify her. I don't think any realm, including Tanoria, will be safe from what is to come. Part of the problem though is that we're still blind. We have no idea which series of events will be the catalyst that sparks something much worse. We also have no idea how much time we have. It could be another twenty years before this darkness is upon us, or it could be tomorrow. Worse, it could be happening right now, right in front of us, and we won't know it until it is too late for us to do anything about it."

Zephyron tossed his head back and gulped the last of his wine. "Listen to me ramble on. This should be a night for us to put these worries aside." He stood, his usual smile once again in place, and his eyes shone with their normal energetic luster. He grabbed her hand and pulled her back out to the dance floor. She swiftly swallowed the last of her wine and deposited her glass on the tray of a passing server.

For the next two hours, they danced and spoke of more mundane topics—food, funny childhood stories, interesting places they'd visited, and people they knew. At times they changed partners, and Aria found herself paired with Kiem on multiple occasions. Each time the crown prince spoke of something different—his life in Aloazai, trade arrangements with different provinces, his training with the Order of the Rose, his father's recent birthday banquet. Aria struggled to focus on his words despite his best efforts to impress her. She nodded her head and commented where appropriate, but his interests and hers had little in common. Maintaining the facade exhausted her, and she found herself wishing she had shard beasts to fight instead.

The one item Aria did note though was that Kiem never once mentioned his current mission but neither did she ask. On several occasions, however, he mentioned Kharra: sometimes to compliment her appearance, sometimes to comment on her intelligence, and sometimes to share something witty she had said. The boy was besotted with Aria's companion.

A lull in the music, enforced by a break taken by the musicians, afforded Aria the opportunity she needed to meet up with Kharra and Zephyron. She informed them that she would be retiring for the evening. They both latched on to her suggestion and thought it best that they also get some rest. Without saying farewell to the prince, the pair slipped away.

Aria found Kiem. "Crown Prince Kiem," she said, "I need to be heading out. I have many long days of travel ahead and need to rest."

Kiem frowned, looking very much his age. "This night ended too soon. Is Kharra still here?"

Aria shook her head. "No, she was very tired, though she looked to have enjoyed her evening."

"A shame that I did not get to say my goodbyes," he said, genuinely crestfallen. A moment later his eyes lit up. "Would you do me the honor of stopping by my encampment in the morning on your way out of the city? I would love a chance to say my proper goodbyes to the lady."

Aria smiled in spite of herself. "I think we can arrange that." Aria bid the prince farewell and returned to her own inn.

Back at the Wild Mercer, all three of the companions changed out of their nice clothes and into more comfortable attire, but despite all of them wanting to rest, they found themselves gathered in Kharra's room. Aria sat on a small cushioned chair beside an equally small table. Zephyron leaned against the wall beside the room's small window. Kharra sat on her bed, her expression distant, distracted.

"We touched on this once in the past, but have you ever heard of anyone in Tanoria having any type of leyoen-like abilities?" Kharra asked.

Aria gave a slow half shake of the head. "No, why?"

Kharra's face grew tight, and she rocked slowly back and forth on her bed.

Aria continued. "The only thing remotely special here are the abilities relating to the use of the crystal shards. Kruustas are the most unique of the group because the shards become part of our bodies. Priests learn to commune with the shards in the temples, and shardhealers are able to use crystals in healing. Beyond that…I'm unaware of anyone in Tanoria having anything else, and nothing similar to any of your abilities."

Kharra stopped rocking, crossed her left arm across the front of her body, and held the elbow of her right. She bowed her head over her right hand and bounced her thumb on her lip. "It was very weak, but I'm quite sure that I sensed it in the prince. I don't even think he knows he has it, and I have no idea what type of ability he may have." Kharra looked at Zephyron.

Zephyron shrugged in return. "I'm just as baffled as you. The only time I know that people with leyoen came to Tanoria was over a century ago when the Sauru pursued one of the Betrayers here, but as far as I know, every single one of them was killed on a mountain. If this strain of leyoen is part of the imperial family, then it may very well predate all of that."

Kharra slipped off the bed and walked over to Aria. "I have not sensed anything from Aria nor any of the priests, at least nothing that seemed like leyoen." She looked into Aria's eyes. "Would you mind if

I touched your face so I could look a little deeper? Physical contact allows me to look deeper than normal. Perhaps I can find something similar to what I sensed in the prince."

Aria studied Kharra curiously. "Sure."

Kharra placed each of her hands on either side of Aria's head and closed her eyes. Unlike Zephyron's touch, Aria felt nothing unusual in the contact. The woman's fingers were both delicate and strong and her contact warm. After a few moments, Aria's right hand, the one with her crystal shard, tingled, sending a brief chill up her arm and along her spine.

Kharra released her hands from Aria's head and opened her brown, moist eyes. "There is something in you as well but not quite like what I sensed in Kiem. In him, I detected leyoen. I'm not certain what I just detected in you. I sensed the power of your shard, which is actually woven throughout your body. It seems like there may have been something deeper, but it's obscured. When I tried to follow it to the source, I met with some type of resistance. I pressed against it a little bit, but it seemed to push back. I didn't want to force my way through; I don't know what effect that might have."

"That must have been the tingling I felt from my shard."

Kharra's eyes widened. "You felt it?"

Aria nodded. "At least my shard did."

"Interesting," said Kharra. "Would you mind if I tried to go deeper?"

"Go ahead."

Kharra placed her fingertips along Aria's temples once again and closed her eyes. Her brow furrowed in concentration.

Aria waited patiently, resisting the urge to shift or fidget. She caught Zephyron watching the two of them, but his expression gave nothing away. Without warning, Aria's entire nervous system felt as if it had been dunked in a river of snowmelt. Her vision blurred momentarily, and she gasped.

When her vision returned, Kharra stood before her with one hand over her mouth and a worried expression on her face. Zephyron was kneeling beside her with one hand on her shoulder and another on her arm.

"What…was…that?" she asked, her words moving slowly between gasps of breath.

"I have no idea," said Kharra. "I'm so sorry. That's never happen before." Kharra's hands went to her head, and she began pacing.

Aria's head cleared. "Is something wrong?"

Kharra shook her head. "No, I don't think so. But you have a block of some sort."

"What is a block?" Aria asked with growing confusion.

Kharra stopped and looked at her. "Someone…" Kharra began pacing again. After several long moments, she stopped and looked at her once again. "Someone very powerful put something in your mind so you couldn't access it."

"My mind? Why would someone want to do something to my mind?"

Kharra threw up her hands and exhaled with frustration. "I have no idea. This whole thing keeps getting more complicated."

Kharra returned to her seat on the bed. She pulled her legs up and crossed them in front of her. "I am really sorry."

"Don't be. If there are questions, then I want answers just as much as you. If someone messed with my mind, I would like to know who and why."

Zephyron patted her arm and moved back to the window. Silence shrouded all three of them for many minutes.

"What is the significance of Kiem having leyoen?" Aria asked, more to break the uncomfortable silence than anything else.

Zephyron left his spot beside the window and moved closer to the two women. He cleared his throat. "People with leyoen are those who have a natural connection to Mattekan, our world. It is through them that it expresses its needs, and from them, Guardians are called. That is how it protects itself and adapts. As we learned from Marimon, the continent on which Kharra grew up, those who can't 'hear' Mattekan will at some point bring harm to it and, over time, potentially try to kill it. If it dies, so does all other life.

"For thousands of years, the number of people who possessed leyoen grew, but there were those who stopped believing in the symbiotic relationship we have with our world and saw only the power they had gained. They were the ones who brought upon us war and enslavement. Now there are probably less than a thousand people in the world who have leyoen, and the Guardians are almost extinct."

"Part of my ongoing quest," Kharra added, "is to find all of the scattered leyoen tribes and bring them back together. My mother fought for over a hundred years to protect our bloodlines, and I vowed to continue her fight. Much of the world is now controlled by those who sought to extinguish those bloodlines or use them to further their own conquests. Scattered, leyoen will continue to dwindle and die out. Together though we can work to set the world right again.

"The fact that I've sensed leyoen in someone in a place where none was thought to exist gives me hope—maybe even more allies."

Aria nodded. "I see," she said. "But what do you hope to gain by finding people here? Most of these people don't even know there is another land. They won't leave to fight in some war that doesn't concern them."

Zephyron, his arms crossed in front of him, cleared his throat. "I think Tanoria has been lucky until now. As I mentioned before, there is a darkness growing. I feel it here even more than I did in Aerous. When the time comes, I don't think Tanoria will be able to avoid becoming involved.

"Our objective right now is to reach Ei'ars'anu." Worry lines creased the Guardian's forehead. "But I won't deny that there are connections here I can't yet discern. I suspect the prophecy that brought us here is but a small bit of the equation, and I hope the picture will become clearer once we reach our goal."

With their collective quest for answers only creating more questions, the three travelers each retreated to their rooms, hoping clarity would form after a good night's rest, but Aria found rest an elusive beast. Kharra's discoveries disturbed her. Someone had tampered with her mind. Who in Tanoria had such an ability? Why would they go through the hassle? How long had it been that way? What effect did it have on her?

Staring at the ceiling of her room, Aria scolded herself. Whatever was done, was done. She had been living with it for years, possibly her whole life. She recalled vivid memories of her past and, to her knowledge, never had problems thinking clearly. So if something was wrong with her, there would probably be some symptoms, right? At last, far later than she intended, sleep claimed her.

10

IN THE FOG

Aria's eyes sprang open. Her senses flared to life, and her body pumped with adrenaline before she threw back the covers. With practiced hands she donned her gear in the early morning darkness and rushed from the room, only vaguely aware of a gentle probing touch on her mind. Five minutes had not passed before Aria rushed out the door of the Wild Mercer and into its adjacent stable. Xierex sensed his rider's mood and fidgeted excitedly in his stall as Aria threw open the door. Without bothering with a saddle, Aria vaulted onto his back, and the two sped away, scaring a sleepy stable boy who arrived to inspect the commotion.

The thin line of predawn light outlined the eastern portion of the city skyline, but Aria turned west, riding into the still-darkened sky. Only a sliver of Wei's orange shape hung visibly; the other two moons had already set. The air smelled damp though no clouds were evident, and a chill breeze swirled in from the west, meeting her head-on. Only the rhythmic beat of Xierex's hooves and the whistling of rushing air reached Aria's ears.

A sudden realization occurred to her. Because of the sense of urgency she had met with upon waking, she had rushed off and forgotten to say anything to Kharra or Zephyron. Too far to turn back, she gave a determined growl and pressed onward.

Aria glanced down at the crystal shard in her hand, confirming what she already felt. The shard swirled with a mixture of red and orange—shard beasts. Surprisingly her sense of location told her the shard beasts remained a considerable distance from the Wild Mercer, but she felt them as intensely as if they were beside her. There were not many, but what she sensed was strong. Xierex raced through the western gates with the on-duty guards having no time to react to their passing before they sped out of sight.

After five minutes of pure sprinting, Aria slowed Xierex to a trot as she surveyed the area. Thick fog rolled in around the zegu's legs. Aria reduced his speed further as the billowing misty blanket continued to grow, limiting her visibility considerably.

A low groan caught Aria's ear. She kneed Xierex gently in the direction of the sound. Within a few steps, they came across a young man—a soldier, going by his uniform—lying on the ground and pressing his hands against his abdomen. Aria leaped from Xierex's back and knelt beside him. She pressed her hand against his wound though she knew the effort to be futile. The pallor of his skin, if not the puddle beside him, told of how much blood he had lost. The best she could hope to do was give him some amount of comfort.

"What happened here?" she asked, taking in the circular rose emblem on his tabard.

The young man, not much more than a boy, failed to see her at first. Then his eyes fluttered into focus. His gaze caught the shard on her hand, and he smiled. "Kruusta," he whispered, relief evident in his voice. "We were attacked. Shard beasts."

"How many were there?" she asked.

"The fog...couldn't see..." he rasped.

"Do you know what kind they were?" she pressed. She felt guilty questioning the poor kid while he bled out, but she needed information.

"No," he whispered in response. "Very fast."

Aria glanced about the area with her eyes and scanned it for shard beasts with her senses. She spied no other soldiers and sensed no specific shard beasts, but the sense of approaching danger nagged at her. She glanced at her hand. Her crystal continued to swirl with its reddish-orange hue.

Aria glanced back down at the young man and sighed. The breath of life had already left him. Sympathy and compassion turned to anger as Aria summoned her krusword. Its power flooded through her, and she savored it. She closed her eyes and stretched out her kru-usta senses, searching for the source of the danger she felt pressing closer. Still, she could pinpoint nothing.

Kharra's door swung inward, admitting a fully clothed Guardian. A growl accompanied by unsavory words escaped Kharra's lips, caus-ing Zephyron's white eyebrows to climb to their apex. She blushed. "Sorry." Kharra threw up her hands. "I can't get through to her."

Zephyron paused. "She's blocking you?"

Kharra scowled and chewed at the inside of her bottom lip. She reached out with her mind to Aria once again, allowing her con-sciousness to travel outward with practiced skill. As before, something rebuffed her, but what that something was, she could not identify. It was not like a shield, which was almost like a tangible obstacle her mind could sense. No, this was different. She still sensed where Aria was; shields obscured that at the same time they obscured the mind. This felt more like her mind voice was being drowned out by some-thing else. To her knowledge, and with Zephyron's affirmation, no one in the world was better than she at mind seeking, or empathy, for that matter. Did this have to do with whatever she touched in Aria the night before? Maybe, she thought to herself though she did not really believe so.

Kharra set her chin and shook her head. "Yes and no. I don't have time to explain. I can't seem to get her to hear me, but I can tell where she went." She grabbed her cloak and rushed past Zephyron. "Let's go."

The tall Guardian followed without a word.

❧

Several long moments passed with no additional information, not even a direction. Then without warning, a surge of power flooded through Aria, knocking the air from her lungs. She stumbled forward, smacking her right knee down into the damp earth. She used her left hand on the ground to stabilize herself.

Aria shook her head clear, and within moments her awareness grew infinitely sharper and more distinct, identical to her experience back in Braylore. Then she knew. Without her making physical contact or trying to reach out for more power, the shard from the city's temple four miles away had reached out to and connected with her. Giving silent thanks, she focused on identifying the danger.

With the shard's assistance, clarity formed. The danger lurked somewhere in the fog, was the fog. Utilizing her additional power, Aria allowed an image to form in her mind. She opened her eyes and maintained the image. As she opened them, a shape coalesced before her, something Aria had never before seen—a visage to give children nightmares.

Vaguely humanoid in shape and proportion, there the similarities between the creature and a person ended. It stood almost twice Aria's height, and its entire body shimmered with a crystalline gleam. The sleek torso gave way to elongated legs, but where knees should have been, the bottom limbs tapered into a dark mist that billowed like a flowing robe. Long, narrow arms swayed as if on the ocean, and the hands resembled those of a clawless prism wraith. From the shoulders came six long crystalline protrusions fanning out above the creature and to either side, reminding Aria of an insect getting ready to take flight. Because of the density of the fog, though, she could not see the terminal ends of the protrusions. Though the shard beast wore no clothing, its head appeared cowled in contrasting crystalline colors of light and dark blues. From within the cowl burned two violet eyes. The mist swirled about the creature like a fond pet.

The creature reached a hand toward Aria, and the portion of the fog in front of its hand grew denser. Instinct propelled Aria's feet to move, throwing her into a roll just before a lance of crystal erupted from the spot and skewered the ground upon which Aria had been kneeling. It retracted just as quickly. A second lance erupted from another patch of dense fog to the creature's right. Aria brought up her krusword just in time to deflect it.

Having never encountered this type of creature before, Aria possessed no knowledge of its strengths and weaknesses, but within moments she ascertained that the speed of its attacks was one of its strengths. Small wonder the young soldier never saw what hit him. The creature itself barely moved except to gesture with its hand in Aria's direction. A third lance erupted from another patch of fog, this time to its left. Again Aria deflected the attack.

Having seen enough, Aria rushed the creature, hoping to bring it down with haste. As she leaped into the air to strike a heavy blow, the creature dissipated, its form vanishing into the fog. Pain laced through Aria's back as one of the crystalline lances pierced through her side, but her forward momentum prevented the creature from landing a perfect blow through her back. The creature now hovered near the lifeless form of the young soldier, it and Aria having changed positions. Aria charged the creature again, but like before, it disappeared into the mist. Ready this time Aria twisted and blocked the lance that struck at her from her right side.

Remembering how she had caused the creature to appear the first time, Aria drew on the energy borrowed from the city shard and in her mind focused the image of the creature. A third time, Aria rushed at the creature. This time, when it tried to disappear, its image wavered for a moment but remained in place. Aria's blow with her krusword struck against its torso. The creature hissed and batted at her sword with one of its arms. Before she could pull the blade free, two of the protrusions from its back lowered, and two lances came toward Aria, one from each side of its body. Desperate to avoid the deadly cross attack, Aria threw her weight against the creature, forcing it backward. Though the maneuver likely saved her life, it also caused her to lose her concentration. The creature disappeared into the fog before hitting the ground, sending Aria into a rolling tumble.

With her still-heightened senses, Aria detected Kharra and Zephyron's swift approach from the south. Only a small part of her brain even wondered how they knew where to find her. In the three weeks she had been with them, accepting their resourcefulness had become the norm. Aria detected the approach of one other, this one a rider from the west—another kruusta, in fact. The fog thickened. Because of her connection to the shard, it did little to hinder Aria's perception of the area around her. The others would not have that advantage.

Aria turned, vaulted onto Xierex's back, and kneed him into a run in the direction of Kharra and the Guardian.

Aria, came the expected and very worried mental voice of Kharra.

Before Kharra could say more, Aria responded, *Stop where you are. I'm heading your way.*

A crystalline lance flew at Aria's head from her right, but she deflected it with an upward swing of her krusword. A second lance appeared directly in front of her. Aria jerked Xierex to the left as hard as she could. The zegu's eyes grew wide, but he obeyed the command, saving both of their lives.

With her heightened senses, Aria heard the voices long before she arrived. "First off, you will address me by my title. Second, do not tell me, a kruusta, what to do. You and your girlfriend need to head back to the city. Now!"

Despite her focus Aria found it within her to groan at the voice—Targus. She ducked again as another lance struck at her from behind.

"You're already injured. You—"

Though still quite a distance from her companions, Aria used the shard's visual perception and saw the other kruusta's face grow red as he batted Zephyron's hand away. The Guardian stood a foot taller than the kruusta, but Targus stood up straight, trying to minimize the difference. He pressed his chest toward Zephyron. "No one orders a kruusta to do anything," he snarled as he pushed Zephyron back a step.

None of them knew the magnitude of the danger around them. Xierex swerved rapidly to avoid yet another lance. It clipped the zegu's shoulder, but his momentum remained undeterred.

Kharra stepped up. "Kruusta, please. Zeph—" Kharra's words were interrupted as Targus backhanded her away, catching her across the face. Stunned, Kharra only stared at him.

Aria clenched her teeth as Zephyron grabbed Targus by the throat, lifted him from his feet, and then thrust him down to the ground. Keeping him pinned, Zephyron lowered his face to the kruusta's. "Don't you ever hit her," he hissed.

The fog parted before Aria, revealing to her eyes what the shard had already perceived. Without wasting a breath for warning, Aria leaped from Xierex's back as she neared her companions and tucked into a roll, her momentum carrying her practically to their feet. Before she came to a full stop, Aria twisted to her left and blocked yet another incoming lance, this one aimed for Kharra. Zephyron released Targus and stood, summoning his weapon reflexively; he had neither seen nor sensed the attack coming, something almost unheard of for the Guardian. He quickly regained his composure.

"This shard beast is new to me," Aria admitted as her eyes and senses scanned the area. "Somehow it is the fog or at least part of it. It can strike from any direction."

"How do you fight something like that?" Kharra asked, her eyes darting back and forth. "I can't sense it at all."

Aria ignored Kharra's question.

"Aria, are you a sight for sore eyes," said the other kruusta from the ground where Zephyron had left him, wounded in both body and pride.

"Targus, are you still able to fight?" Aria asked as she assessed the injury to his shoulder.

"Yes," he said as he stood with a grunt. "The thing was just here before these two arrived." He practically spat as he referred to Aria's companions. She ignored the attitude. "But I have no idea where it went. I can't sense it clearly."

Aria had fought with this particular kruusta a handful of times in the past, always against shard drakes. A seasoned kruusta with over three decades of fighting experience, he was known for being both a hothead and more than a little arrogant. He readied himself for the attack he knew would come soon. Out of the corner of his eye, he glanced at Zephyron and the Guardian's unusual weapon but said nothing.

The anticipated strike came but from two different directions simultaneously. One hurled toward Targus and the other toward Zephyron. Targus spun and swung down, catching the lance as it hurled passed him. Zephyron swung in defense, his energy blade causing sparks to fly as it collided with the crystalline lance.

"How do we fight this thing if we can't see it?" Targus said, more than a little exasperated.

"Leave that to me," Aria said.

Kharra, Zephyron, and Targus all glanced at her with a mixture of optimism and skepticism. What could a kruusta, a warrior of the blade, do against a shard beast that had no physical form? What indeed?

Aria relinquished her krusword, reabsorbing it back into her shard and drawing a wary look from Targus. "Aria, what are you doing?" demanded the other kruusta.

Aria pushed his voice from her mind. She closed her eyes and drew on the power of both her shard and the shard from the city's temple. With her connection to the city's shard, she easily saw the creature with her mind's eye. She focused on that image, forming it in her mind and willing it to separate itself from the fog.

An intake of breath from Kharra informed her it had worked.

"By the spirits…" Targus whispered.

Aria opened her eyes but kept her concentration fixated on the image. As she did, all of the fog in the area faded away, and before them towered a monstrosity unlike any Aria had ever seen. The body she had previously seen was but a small portion of the actual shard beast.

Before the four of them loomed a humanoid body supported by dozens of thick weaving and slithering serpentine appendages, as if the tails of several giant snakes had come together in a single torso. Overlapping iridescent scales protected the underside of the appendages and the lower portion of the torso. The six shoulder protrusions Aria had spied before were no longer obscured by the fog. Each protrusion revealed itself to be another type of appendage; these ones were long—at least two horses in length—and folded against themselves, facing outward. She now knew where the lances came from. Each one of those appendages hovered at different angles and each was poised to strike out at any moment. Aria already knew how fast they moved.

Without a word Zephyron exploded into action, his blue blade of energy intercepting the first lightning-quick strike of one of the appendage-lances. Crystal meeting energy blade resulted in an explosion of light and sparks. Zephyron allowed his momentum to carry him to the creature's opposite side.

A second lance struck out at Targus. The kruusta brought up his krusword to parry the attack, gritting his teeth as the force of the blow pushed him back. He counterattacked against the lance before it withdrew, but the krusword did no lasting damage.

A third lance struck out at Aria. Seeing the incoming attack, Aria summoned her krusword and brought up her blade to deflect it, but the shifting of her focus slowed her response. The fog instantly rolled back in, and the lance clipped her hip. She yelped as it connected, and her footing slipped.

"Aria, what are you doing?" shouted Targus over his shoulder. "We need your help."

Seeing a fallen victim, the creature snarled and struck at Aria again. This time Kharra stepped in front of her. The creature shrieked in protest as it collided with an invisible barrier. *I got you,* Kharra said to her mind. *Go back to what you were doing and just maintain your focus.* Kharra's mind voice conveyed with it an understanding of Aria's task, even if the others could not see it.

Aria nodded as she pushed herself to her feet and retracted her krusword. Once again she focused her full attention on the unusual shard beast and formed an image of it in her mind.

Two additional lances struck out at Kharra, but they too failed to reach their target. Aria sensed Kharra tensing against the assault, but the young woman stood her ground. Zephyron launched a counterattack at the distracted creature, leaping high into the air and landing a blow against its fused torso. The creature howled in fury, causing the hair on Aria's arms to stand on end. She ground her teeth to maintain her concentration as one of the shard beast's lower appendages whipped around and flung Zephyron away as if he were nothing more than a rag doll. The Guardian flipped backward as he was thrown and managed to land on his hands and feet.

Targus chopped at a pair of the lances as they beat against Kharra's invisible barrier. His krusword connected, slicing through the hard exoskeleton protecting the creature's thrusting limbs. One crystalline lance shattered, spraying out against Kharra's invisible barrier. Another lance struck out at Targus even as the creature recoiled the injured one. The attack came so quick that Targus failed to see it, but Zephyron deflected it just inches away from the left side of Targus's head. The blood drained from the kruusta's face. Targus gave a slight nod of thanks to the white-haired swordsman and shifted to the creature's opposite side.

Zephyron remained to the creature's right while Targus danced over to its left. Five of its six lances were still functioning, but its attacks were somewhat limited by its visual range, which appeared to be no different than that of a human. With their positioning, the two fighters forced the creature to split its attention.

Every instinct screamed at Aria to call forth her krusword and join the fray, but she forced the sentiment away as the shard beast struggled against her hold, its power grappling against her own. Aria's lips curled as sweat beaded on her face and her breathing grew deeper. The creature's true advantage rested in its ability to disappear into and reappear from anywhere within the fog, and it desperately wanted to regain that advantage.

Even with the assistance of the city's shard, Aria's mental endurance struggled against the battle, and she felt herself losing ground against the creature's overwhelming power. Her eyes stung, and her vision and the image she maintained wavered. A swirl of misty vapor seeped into the area, slowly circulating around the shard beast's body.

No longer aware of the fighting around her, Aria snarled in defiance, knowing death hovered just feet away. She closed her eyes once again. The droning rhythm from the clashing of krusword and energy blade against the shard beast faded into white noise, but the birds chittering angrily from nearby trees still came through, an annoyance Aria failed to banish from her thoughts. She poured every ounce of mental strength into maintaining the image in her mind and forcing the creature to remain in its corporeal form.

A hand touched Aria's right shoulder, and an immediate rush of warm strength flooded her body, revitalizing every weary neuron and reinforcing every weakening muscle. Her exhaustion washed away, replaced by a renewed vigor and determination.

As time passed, the sun bore down on Aria's face, burning her fair skin, and sweat ran freely along her brow. Her muscles protested, but she endured. The rhythm of the battle continued to rage around her, but she could not tell who was winning. She wanted to open her eyes, but she dared not; she did not want to risk distraction.

A rush of air brushed her cheek as the sound of crackling energy sizzled beside her ear and intercepted something solid. Nearby, Kharra growled with exertion. Through the chaos swirling about her, Aria fought to maintain her concentration.

Suddenly and without warning, Aria's grasp on the shard beast wavered again. Panic threatened to overwhelm her as it continued to slip free even as she tried desperately to maintain the smallest hold.

"No!" she exclaimed as she fell forward to her knees. She scrambled to reform the image in her mind, but she could not find it. She opened her eyes. Before her, strewn for many yards in every direction, were the shattered remains of the shard beast; their iridescence reflected colorfully underneath the early afternoon sun. It was like sitting in a field of rainbows. Strange how such a hideous and dangerous creature could leave behind something so beautiful.

Aria remained on her knees for several moments, allowing herself to catch her breath. Kharra offered a hand to help her stand, and Aria accepted gratefully.

Targus limped toward the women, his brown hair clinging to his brow. "Aria, what were you doing?" he demanded angrily. "We needed your sword!"

Aria stared at him blankly, not registering the verbal assault.

Zephyron moved to intercept him, but Kharra got there first, stepping between him and Aria. She thrust her index finger into his chest. "We would all likely be dead if not for what she did."

Targus shot a look at Kharra and then back at Aria. "What do you mean? She did nothing!"

Aria placed her hand on Kharra's shoulder, gently guided her to one side, and stepped closer to Targus. Looking down at Kharra, she said, "What I did was not normal for a kruusta. At least I don't think it was. He could neither see nor sense what I was doing."

Targus's scowling brow eased its tension as a look of confusion took its place.

Aria continued. "Do you remember the fog that covered the area?"

Targus nodded, his face dubious as if he was unsure sure how that was relevant to the original question.

"That fog was the shard beast. It was not something the creature created. It was part of the creature. It had the ability to solidify its form in order to attack and disperse again. That is why you were unable to pinpoint its location. The only chance we had of defeating it was to make it stay solid. That is what I was doing."

Targus tilted his head and furrowed his brow. "I don't understand. How did you do that?"

"I do not know. Instinct guided me," Aria answered, though she omitted the part about the shard providing her with insight. Targus lived in a world of black and white. He would not understand an explanation about the shards. "I was somehow able to force this"—Aria waved her hand across the field—"thing to remain in a single, solid form by maintaining an image of it in my head, but if I stopped concentrating, I would lose the image and my hold over it. That's why I could not fight."

All the anger left Targus's face. He shifted his posture and crossed his arms, still watching Aria. "Huh," he said, studying Aria's face.

Aria gave him a slow nod.

"Do you sense anything else in the area?" Kharra asked.

"I sense nothing," Targus responded.

As she had in Braylore, Aria used the additional power of the shard to allow her senses to travel along with the veins that crisscrossed the areas nearby. She sensed her companions in her immediate vicinity, but no other humans or shard beasts. Farther away she sensed normal wildlife. To the east she sensed people and animals moving in and out of the city, going about their usual business.

Aria lifted her head to the southwest. Kharra, Targus, and Zephyron followed her gaze. "There was someone watching us." She pointed up to a steeply rising hill to the west. "From up there. He's gone now though. I believe he headed toward Haan."

Targus looked back at her, pain and weariness evident in his face. "That's where I'm headed. I'm to meet up with Kruusta Jacia in Tara Gol."

Confident that the threat was gone, Aria finally relinquished her connection to the shard, silently thanking it as she did so. She had no idea if such a mundane thought registered with the entity, but it felt right to her. As its power separated itself from her, exhaustion threatened to overwhelm her. She swayed, but Zephyron shifted quickly and steadied her, his hold both sturdy and gentle.

"Are you okay?" Zephyron whispered to her.

"I have to be," she responded so only he could hear as she put a hand on his shoulder to steady herself.

He nodded and released her.

Aria cleared her throat. "We need to search the area," she said to all of them.

The four combed through the area. It was a mostly grassy field with a scattering of big leafy trees forming a perimeter. Aria fought against her exhaustion as she scouted the locale. She found shredded tents, trampled firepits, broken swords—all the signs of some sort of battle.

The group reconvened.

"We found five bodies," said Targus. "Maybe this was just a scouting party and the camp is farther west."

Zephyron shook his head. "No, they were here. There are patches of splattered blood, dozens of firepits, and fresh supplies scattered for a mile in every direction. They were hit some time in the middle of the night."

"So where are they? Surely there would be more bodies?" Targus questioned. "Five hundred troops, you said? I don't see any horses. Even if someone looted them, there would still be more bodies."

To her companions, Aria sent, *Many kruustas rely so heavily on their inherent ability to sense shard beasts that they do not work to hone their tracking skills.*

Aria received a mental acknowledgment from both of them.

"You didn't look close enough," Zephyron said, earning himself a scowl from the kruusta. "There is horseflesh and bits of their hide all about us. Most of that blood is from horses, not people."

Targus scowled at the Guardian. "What are you saying? If the blood is from the horses, where are the carcasses?"

Zephyron leveled his gaze at Targus. "I'm saying something ate the horses, saddles and all. I found enough torn leather bits to piece that together. This whole place is trampled." He pointed to one side of the clearing. "I found the tracks of Prince Kiem's forces coming into the area but not leaving." Zephyron then pointed in a different direction. "And I found several tracks of many somethings leaving the area. I have no idea what they are."

"Show me," Aria said wearily.

Zephyron led them west across the field. "Here," he said, pointing to several large sets of tracks. He moved a short distance to the left. "And see how the tracks here heading into the clearing do not sink as deeply as the ones leaving? That leads me to believe they were carrying something heavier, probably people, on the way out."

Sounding uncertain, Targus said, "Those look like..."

"Splinter maws," Aria finished coldly.

"But that can't be right," Targus said with a frown as he paced around the tracks. "These are way too big."

"What are splinter maws?" Kharra asked.

"They are nasty little shard beasts about the size of a medium-sized dog. They have three pairs of legs, plus an additional pair of appendages along their shoulders that they can use to manipulate their environment. Their maw is filled with hundreds of tiny needle-sharp teeth. The worst part though is that the saliva of a splinter maw induces muscle paralysis and can be fatal if left untreated, not unlike a prism wraith. These tracks are unmistakably splinter maws, only about six times the normal size." Aria moved slowly around Zephyron's discovery, examining the different sets of distinct V-shaped tracks. "There are so many overlapping tracks. I can't really tell how many there are. At best guess, I'd say there were about seventy-five of these things here."

It would seem you do not rely solely on your ability to sense shard beasts, came Zephyron's mental voice.

Aria almost retorted before she realized he was complimenting her. Instead she gave a mental chuckle and responded, *Indeed.*

Targus ran a hand, covered with his own dried blood, through his brown hair. "What in Tanoria is going on here?" he demanded, his voice strained.

Aria shook her head. "We don't know, but we have been investigating the shards and strange shard beast activity since we left Murali three weeks ago. Have you noticed anything strange or out of place with either the shards or the shard beasts?"

Targus stared, his eyes narrowed. "What's wrong with the shards?"

Aria fought down the rage that started to build up within her as she recalled her experience in Murali. "The shard in Murali was dying, and the one in White Bluff was completely destroyed."

Targus's mouth hung open, his eyes wide. "Kruustas Zach and Vera both fell this past week," he whispered, his gaze catching Aria's. She pursed her lips. That made six kruustas who had fallen in the past month.

Zephyron cleared his throat. "Sorry to change the subject, but we have pressing concerns right now. I didn't find Prince Kiem's body here, so we can assume that he's been taken. What are your procedures for dealing with something like that?"

Aria answered, "We need to notify the Order of the Talon garrison in Valmont. They'll probably send some of their people in pursuit of the shard beasts while at the same time passing the message to Valgate, the capital of Aelland. Valgate's garrison is much larger than Valmont's. I assume they'll also send some troops in pursuit and pass word to the emperor in Aloazai."

"How many people would Valmont send?" the Guardian asked.

"Their garrison is small," Aria answered. "So they probably wouldn't send more than maybe a hundred. Valgate could probably send ten times that much if the need warranted it. Aloazai can send thousands if necessary."

Zephyron stepped back and turned to survey the field. "How long would it take word to reach Valgate and for their forces to make their way toward Haan?"

"A messenger riding hard to Valgate could get word there in two or three days," Aria responded. "The forces there would have to mobilize and then march out. I suspect it would take them at least a week and a half, probably close to two to reach where we are now. Aloazai is much farther."

Zephyron sighed. Aria noted the conflict etched on his face. He looked to Kharra, and she gave him a slight nod. Zephyron said, "That's too long, and seeing what was done here, there's no way a small force from Valmont will have a chance against whatever attacked Prince Kiem's camp."

Zephyron glanced at the other kruusta. "Targus, could you ride to the garrison in Valmont and inform them of what transpired here? The three of us will pursue these creatures and hopefully locate Prince Kiem and his people."

Aria winced inwardly, but the arrogant retort never came. Still holding a bloody rag to his shoulder and favoring his left leg, Targus gave a resigned sigh and nodded.

"Who in Tanoria are you?" Targus asked. After fighting side by side with the Guardian, even the arrogant Targus understood Zephyron was no commoner.

"I'm just a friend," Zephyron answered. "My name's Zephyron, and this is Kharra," he said with a gesture. "We're trying to help your prince. Now please, it's paramount that you inform the garrison in Valmont and get yourself healed."

Targus nodded. "You're right. I'm sorry for how I reacted earlier." He turned to Kharra. "And please, forgive me. I didn't realize what I was doing when I struck you. My actions were unacceptable." At Kharra's gentle smile and nod of acceptance, Targus turned back to Zephyron. "Few common folk know how dangerous shard beasts truly are. It's a kruusta's responsibility to keep them from getting themselves killed, but you're not common folk."

"I'm just a fighter," answered Zephyron. "But those shard beasts are getting farther and farther away from us. We need to leave now, and we need you to get word to others about this incident."

Targus nodded again. "Agreed. Good luck to you," he said and extended his arm out to Zephyron. The Guardian took it and the two shook. Dropping Zephyron's arm, Targus asked, "Do you need my horse? I did not see another mount."

"No, we're fine," Zephyron responded. "But if you could, please leave word with the Wild Mercer that we'll be out for a few days."

"Very well," Targus said as he turned. His eye caught Aria's. He actually blushed a little bit but just nodded at her as he collected his horse, which was grazing a short distance away. The kruusta mounted and, with a wave to the party, kicked his horse into motion.

With Targus out of sight, Aria sagged. She tried to brush it off with a display of levity, chuckling lightly to herself, but the attempt cost her. She winced.

Both Zephyron and Kharra turned their heads toward her.

"I never thought I'd see the day when Targus was humbled. Sadly, arrogance among kruustas is not uncommon."

"You never were," said Zephyron.

Aria sighed, her smile fading. Her gaze fell to a small bloodstained patch of grass. "For much of our lives, kruustas live a very solitary existence. We have powers and abilities no one else has, and we do a job no one else can do, that no one else wants to do. Facing down monsters that frighten other people is what we have to look forward to every day. Then at the end of it all, we know that each of us has a destiny to become monsters ourselves. Common people want nothing to do with us until we are needed to save someone or something."

Kharra stepped up beside Aria and rubbed her arm. "That type of existence," the young woman began, "does a number on a person's mental health. Each of you learns to deal with it in your own way. Some, like Targus, they need to be validated and acknowledged by others. Yet I suspect that there are others, like you, who wrap themselves up in their duty and accept their isolation."

Aria looked down at Kharra and patted the woman's hand. "At times it kills me that people fear me, that I am so different. I remind myself that I do this so others can live without fear and the constant threat of danger. I've long since accepted my destiny. We each have our roles to play."

Aria shook herself. "Now let's get going while the trail's still fresh, and thank you for helping. I know it pains you to divert from your own mission."

Zephyron smiled. "It's the right thing to do."

11

THE TRAIL OF BLOOD

The shard beasts had no reason for stealth, so following the trail proved quite easy. It was early afternoon when the trail connected to the Rajeen Highway, the major road linking the province of Aelland to Haan.

Zephyron slowed his pace and sniffed at the ground with his sensitive nose. A snarl escaped his throat. Kharra leaned over his shoulder and grimaced. Aria dismounted to more closely inspect their discovery. It was a forearm. Shredded flesh and splintered bone protruded from under both the coat sleeve and the mail at what should have been an elbow. Aria rolled the limb over with her toe revealing the brass single-star insignia of an Order of the Rose officer on the cuff of the blood-encrusted white sleeve.

Aria looked at her companions. In his tigron form, Zephyron gave no expression. Kharra's, however, mirrored Aria's own apprehension. Without a word Aria climbed back onto Xierex's back and nudged him into motion.

Aria rubbed her fingers in circular motions around her temple in an attempt to push away the dull throbbing that persisted behind her eyes. Perhaps exhaustion had caused the headache, or maybe it had to do with drawing upon so much power during the fight with the fogbeast.

"Here, take this," Zephyron said, offering Aria his waterskin. "You look dehydrated."

Aria looked up at the Guardian, not quite focusing on his face and not quite registering what he had said. Backed against the fire-light of their campfire, his face lingered in shadow, but a halo of some sort shimmered about him, not unlike those that form about the sun or moon just before a rainstorm. Her eyelids felt heavy and her eyes strained. At last his words registered, and she accepted his offering with thanks.

The Guardian continued to watch her. "Are you okay?" he asked.

Aria nodded once. "Just tired, I think," she responded. She lifted up the waterskin. "And thirsty."

"I'm not surprised," Kharra added from her spot beside the fire. "I don't know what ability that was you used today, but I felt the toll it was taking on you. That was a lot of power you were wielding." Kharra shook her head slightly. "I'm actually surprised you haven't already fallen over. I'm practiced with the powers of the mind, and even I find that sustained level of activity exhausting. In some ways it's even more draining than physical activity."

"I was connected to Valmont's shard. I didn't ask for it or reach for it. The shard itself connected to me."

Kharra nodded. "I can detect the difference in you when you're connected to one."

Aria sighed. "I don't know what this new relationship is that I have to the shards, but I think I prefer the use of my blade. It's far less taxing."

Zephyron sat back down in his spot beside the low fire, a wry grin on his face. Aria raised an eyebrow at him. His grin grew larger, and he shook his head. "You sound just like I did when I first began my training as a Guardian."

Aria smirked at him but then grinned back, if wearily. The Guardian's lighthearted nature was infectious. She looked down at her hand. The silvery-white tendrils had grown thicker, looking almost like a giant spider web weaving up and under her sleeve. Her time continued to grow shorter.

Zephyron and Kharra both watched her as her smile faded, each of their faces unreadable. Had they discussed the method with which they would eliminate her when the time came? She hoped so. While the shard beast they fought together was deadly, it still did not measure up to a converted krumetus. As far as Aria knew, no shard beast was more powerful than a kruusta who had finished their conversion. Death always soon followed such an event.

Late afternoon on the second day of hard riding, the trio reached the outskirts of Tara Gol, a village of middling size with a population somewhere between that of Murali and Braylore. The people of Haan were a reserved lot, always protective and slightly distrustful of lowlanders. Still, there should have been at least some activity along the road or around the buildings as Aria and her companions walked into town.

"I don't like this," Aria whispered, though her voice sounded loud to her ears.

Kharra shook her head. "I sense nothing."

"Let's spread out," Aria suggested. The other two nodded, each heading off in a different direction.

Aria tied Xierex to a hitch outside the Silverstone Inn and summoned her krusword. A chill swept through her as its power flushed through her body. With her empty hand, she pushed open the inn's door. It caught against an overturned chair. Aria nudged the door open farther with her foot, keeping her sword ready, and she stepped into the dark interior of the building. She did not see anyone, living or dead, but it was clear a fight had taken place within. Most of the benches and tables were overturned. Multiple ale pitchers dotted the floor, broken, and nearly every keg was smashed. Aria noticed the lack of liquid in or around any them.

Aria moved to the hearth in the back of the room. With the brisk mountain air, one would assume a hearth would be kept warm, but this one had not been lit in some time. She inspected the kitchen next. Like the hearth, the oven coals were cold. She moved back out into the common room. From the sunlight trickling in through the front windows, she noticed a few strands of a spider's web connecting the kitchen's door with the inn's bar. She ran her fingers along the bar top, taking away a layer of dust. She stared at her fingers and frowned.

Aria moved up the stairs to the inn's second floor, checking each room she passed. Still, she found no one, but she did find more chaos like she had seen in the common room. In some rooms the sheets were shredded. In others beds were overturned. In two, vanities were shattered. Finding no answers and acquiring only more questions, Aria departed the inn.

Kharra stepped carefully through the front door of the medium-sized home.

"Hello?" she called, even as she scanned the vicinity with both her mind seeking and empathy.

Kharra looked through the front room, the dining area, and the kitchen. She found no people, but evidence suggested a struggle—window glass covered the floor, as did splintered tables, shredded chairs, smashed plates, and broken pottery.

Kharra climbed the steps on the opposite side of the front room. "Hello?" she called again. With each room she checked above, she found only the same chaos as below. She paused in a doorway as something red caught her eye. She reached down beneath the shredded footboard of the bed and pulled free a small doll with a red dress. Then she realized the dress was not red but rather stained with blood.

Kharra stood there and closed her eyes as the haunting memories from four years before rushed back to her, memories she had long thought defeated.

"Calim! Bette!" she called. There was no answer. She looked in the front room, in the dining room, and in the kitchen. There was no sign of her parents, but there had been a struggle. Tables and chairs were overturned. Glass from the windows littered the floor. Pottery and plates were shattered. She ran upstairs, taking two steps at a time.

Kharra blinked tears away as she fought back against the memories.

At last, under a pile of five bodies, she found Bette. Her skirt was bloody and torn and half her face blackened from a blow. Tears filling her eyes and her throat swelling, Kharra pulled Bette free from the others and dragged her lifeless body over toward Calim. She barely made it to Calim before she sank to the ground beside the two people who had taken her in and raised her after her mother had died. Kharra screamed as loud as she could and then screamed some more.

Kharra ground her teeth, but the memories continued flooding back unbidden.

"How did we miss one?" one of them asked.

"I don't know," another responded. "But we better capture her and put her with the rest before Xareen finds out."

Kharra looked at each of them. "Why?" she shouted at them. "Why did you do this? What have we done to you?"

"It's not about what you've done. It's about what you're worth."

"You didn't have to kill them!"

"The ones who are dead are the ones who resisted. Come along quietly before you end up the same."

Three of the seven men approached, each with their swords drawn, while the other four remained with their horses. Kharra stared at them, trembling with both grief and rage. "Why!"

Kharra trembled, and the boards of the floor and walls began to shake in response, a little at first and then with growing intensity.

The crackling flames swallowing the surrounding buildings responded to her, flaring up even higher into the sky. The heat licked her skin, and she welcomed it. She lashed out mentally at anything and everything in the area, wanting to inflict the same pain on them that she felt in her heart.

Kharra's lip curled to a snarl as she fought back against the horrible images assaulting her mind.

Just the leader remained. Fear filled his eyes, uncertain from where the next attack would come. He turned to flee, but a horse reared and kicked him to the ground. Scrambling backward, trying to get out of the way of its flailing hooves, he spared a glance at Kharra. "What are you?" he yelled with wide-eyed terror.

Kharra forced herself to take long, controlled breaths. Her trembling vanished, and the house calmed, becoming quiet once again. With a sorrowful sigh, she put the doll on the bed and left to rejoin the others.

An hour later Aria and her companions reconvened in front of the Silverstone Inn. Between the three of them, they had searched the majority of the buildings within the village proper. Like the inn, they had found no one, each building devoid of human life.

"What in the world is going on here?" Aria asked, half to herself and half to the others, hoping they had more insight to the problem than she did.

Zephyron shook his head, looking just as perplexed, and Kharra looked introspective.

"I know the shard beast trail came straight through the town, but I don't think they stopped," Zephyron said.

"I agree. Whatever happened to the people here wasn't recent. Based on what you learned from Kiem last night, who knows how long ago this occurred?"

Kharra frowned. "I can't sense shard beasts like I can humans and animals, so I can't tell how far away they are."

"Without a temple shard to enhance my sensing range, I'm limited to about a half mile, and unfortunately there are no nearby shard temples. There are a few farther into Haan but not in this region." Aria frowned at her own words.

"What?" asked Kharra.

"I just realized what I said, like connecting to shards is something I do on a regular basis."

"It's a new ability you're developing," stated Kharra matter-of-factly.

"At this point in my life?" Aria retorted.

Kharra shrugged. "Latent abilities are rare but not unheard of among leyoen users. It's not unreasonable to think kruustas are similar. You are, after all, the oldest living kruusta. Who's to say what you might still develop?"

Aria admired Kharra's optimism, but her own gut told her that whatever this connection was she had to the shards, it was not something normal. She had always felt that she had more than enough power from her own personal shard. Recently though she had come to realize that some circumstances required more than she could give. As such, she appreciated the extra power when she needed it, but it also concerned her since it seemed to further accelerate her conversion. Even though she was prepared to accept her fate, she preferred it not come sooner than necessary.

Rather than responding to Kharra, Aria said, "I think we should move on."

Both Kharra and Zephyron agreed.

The first stars were beginning to fill the dusk sky when Aria at last sensed the presence of shard beasts. "We're getting close," she announced. Kharra nodded in response, and both Zephyron and Xierex picked up their pace.

The group finally caught up to the shard beast pack that evening, when the three moons were at their fullest. Aria, Kharra, and Zephyron, back in his human form, observed the creatures in their unusual procession from their concealed vantage point high among the trees on a hill overlooking the road.

Aria counted fifty-six splinter maws, more than she had ever seen before in a single pack and each larger than Xierex. What Aria found even more disturbing was their organized column, each walking one in front of the other. Jagwolves were the closest of all of the shard beasts to having any semblance of organization, running in loose packs not so different from normal wolves.

"There're people with them," Kharra announced. "A lot of them."

Aria and Zephyron both looked down at the shorter woman. She held her eyes closed and her head tilted slightly to the right. They then both looked back down at the long line of splinter maws. Though the distance was great, Aria saw what appeared to be people lying across the backs of the creatures. The shoulder appendages of the splinter maws kept the people in place.

"Most are unconscious," said Kharra. "I can't pick up many thoughts. They're in some sort of haze, but their fear is very strong."

"Is Prince Kiem—" Zephyron began.

Kharra held up a finger, and her brow furrowed. She sighed. "I can't tell," she said, disappointment evident in her tone. Kharra opened her eyes and scowled toward the passing creatures.

"Never in all my years as a kruusta have shard beasts ever taken captives," Aria said. "I have no idea what this even means."

Zephyron crossed his arms. "I guess we'll just have to find out."

Aria glanced at the Guardian sideways. "What do you suggest? Should we follow them to where they're going? Or should we attempt to rescue the captives?"

"How difficult are splinter maws to fight?" Zephyron asked. "Normally, I mean."

"Not really difficult at all for a kruusta. As I said, normal ones are no bigger than a dog, and while they do sometimes hunt in packs, there are usually less than twenty together at any given time. They are not terribly bright, just voracious...oh, no."

"What's wrong?" Kharra said suddenly, her eyes flashing open and her face transfixed on Aria's expression. Zephyron glanced at

Kharra and then looked at Aria. He had not picked up on Aria's sudden anxiety, but Kharra's empathy certainly had.

Aria licked her lips. "Splinter maws are voracious eaters. This behavior, it's not normal for them. That suggests to me that perhaps someone is controlling them, much like the shard drakes in Murali. What if there are periods of time when that control slips a little against that natural instinct?"

This time it was Zephyron who blanched. "That arm…"

Aria nodded.

Zephyron rubbed his forehead. "I think our decision has been made for us."

Kharra did not hide her pained expression nor her resigned sigh.

As much as Aria disliked their odds for success, she found herself nodding in agreement. She brought her finger and thumb to her chin and thought for a moment. "We can't run in there blindly," she said at last. "We could quickly find ourselves overwhelmed, and if they are being controlled, then we have the controller to worry about. I don't know what the range is on their ability, but I'm guessing it can't be too far. The shard drakes attacked me within Murali, which was only a few hundred yards from the temple. They then chased me for several miles afterward, but I think once they were called to the village, their natural instincts took over. For the controller of these splinter maws to keep them from eating the captives, my guess would be that he or she would not be very far away from them. Also, someone was observing us when we fought the creature in the fog, though they left before we finished."

Kharra nodded. "That's probably not a bad assumption," she agreed.

"So," Zephyron started, "we find this controller, take him out, and then…what?"

Aria tapped her finger against her cheek, her eyes staring in the direction of the leaf-covered ground but not focusing on any one thing. "We don't know what might happen if we killed this person.

The splinter maws may just go on a rampage and eat all of the captives. But...I have an idea."

Both Kharra and Zephyron looked up at her.

Aria frowned. "I don't know if it'll work..."

"I've got nothing," said Zephyron. Kharra shook her head, indicating the same.

"We whittle them away. They don't know about Zephyron's talents, so we use your tigron form. You run in, make like you're a savage, hungry wild cat looking for something to eat, and then get out."

"Ah," said Zephyron. "And you think they will send a few of their splinter maws after me?"

Aria nodded. "I do. Kharra and I will situate ourselves in specific spots on either side of the trail. You lead the splinter maws to us, and we take them out."

"And in the meantime," said Kharra, catching on, "Zephyron repeats the behavior in the other direction?"

"Yep. I think we'll get a few passes before the controller wises up and changes his tactics. Like I said, I'm not sure if it'll work."

"Actually, I think it could," Zephyron replied.

It did not take the trio long to locate the controller, or rather controllers. There were five of them in total, and Aria's stomach sank as soon as she saw their robes—four blue and one blue with a yellow collar. It revolted her that they did not even attempt to obscure their association with the Order of the Shard. Like Priest Malechi, the four in solid blue each wore a thin glowing bracelet on their wrists. The fifth one, identifiable as a shardhealer by his robes, did not. Aria had hoped, naively, that her encounter with the corrupt priest in Murali had been a fluke. How could this type of corruption have spread without her being aware of it before now? She suppressed her personal disappointment. She needed to focus on the job at hand. Her mind was already weary, and she did not need any additional distractions.

I'm in position, came Zephyron's thought.

I'm ready here, Aria responded, utilizing Kharra as her mental conduit. How comfortable she was becoming with this mode of communication.

As am I, Kharra added.

Less than thirty yards in front of Aria rode the five robed riders. One was nodding off in his saddle. A second priest and the shard-healer were riding quietly, keeping their eyes trained straight ahead. The last two priests were conversing together in hushed tones. Their voices were too quiet for Aria to make out what they were saying.

From out of the brush beside them pounced a giant savage white cat, its fur practically glowing under the light of the moons, snarling fiercely and raking its claws into the hindquarters of one of the passing splinter maws. The shard beast howled in pain and reflexively turned to defend itself. The cat, though nearly equal in size with the creature, was too quick and bounced around to its opposite side. It attacked the shard beast again, this time in its right front shoulder, before the priests even realized the attack had taken place.

The two priests who had been conversing shouted at the cat and rushed toward it with their horses. The shardhealer said nothing but fought to control his spooked horse. The priest who had been dozing almost fell out of his saddle as the fourth priest slapped his arm. The sleepy priest sat up, finally alert to the attack. He shouted at the three nearest shard beasts in addition to the one under attack to retaliate against the cat. His bracelet glowed brighter as he issued the command.

Seeing its peril, the cat bounded out of the way of the new attackers. It hissed and swatted at the face of the nearest splinter maw, connecting with its eye. The cat's white paw came away with greenish gore. The creature flinched, reared its front two feet off the ground, and howled savagely. It shook its head back and forth, splashing more of its gore across the ground, clearly unaccustomed to such pain.

The three other creatures tried to push each other out of the way in an attempt to get at the cat. Instead of standing its ground, the cat turned and fled into the brush. The four splinter maws pursued.

Aria adjusted her grip on her krusword as she waited for the white streak to pass by her. So quickly he moved that had she not been ready for him, she would have had no chance to move into action in time. As Zephyron passed, Aria stepped toward the crashing footfalls, arced her krusword upward, and sliced through the throat of the first splinter maw before it even realized she was there. The creature crashed chin first through the brush; it would not get up again. Its shoulder appendages fell away, and the people who had been restrained on its back slid off. All were still unconscious, but Aria had no time to spare them attention.

The second splinter maw crashed through the brush on the heels of the first. Ignoring its fallen companion, the beast launched its slavering, tooth-bladed maw toward Aria's face. The kruusta stepped to the side at the last moment, sliding her krusword down low along its shoulder. The undergrowth kept the beast from turning, and it snarled furiously as it became tangled in the surrounding branches. Out of the corner of her eye, Aria saw the white cat back among the main column of shard beasts, attacking them in seemingly random fashion. The priests were shouting at each other as much as at the creatures they were trying to control, though Aria could not make out the words.

Without waiting Aria met the third splinter maw head-on, driving her krusword through the roof of its mouth as soon as it opened to snap at her. She withdrew her weapon, flinging the smelly gore from her blade, and rushed to intercept the last of the four creatures. This one slowed before meeting its attacker. Its beady black eyes stared at her down its long, ridged snout. Aria crouched low with her krusword poised in front of her as she stepped around it. The creature bucked its head and snorted. It attempted to back up a step but caught itself on a branch. The creature panicked and began swinging its head from side to side. Aria took advantage of its predicament to slash at the hamstring of one of its far back legs. Though covered in a fine-scaled shimmering skin of crystal, armor enough to resist simple attacks from basic steel weapons, the splinter maw had no resistance to a krusword. Its back leg buckled, and before it could compensate, Aria slashed the hamstring of one of its middle legs as well. The shard beast stumbled to the left beneath the burden it carried on its back and its own unnatural bulk.

As the splinter maw thrashed on the ground, Aria moved in to relieve it of the three people it carried on its back, dragging them one at a time through the undergrowth toward a clearing just a few yards away. As she returned for the last of the three individuals, she slashed the beast's neck and put it out of its misery. She located the soldiers who had been on the backs of the other splinter maws and dragged each of them to their comrades. While such work would have proved difficult for an ordinary human, with her kruusta-enhanced strength, the activity provided only a mild workout.

Incoming! called Zephyron's mental voice. As before, he sped past her in a blur, a bolt of white lightning. He vanished long before the next splinter maw stumbled into view. The smaller versions of the creatures were quite nimble, but these were among the clumsiest shard beasts Aria had ever faced. Still, their sheer size and dagger-long teeth were enough to keep any fighter respectful. This time Aria was facing six of the beasts, but due to the snarl of trees and undergrowth, they could not use their numbers against her. She and Zephyron had carefully selected their place of ambush, and their plan was being executed even better than they had hoped. In less than fifteen minutes, six more shard beasts lay dead and twenty more soldiers had been dragged into the safe area.

With each of the soldiers safely out of harm's way, Aria made her way back toward the road so that she could further assess their progress. All of the priests had dismounted. One of them was struggling to calm the panicking horses. Two of them were shouting back and forth at each other, one pointing aggressively out into the surrounding trees. One pointed at his bracelet and then threw his arms up. Aria caught the words "cat," "maw," and "prince," and started to piece together the context of the argument. She also noticed that the line of shard beasts had diminished significantly.

How are you doing over there? Aria thought, hoping Kharra was able to pick it up.

The ninth one is about to fall, Kharra replied. *And we've got Kiem,* she added hurriedly. *How are you holding up?*

That's great. We've cleared out about a third of the shard beasts they had. I'm clear at the moment. I have thirty-nine soldiers over here, but none of them are awake yet. Now I'm watching the priests. We've definitely thrown a tangle into their plans.

Oh? Kharra responded. *We're done here now, by the way.*

Great, she responded.

Aria listened as the arguing between the priests escalated. Priests and shardhealers in the Order of the Shard only had very basic combat training. These priests relied on people's fear of the shard beasts and their own control over the creatures to keep problems away. With their weapons running off and not returning, they were becoming unnerved. They somehow knew the beasts were dead. One thing was clear—they had specific instructions regarding Kiem's capture.

Aria felt the other woman's mind fade briefly and then return with a mental chuckle. *It seems they're afraid to go off into the trees. They believe there's an entire pride of insane giant white ghost cats that they're now calling "shard eaters."*

Aria found herself grinning at the description of Zephyron's hit-and-run tactics of attacking them rapidly from different places up and down the line of shard beasts.

If Zephyron attacks again, Kharra sent, *I don't think they'll send the shard beasts after him. It looks like they're going to round them up, use them defensively, and camp nearby. They don't seem to care much about the rest of the soldiers, but they need to track down Kiem. Since the shard beasts that chased Zephyron ran off in all different directions, they're going to have to spend some time searching for him.*

Aria thought for a moment. *Before they can collect themselves enough to search, we should probably try to get the prince and soldiers on their feet and withdraw from this place.*

Kiem is going to want to rescue the rest of his men, Kharra said.

I know, Aria responded, *but we don't want them near enough to find the prince.*

I agree, Zephyron added. *Let us retreat to our rendezvous and regroup.*

The three companions met up together and, with the assistance of Kharra's mental coaxing, roused the soldiers from their stupor. Despite their confusion, the large group followed Zephyron's lead to a spot he deemed far enough away from the priests. When they finally stopped, Aria fended off questions from Kiem as she wiped down Xierex. She understood the prince needed answers, but every muscle in her body ached, as did her head; she struggled to think straight.

"Crown Prince Kiem," said Kharra as she walked up beside him. "Kruusta Aria's exhausted. Let's allow her some rest. I'll do my best to answer your questions."

"Oh, of course. My apologies, Kruusta. You go get some rest."

"I will." Aria placed her fist over her chest and bowed her head in salute as Kharra led the prince away. She did not even recall climbing into her bedroll before slumber overtook her.

12

THE RESCUE

The biggest shard Aria had ever seen loomed before her. She peered up at its thirty-foot height, noting every edge and facet. Unlike other shards, this one was dark, nearly black. The blackness though was not solid. Within the tall structure, just beneath the surface, the blackness swirled. She had no idea what that implied. Aria placed her hand on the shard and closed her eyes. As in Braylore, her awareness flowed outward from her and melded with that of the shard. She felt a rhythmic beat. A heart, she determined. It was slow and steady, comforting. She allowed her senses to expand. Beside the shard was someone or something, but it was encased in crystal, both in the physical sense and in the metaphorical sense of the mind. It too was shrouded in darkness. The crystalline veins surrounding the cavern pulsed with the same swirling darkness.

The beating intensified, growing louder and stronger. She could not place the source. Aria opened her eyes and pulled her hand away—or tried to pull it away. Her hand was somehow attached to the larger shard. She saw that the crystal embedded within her hand had released its own substance, the very same substance used to call forth her krusword. Instead of a sword, though, the substance had covered her entire hand and fused with the shard before her. She tugged on her hand, but the substance from her crystal continued to discharge, and the mercury-like liquid rolled farther up her arm. Connected as it was to the shard, the substance began to change color from its normal bluish green to the same dark hue as the shard.

Aria began to panic. She put her metal-heeled boot up against the shard and, with all her strength, pushed with her foot. At last the hardening substance shattered. She pulled away forcefully, falling down to the ground. But despite the severed connection, the substance from her shard continued to roll out and cover her arm. It moved up and over her shoulder, across her chest, and down the other arm. Soon her entire body was coated. Her skin ignited in burning agony as if her flesh was being devoured by the substance that now coated it. She screamed as she fought to tear it from her body, but she could do that no more than she could remove a limb. Her back erupted in pain as if stabbed with several swords. Her throat grew hoarse. Finally though her screaming stopped. It was not for lack of trying but rather because sound no longer came from her throat.

Aria looked down at her hands or what had been her hands. In place of her once strong, delicate fingers were long, needle-like ebony-black claws, each razor-sharp. She looked up at the shard to which she had been attached and saw her reflection. Six protrusions splayed out on her back, three fanned out to either side. Her facial features were alien, inhuman. Her teeth, like her fingers, were needle-like and pointy, capable of tearing flesh from any creature. Her eyes burned violet, though they seemed devoid of emotion. She tried to scream again, but all that came out was a hiss.

A misty fog rolled into the area. It began to swirl about her hands and feet. It lifted her from the ground and carried her away from the shard. She attempted to move away, but her body would not respond to her.

The smell of cooking meat dragged Aria from her unpleasant dream. She opened her eyes slowly, thankful for the shade of the tree limb above her. The morning sun was bright and the sky clear. Aria sat up and rubbed her eyes. Her head still throbbed. She could not tell if it was due to her exhaustion or her excessive use of power—perhaps a little of both.

To Aria's surprise the clearing was bustling with activity. It took her a moment to locate her traveling companions. They stood on the far side of the clearing, speaking with Kiem. The crown prince's face burst into a smile when he saw her approach. A red line ran down the side of his face from his temple to his jaw. He was going to have a scar.

"Kruusta Aria! We were just talking about you," he announced enthusiastically as he waved his arm for Aria to join them.

Aria put on her best smile. "Good things, I hope," she said, trying to keep her tone lighter than she actually felt. Zephyron smiled at her, but Kharra's expression remained unreadable.

"Of course," Kiem responded. "You, all of you," he added, with a gesture to Kharra and Zephyron, "saved our lives. We are forever in your debt. Lady Kharra and Master Zephyron were filling me in on the situation. You have saved so many of us, but I need to go back for the rest of my people. Their lives depend on me."

Aria nodded, both in agreement and in approval. Kiem was so young yet so understanding of his responsibility to his people. "We figured you would want to go back for your soldiers, and we won't leave until we've rescued everyone we can."

Kiem ran his hand through his cropped blond hair, his facial features relaxing minutely as he did so. He looked back across the clearing. "I am truly grateful for your assistance."

Kharra continued to watch Aria. The kruusta had the distinct impression the younger woman was scrutinizing her. Kharra's mouth twitched upward at one corner.

"So what's the plan?" Aria asked.

Prince Kiem gestured to Zephyron, who nodded to him in acknowledgment. "We're working on that right now," said the Guardian. "The priests are still camped a little farther up the road near where we left them, in a big clearing with the remaining shard beasts rounded up around them. It looks like they're taking turns searching for the prince. Originally they were going out alone, but after they found the remains of our handiwork, they began taking one or two maws with them. The other priests wait behind with the remaining maws and keep the rest of the soldiers subdued.

"At the very least, they're confused. One of them suspects human involvement due to the lack of bodies and the swordlike cuts on the maws on Aria's side. The others disagree and have concluded that the crazy 'shard eaters' prefer human flesh after all."

Zephyron nodded toward Aria. "You are the foremost expert on shard beasts. What do you suggest?"

Aria crossed her arms and twisted her lips. "Shard beasts don't have human controllers. There should still be thirty-seven of those things. We could possibly pick off the ones that go with the searching priests, but they'll call off the search if one of the priests also fails to return."

"Well, we have you and the soldiers you already rescued," the prince began. He looked at Zephyron and Kharra. "Do you two fight? You never mentioned it in our discussions the other night."

Zephyron gave the prince a silent nod. Kharra nodded as well, but she continued to watch Aria. The kruusta resisted the urge to shift under the other woman's scrutiny.

"That gives us seventy-six fighters," the prince said. "Can't we just hit them head-on? We outnumber them two to one."

Aria almost gaped at him, but she schooled her expression. "I appreciate your confidence, Prince Kiem, but these are shard beasts we're talking about."

The prince pursed his lips. "These men and women are highly trained fighters. Don't mistake the ambush on our camp as a sign of our inability to hold our own."

Aria held up a hand. "Prince Kiem, I meant no disrespect, and I don't doubt the fighting abilities of you or your soldiers. But fighting shard beasts is very different than fighting people. They're also very different from hunting animals. These particular shard beasts are likely stronger than anything you've ever faced."

"What better way for us to learn of our weaknesses?" the prince asked. "How are we to improve if we do not push ourselves to fight something stronger than us?"

Aria sighed. Responsible but still young, holding to a young person's ideals.

Zephyron cleared his throat. "Kruusta Aria, could I speak with you a moment?"

With a nod Aria drifted away from the prince. Zephyron moved along beside her. She gazed out across the clearing. The soldiers, many of them young, were finishing up the last of their meals, food likely provided by Zephyron since their own supplies had been lost. They gathered in small groups, discussing their experience and the battle to come. More than a few eyed her and the impossibly tall, white-haired man beside her. Even dressed as he was in his simple tan tunic and loose-fitting gray breeches, he carried a regal air about him. He looked more a nobleman than a fighter. Most of them had not been at the Golden Horseman, and they had no idea what a man of such bearing was doing counseling their prince on combat tactics.

"You can't really be considering this," she said, her tone half-questioning.

"I've been keeping tabs on the priests. They haven't budged from their defensive position. One of them checks the prisoners every so often and appears to administer something to them. I'm assuming whatever he's giving them is keeping them sedated."

"That's a shardhealer, not a priest," Aria corrected.

Zephyron raised an eyebrow at her.

Aria clarified. "They usually start off as priests, but then they show talent for using the special crystal healing implements. They treat injuries and ailments others can't. There aren't many shardhealers, and I don't really know how their skill works."

Zephyron waved away her explanation, indicating that they had more pressing issues to discuss. "I don't know how long they intend to keep searching," he said, "but based on the snippets of conversation

I've overheard, they're loath to even consider returning without the prince. I suspect they'll spend at least an entire day, maybe more, searching for him. I'm also fairly certain that my attempts to draw them out in small groups will no longer work."

"Couldn't we just wait them out?" Aria asked. "Wait for them to depart, whenever that is, and then we can hit them while they're strung out."

Zephyron pursed his lips. "We could, but it would come at a price."

Aria narrowed her eyes, realizing what he was getting at. She again recalled the arm they had found and blanched.

Zephyron saw her expression and nodded. "You were correct yesterday. Though the shard beasts are being controlled, some of their natural urges, such as the need to eat, are still intact. The longer we wait, the more soldiers will be used to sate the creatures."

Aria stared off into the surrounding trees and rubbed her temples with her thumb and middle finger. "You realize these kids have likely never seen a shard beast in their lives, let alone fought one? Fighting beside you, I sometimes forget you're not a kruusta. You have advantages other humans do not. You're able to keep up with the shard beasts' speed and strength, and your weapon is able to penetrate their armor. These soldiers will have neither of those advantages. If these were normal-sized maws, then a group of the soldiers might actually be able to pick off a few of them, but these shard beasts are some sort of mutation. Many of these soldiers will likely be killed if they try to engage the creatures."

Zephyron nodded again. "I know. I've said as much to the prince, but he'll go forward with an attack without us if we don't include them in our plans."

Aria sighed and nodded.

"Youth," Zephyron added with a chuckle that she knew was for her benefit. They had only known each other for a few weeks, but he understood her well; no kruusta had ever been a child.

Aria smiled weakly in return. "So how do we do this?"

"The shard beasts are being controlled by the priests, and those priests are just men. From what little I've seen, they don't even seem like soldiers."

Aria tilted her head to the side. "They have all those shard beasts. They don't need to be soldiers."

"True," said Zephyron, "but they aren't used to commanding a battlefield."

"Oh, I see what you're getting at. They aren't going to be very good at dividing their attention during the fight."

Zephyron nodded. "Right. So we get the priests to focus all of their attention on you. Really focus. Then I can bring Kiem's soldiers in from a flanking position. They should be able to engage with little risk to themselves."

Aria put a finger to her lip as she thought. "Because...the maws won't defend themselves while their impulses are being overridden by the priests."

"Exactly."

"Let's get going then." Aria's stomach growled.

"After you eat..." said Zephyron with a raised eyebrow.

Despite the grim situation, Aria found it in her to smile a little. "After I eat."

Are you sure you want to go through with this? came Kharra's mental touch.

We don't have much of a choice, Aria replied. *This is the best we could come up with that would allow Prince Kiem and his soldiers to participate while hopefully keeping their losses at a minimum.*

It's you I'm worried about, not them.

Thanks, Aria replied. Because she had been on her own for so many years, she still found it difficult to accept that anyone would care so much for her well-being, particularly when she did not have much longer to live anyway. She wondered, not for the first time, how much she had missed from life's possibilities because of Tanoria's isolation from the rest of the world.

Ready? Aria asked both Kharra and Zephyron. With their mental assent, Aria nudged Xierex into motion. The zegu burst down the hill north of the priests' defensive encampment. As one, the four priests and the shardhealer turned to face their attacker. Where they expected a savage white cat, they found themselves faced with a furious kruusta. Before they could react to her presence, Aria charged the closest splinter maw and sliced it across the throat as it reared to defend itself.

"Are you crazy? What are you doing?" one of the priests shouted. The other priests kept their silence but glared at her.

Aria spun Xierex around. "I denounce all of you as priests and shardhealers of the Order of the Shard. What you are doing is against our laws, and I am here to put an end to your treachery."

"We are not—" retorted the priest.

Aria cut him off with the harsh command of her voice. "Don't waste your lies on me! You control these shard beasts. I was in Valmont when you attacked these soldiers. I fought against your fogbeast, which has been destroyed." She glared at each of them in turn. Her look alone revealed to them that she knew the truth of their intentions.

The shardhealer averted his gaze from her. Two of the priests licked their lips nervously. Another one shifted uneasily. The fourth priest, who seemed to be in charge, glared at her. "I'm sorry it has to come to this," he said without a hint of actual compassion. The bracelet on his wrist began to glow, as did the bracelets of the other three. The shardhealer tried to cower near the horses, but all five of the animals screamed in terror as every single one of the shard beasts turned toward the kruusta. The shardhealer stumbled out of the way, shuffling toward the brush along the side of the road.

Aria wheeled Xierex around to make some space and then launched herself from his back. She summoned her krusword and engaged the nearest beast. It snapped at her with its slavering maw, but she sliced it across the face, severing its snout. The creature howled and thrashed and ran from the fight. Xierex reared at one that came for him, bashing it in the eye with his razor-sharp clawed hooves.

With all attention focused on her, neither the priests nor the shard beasts noticed the attackers that charged at them from behind. Led by the tall, white-haired Guardian and his electrifying blue energy blade, the knights of the Order of the Rose in groups of seven or eight separated out and attacked a single shard beast from behind. The shard beasts, all having been ordered to attack the kruusta, did not respond to this new threat.

The priests placed so much focus on destroying Aria that Zephyron killed one of the beasts and the soldiers had at least one more disabled before the priests realized something was attacking their flank.

"Get them!" the lead priest said to two of the other priests. On that command, half of the shard beasts that had been focused on Aria turned away to address the new battlefront.

But to the priests' confusion and the shard beasts' dismay, while the beasts lunged and snapped at the soldiers, they failed to make contact with their quarry. Something unseen was preventing their attacks from landing. Tanoria had never seen the likes of either Kharra or Zephyron.

Aria could no longer pay attention to the other half of the battle. She had more than a dozen shard beasts rushing at her from every direction, and she pulled back all of her mental energy to concentrate on the fight at hand. These beasts were stronger and bulkier than the average creatures of their kind, but Aria compensated for the difference. Her movements picked up speed, and she flowed in and out of the attacking creatures. She launched herself over the top of one, using her momentum to bring her blade down into the spine of another all the while avoiding hitting any of the captive soldiers still attached to its back. She rolled away from the beast and came up under the front shoulder of another, dropping the creature to its chin. The beast turned its head to snap at her, but she thrust her blade into its beady black eye and then its brain. The creature howled in pain and then ceased moving.

The song of her krusword grew in Aria's mind and ears. Away fell the other sounds of battle—the cries of pain from soldiers, the growls and snarls of the shard beasts, the clink of metal against crystal, the shouts of human voices, the crunch of gravel underfoot. Aria followed the rhythm of the song and allowed it to guide each thrust, twist, jump, slide, slice, and jab. Like the sounds, time also fell away. When dancing to the song of the krusword, time ceased to exist. There was only the dance. Her body flowed to the rhythm of the song.

At last the song stopped, and Aria's senses rushed back to her in force. She looked about. Soldiers and priests alike were staring at her, more than a few displaying fear. Kharra watched her impassively. Zephyron stood off to the side, a lopsided grin on his face.

One of the priests fell to his knees, still staring at her. "I have seen kruustas fight many times," he said. "But I have never witnessed anything such as this. Kruustas are strong, but this..." The man's voice trailed off.

"Well, I had help," she said with a gesture to the soldiers.

Prince Kiem, sporting a new gash across his forehead, cleared his throat. "We only disabled four of them. Zephyron had to finish them off for us. He killed three on his own. The rest were yours."

"Who are you?" the lead priest asked.

Aria debated not answering but found herself saying, "Kruusta Aria."

The man paled. "They told us—we heard you were killed in action, that you fell fighting shard drakes."

"You heard wrong," she said, her voice cold and her glare boring into the man. "Prince Kiem, you're welcome to take these men into custody."

The lead priest shouted something to the others. Before anyone else had time to move, each had pulled out a crystalline dagger and plunged it into his own heart. So unexpected was the action that even

Kharra, with her mind moving abilities, was unable to react in time to stop any of them.

"Find the shardhealer," said Aria.

"Here," said one of the soldiers.

Aria walked over to him and frowned. The shardhealer, or what was left of him, had been trampled several times during the fighting.

"Okay, men," said Prince Kiem. "Let's get our people free of these things and get our wounded back to camp."

"How many did you lose?" Aria asked as Prince Kiem approached their campfire. The prince looked haggard, his eyes darkened and puffy. He looked at least ten years older than his eighteen years, if not more.

"Two-hundred thirty-seven," he whispered, his voice raw and hoarse. Aria barely heard him.

"I'm very sorry for your loss," said Kharra. From the log on which she sat, she reached her hand out to his in a comforting gesture. Aria noticed the tenseness in Kiem's shoulders relax, and he managed a thankful smile.

"Thank you," he said. "It would have been much worse had you three not come for us. I am so very grateful and in your debt." He looked at Zephyron. "I knew you moved like a fighter when I met you. I have no idea what type of weapon that was you had, but it was amazing to see. Knowing that you are not a kruusta and seeing you slice through those shard beasts to keep my men from harm's way, you have my utmost respect." The prince then turned his head toward Kharra, looking her straight in the eyes. "I do not know what it was you did during the fighting, but I know you did something to keep those creatures off my men and me. Thank you." At last he swiveled his head to look at Aria and stepped closer to her. He put his hands on the outsides of her arms. She could almost see the awe in his eyes flashing in the firelight. "I don't care what people think about kruustas. I don't care what might happen in the future. Today you were our guardian spirit. You moved with a grace and precision that I could only dream about. You have my most heartfelt and deepest thanks, and I wish you the brightest future. For all that you have done for Tanoria and for me, you deserve a happy ending."

Aria smiled as she fought the lump that formed in her throat. "It was my pleasure," she said with a cracking voice.

Zephyron cleared his throat. "What will you do?" the Guardian asked.

The prince sighed. "I need to continue on with my mission," he answered. "I have to find my brother and sister, and I need to find out what happened to the people of Tara Gol. I never expected this type of setback. I have only half the force I started with, and I have not yet made any progress toward finding them." The poor young man looked defeated. Kharra rubbed his hand again and offered him an encouraging smile.

As if a switch was flipped, the prince looked up at the group with a new light in his eyes. "I am going to return to Valmont so those who need further aid can get it. I'll then go to Valgate to requisition three thousand soldiers from their garrison. General Cardemon will not like it, but he is a loyal soldier. Once he hears what we encountered, he will not resist. I will return to Haan with a greater force and unravel this mystery. I will also send an update to my father. It will be a while before he receives it, but he needs to know that something is not right in Haan."

Zephyron nodded. "You are a brave man, Prince Kiem," said the Guardian, "to face what you have faced—something not many others have done—and survive."

"Thank you for saying as much. It means a lot. It has been a long day. If I don't see you in the morning, I wish you well on your own quest." The prince turned and left.

After the young prince disappeared from the light of their fire, Aria asked, "What did you do to him?"

"I just eased his fear a little," said Kharra, "and gave a little boost to his confidence. The decisions he made were his own."

"Interesting," Aria responded.

"What are your plans for us?" Kharra asked.

Aria chewed on Kharra's question. She had long ago learned that if too many things seemed like coincidence, then coincidence likely had nothing to do with it—the dying and damaged shards, the glowing bracelets, the corrupt priests, the strange shard beasts, the dying kruustas, the presence of Kharra and Zephyron, and even the development of her newfound abilities. She'd had suspicions before that certain things could possibly be related, but there was simply too much now to even doubt it. Despite that, she still had no idea how it all fit together. Tanoria was a big place, and there was no way that the three of them alone could follow every lead back and forth across the land.

Aria recalled her dream from the previous night. She knew the shard she had seen in it was the Dragon Shard in Ei'ars'anu, and she knew even that was somehow related. "With the prince and his men out of immediate danger, we can continue with our mission," she said. She hoped that by continuing, she would finally start getting some answers that made sense rather than more questions.

13

THE ACADEMY OF THE SHARD

Aria reined in Xierex as they topped the crest of Voralan's Rest, a hill known for an ancient battle that once took place upon its slopes. Voralan, a general of the Quan'li forces from thirteen hundred years before, stood with his soldiers against the overwhelming numbers of the Thorum Crusade. Thorum, a would-be usurper and a butcher of innocent civilians, had marched his crusaders into the Quan'li Province with the intent of toppling the then small capital city of Quan'li'ru and killing its newly ascended child king.

Voralan and his men all perished, but they fought with such strength and courage that they crippled Thorum's much larger force and delayed the advance long enough for the forces of three orders— Shard, Talon, and Heart—to arrive and rout the invaders. The child king grew up to become one of the best rulers in the history of Quan'li, and as part of his appreciation for the assistance from the three orders against the Thorum Crusade, he set up academies in his city for each of them.

Situated along the banks of the Wan River in the center of the province, Quan'li'ru had grown to become a major trade center, one respected by the other provinces. Behind the city's great wall lived over five hundred thousand people, and even with such a great population, the citizens enjoyed ample space. Wide stone-paved avenues lined with trimmed trees ran through the heart of the city, allowing for ease of access to any of its dozens of marketplaces. Great white-domed structures intermixed with streets of gated estates. People of the city often found enjoyment in one of its many parks, lakes, or amphitheaters. In the center of the city, the walls of the majestic hip-podrome, with its many pennants flapping in the wind, rose above everything else.

Many people considered Quan'li'ru to be a great city. Gazing down over the place where she had grown up as a child of the order, memories came flooding back to her, not all of them pleasant. For that reason she avoided the region whenever possible. Training to be a kruusta had been brutal and painful. They said such training was necessary so the kruusta could grow up to survive against the beasts they were meant to fight, but Aria had always believed in other ways to achieve the same results. She had never voiced her thoughts though. No one had. Questioning the trainers only brought more pain. Despite that, few kruustas reflected on their training with regret or anger. They understood that they had been trained to become pow-erful weapons, something that could not be achieved by being soft.

"Below is the city of Quan'li'ru, capital of the Quan'li Province," Aria announced as she dismounted.

Kharra and Zephyron, the latter having already taken on human form, stood beside her to gaze down upon the expansive hub of civi-lization. "It's almost as big as Galirna," said Kharra.

"It's pretty big," Zephyron agreed. "It is unfortunate though that you weren't around to witness Aerous's splendor before the war. We once had cities so vast they would make this seem a tiny village in comparison."

Aria tugged on Xierex's reins and began going down the hill. Isor had finally disappeared beyond the Ferthin Mountains, casting the entire range in a black silhouette as the sunlight struggled to remain. As Isor dipped farther, the light became pink, reflecting off the thin clouds dotting the sky. Across the city below, lights flickered on as the lamplighters went to work and laborers returned home. Aria felt a dull ache in her stomach as they approached, but she forced it from her mind. She scolded herself for being anxious about returning to the place she had spent most of her childhood.

The guards at the gate saluted Aria when they caught sight of her medallion. One even smiled. Unlike other places, the citizens of Quan'li'ru did not outwardly fear kruustas. Having the school located within the city desensitized them to the unusual nature of a kruusta, and the people here had become accustomed to seeing them as humans rather than unfeeling monsters. Aria nodded to the guards, tucked her medallion back under her belt, and continued through.

Though many of the buildings had been changed, replaced, demolished, or upgraded since she had last been to the city, the path to the academy grounds remained the same. Aria allowed her feet to guide her through the streets even though her eyes occasionally doubted the direction they chose.

The Academy of the Shard came into view as the last of the sunlight faded beyond the horizon. The campus faced the wide-open Liolton Square, named after Priest Liolton, the first headmaster of the institution. The hundreds of candles and lanterns that lit up the face of the school's buildings also illuminated the square. Aria recalled the times she had been assigned to the lighting of different sections, a task each trainee rotated through as one of their many duties. The light cast the academy's facing in a silvery-golden glow, making its spires and arches shine as bright as the moons. In terms of style and architectural grandeur, the Academy of the Shard in Quan'li'ru topped all but the Temple of the Prime Shard in Aloazai.

Aria's neck tingled as she peered up at the towering edifice. True, she had a number of bad memories during her years of training, but she had some good ones as well. If nothing else she always found the order's architecture to be inspiring and uplifting.

Leading Xierex and her companions across the square, Aria noticed they were earning themselves looks from the local passersby. Some of them nodded to Aria, but many stared at Zephyron. Was it the pure white hair, something unheard of on someone who appeared so young? Or maybe it was his height? Aria thought of herself as tall, but he stood more than a head taller. Zephyron never seemed to notice the attention. Xierex also earned himself a few stares. Though zegus were not unheard of, they were considered somewhat exotic. Most kruustas rode horses, but Aria had a reputation within the order as being different.

At the gates of the academy, the trio was greeted by a gangly youth with big ears and freckles. The poor kid would never be able to blend into a crowd. "Good evening. I am First Acolyte Dolson. Do you have an appointment?" The title of first acolyte went to those who were next in line to be raised to full priest. Given his title, Dolson must have been seventeen, though he looked to be thirteen at most.

Aria pulled her medallion from under her belt.

"Oh, Kruusta, forgive me!" he said, flustered. "I didn't recognize you in the darkness, and I wasn't informed of additional guests tonight. I will have your quarters made up shortly. What is your name, if you don't mind?"

"Aria," she said plainly.

The youth's mouth hung open. "Aria Moonblade?"

"Is there a problem?" She disliked the nickname that people had attached to her, but she had stopped fighting against it long ago.

"No, not exactly. I've just read so much about you. The things you've accomplished. It's very inspirational. I never thought I would get to meet you in person, especially after last week."

"What happened last week?"

The acolyte frowned. "I saw your name on a list in Priest Worrel's study."

"Is that unusual?" she asked.

"Well, it was a list of recently deceased kruustas: death in the line of duty, killed by a shard drake."

Aria glanced at her companions. Zephyron's deductions had proved accurate. She had not returned to Murali after the drake attack, so Malechi had assumed that she had perished and reported it as fact. "Are any other kruustas here?"

"Yes, there are three others. Kruustas Zai'il and Tual arrived yesterday and Kruusta Rauss just today. They are set up in the east wing." Dolson looked at Kharra and Zephyron. Smiling politely he asked, "Are you both kruustas too?" Though neither of her companions had a crystal in their hands or carried themselves like kruustas, it was uncommon for those of their profession to travel with anyone other than another kruusta.

Kharra began to speak, but Aria intercepted her. "No, but they are traveling with me. They will also need rooms."

Dolson's smile grew wider, particularly when his eyes met Kharra's. "That won't be a problem. We have plenty of space. Would you like me to show you there now?"

Aria studied Dolson, disliking that recent events had her suspecting everyone's motives. A movement to her left caught her attention. She looked to the side and saw Kharra's slight nod. Aria relaxed.

"I need to stable Xierex here," Aria replied as she patted the zegu on the neck. "He's a bit temperamental around strangers. I know the way to the east wing. Why don't you take my friends here to their quarters, and I will catch up as soon as I tend to Xierex."

"Certainly, Kruusta," he replied with a bow. He waited for Aria to remove their packs from the zegu's saddle and hand them off to their respective owners. Once she was finished, he made a sweeping gesture with his hand and said, "This way."

Aria watched as the three of them walked out of sight. Just before her companions rounded the corner, she saw Kharra elbow Zephyron in the ribs. Aria shrugged and headed toward the stables.

The stables were simple yet comfortable, with floors covered in packed dirt loose enough to absorb shock but hard enough to avoid slipping. The high ceiling allowed for plenty of air flow. Evenly spaced hooded sconces provided visitors with plenty of light by which to see while at the same time reducing the risk of accidental fire. Each stall was wide and deep and bedded with fresh-laid shavings.

The on-duty stablehand approached Aria as she stepped through the doors. The lad, however, was more than happy to allow Aria to stall her own animal when he realized the visitor was leading a zegu. It was apparent he had never seen such a beast before, but he knew of their reputation. While he did not want to interfere, he hung by close enough to watch. Only a few horses were still awake when they arrived. Their eyes grew wide upon seeing the zegu, not sure what to make of him. Xierex knew what horses were and worked with them without issue, but they did not always share the sentiment.

The stablehand spoke to Aria as he watched her care for Xierex, and she was happy to let him. Frequently, staff personnel like stablehands and servants saw and heard more than people realized. Aria discovered quite a bit of information from the lad. She learned three additional kruustas had died since she had left Targus in Valmont, including Kruusta Jacia, the one Targus was supposed to meet in Tara Gol. Aria also found out the krusword trainees, those who had already obtained their kruswords but had not yet been named kruustas, had all been experiencing recurring nightmares over the recent months. The acolytes and the younger trainees had not had them. In addition to the nightmares, three of the krusword trainees had disappeared over the past two weeks. While it was not uncommon for trainees to run away, they almost always returned within a few days.

With Xierex fed, watered, and brushed, Aria thanked the stablehand and left him with a small sack of sausages from the last village they had visited. She welcomed him to help himself to them but informed him that they were actually treats for Xierex. Zegus were omnivorous, and Xierex had a particular fondness for sausages. Aria left the stablehand with instructions that if Xierex became rambunctious, he just needed to give the zegu a sausage, and he would calm down.

Aria found the guest wing without trouble. First Acolyte Dolson was awaiting her arrival in the hallway and showed her to her room before he excused himself to attend to other errands. Aria searched for Kharra and Zephyron in the rooms Dolson had pointed out, but neither was there.

Dining hall, said a voice in her head. Aria could now easily identify Kharra's mind seeking.

Uncertain whether she would be heard, she thought, *Coming,* in response.

Though spacious, the guest wing's dining hall was nowhere near as large as the main dining hall. Except on special occasions, guests dined separately from the acolytes and trainees. That included kruustas or priests who had journeyed from other temples or provinces as well as any family members of the trainees or important dignitaries who might come to seek the aid of the order. The dining hall had two long wooden tables, each able to hold sixty people total. She found the hall about a quarter filled when she arrived. She spotted all three of the other kruustas sitting together as well as Kharra and Zephyron not far away.

Zai'il leaped from her seat and rushed over to Aria, smothering her in an unexpected hug. "Aria! You're alive!"

Aria laughed in spite of herself. "Apparently, rumors of my death have been greatly exaggerated."

Zai'il had arrived at the academy at the age of five the year before Aria had been named a kruusta. The young girl had cried every night for her family and struggled daily with her training. Aria took a liking to her back then and became her mentor. Later, when Zai'il was named a kruusta, she tracked Aria down to thank her in person for the help, for giving her the strength and courage to succeed through her training. For a time they had even traveled together, though their assignments eventually split them apart.

Aria returned the embrace and then held the dark woman at arm's length. "Zai'il, you're looking well." Her short brown hair, dyed white, resembled the spiky shards of a broken crystal, and her honey-brown eyes radiated energy and vitality.

"You too considering we'd all heard you were dead."

Aria approached the table where the other kruustas sat and gestured for Kharra and Zephyron to join her. Rauss nodded a greeting from the opposite side of the table, and Tual shook her hand.

Tual was a short man, not much taller than Kharra, with close-cropped dark hair and equally dark eyes; a lean, wiry frame; and muscular limbs. Aria had fought with him once in the past, about ten years before. He had faced his first shard drake in that encounter.

Aria knew Rauss by name, but they had never crossed paths. He was only in his fourth year as a kruusta, and his face still held a lot of its boyish softness. His green eyes, however, were not soft. They had endured kruusta training and had seen much fighting since he had been named. His reddish, short-cropped curls, still wet from a recent bath, clung to his forehead. The traveling life of their occupation meant many days of bathing in creeks, rivers, and lakes, so a real bath was always a treat.

Aria introduced Kharra and Zephyron and explained to the other kruustas that the travelers had hired her to guide them through territories infested with shard beasts, though she left out the specific details. It would not be the first time people—generally the wealthy—had sought the services of a kruusta. It was usually for protection and sometimes just to make them appear more important than they were. The three kruustas were not interested in Aria's companions. They had more pressing things on their minds. They were, however, concerned about saying too much in front of the strangers.

"Don't worry, they're good," Aria said on their behalf. "They already know some of what's going on."

Tual frowned, but he did not argue. He said, "It's good to see you alive. Five others are still dead."

"That makes nine in total," said Zai'il. "What in Tanoria is happening?"

Aria started to answer, but a now familiar voice filled her head. *People nearby are listening to our conversation.*

Aria gave a slight nod. "I don't know," she said in response to Zai'il's question. "The order is just having a run of bad luck, I guess. Enough of this depressing talk. We're travel-weary. Zai'il, let us head back to my room, open a bottle of that fine liquor you favor, and reminisce about old times." Many people knew Zai'il and Aria had once traveled together, so such a request would not seem out of place.

Zai'il raised an eyebrow, knowing it was unlike Aria to dismiss something of importance. Aria gazed at her intently and pursed her lips. She then flicked her eyes to the side quickly. All three of the other kruustas indicated they understood. Tual, Rauss, Kharra, and Zephyron each announced they were retiring for the evening while Aria and Zai'il planned to meet in Aria's rooms.

Aria headed to her quarters. Intended for extended stays, the guest rooms were designed to be a home away from home for visiting kruustas, priests, dignitaries, family members of trainees, and merchants doing business with the order. Each guest's quarters consisted of multiple rooms, including a receiving room, a sitting room with a stone fireplace, a bathing room, a small dining area, and a bedroom. As an added bonus, the walls and doors of the guest rooms were thick and well insulated. If whomever Kharra sensed from the dining hall did not believe their ruse and tried to listen, they would have difficulty hearing anything.

Zai'il arrived a short time after Aria, liquor bottle in hand. As promised they shared a drink and began rehashing stories of old times, laughing loudly on occasion for good measure. Anyone listening would assume they were getting drunk. After a while the other four from the dining hall arrived one at a time. Each had been careful to avoid being seen, though only Kharra could confirm their spies had given up for the evening. Still, once everyone was present, Aria closed the wooden door to the receiving room to provide an extra buffer between the front door and where they were gathered in her sitting room.

"Would you mind telling me what all this is about?" asked Tual once everyone had settled down.

Kharra responded, "We had people listening to our conversation." Tual peered at her questioningly, but she did not clarify.

Aria took up the conversation. "Based on what we've seen so far over the past several weeks, we believe the deaths of the kruustas and some unexplained events with the shards might be connected. The shard in Murali was dying, and when I discovered the truth, Priest Malechi somehow summoned three shard drakes to attack me and the village."

As Aria explained, Tual did not watch her but rather Kharra and Zephyron.

"He summoned shard drakes? How is that even possible?" asked Rauss with a hint of trepidation in his voice.

"I don't know how, but I am certain he did it. As for how I survived, I have Kharra and Zephyron to thank for that. Had they not shown up when they did, I would be dead right now." The three other kruustas looked at them appraisingly. "From what we've been able to gather so far," Aria continued, "there seems to be some sort of corruption in the priesthood."

"Oh, good spirits," Rauss said, running his fingers through his reddish locks as he came to his own conclusion. "I can't even contemplate the possibility of corruption. These people have been our family. They are the voices of the Great Consciousness! Why would they do such a thing?"

"One incident does not mean the priesthood is corrupt," said Tual. "Perhaps that priest acted alone."

Aria continued. "A second shard we encountered had been destroyed, and prism wraiths overran the village, killing many of the villagers. We don't know how that happened either, but they can't be a coincidence."

"I think you're right," Rauss conceded. "One of the villages I passed through had been completely deserted, and the shard was dead, appearing no more than a rock."

Tual's eyes bored into Zephyron as he answered. "I haven't encountered anything odd with the shards, but I did encounter a large pack of jagwolves near Barsway. There had to be near a hundred of them. I only managed to pick off a few of the stragglers before they outdistanced me. I have never seen so many in one area before nor have I seen them so far east or at such a low elevation. Still, I haven't given it much thought until now."

Aria glanced at her old partner. "What about you?"

Zai'il bit her lip. "Now that I think about it, I did visit a shard temple about three weeks ago. I always like to check in with the priests as I pass through the villages. While speaking with Priest Graejen, I thought I saw a crack running down the length of the shard. Isor's sunlight had been pouring in through the windows, so I discounted it, thinking it had just been a trick of the light. But reflecting back, I am certain it was a crack."

"So are the priests doing this?" asked Tual with skepticism.

Zephyron shrugged but responded, "We found the remains of the White Bluff priest in the blast debris. If he had been the cause, I imagine he would have tried to get away. So if there is some corruption within the priesthood, then it may not be all of them. We've learned to identify those who are corrupt by the crystalline bracelets they wear that glow when they are controlling shard beasts. We only know of Priest Malechi in Murali and the three plus one shardhealer we intercepted in Haan for certain. The shardhealer was not wearing a bracelet, so there may still be others who do not give themselves away as readily.

"As for why, who knows? In the end, they are still people, and people are capable of corruption." Zephyron sighed. "Even Guardians are not immune to corruption," he added sadly.

"Who?" asked Rauss.

Zephyron waved the question away with his hand.

Aria informed the group about what she had learned from the stablehand, which led to another flurried round of speculation and questions. The volume in the room grew. Kharra cleared her voice. Everyone stopped talking and looked at her. "Our mission—"

"Kharra," said Zephyron, trying to interrupt.

Kharra held up her hand, and Zephyron grew silent. His eyes said he wanted to protest, but he deferred to Kharra's judgment, something Aria found peculiar since she was so much younger. "Our mission is taking us to Ei'ars'anu so we may retrieve an artifact known as the Heart of the Sauru. We don't have all the details on what that is exactly, but from what we've been able to piece together, the Heart has the ability to influence crystal. We believe it was somehow used for vile things in the past. I believe it is being used for that again, and those using the Heart now are causing damage to your shards."

Zephyron closed his eyes and hung his head. This was the first Aria had heard of these specific details, and she felt a hint of annoyance flare in the back of her mind. She forced the emotion down.

Zai'il scowled and glanced at Aria. "That is a suicide mission. Why would you agree to take them there?"

"I owe them a life debt."

Zai'il looked at Kharra. "You don't save a life just to ask them to throw it away again."

Kharra stared at her defiantly. "I intend for us to live. No one is throwing away their life."

Zai'il turned back to Aria. "Where did you find these people? Do they not know anything? No one goes to Ei'ars'anu and lives."

Tual tensed, appearing suddenly dangerous. "Why do you want this Heart?" he asked, his voice more a hiss than a whisper.

"The artifact is key to undoing something that was done a long time ago," Kharra answered.

Tual glowered at her, his eyebrows drawn together. "How do we know you are not the ones intending harm? You're not from the order, yet you come here claiming our organization has somehow been corrupted? You speak of an artifact that is destroying our shards, something I have never heard about. And you want one of the most renowned kruustas in history to take you to a place knowing such a mission is suicide?"

Kharra regarded him, her eyes searching. She moved toward him, but he jumped backward and brought forth his krusword. Before anyone could blink, Zephyron had summoned his own energy blade and stepped in front of Kharra. If Tual looked dangerous, then Zephyron looked deadly. His blade, like tightly controlled blue lightning, crackled with energy. His eyes, normally blue as the summer sky, flared with the same energy dancing along his blade. Aria sensed the power Tual held through his crystal, but it was just a trickle compared to what she felt radiating from Zephyron. Tual felt it too, and he had no illusions as to who would win should they come to blows. Despite that, he held his sword up, prepared to defend himself.

"Who are you people?" Tual demanded.

"Tual," Kharra said as she placed her hand on Zephyron's back. Zephyron dismissed his blade, reabsorbing the energy back within his body. The energy blade, Aria had learned, was one of the abilities he had gained when he had been called to be a Guardian. His eyes also dimmed. "May I approach you?" Kharra asked.

Seeing Zephyron back down, Tual relaxed. He reabsorbed his own krusword and nodded. "Don't worry," Kharra reassured him. "I won't harm you." She placed each of her hands on the sides of Tual's temples and closed her eyes.

After a minute Kharra pulled her hands away and opened her eyes. Tual backed away and eased himself into the chair behind him, tears forming in his eyes.

"What did you do to him?" Zai'il asked. Rauss's eyes narrowed.

"I did nothing to him," Kharra whispered in response.

"She showed me…" Tual started but trailed off.

"Showed you what?" Rauss and Zai'il asked in unison.

Tual stared up into Kharra's eyes. "I…I don't know how to explain it. It's like you…you bared your soul to me. I don't know how you did it, but…" He looked at the two doubtful kruustas. "We can trust her."

Both of the kruustas began to speak at once, but Tual raised his hand to stop them. "I can't explain, but what she did…I just know in my bones that we can trust her." He looked at Kharra. "I-I'm sorry I distrusted you."

"We're friends," said Kharra with a smile. "Apologies are not needed."

Zai'il sighed. "I trust Aria with my life, and I have never known her instincts or judgment to be wrong. If she believes you, so do I."

Rauss stared at Kharra for several long moments. Then he shook his head and shrugged. "How do the dead kruustas fit into this?"

Kharra shrugged. "I have no answer to that, but I don't think anyone in this room doubts they're related."

"So how do we approach this?" asked Tual, his voice conflicted and subdued.

"We need information," said Aria plainly. "That'll require some investigation."

"Without arousing suspicion," Zephyron added. Everyone in the room nodded.

Zai'il smiled. "Divide and conquer." Tual raised one dark eyebrow at her. She shrugged. "We keep it casual. Chat with some of the priests and the other guests here but not all together and not all at once. Some of us also know people around the city. We can chat with them, see if they've heard anything out of the ordinary. Between the lot of us, we're bound to learn something."

Aria nodded. "That sounds good."

"I also want to add," said Kharra, "we had watchers earlier this evening. I suggest we avoid gathering in a large group again for a while, at least until we have some solid information."

"If I may ask," said Zai'il, "I'm usually a pretty keen observer, but I didn't notice anyone paying us any special mind. What made you think we were being watched?"

"I can detect other people's minds with my own mind."

"Rather straightforward," said Aria.

Kharra shrugged. "I already know I can trust everyone here."

"From our...minds?" asked Zai'il.

Kharra nodded. "Don't worry though. I didn't read your thoughts. Just your intent."

"Read our..." Zai'il glanced at Aria.

Aria gave her a reassuring smile. "It took a little while for me to get used to it, but both Kharra and Zephyron are good people."

"I've never heard of anything like that before," said Rauss with more than a hint of doubt. "But if the great Aria's good with the explanation, then I am as well."

Aria raised an eyebrow at him.

Rauss smiled, and it almost looked out of place on his previously serious face. "Meant as a compliment."

Aria said, "While neither she nor Zephyron are kruustas, both possess unique abilities. I've seen them in action."

"Well then I'm glad they're on our side," said Zai'il with a grin, her levity breaking up the fog of disbelief.

Kharra stifled a yawn.

"That's our cue," said Zephyron. "I think we've accomplished all we can right now. I'm going to get some sleep."

"Me too," said Kharra. Rauss and Tual echoed the sentiment, and one at a time, all three of them departed.

Aria sighed.

"I'll drink to that," said Zai'il as she sipped from her glass. "What exactly have you dragged me into this time?"

"What indeed? This hole keeps getting deeper."

"And these new friends of yours, are you certain you can trust them?"

"Absolutely," Aria responded without hesitation.

The two of them chatted about more mundane topics as they finished off the bottle. At last Zai'il departed, leaving Aria to her own thoughts, thoughts that would keep her up for many more hours before sleep finally claimed her.

14

NIGHTMARES

"I'm going to let you take the lead on this one," said Zai'il. "I'm not so good with children."

Aria chuckled softly as she paused and peered up at the shop sign. "Are you sure this is the place?" she asked as she and her two companions walked through the front door.

Kharra nodded as her eyes scanned the shop. Zai'il followed close behind.

"Oh, hello there," came a kind masculine voice from the back of the shop. "I'll be there in a moment."

Kharra nodded as her eyes scanned the shop. She passed by a large rack displaying long leather tunics, each dyed a different and distinct color. Some were plain, and others sported decorative collars, lapels, woven cuffs, tooled leather belts, and more.

"Hmm," said Kharra as she glanced at Aria and then back at the tunic in front of her. "I think this light lavender tunic would go well with your eyes. I like this black one too." She rubbed the material of the cuff between her index finger and thumb. "Very soft."

"Kharra, I don't really—"

Kharra chuckled. "Don't worry. I'm joking. It is soft though." Zai'il snickered at Aria's fluster.

"Ah, welcome," said the man as he neared.

Aria turned to see his approach. He looked to be in his early forties with a few pieces of gray beginning to poke through his otherwise black hair. His hands were rough and calloused but strong.

The man nearly stumbled when he saw Aria and Zai'il. "Uh, oh, Kruustas, I-I'm sorry. I didn't realize…I mean, I didn't mean to make you wait." The man alternated between licking his lips and swallowing, shifting the weight between his feet as he did so.

"I am Kruusta Aria. This is Kruusta Zai'il, and this is Kharra. We are…" Aria paused.

"How is your son, Master Fornsworth?" Kharra asked, earning herself a surprised blink from the two kruustas.

The man froze, his eyes wide and his mouth open. He glanced at the kruustas, at Kharra, and then back at the kruustas.

"How did you…I haven't said…"

Aria studied Kharra, curious about the younger woman's approach. Zai'il remained silent but watchful. Keeping her gaze on the man, Kharra pursed her lips and tilted her head like a disappointed parent.

The man's panicked eyes rested on Aria. "I-I'm so sorry, Kruusta," he said. "We, we didn't know what to do. He only arrived here the night before last. We…we were going to send him back after he had some time to rest and had a home-cooked meal. He…he's a good lad. He just had a scare is all."

Aria raised an eyebrow at the man, and he cleared his throat again. Aria pursed her lips. "Master Fornsworth?"

"Please, call me Elias," said the man.

Aria nodded. "Elias, I'm not here to punish your son, but if he's run away, he will need to return."

The man's shoulders drooped a little bit, but he nodded.

"Do you think, perhaps, we could speak with him?" Zai'il asked. "Maybe we can find out what scared him or at least ease his fears. Kruusta training can be difficult and demanding, but I'm sure he's a tough boy or he'd not have been selected."

Elias nodded again, his head moving with slow resignation. "He's with his ma upstairs. Follow me. I'll take you to him."

Zai'il, Kharra, and Aria followed the leather worker through the back of his shop, past all the premade tunics, vests, cloaks, breeches, belts, bags, and more, past a table stacked full of tanned hides, and up a set of wooden stairs.

The man opened the door at the top of the stairs and held it open for the three women. They entered into a wide sitting room lined with multiple leather seats, most of which were thick, stuffed, and worn from use.

"Alyse, Jorun, could you come to the front room?" he called.

A woman with plain brown hair pulled up and bundled atop her head stepped into the sitting room from a doorway in the back. "What do you—" she started but saw the kruustas and stopped. Then she broke down into sobs.

At the same time, multiple pairs of thudding feet pounded down a different set of stairs. From a hallway to the left of the sitting room emerged two children. One was a dark-haired boy who looked to be in his midteens and another was a younger girl, no older than ten.

"Whatcha need, Pops?" said the boy without looking at the guests.

The young girl saw Zai'il and yelped. She then ducked behind the boy.

The boy finally looked at Aria and immediately paled. His eyes grew wide with terror, but he stayed his ground. Aria noticed a relatively fresh wound on his right hand and the unmistakable sparkle of crystal at its center. Silence hung heavy in the room as Aria worked to find the right words to not frighten the boy further. Zai'il's eyes wandered up to the ceiling, trying to avoid adding to the tension.

Kharra stepped forward. "Hello, Jorun. My name is Kharra, and these two ladies are Aria and Zai'il." Kharra extended her hand casually to the boy, who stood of a height with her. "We're not here because you're in trouble." She glanced at the two parents and then back at the boy. "We're just here to talk."

The boy blinked at Kharra's extended hand and then slowly took it in his. The tension in his entire frame eased. "You...you're not a kruusta?"

"Nope."

The boy's brow scrunched. He looked at Aria and then at Zai'il. "But you both are." It was a statement, not a question.

They nodded.

"And you didn't come here to take me back?"

Aria thought for a moment before answering. "You will eventually have to go back to finish your training." The boy's brows shot up, but Aria smiled. "But I am more concerned about your well-being. Something scared you. Why don't we all sit down, and you can tell us what caused you to run away?"

"You people are monsters, that's what's caused him to run away!" blurted a red-faced Alyse. "You're terrorizing children."

Zai'il's brow angled downward. Aria stared at Alyse and forced down the anger that suddenly welled in her. She felt something touch her elbow and glanced down to see Kharra's hand. Aria took a long, silent breath and relaxed.

"Mrs. Fornsworth," Aria started, "the Order of the Shard was founded to protect people from shard beasts, but it's an organization run by people. People have faults. I won't pretend that I think everything is okay at the academy at this moment, but I really do want what is best for your son. Right now that means finding out what's really going on there and what caused him to have such a fright. Please, if there's something wrong at the academy, I want to get to the bottom of it. The academy is supposed to be a place of learning and training, not fear."

The redness remained in the other woman's face, but the tension in her body relaxed. She exhaled loudly, nodded stiffly, turned on heel, and exited the room. The young girl who had been hiding behind Jorun dashed through the same doorway after the woman.

Aria turned back to the boy. "So are you okay if we ask you some questions?"

Though fear still lingered on his face, he nodded tentatively.

"Please have a seat," said Elias.

Aria and Kharra each picked out one of the thick-cushioned chairs placed on either side of a low rectangular table. Elias sat on a light tan sofa, and Jorun sat beside him.

"I'm fine," said Zai'il as she took up a standing position against the wall opposite the sofa.

As everyone settled in, Aria said, "Congratulations on your shard."

The youth smiled, the unexpected compliment putting him further at ease. "Oh, thank you." He blushed.

"It looks like it hasn't finished healing yet. You must have received it fairly recently."

Jorun nodded. "It hasn't even been a full moon cycle since I received it."

"We all attended the ceremony," said a much calmer Alyse as she returned to the room. "It was quite lovely." Alyse sat upon the sofa beside her son, opposite her husband. The young girl climbed onto Elias's lap.

Aria gave a tight smile to the clearly worried mother. Then she turned her attention to Jorun and asked, "So, Jorun, what happened that gave you such a fright?"

Jorun stared down at his hands, and silence fell in the room as everyone waited for his answer. He took a deep breath and exhaled. "I-I've been having nightmares nearly every night since I received my shard. Horrible nightmares."

Kharra furrowed her brow. "What can you tell us about your nightmares?"

Jorun frowned. "I can't remember them very well. What little bit I do remember...I'm always in a room with thick stone walls and dim lighting. There are people, but I can't tell who they are. My body always hurts something awful, but I can't tell why. Then my vision gets blurry as if I'm looking through murky water. I see shapes, forms of some sort of creatures moving all about me, but it's too blurry to tell what they are." He sighed. "I'm sorry. That's about all I can remember."

"What about the other nights?" Aria asked.

The boy looked at her quizzically. "Every night I have nightmares, and every night, the nightmares are the exact same thing."

"He looked horrible when he arrived, Kruusta," said Alyse. "But he slept soundly through the night and well into yesterday afternoon."

"Did he have nightmares?" Aria asked.

"I don't think so," the mother answered with a shake of her head. "I don't think he moved at all. He looks much better today."

Aria drew her lips taut. She glanced at Zai'il. The dark woman's nose and lip barely contained her snarl. Then she looked at Kharra sitting on the chair on the opposite side of the table and held her gaze. Without any mind seeking involved, she knew all three of them had drawn the same conclusion.

Kharra shifted her gaze from Aria to the boy. She did not even have to delve into Aria's thoughts to know Aria held suspicions similar to her own. Kharra took a deep breath. "Jorun, I've been gifted with a very rare ability. In some ways it's like a shardhealer's, except I don't need to use crystal tools. If you let me, my ability will allow me to actually see what you dreamed. Would that be okay?" She looked from the boy to both his parents.

The boy looked first at his mother, then at his father, and then at his sister. Seeing the young girl's worried face, the boy smiled a little bit. He looked back at Kharra, licked his lips, and nodded.

Kharra nodded in return and stood. "I'll need to be able to touch you—your hands will do."

"Oh, come take my seat," said Alyse as she stood.

"Thanks," Kharra replied as the two women changed places.

Kharra sat down beside Jorun at an angle. She caught a glimpse of Zai'il leaning forward slightly, observing them. Jorun mirrored her position so the two of them were mostly facing each other. Kharra held out both of her hands, palms up. "If you could just place your hands in mine and close your eyes, I'll begin."

With no further hesitation, Jorun did as requested.

"Take long, slow breaths and relax," Kharra said softly.

Again he did as she instructed. Once he was relaxed, Kharra closed her own eyes and allowed her consciousness to extend from her mind down into his. While she could see into a person's mind without touching them, the physical contact made it much easier to get past any resistance or barriers the person may consciously or subconsciously have in place. She compared it to the difference between looking down into water at some fish below and being under the water with a glass mask on and seeing the fish right in front of her. The barrier that was the water's surface was removed simply by submerging. Likewise the person's natural mental barrier was removed with the contact, the equivalent of being submerged.

With efficiency Kharra navigated her mind through the boy's conscious mind and down into his subconscious. She sifted through his memories of his days of training and discipline. Down further she went, searching for anything that resembled his description. After several minutes she found what she sought. Her heart sank. She dared to hope she was wrong, but her theory had proved correct. Well, not quite. It was even worse. Her eyes snapped open with alarm.

"What's wrong?" Aria asked, sensing something out of place.

Instead of answering, Kharra said, "Jorun, can I see your back?"

The boy turned and lifted his shirt. Kharra gasped at what she saw, as did both Aria, Zai'il, and the boy's mother. Scalelike bluish crystals completely covered his shoulder blades.

"What in the world is that?" said Alyse, her voice rising an octave.

Standing across from her, Kharra saw Aria's face grow dark. She showed no other outward signs of emotion, but to Kharra's sensitive empathy, the kruusta was radiating rage. Kharra knew it was for the well-being of the family that Aria said nothing.

Through the rest of the conversation with the family, Aria had struggled to smile politely and keep her tone light. Now that they had bid them farewell, Aria strode purposefully in the direction of the academy without bothering to school her face to hide her anger. Not even possessed of his shard for a full month, and Jorun already showed signs of conversion. Whatever was going on with her order, she knew it was also somehow involving innocent kids like Jorun. Unacceptable did not begin to cover it. Aria envisioned putting her fist into the face of the very next priest she encountered.

"Aria, wait up," said Kharra as she quick-stepped after her. "Don't do anything rash."

Without turning Aria stopped to allow the shorter woman to catch up.

Kharra's hand grabbed her arm gently and turned her. Aria was surprised that she remained angry; Kharra had not used her empathy to calm Aria as she had done in the past. Zai'il, Aria noticed, hung back.

In a low voice, Kharra said, "Not everyone is involved, and you still need more information."

Aria took a deep breath and allowed herself to calm a little. "I know."

Composed, Aria began walking again at a much more normal pace. Kharra remained at her side, and Zai'il sped up to join them.

"Can this conspiracy run so deep that they are targeting trainees?" Aria asked.

"Part of me is having trouble believing it," said Zai'il. "But we all saw the same thing. This goes way further than we suspected."

"I'm sorry, Aria," said Kharra.

Aria glanced down at the young woman. "For what? You did nothing except confirm what I already knew."

Kharra shrugged. "I'm sorry that you have to go through this. Both of you. I know this organization is like family to you both."

Zai'il said, "That is kind of you to say."

Aria nodded and managed a weak smile. "Thanks." She shook her head. "It disgusts me, but there is no use denying what is. We need to figure out exactly what they are doing and why."

Kharra's head bounced in agreement. "And that will require a deeper investigation." The younger woman's lips twitched up at both corners.

"I know that look," Aria said. "It's the same one Zai'il used to have…"

"I had a look?" asked Zai'il with a raised eyebrow.

Aria nodded. "Yep, you had it any time you were about to do something that would get you in trouble. So, Kharra, what are you up to?"

"I think I have an idea how we can get more information." Kharra's tone held a hint of playfulness.

"Would you care to elaborate?"

"I'm going to spend a couple of days among the trainees."

Aria's brows came together. "I was going to start interviewing them tomorrow."

Kharra shook her head. "No, they'll be guarded if either of you go. Zephyron would probably have a similar effect. No, I'm going to spend some time with them by myself. I'm near enough to many of them in age, and I don't carry with me the aura you all carry."

"Huh? Aura?" Aria asked, confused.

"You kruustas and Zephyron have had decades of battle experience, and you all radiate an aura. I don't know if it is confidence or danger or something else, but even people who don't have my gifts can feel it." Kharra lifted her palms up and out. "I don't know. People are either intimidated by you both or act deferential around you."

Aria raised an eyebrow at Kharra. "But not around you?"

Kharra batted her eyelashes and said, "I'm just a girl who might need a young, strong man's protection."

Zai'il laughed. "Oh, that type of trouble…"

15

DISRUPTION

Aria paced around her room as she absorbed the words of Kharra's report. All eyes watched both of them. She paused and looked at the shorter woman. "Are you certain?" she asked.

Kharra nodded.

Of course she was certain. In the assessment of people, Kharra had yet to be wrong. Over the past several days, their small group had taken to socializing with a variety of people both in and out of the academy. Inside, they mingled with students, acolytes, trainees, priests, and staff. Outside, they visited local establishments—taverns, inns, shops, even guard posts—to learn if anyone had observed anything out of the norm with regard to the academy or its members.

Charmed by Kharra, First Acolyte Dolson had been eager to give her a thorough tour of the expansive academy grounds, and when asked, Dolson had introduced her to a number of the krusword trainees.

Aria originally thought Zephyron to be the more charismatic of the two, but then she caught a glimpse of Kharra taking lunch with no less than a dozen trainees plus Dolson. Maybe Aria had been wrong because Kharra always seemed so reserved.

"I've spent the last three days around them," Kharra began. "All of them are hazy about specific details, and each one wakes up in the morning in his or her bed, making them believe they've been dreaming. However, all of their so-called nightmares are exactly the same—same people, same locations, and same experiences. Their descriptions are exactly the same as Jorun's, the krusword trainee who ran away."

Aria glanced at the others. Rauss's face simmered with anger. Zai'il's expressed disappointment. Tual's looked calculating. Zephyron, who was always smiling and witty during normal, casual conversation, showed the same intensity he did when any situation became serious. At least his eyes are not glowing, Aria thought. While she knew she had nothing to fear of Zephyron, seeing those eyes for the first time when he was facing down Tual had haunted her for the rest of that night.

"We can't let this continue," Aria said at last.

Rauss nodded. "Something needs to be done."

"Our biggest problem is knowing who we can trust," Zai'il added with a hint of sadness. "Is the entire priesthood involved with this?"

"I don't think so," Kharra responded.

Aria shook her head. "There were several between Murali and here who did not appear to be involved."

"I interviewed a few here," said Rauss. "Surreptitiously, of course," he added hastily. "I did it under the guise of a younger kruusta needing advice. For the priests, I think those bracelets you mentioned are the key. The ones without the bracelets seemed oblivious. The ones with them, while not outright suspicious of my various questions, brushed me off or made excuses to be elsewhere."

The others listened as Aria laid out her plan. Their goal that evening would be to search about discretely and find out where the trainees were being taken. One at a time, her companions and fellow kruustas left her rooms and headed to their assigned areas. With just the six of them, they would be hard-pressed to cover every crevice in the massive academy complex.

When the last person departed, Aria focused on her own assignment. She pulled on her new brown doeskin breeches. The soft, supple leather fit perfectly. They, along with a few other items, were a gift from Elias Fornsworth. She started pulling the matching long-sleeved tunic over her head, but she caught her reflection in the room's mirror and stopped. She lowered the tunic and approached the mirror.

With her right hand, Aria traced over the shards protruding from her left shoulder. Since White Bluff, they had continued to grow a little each day. The white tendrils on her arm had finally met up with the shards. One might almost mistake the texture for a sleeve if they ignored the prismatic reflection and mirrorlike sheen. Soon no skin would show. Aria would not be able to keep her condition hidden from the others of the order much longer. The sooner they dealt with the issues within the academy, the sooner they could be away from the city, and the happier she would be.

Aria refocused her mind and finished dressing, donning her thin leather spaulders, which had been cut to accommodate her shards, and her cloak. She needed to deal with the problem at hand and not allow herself to be distracted. These kids were her current priority.

Aria cracked her door and slipped out into the night. Without the usual moonlight, the shadows from the torchlight along the arches and hallways stretched much farther than normal. Moonless nights only happened once every three months, and Aria was grateful for the darkness. She skirted the edge of the large quad that separated the different wings, thankful Master Fornsworth had included a pair of soft-soled black deerskin boots. They were much easier to keep quiet in than her normal traveling steel-tipped boots.

For two hours Aria stalked the hallways and rooms of the north wing. In and out she slipped among the shadows, not certain what she was looking for but confident she would know when she found it. She entered the cavernous assembly hall, the only enclosed room in the academy capable of holding all residents, instructors, staff, and visitors at the same time. Over one hundred pillars supported the vaulted ceiling of the massive chamber. The nave of the room was vast and, during the day, bright with hundreds of panes of stained glass lining the upper level. When the sun was high, one could not help but feel uplifted by the brilliant, colored light, but on a moonless evening like tonight, the chamber was as dark as anywhere else.

Aria approached the large shard, drawn to its pulse of life. Before Murali, she had never sensed the shards, and the only pulse she felt had come directly from the crystal in her hand. Ever since White Bluff, the call of the shards tugged at her soul, some opening to her without her even trying. Now their pull grew stronger. It would be so simple to open herself up and let the rapture of its power fill her. Why not? It wanted her and would embrace her. She shook her head clear.

For sixty-seven years, Aria had served the order, taking up the lonely life as a warrior against dangerous shard beasts so other people might live normal lives. In that time she had acquired few acquaintances and fewer close friends, and she had been without family since her childless brother had died twenty-three years earlier. People had feared her and most had never wanted to get close enough to become a friend. She never knew what she had been missing. That had changed nearly six weeks ago when she met Kharra and Zephyron. In such a short period of time, they had become her good friends. She now understood what it was to care for people, and her heart clung to that as tightly as the shard's call. She did not yet want to let go of it, of that feeling, so she would hold off conversion as long as possible.

Aria placed her hand on the shard more as a gesture of sentiment than a need to commune, so she was not prepared for the barrage of imagery that assaulted her mind—cells, cages, tables, vats of a boiling silvery substance, screaming, crying, a lifeless emaciated body against a wall. Aria pulled her hand away, staggering backward as she did. Her hand throbbed. She glanced down and was shocked to see the crystal pulsing bright red. She had never seen that color before, but she knew the meaning. Whatever was going on here, the shard was furious.

Aria turned and ran, not caring if anyone saw her. If they did, she would be just a fleeting shadow, here one moment and gone the next. Aria sprinted across the quad, through the south hall, left at the end, down a flight of stairs, another left, through the library and several study rooms. She was unfamiliar with the areas through which she ran, but the shard had shown her where to go. Down three more flights of stairs, Aria came to halt, her path barred by a locked metal door. Failing to find a key or other mechanism to open the door, Aria paced back and forth.

A shuffling of footsteps caught Aria's attention. Her eyes darted along the hall, and she spotted a decorative alcove with a statue displaying some ancient order priest. She ducked into the space and pressed herself against the wall on the far side. From the shadows she counted twenty people as they passed: seven priests and eleven krusword trainees. Aria growled under her breath at not being able to see their faces.

The door slid open, and the large group entered. When the last priest shuffled past Aria's position, she stepped out from her cover, staying far enough behind to avoid notice. The door fell closed, but Aria caught it with her foot. She waited for a few moments and then inched it open carefully, thankful the well-oiled hinges did not creak. The opposite side of the door revealed another hallway. The group was no longer in sight. Aria slipped through, keeping a careful eye on the series of doorways dotting either side of the passage.

Aria inched up to the first doorway and peered in around the corner, discovering a small, dimly lit storeroom with a neatly arranged assortment of barrels, crates, shelves, jars, and other similar containers, some filled and some empty. She moved into the room to give herself more cover while she strained to listen for sounds deeper within. She heard muffled voices, but they were too distant to distinguish clearly.

Aria advanced farther up the hall, passing another set of doorways. Both looked to be offices of some sort. A part of her itched to riffle through the scrolls on the desks to collect more information, but a deep sense of urgency prodded her to keep moving forward. She paused as a familiar tingling sensation tugged at her mind. A shard beast was nearby, but its aura was so faint she barely sensed it.

The fourth doorway revealed a large room, longer than wide. On the far wall were a series of holding cells and within them, seven of the trainees. Most of them sat on the cold stone floor, dazed, though they appeared unharmed. Four of the trainees, however, were missing, and none of the priests were present. Against the near wall were several wide tables, each covered with a variety of tools, implements, crystals, boxes, clothing, and more.

Aria stepped into the room and caught sight of a worn wooden door at the other end. She moved past the trainees, who paid her no attention, and toward the door. Two steps from her destination, a spine-chilling scream, followed by the loud shuffling of several feet, stopped her in her tracks. Panicked, Aria slid under one of the tables and pressed herself as tight against the wall as possible. The door burst opened, revealing a pair of fast-moving feet and the hem of a priest's robe. A second person followed and stopped quickly.

"No, let go of me!" said a young male voice on the verge of hysteria. Aria dared to lean down farther to catch a glimpse of his face. Her breath caught when she recognized First Acolyte Dolson. His face was red, his eyes filled with tears.

"Dolson, stop!" Aria identified the second voice as Priestess Pleria, one of only three female priests currently residing at the academy. The priestess grabbed Dolson's shoulders and turned him around.

"I can't do this anymore! I won't be a part of this. Those are my friends in there!"

A third pair of feet walked into the room. Priest Kilgor growled, "We have been too lenient allowing acolytes to socialize with the trainees. We're going to put a stop to that."

"Kilgor," said Pleria, "go back in the room. Let me handle this."

"Very well, Pleria. You are his sponsor. He is your responsibility."

"I know. I'll handle it."

Priest Kilgor huffed and returned through the door.

The priestess closed the door and dragged two stools away from the wall. "Have a seat," she said to Dolson.

"I don't want to sit. I want out of here."

"Dolson, sit down."

The acolyte finally sat, allowing his weight to drop onto the stool. The priestess sat on the other stool. "This is wrong," said Dolson. "And you know it. Why is this allowed to happen?"

Pleria's response was very quiet. "I agree with you. This is wrong, but I am not in a position to change it."

"Why not? Just stand up to them!"

The woman sighed in disappointment. "Honestly, I'm afraid. Going against them means fearing for my life and the lives of my family."

"If this is what is required for me to be raised, then I would rather die."

"You are a braver soul than I, but don't throw your life away. I need someone like you to help me end this. Maybe one day we can. For now I need you to go through with this."

Aria weighed her options. Slowly she slid her way out from under the table. "I think I've heard enough," she growled.

"Aria!" said Dolson, nearly falling off his stool.

Pleria glanced at the door and back at Aria. She grabbed Aria's arm and pulled her to the other doorway. "Aria, you shouldn't be here. It's not safe for you."

Aria glared at Pleria. The shorter woman let go of her arm and stepped back, fear evident in her dark-brown eyes.

"What—" Aria's question was cut off by another shrill scream leaking out from the other room. Aria moved around Pleria and toward the door.

The priestess grabbed her wrist again. "Aria, please don't. You don't understand what you're getting involved with."

"That's irrelevant. I've been involved since Priest Malechi tried to kill me." The dark-haired woman gasped in surprise. So not everyone knew. "Whatever you're doing to these kids ends now."

"The process has already been started. It can't be reversed."

Aria looked at her in horror. "What process?" Pulling free from Pleria's grasp, Aria rushed for the door, calling forth her sword as she did.

Throwing open the wooden barrier, Aria was greeted by five annoyed stares, but it was not the priests who caught her attention. Terror gripped her stomach as her eyes settled on the three krumetus standing submissively off to the side. When she thought the nightmare could not get worse, the trainee who was strapped to a slanted table in the center of the room started to thrash. The boy's skin changed from a soft tan to an opalescent white. His arms and legs began to elongate as shards erupted from his skin. Within moments, the crystal tendrils worked their way up his neck and across his face. His eyes glazed over as the crystal took hold. The boy arched his back and wailed a single note so long and painful it cut Aria deeper than anything she had ever felt.

Shouting in rage, Aria rushed to the table.

"Stop her," Priest Kilgor ordered.

Dodging the priests as they attempted to grab her, she sliced the bonds holding the boy down. Then she realized her mistake. She was too late; the thing on the table was no longer a boy. The newly formed krumetus swung its sharded arm at Aria, backhanding her across the chest. The forceful swing sent her flying against the wall. The creature broke the last strap holding it down and climbed off the table, landing on the ground with a thud.

"Contain it!" Kilgor shouted.

The sharded behemoth grabbed the nearest priest and threw him into a glass cabinet. The man's head shattered the glass, leaving behind splatters of blood. He fell over in a heap.

"Too late!" shouted one of the other priests as he ran for the door. The three remaining priests followed.

The krumetus aimed a long, clawlike hand at the fleeing men and from it erupted a spikelike projectile, impaling the last priest through the back. The others did not slow. They ran through the holding room and up the hall. The creature moved after them, not running but pursuing with swift, purposeful strides.

Aria glared at Kilgor as she hurried after the beast. The man's balding head held not a drop of sweat. His face showed no concern.

If anything, he simply looked annoyed. Aria ground her teeth and rushed through the door. She caught sight of Pleria and Dolson hiding under the table. Pausing, Aria grabbed Pleria's arm and pulled her out.

"Get those trainees out of here," Aria demanded. Pleria nodded weakly, her disheveled black hair falling across her eyes.

A crash up the hallway caught Aria's attention. She sprinted to catch up. The metal door that had barred her way had been knocked off its hinges. Beneath it was one of the priests, bloodied and unmoving. She continued running, down the passage and up the three flights of stairs. A third priest lay at the top of the stairwell, blood pouring from a gouge in his head.

Aria sensed the creature pulling away from her. She drew deeper on her crystal to push her legs faster. A bell sounded, followed by dozens more. At least one of the priests survived long enough to sound the alarm. Under normal circumstances, she would be happy for the toll, but now she cursed under her breath. The alarm would bring people out of their rooms and into harm's way.

Aria retraced her earlier steps through a series of study rooms, through the library, back down the hall, up another flight of stairs, down another hall. At last she emerged on the main level. Directly across from the stairwell, she found the body of the fourth priest, or what was left of him. His severed arm still dangled from the alarm cord while the rest of his unmoving corpse lay shattered against another wall.

Shouts and screams drew her attention north toward the quad. Hurdling benches and dodging confused students, Aria dashed out to face the creature she had unwittingly unleashed. She was not the first kruusta to arrive. Rauss danced around the beast, which had grown larger since Aria had first seen it. The krumetus drew itself to its full height, dwarfing Rauss, who was only a third of its size. The creature stomped, sending a shock wave outward and knocking Rauss off his feet. Several spectators also lost their balance. Rauss had never seen a krumetus before and was still dazed by its initial attack. Aria sprinted to his side and pulled him out of striking range.

The krumetus bellowed at Aria's interference, and its faceted eyes studied her every move. Aria let go of Rauss just in time to block the creature's slashing swing. The force of the blow pushed her back, but she kept her footing. Its other arm came around with blinding speed. Aria adjusted to deflect it. The strike threw her against the fountain in the center of the quad. How something so large moved so fast was beyond her.

The creature of pure, solid crystal drew back and then pounced. Its foot hurtled down toward her. She dodged away from the crushing force, rolling across the ground as she did so.

Rauss rejoined the fight. He stood opposite Aria, attempting to penetrate an area along its back. Rauss lunged, slicing at the creature's hamstrings. The krumetus roared with anger, turned, and slapped Rauss across the chest faster than he could bring his sword back around. Rauss flew backward against a pillar. The creature swiveled toward Rauss, and with an extended claw, launched its crystalline spear at the stunned young kruusta. Aria leaped to intercept the weapon, but she failed to reach it in time. She struck the claw and used her momentum to keep moving past, but the spike, with a diameter larger than a fist, impaled Rauss in the chest.

Aria slid to a stop beside Rauss and tried to pull the spike from his ribcage. Blood splattered from his lips and his head went slack. Aria ducked for the blow she knew was coming.

"Noooooo!" came a roar from the halls as Zai'il launched herself over a hedge and onto the creature's back. With one free hand, Zai'il clutched one of the shards protruding from the beast's shoulder, and with the other, she drove her krusword down onto its head. The krumetus bellowed, reached around on its back, and grabbed a hold of Zai'il. It threw her across the quad like she was nothing.

The beast moved toward the fallen kruusta, but a quick series of slices along its elbow from Tual drew its attention. Zai'il regained her footing and danced to the opposite side of Tual. Aria joined them, taking up a position at the creature's back. The three kruustas did their best to stay out of range of its arms. Both claws sported three bladelike shards, each one as sharp and deadly as a sword. Every time the monster focused its attack on one kruusta, the other two initiated a number of quick strikes at its flanks.

The fight took on the cadence of a dance, back and forth, in and out, only much more deadly. Slowly they began to whittle the creature down, the damage from their kruswords chipping away a little bit at a time. The krumetus, however, scored several hits on its attackers as well. It tried using its shock wave, but the three experienced kruustas were ready each time. Zai'il and Tual jumped away when they came. Aria simply steadied herself and absorbed them. That earned her raised eyebrows from the others. This was going to be a fight of endurance.

A number of krusword trainees who had been spectating from the sidelines called for their swords. They had been watching the kruustas' tactics and started to mimic them. Aria thought to send them away but then changed her mind. Though they were all relatively weak, their kruswords would still cut the creature.

Bluish-green ooze seeped from dozens of cracks in the creature's armor. This krumetus was young and had not learned how to tap into its regeneration or any number of other abilities a more experienced one might develop. Though its attacks were still faster than a human's, the beast's strikes slowed. A wave of power surged from Aria's right. By the time she turned to look, Zai'il had launched herself at the monster, her dark form all but a blur as she moved past. With a final strike, she severed the krumetus's head. The creature staggered forward two steps and then fell.

The cheers of hundreds of students and trainees sounded along the quad. The trainees who had participated in the battle looked shaken and white-faced, but they turned and hugged those who stood beside them. Some sat and cried.

Tual and Zai'il were both covered in cuts and bruises. Tual's arm ran red with blood, and Zai'il sported a deep slash against her temple. They both took a moment to survey the creature. "Where did that come from?" Zai'il asked.

Aria barely heard her as she looked around the quad. They had won against a krumetus, but something did not feel right. What was this sensation? Where were Kharra and Zephyron?

⅊

Lukav watched the battle below unfold with keen interest. He rubbed his chin thoughtfully and asked, "Kilgor, who are those two?"

"I don't know, Oracle Lukav. They accompanied Kruusta Aria into the city. From what I am told, they hired her as a guide, maybe as protection. I don't know for certain."

"I don't think they need her protection."

The tall man with the long, thick white hair spun, sliced, dodged, parried, jumped, and turned with such fluid movement that the scene was mesmerizing to behold. Not only did the man keep up with Lukav's three krumetuses, but his crackling blue blade inflicted significant damage to them.

Lukav's attention jumped to the young woman. She did not carry a weapon, but every time he directed one of the krumetuses toward her, the beast for some reason failed to get close to her.

Lukav frowned. There was something familiar about how the man moved. Searching deep into long-forgotten memories, realization sparked to life. The white hair. The young face. The incredible height. Suddenly the flicker of a memory came to him. That man had served as Avesa's lieutenant when the Great War first started over a hundred years ago. Lukav believed they had all been destroyed. How in the world was he still alive? Why was he here? Or better yet, how had he discovered Tanoria? Only Guardians had the ability to travel to and from the shrouded land, and they were all but extinct.

Lukav glanced at the young woman again. What of her? A second realization sank in. She possessed leyoen. He did not know why he was unable to sense her power, but he knew for certain she was using mind moving. That would explain why he had occasionally seen one of the krumetuses fly backward as if hit by an incredible force and why another would quit moving completely.

Suddenly one of the krumetuses exploded in a shower of crackling blue sparks beneath the man's blade of energy.

"We can still salvage this," said Kilgor, his voice sounding weakly hopeful.

"For your sake, you'd better hope so." Lukav glared at the bald priest.

"The students we can handle, but those kruustas know too much. We need to bring them down. They have been fighting the wild krumetus in the quad. If we move now, they won't have time to recover."

Cursing the distraction, Lukav willed the krumetuses to break away and head toward the quad.

The scene erupted in slow motion. Trainees clapped and shouted. The alarm bells continued to echo through the night. Tual moved to inspect Rauss's body. Zai'il started across the quad toward Aria, but before she took two steps, a crystalline spine impaled her in the upper right section of her chest and launched her backward. She screamed as it pinned her to the wall. Aria could not tell if the injury was lethal, but the roar behind her demanded her immediate attention.

Both Aria's crystal and rage flared to life. She spun around and brought her sword up just in time to catch a krumetus leaping down upon her from the top of the tiled overhang that covered the quad's bordering walkways. Aria and the beast tumbled over together. She rolled out of range just as its massive claw slammed down.

A second krumetus, the one that had attacked Zai'il, jumped down off the roof and landed beside the fountain with thunderous force. The crystalline giant bellowed at the students on the sidelines, causing the audience to scream and back away. Within moments Tual maneuvered himself between the monster and those it wanted. The beast slashed at him. Tual blocked the attack, but his face contorted in pain as he absorbed the shock.

Aria scrambled to her feet to meet the one that had tackled her. It turned and charged. Aria dived and rolled out of the way. The creature's momentum carried it in range of Tual, and the dark-haired kruusta found himself facing two of them. He parried and dodged the attack of one, but as he did so, the other sliced through his chest with its sharded claws. Tual fell forward.

Only a handful of seconds had passed since the new attack had begun, and already another kruusta lay dead. Aria wanted to crumple where she stood. It was her actions that had allowed them to go free; these deaths were her fault.

The two krumetuses turned as one toward Aria. They strode in her direction slowly, menacingly. Aria glanced about the quad, seeing the fearful, tear-filled, hopeful eyes that stood witness to the evening's battle. Pity and guilt could wait. She needed to keep fighting. Aria prepared herself for their charge, but nothing came.

Instead the two hulking monsters lifted their claws and began shooting spines—not one or two at a time but dozens. Aria fought on the defensive, deflecting each spine that came near. They flew faster and more frequent, and she willed her arm to speed up in response. She became her blade. The crystal began to sing, and she swam in its melody.

Suddenly the spines stopped though the krumetuses had not halted their attack. They snarled but not at Aria. A few moments passed before she noticed Kharra moving past her. "Sorry we're late," said Kharra, sad but determined. The concentration behind Kharra's eyes indicated she was holding the creatures at bay with her mind. "We were fighting three of them over on the west courtyard. We killed one, but these two fled."

From the corner of her eye, Aria caught a streak of white and blue. Zephyron's energy blade spun into view. The two krumetuses whipped around to face the new assailant. One charged Zephyron, but he leaped not to the side but over the top of the creature. Flipping head over feet, Zephyron landed on the run and continued on to the second beast. Not expecting the assault, the creature failed to protect itself from the approaching blade. The weapon connected with the creature's thick crystalline arm, creating a shower of sparks that lit up the entire quad.

The beast moved backward slowly. Unusual behavior for a krumetus, Aria noted. Suddenly Kharra crumpled. Beside her stood Priest Kilgor, holding what looked to be a long crystalline knife.

Before Aria had time to react, the krumetus Zephyron had jumped over scooped Kharra up in its glass-like claws and in a bound, leaped up to the roof and continued on out of sight.

Sensing something wrong, Zephyron spun around. As he did so, the krumetus he was fighting sliced him across the shoulder and down along his back. Zephyron fell, his crimson blood spilling out upon the gray flagstones.

Kharra's deflection and Zephyron's interception of the krumetuses had given Aria enough moments to collect herself. She whirled her sword around in her hand and approached the beast. It watched her warily. The creature sidestepped, circling her as she circled it. Finally the monster struck, jabbing directly at her and causing the shards on one of its claws to extend unnaturally far. The action came so fast that Aria did not see the motion, but she sensed it, giving her just enough time to twist away. The other claw swung horizontally from the right, and her twist collided with it before she could correct her movement. Luck was with her though, and the strike landed against the shards in her own shoulder. The attack cut through her new tunic, but she remained unharmed.

Aria retaliated with attacks of her own, ducking under the creature's left arm and slicing where the arm connected with the torso. Human or shard beast, that area hurt. In pain, the monster's inhuman reflexes brought its jagged elbow down on Aria's back. She staggered forward before being thrown off her feet. She rolled with her momentum to avoid injury but found the creature already beside her as she attempted to stand. Its longest claw, somewhat resembling a krusword, stabbed through her just beneath the collarbone. A collective gasp echoed off the area's stone walls. The krumetus lifted her off the ground with its swordshard and flung her to the opposite side of the quad. She landed on her shoulder and tumbled a number of times before coming to a stop against the wall.

Before she fully regained her senses, flames of pain shot up through her leg as the beast slammed its claws down on her hamstring. She screamed. Once again the creature lifted her up and threw her. This time she was ready for the landing, but her injured leg failed to respond to her. Unable to catch herself, she collided with the fountain.

Dazed, Aria ignored the sting of blood dripping into her eyes. She saw the beast's reflection approaching her from behind, walking deliberately toward her. Between her head, her leg, and her shoulder, she struggled to get her body to respond as she wanted. The creature knew she was finished. She managed to twist herself around to face the monster and meet its eyes, eyes that just a few hours ago had been that of a young boy. Now those eyes were cold, calculating, and inhuman.

The krumetus lifted its claw to finish her. Aria steeled herself for the blow that never came. Instead the distinct *ting* sound of something colliding with the crystal, with its head, drew the creature's attention away. To the side of the quad, awkward yet fearless, youthful but possessed with the determination of a seasoned warrior, stood First Acolyte Dolson. He held a crossbow, one designed to fire crystal-crafted bolts.

Dolson reloaded the crossbow and fired again, this time hitting the krumetus in the chest. The beast broke the shaft protruding from its chest and threw it aside. The bolts were designed for much smaller shard beasts, not krumetuses. Dolson knew that. The creature stomped one of its clawed feet in his direction, thrust its chest forward, swung its arms wide, and bellowed at the acolyte. Dolson reloaded and fired again. The shot hit the creature's arm.

Dolson was buying her time, distracting the beast so she could get free. He did not know how bad her injuries were, but she was not about to let him throw away his life for her sake. Aria closed her eyes and pulled deeply on the power of her crystal. It answered her, giving her all the power it had, but it did not end there. Her crystal called out to the shard, the one with which she had connected earlier, and the shard responded. She drew the shard's power into herself, drinking it even deeper. Every fiber of her being came alive. The pain overwhelming her just moments ago disappeared. She could hear the breathing, the heartbeats, and the tears of all those who watched. She could smell the blood of the fallen kruustas and the wet stones that had been splashed by the fountain's water. Aria opened her eyes.

The creature charged Dolson. The young man never flinched. Instead he held his crossbow steady and faced down the menace that rushed at him, knowing he would die for his actions. Aria could not let that happen. She clutched her sword in hand, and with speed she never knew a human could possess, dashed over to Dolson. Aria pushed him out of the way and took the full force of the krumetus's charge. She clung to its head and beat down on it with her weapon. The beast grabbed at her and flung her aside. She landed lightly on her feet and ran back at the creature. Not expecting such a tactic, the beast attempted to deflect her blow, but she adjusted her attack at the last moment, striking its arm in the same place Zephyron had struck earlier. Her blade sliced through cleanly. The arm, from the elbow down, fell to the ground.

The krumetus howled in pain and swung at her with its other arm. It was too slow. Aria moved around behind the beast, slicing its knee as she went. The knee buckled. It swung at her again, and again it missed. Its movements had slowed so much that Aria had no problem reading them. She danced around the creature with practiced steps, her sword swirling in a blur of motion. The song of her crystal harmonized with her movement. The beast had difficulty following her. It attempted to shoot a spike at her, but she swiped it aside with little effort. In the same motion, she lopped off its other arm. Before it even realized the second arm was gone, Aria leaped onto its head, and with a two-handed grip, she drove her krusword down through its skull. She heard the crunch of the crystal and the squish of its brain as the sword sank down. The creature toppled over, and Aria jumped free before it hit the ground.

Nearby a cacophony of shrills and shouts assaulted Aria's ears, challenging the song of battle to which she danced. With the rage of the shard still flowing through her, Aria turned and took three steps toward the noise. Colors—blue, green, and yellow—swirled in front of her. Unsure of what they meant, Aria paused. The sounds assaulted her ears once again, and she shouted in response. The colors faltered, and the sounds disappeared. Something touched her arm, giving her pause. Slowly the world came back into focus. The sounds she had heard had been students cheering for her success. They were silent now, all staring with mouths hanging open, confusion and fear evident in their eyes.

Aria glanced around. Blood splatter dotted every part of the quad's stone walkways. The fountain's masonry spread out across the quad, shattered into hundreds of pieces. Several walls were now nothing more than piles of rubble. Aria peered at her arm and the hand that touched it. It was Priestess Pleria. Her face showed a mix of fear, relief, and disbelief. Dolson, a short distance away, dusted himself off from her rescue. Aria saw the bodies of her fallen companions, and a heavy pang of sorrow and guilt for the loss of their lives assaulted her heart. Then a moment of elation coursed through her body when she saw a pair of healers move an explicative-shouting Zai'il onto a stretcher. Aria blinked, finally allowing herself to breathe but not daring to allow herself to relax.

As quickly as it had flooded into her, the power of the shard seeped away. As it withdrew, she felt herself falling, but she could not summon the will to catch herself. That was when the blackness overcame her.

16

THE MONSTER WITHIN

K harra watched the man who paced just out of her kicking range. She was hanging by her wrists in rusted wrought iron shackles. Their chipped edges scraped on top of the abrasions she had already acquired from the monster that had brought her to this place. She had been unconscious during the trip, only waking up after arriving, and she had no idea where she was or how far they had traveled. When she awoke, she had found a crystalline collar around her neck. It was not unlike the ones used on the Vadari, leyoen users enslaved to serve Xareen, except this one was much cruder. The device blocked her mind moving ability but not her other abilities, for which she gave a silent thanks.

The floor and walls looked to be made of a natural cave, though shaved and smoothed down by the hands of men. The air was cool but not cold. There was only one way in or out of the room, through an arch made from a natural crystal formation and no door. On the far side of the room stood three crystalline statues. They were tall and humanoid in shape but with arms and legs too skinny and spindly for any human. Illuminated crystals provided plenty of light for the area. Crystal-powered technology had been common in Marimon, but this was the first Kharra had seen of it since coming to Tanoria.

The man stopped and eyed her. He had a lean face with a hawklike nose, fine cheekbones, and blond hair. "Why are you here?"

"Because you brought me here," Kharra replied neutrally.

The collar around her neck sent shocks through her body. Unprepared for the assault, Kharra screamed. "Don't play games with me, girl. I meant in Tanoria. How did you get to Tanoria? You used mind moving while fighting my krumetuses." He moved closer and rubbed his finger along the collar. "I'm glad I saved some of these. It's been so long, I don't think I could recall how I made them." He grabbed her hair and pulled her head back. Bringing his face close to hers, he said, "You are not someone I know, and the people in Tanoria do not possess leyoen. So I know you're not from here." He released her hair and began pacing again. "Tanoria is protected by ancient powers far greater than you could ever comprehend, making it impossible for humans to find this land, even if they knew where to search." He waved his hands off to the side to indicate some far-off location. "So how did you get here?"

"Why do you care?"

The man stepped closer, and his eyes narrowed. "Because this is my land. Your kind does not belong here. So I ask again, How did you get here, and why are you here?"

Kharra met his gaze. With a snarl she said, "I am searching for a family heirloom." Not the truth but not entirely a lie either. She needed to share just enough to convince him that the artifact only held value for herself.

The man studied her. "That must be a valuable heirloom for you to come so far, to a land most do not even know exists."

Kharra glanced down, allowing him to witness a sadness only partially feigned. "My family died a long time ago. I don't know why. I learned that they died in part because of this heirloom. If I find it, I may be able to find out why and how. I need closure." Some truth.

"And the white-haired man who was with you? Why is he here?"

Kharra's heart thudded in her ears. She had no idea if Zephyron had survived the attack. He was a Guardian but not unkillable. "He is a teacher and a friend. He would not allow me to come alone." All true.

"Why do you travel with a kruusta?" he pressed.

"As you guessed," she began, "we are not from this land. We hired her to be our guide."

"Unfortunate for you."

Kharra screamed as shocks lashed out through the collar.

Voices, muffled and unclear. Scraping of slippered feet. The strong but pleasant smell of balsam filled the air. It was accompanied by the not-so-pleasant stringent odor of alcohol. Aria's head pounded, throbbing with her pulse. For a moment she felt as if she had been floating. Her muscles tensed, and the floating sensation disappeared. As her consciousness clawed to assert control, she recognized a bed and pillow beneath her. Slowly she sent the impulse for her eyelids to open, but they were heavy. A crack was all she could manage before light assaulted her, racking her in dizzying pain. She closed her eyes, but she was too slow. The throbbing in her head intensified. She had never had a hangover before, but she imagined this was what one felt like.

"She's stirring," said an unfamiliar voice.

"Aria," whispered a gentle, fatherly tenor. Something warm pressed against her cheek and then her forehead. "The fever has gone."

Aria worked her tongue, but her throat was dry and swollen. Cold metal touched her lips. Her tongue responded. Cool water dribbled down her throat. She swallowed, savoring the moment. She drained the entire cup in a matter of seconds.

Aria forced her eyes open a second time, slower than the previous attempt. The light was not as intense and much less painful. Her head continued to throb. Aria blinked several times. With each blink more and more things came into focus—faces, the window, tables, shelves, jars, canisters, and bowls. Beside her sat a middle-aged man with warm brown eyes and graying hair. He smiled when she looked at him. Two priests stood nearby, their blue robes hanging loose around their feet. They both appeared to be in their third or fourth decade. Neither had gray nor thinning hair, but each watched her with dark eyes that spoke of experience. The creased brow and pursed lips of one of the priests told her of his concern. She could not even recall his name. The other, Rensin, studied her but fingered a long dagger he held in his hands.

Aria inhaled deeply, but an unpleasant pressure built in her lungs, so she stopped. She struggled to sit up. The kindly-looking man assisted her while saying, "You should probably continue to rest. You've been through a lot."

"Where am I?" she asked weakly. "How did I get here?"

"You are in the infirmary. You have been the talk of the academy for days. Forgive my manners. I am Shardhealer Fehrun." Shardhealers were widely respected among the order. Many priests and kruustas learned how to concoct medicines with herbs, create salves, or treat injuries, but those who had the calling to become shardhealers used crystals in their treatments, though not embedded ones like those of the kruustas. Shardhealer talents were rare and valuable. "These two are Priest Rensin and Priest Tronnick." Fehrun gestured to the other men.

Aria studied the elderly man, trying to recall what events may have driven her to the infirmary. As she beheld him, she noticed a faint wisp of color, yellow, swirl about him, but it disappeared as quickly as she saw it, leaving her to wonder if she had seen anything at all. She closed her eyes, trying to force the throbbing to subside.

"How do you feel?"

Aria opened her eyes. "Like I've been trampled by a stampede of zegus. I think my head will split open at any moment," she groaned.

Priest Tronnick's face grew alarmed, and Priest Rensin gripped his dagger tighter. Healer Fehrun put up his hand, and they relaxed. Aria glanced at the two priests and back at the healer. "What's wrong?" she inquired.

"Do you recall any of the events that happened the night you were brought here?" Fehrun asked.

Aria leaned against the wall and stared up at the ceiling. She recalled coming to the city and meeting with the other kruustas. As she stretched her mind and forced herself to dredge up whatever she could from its depths, the memories came back to her, slowly at first and then faster. She remembered investigating the basement, discovering Pleria and Dolson, and interrupting some experiment that turned trainees into krumetuses.

First there had been one krumetus, one she had accidentally allowed to escape. The memory and guilt of Rauss falling to the beast bubbled up. They had avenged his death by slaying the creature. They had thought they were done there, but two more attacked. She remembered seeing them in the room where she found the priests. She had been so focused on catching the one that had fled she had not considered the other three. Visions of Tual's death and Zai'il's near death flashed before her eyes. Then Kharra and Zephyron had shown up when the creatures had threatened to overwhelm Aria. They had already killed one of the beasts and were pushing back the remaining pair, but one took Kharra after she was somehow disabled by Priest Kilgor, which distracted Zephyron from his fight. Aria recalled seeing him fall in his moment of vulnerability.

Tears welled in Aria's eyes. So many deaths lay at her feet. At first she thought the memories ended, but no. There had been one more krumetus for her alone to face. It had hurt her so severely she could neither stand nor swing a weapon. She remembered seeing Dolson, armed with only a crossbow and firing at the creature without concern for his own safety. Inspired by his courage, she had called upon the crystal to give her strength. Her crystal had responded. In her need, it had not been just the crystal she touched but the academy's shard as well. It had loaned its vast reservoir of power to her.

Aria's stomach suddenly overwhelmed her with nausea, and a cold chill washed over her. Alarmed, she stared at Healer Fehrun and then at the two priests. Aria threw off her sheets. A twinge of panic set in as she turned her eyes to her left arm. Unlike the krume-tus she fought, her arm still resembled that of a human's, only made entirely of crystal. She suspected the full, hideous mutations would not happen until the person lost hold of their humanity. Aria traced the crystallization from her fingertips, up her arm, over her shoulder. She touched the spot where the krumetus had stabbed her beneath the collarbone, but it had crystallized as well. She followed the line of her neck, slowly running her fingers along the crystalline tendrils. She licked her lips.

"I need a mirror."

Healer Fehrun studied her, worry setting into his eyes. "Perhaps you should rest for now."

"Please just get me a mirror."

"Very well," he said, nodding to Tronnick.

The priest moved to the end of the long room and grabbed a mir-ror from a table. He returned and handed it to Aria.

Aria took a few deep breaths and then lifted the mirror. She sat on her bed, stunned by what her eyes saw. The crystalline tendrils had spread up her neck, over her cheek, and covered her left eye. The effect was both fascinating and terrifying at the same time. Her entire eye was now made up of the crystal. She touched the spot with her right hand, the warmth from her still human hand quite palpable. The crystalline skin had not lost its sensation. She tried to poke and pinch at it but could not. She closed her right eye and then her left, right eye, then left. Her vision was the same as ever. How was that possible?

Now she understood the behavior of the two priests and why they were in the room. They likely expected her to be completely con-sumed at any moment. At the slightest indication of the process con-tinuing, they would use their crystalline daggers to kill her before she became a danger. So many thoughts and emotions swam through her head, she thought she would lose herself in the flood.

Aria began to cry, and to her surprise, the crystallized eye was still able to shed tears. "I'm sorry. All of this is my fault."

"Not so, my child," said the shardhealer. There were times when Aria would have laughed at someone calling her a child. They tended to forget she aged much slower than they. "Your actions exposed a cancer that has been eating away at the inside of our order. Priestess Pleria spoke on your behalf and had many things to say about what has been going on. We search for Priest Kilgor as we speak, as well as for his accomplices. Many within this academy's grounds were killed by the krumetus three nights ago, but many others are spread out across Tanoria. Some are at the other academies while more still reside at various shard temples. Pleria did not yet know of their full agenda or of the entire list of those involved, so we move discreetly for now."

Aria fought through grogginess and swung her legs off the bed. Fehrun placed his hand against her chest, and she paused. "Hold up, you still need to rest. Whatever you did the other night to defeat the beast has had significant side effects. Not just the crystallization, but it drained you so thoroughly we thought we lost you a few times. You must stay here for your own safety." And for the safety of others, she was sure he left unsaid.

"Shardhealer Fehrun, thank you for the wonderful care, but I have a friend who needs my help. I've already wasted far too much time here. I need to be going." She stood, pushing his hand aside in the same motion. She grabbed a robe from a hook on the other side of the room, put it on, and headed for the door.

Priest Rensin moved next to her, grabbing her arm. "We need you to get back into bed," he said firmly.

"Unhand me," she demanded in a low, steady voice.

Rensin's hand tightened, and Tronnick grasped her other arm. They attempted to drag her back to the bed. Calmly, she tried to twist herself free.

"Try to hold her," said the shardhealer. "I am going to have to sedate her again."

Aria twisted harder, kicking over a table as she did so. A number of glass jars and canisters hit the stonework floor and shattered.

Priest Rensin twisted her arm in the opposite direction, forcing her toward the ground. He put his foot against her right shoulder. Had she not had some of the last dose of sedative still flowing through her system, he would have been no object for her, but in her current state, her limbs were uncoordinated and sluggish to respond. Healer Fehrun maneuvered closer with a long crystalline rod.

The wooden door crashed opened. "Take your hands off of her," thundered a voice so full of fury and rage she did not immediately recognize it.

Both priests released her arms, and the shardhealer stepped away. She stood, finally able to see the person to whom the voice belonged. Incredibly tall, white hair slithering around his waist, eyes blazing like blue furnaces, Zephyron looked like everything the tales about Guardians said they were. At that moment in time, he appeared to be an angry god who had come to deliver his wrath upon civilization. Just behind him stood Zai'il, her entire right shoulder wrapped in bandages.

Priest Tronnick paled as he pressed himself up against the wall. Priest Rensin clutched his dagger. Shardhealer Fehrun struggled to find his voice. "Please," he said weakly, "we need to keep her here. Her condition...I have never seen a kruusta's condition so far advanced while they are still in control. We can't risk—"

"I will take responsibility for her," Zephyron said.

"Sir," the shardhealer countered, his voice quivering, "you don't understand. If the crystal takes over, she will become more dangerous than the ones that attacked the other night."

"I'm aware of her condition. Aria, let's go."

Needing no further prodding, Aria dashed for the exit. Without turning she uttered, "Thank you for not killing me just yet, Shardhealer Fehrun." Aria slipped around Zephyron and passed Zai'il out the door.

Aria ignored the cold stone floor on her bare feet as she strode across the academy grounds toward the guest wing. Zephyron and Zai'il moved up to either side of her. "Thank you," she said, staring down the hall as she walked. People stared at her as she maneuvered in and out of the busy noontime foot traffic, but she forced herself to ignore them.

"That's what friends do," said Zai'il.

Aria nodded.

Zephyron spoke up. "I've spent the past three days searching for Kharra without any luck. She is neither in the city nor anywhere within five leagues of here. I need your help to find her."

"Of course, it's the least I can do," she said. Images from three nights ago flashed through her mind. If she had just waited and not confronted the priests by herself, then Kharra would not have been taken and the other kruustas would still be alive.

"It is my fault those beasts got loose," she whispered.

"Not true," said Zai'il.

Zephyron nodded in agreement. "Don't blame yourself. From what the priestess said, your actions saved at least seven trainees. And the situation was not your fault. If you're going to blame anyone, blame the corrupt priests."

They reached the quad, and Aria's steps faltered. Though the fountain and walls had been repaired, the flagstones were still stained with blood. She closed her eyes, and her head swam with emotions. The cost of her actions had been great. How could she value one person's life over that of another? Isor's brilliant radiance shone down on her face, intensifying the focus of her thoughts. She swallowed around the lump in her throat. Zai'il put her hand on Aria's shoulder, and Aria opened her eyes and glanced at her friend. Zai'il gave her a nod of encouragement and understanding. Aria continued toward her rooms as Zephyron and Zai'il followed quietly.

In her quarters, she packed her gear while Zephyron waited with his back to her. Zai'il stood beside Aria's wardrobe and watched. As Aria dressed in something more suitable for travel, she asked Zai'il, "You're not going to try and stop me?"

"Nope."

"Why not?"

"Because I know it would be pointless. Besides, I know I'd do the same if I were you, and you were the one taken."

"Are you coming?" Aria asked her.

Zai'il shook her head. "I don't recover as fast as you do. Healers say I have a punctured lung and that nearly all of the muscles in my shoulder have been torn. So I'm no good in a fight right now. I think I'm going to stay here and help Pleria."

Aria looked to Zephyron. "The healer was right, you know. The crystal's progressed too far. I'm a danger to everyone around me."

"I'm willing to take that chance," the Guardian responded. "Kharra and I both need you. Besides, I don't give up on friends."

"Zephyron there is convinced you can beat this conversion," said Zai'il. "If anyone can, it'd be you."

Aria finished lacing her boot and looked up at Zai'il. She saw colors like she had with the shardhealer. Except around Zai'il, they swirled around her in green. She glanced at Zephyron. The colors appeared around him as well. They swirled in a pattern of blue and white, interweaving with each other. She blinked, and the colors disappeared.

Aria turned to Zai'il and hugged her. "Thank you, my friend."

Zai'il returned the embrace with one arm. "Of course. You are like family to me. Please be safe." Zai'il excused herself from the room, leaving Aria and Zephyron alone.

Aria placed her hand on the closed door and lowered her head. She took a deep breath and returned to Zephyron. "Look at me. Look at my face. It's hideous. I am becoming one of those monsters. My entire life has been sworn to protecting people from shard beasts. I can't allow myself to become the thing I'm trying to protect them from. I don't want to hurt or kill some innocent person."

Zephyron approached her, grabbed her shoulders, and leaned over slightly so that he was level with her eyes. "I won't let that happen. You've lived your life protecting others, never looking for anything in return. The people you seek to protect fear you because they think you will become this monster you believe you are destined to become. I don't know why this thing happens in your land, but I do know more about Mattekan than almost anyone else in a way only a Guardian can understand. The crystals and shards are not evil nor does their influence become evil over time. They are things of beauty and life. Something else is causing this corruption to both them and you. I will not allow you to become a monster and neither will Kharra.

"And for the record," he added softly, "your face is beautiful."

Zephyron's words reverberated down through Aria's soul. Stunned, she stared at him for several moments, ignoring the tears streaming from her eyes. She knew without a doubt he meant them. His arms embraced her, enveloping her in their warmth and strength. She put her face against his shoulder and continued to cry. Nothing had ever caused her so much terror as the thought of becoming a monster.

"I will help you fight this every step of the way," he whispered.

Aria steadied herself and regained her cool kruusta composure. She checked the rooms one last time. A tendril of pain washed over her as she glanced at the area where she had met with the other kruustas. She would not let the loss of Tual and Rauss be wasted.

17

COLORS OF THE HEART

Kharra still hung in her shackles. She had lost track of time. Each day the man returned to question her and bring her pain through the crystal collar. She would scream until her throat became raw. In the lucid moments between the pain, she wished for her sister's ability to resist it. How she missed her sister. Jayde was the strategist and the fighter. She likely would have already figured out a way to escape.

Kharra's answers never changed, but her captor seemed to find pleasure in hearing her scream. During one of the sessions, a second man had walked into the room. "Oracle Lukav," he began. A short man, round of face and bald, he wore the blue robes of a priest of the shard. He glanced at Kharra. His eyes flicked to her collar and then he looked at Lukav. "I have reports telling me all three of the krumetuses were destroyed. Two of the kruustas died as well, but two survived, Kruusta Zai'il and—"

"Aria?" asked Lukav, turning to the priest.

The priest nodded.

"Figures," Lukav spat.

"There is some good news though."

"What could that be?"

"They say Kruusta Aria is in the process of conversion, but they don't understand how she retains her humanity, the condition is so far advanced."

"Is that so?" said Lukav with a vile grin. "Makes sense. She is already the oldest living kruusta. To survive such an encounter, even someone of her experience would need to draw on a considerable amount of power." He peered at Kharra, his smile still intact. "This might actually work out nicely."

Kharra stretched out her mind and scanned his surface thoughts. The collar grew cold around her neck but did not interfere. Kharra sensed leyoen in him, though weak. She took satisfaction in knowing he would not sense hers. She had discovered four years ago that no one, not even her sister who was quite powerful in her own right, possessed the ability to detect Kharra's leyoen except in specific situations. The only one who had ever demonstrated a way to even sense Kharra was Aria, through the use of one of the large shards. Then she froze.

This conversation with the priest had brought new information to the surface of Lukav's mind. His unique ability allowed him to control and manipulate small bits of crystal.

Even in her state of pain, Kharra's mind worked well enough to fit pieces of the puzzle together. She now understood that Lukav compensated for his own weaknesses by creating devices that amplified his meager ability. With them, he could not only control shard beasts but allow others to control them as well. Lukav could not manipulate a kruusta who possessed the free will of a human, but if they lost their mind to the crystal, he would be able to assert complete control over them.

Kharra now also understood that the krumetuses' power levels differed based on the kruusta from which it came; the more powerful the kruusta, the more powerful the krumetus. Lukav believed that Aria was the most powerful kruusta to ever live. If Aria lost herself, Lukav would then have control of the most powerful krumetus the world had ever seen. If the group of four kruustas had had so much difficulty with the ones created from trainees, who would be able to stand up to the one created from Aria?

The priest continued, "Aria and the white-haired man departed from the city three days after we left."

Lukav chuckled and ran his finger along Kharra's chin. "They are coming for you. Your interference set me back months, if not years. I will exact the cost from you one way or another."

Another shock came through the collar, but this time Kharra resisted the urge to scream. Through the pain her mind raced. She needed to escape.

Aria let Xierex have his rein. The poor zegu had received no exercise while she had been in the infirmary, and he wanted to make up for it. Head down and horns back, he propelled himself forward with the ease of a deer. People often wondered how such a massive beast could run so fast. His legs were powerful, certainly, but he also carried the added weight of the thick crystalline-plated armor along his chest and neck. The crystal of his natural physiology was what provided him with the extra surge of power needed to sustain greater speeds. She had not made the connection before, but now she understood with absolute clarity.

Aria glanced at Zephyron. His sleek cat form loped easily beside her. His transformation between human and tigron continued to amaze her. His shoulders moved rhythmically back and forth beneath his white fur. Without Kharra, they were not able to carry out silent conversations. Zephyron's mind seeking ability was limited to those who had the ability themselves. He claimed he could detect the thoughts of those who did not have the ability, but it required a lot of concentration on his part, something difficult to maintain while they ran.

As she rode Aria gave more thought to what Zephyron had said. The shards were not evil nor did their influence become evil over time. Zegus lived long lives with crystal as part of their bodies. They never became monsters—well, not real monsters. Some people might be frightened of the wild ones. They might fight to protect their young, but the behavior was no more savage than any other wild animal.

Something must have happened during the Battle of Death's Pillar that affected only kruustas. Shard beasts existed long before then but not the krumetus. More than before, Aria was convinced that the events of the battle were also related to the story Zephyron told about the Sauru going mad. The blue and white colors swirled about Zephyron again and disappeared just as quickly. Aria looked away, back at the road ahead. Without asking him directly, she sensed Zephyron also believed the two things were somehow related.

The colors were coming more frequently, always when she looked at a person. They had started right after she had defeated the last krumetus. Though she had no idea why they appeared, she suspected they had something to do with her crystalline eye. Maybe Zephyron would know more.

Xierex ran for three hours before finally tiring, his pent-up excitement exhausted at last, but the lightness of his steps indicated he still had plenty of energy. He snorted when they slowed, which was his way of saying thanks. Long shadows spread over the road as darkness crept up on them. Wei's moonlight was the only light tonight. With the other moons present, Wei's light augmented theirs, but by itself, its dull orange cast made the terrain more difficult to make out than with no moon at all. Aria spotted a good area to camp, reined in Xierex, and dismounted.

Zephyron, now in human form, joined her. She could never tell if his clothes came as part of the transformation or not. When she asked about it before, he had grinned and said, "Magic."

Their camp remained simple—two thin bedrolls, a small fire, and a pot for tea. They still had a bit of the tea they had acquired from White Bluff. Their food came from whatever Zephyron caught. He attributed his uncanny ability to find food to his tigron nose. They finished the last of a ground rover that was Zephyron's most recent triumph. The large rodent's layer of fat served to flavor the meat without needing any additional spices. Though remarkably tasty, Aria did little more than push her food about her plate. She had not had much of an appetite since leaving the city. The warm tea, however, brought comfort. She drank plenty, savoring the mild sweetness of the added honey and hoping the beverage would help her relax.

Though full into spring, the night air still held a bit of a chill. Aria gazed over the fire at the white-haired Guardian. He had been right. The things she had learned from both him and Kharra had changed the way she viewed the world. Most of the people of Tanoria would have trouble accepting such a new perspective. She found herself wondering what other parts of the world might be like: the people, the animals, the food, the clothing. She'd learned about Kharra and Zephyron's own battle against an enemy whose goal was to destroy entire civilizations.

Aria stirred her tea with a stick of cinnamon, keeping her eyes and thoughts on Zephyron. The blue and white colors swirled about him again, subtle and conforming to the contours of his body but noticeable.

"According to the information Pleria provided," he said as he poked the fire with a short branch, "we should be nearing the south end of the Urshaw Caverns. I suspect we'll reach the entrance early tomorrow."

He looked up when Aria did not respond. The firelight caught his sparkling blue eyes, and the curiosity dancing behind them was evident. "What is it?"

Aria blinked. "What? Nothing."

Zephyron smirked and sat down on his bedroll. He crossed his legs and draped his hands over his knees. "Nothing indeed. You've been staring at me on and off for the past week. What do you see?"

She studied him a bit more, biting the inside of her lip. "Ever since the fight, I've been seeing colors around people. At first I only saw them once in a while, so I thought they were some sort of trick of the light, but I've been seeing them more often lately. I don't know what they mean. I fear it's part of the process of losing my sanity."

It was Zephyron's turn to study her. He poked at the fire again. "What do you feel when they appear?"

Aria furrowed her brow and glanced into her cup. Taking a sip of her tea, she gave the question thought. She did not feel sad or happy or angry or anything when she saw them. They were just colors. Then it dawned on her. She looked up at Zephyron. "I had not thought about it before. Now that I think about it, I…" She struggled with putting it into words. "I'm not entirely sure, but when I see the colors, it is like I am seeing into the person's intent or their purpose. I'm not sure how else to describe it. It is as if a voice is whispering something to me about that person."

Zephyron smiled, but it was the type of smile that said he held a secret that she did not. She hated it when he did that. Here she was, eighty-five years old with sixty-seven years of experience as a kruusta. She had already outlived many people she had known over the years, and she was used to others deferring to her wisdom and judgment. Yet she often felt like an uneducated child around the Guardian. He never gloated about his knowledge, but his extensive experience allowed him to perceive what others did not understand. It annoyed her to discover how much she did not actually know. One thing that had surprised Aria, however, was that Kharra was only twenty-two years old. Yet Zephyron deferred to her quite often.

"What do you know of your family history?"

Aria frowned. "Not much at all. My mother died before my first naming day. My father, a kruusta himself, left me with his sister, Erita, and her family so he could continue his duties. He died when I was three. I can't even recall what he looked like. Some of my earliest memories are of my aunt telling me stories about my mother.

"Aunt Erita said she carried a pair of swords like she was some sort of fighter, but she was certain my mother wasn't a kruusta, didn't belong to the Order of the Talon nor any other type of militia. My aunt often mentioned how beautiful my mother was and how she loved her accent."

"Accent?" asked Zephyron.

Aria shrugged. "There are a number of dialects around Tanoria. You and Kharra both have them, though they're not too pronounced."

"I didn't even realize I had one."

Aria chuckled. "I travel from town to town around Tanoria. I don't generally give them much thought."

"So," said Zephyron, "about your story?"

With a nod Aria sipped her tea and continued. "Like most people, my dad's family feared kruustas, him included. Aunt Erita tried to hide it from me. She tried to keep her words about my father positive, but every once in a while, she'd mention how she didn't understand how my mother could fall in love with him, a kruusta.

"The order came for me when I turned five, and I've been with them ever since. I had a brother, Delf, whose mother was different than my own. He was two years older than me and raised by his mother. According to him, he was the result of a one-night stand, but my father made sure Delf was provided for. My brother knew little of our father and nothing of my mother."

Thinking of her brother brought a smile to Aria's face. They had not grown up together, but they had become friends as they got older. He had joined the Order of the Talon when he had come of age, and their paths had crossed many times over the years. He had been a good swordsman, and their reunions had involved sparring matches as a means of showing each other how much they had improved. He had never resented not being chosen by the Order of the Shard. In fact he had respected their father's duties and hers. Most importantly, he had never shown fear around Aria.

"Why do you ask?" she inquired.

"Hm." Zephyron knuckled his head and actually blushed, though the firelight concealed it. "Your ability reminds me of someone I used to know." He tossed the stick into the fire. A boyish grin crossed his face, and his eyes twinkled as he dredged up the memory. "She was one of Avesa's personal bodyguards."

"Who was Avesa?"

"Avesa il Marquin, Kharra's mother. She was the leader of the Zumai before the war began over a hundred years ago and throughout its duration. I was her second-in-command back then, before I became a Guardian. Avesa had three bodyguards, two men and a woman, all Sauru swordsaints. The woman's name was Dalia. One of her abilities was called heart seeking, the ability to understand a person's heart by reading the colors it gave off. When she was not on duty, we used to sit someplace overlooking an area where people gathered. She would tell me what she viewed. She said my colors were blue and white, the heart of a Guardian. I never thought she meant literally. A handy ability for a bodyguard, she instantly knew whether or not a person interacting with her charge meant harm."

"You were friends with her, then?" Aria asked.

"I, uh,"—he blushed further—"courted her for a while. It was only for a short while though. We had a mutual separation and remained friends. She ended up marrying Corigan, one of the other bodyguards and had a beautiful daughter by him."

Aria found herself beaming through tears threatening to release. She had never cried so much as she had since meeting Kharra and Zephyron.

"What's wrong?" Zephyron asked.

Aria responded with a half chuckle and said, "I'm feeling oddly sentimental. I'm just really happy that I'm not going crazy. And for the record, your colors are still blue and white."

Zephyron smiled at her. "You're not losing your sanity. You are manifesting a leyoen ability. I find it odd, though, that you are only now beginning to manifest it. Usually a person gifted with leyoen shows signs of their gift during their teens. If I recall correctly, Dalia could call upon or dismiss her ability at will. If the colors bother you, I bet you can do the same."

Aria nodded as she lifted her left hand in front of the firelight. She had been avoiding looking at the parts of her that had crystallized, but ignoring the problem would not make it go away. The light from the fire, though distorted, illuminated through her iridescent skin. She turned her hand over and looked at her palm. She flexed and extended her fingers. They moved and felt like they always had. Her tactile sense had not changed, though the area was much more resistant to pain.

After a period of silence, Zephyron said, "We didn't come across you randomly."

Aria looked up from her hand. "What do you mean?"

The Guardian pursed his lips. "Kharra was drawn to you." Aria raised an eyebrow, which Zephyron acknowledged with a nod. "First it was dreams. They were never super clear or very complete, but they always left specific impressions with her when she awoke. She knew she had to come to Tanoria to find you even though I'd never even told her about this land's existence. Once we arrived here, she chose a route that led us straight to you rather than to Ei'ars'anu. When I asked her about it, she said she was drawn to you, but she didn't know why."

"So Kharra was drawn to my leyoen? I thought she said she couldn't sense it."

Zephyron shrugged. "I don't think it was your leyoen she was drawn to, but it was something about you. Kharra taps in to powers and instincts I don't even think she realizes she has. She, along with her twin sister, Jayde, are the most powerful Zumai I've ever met. Their mother was powerful, but that built up over two centuries. The twins are only in their early twenties."

"Kharra mentioned her sister once in passing but not much about her."

"They didn't grow up together. I didn't even know Jayde was still alive until about four years ago, but they were reunited and took to each other very quickly. Jayde's nearly as powerful as Kharra, though her strongest abilities manifested differently."

Aria nodded. For several moments she went back to inspecting her hand as she silently processed Zephyron's information. Still looking at her hand, she asked, "Can I ask you something personal?"

"Certainly," Zephyron responded.

"What is the relationship between you and Kharra?"

Zephyron sat in silence for a few moments.

"I'm sorry if I've asked too much," Aria said, looking up from her hand.

"No, it isn't that." Zephyron stared into the flames with a crooked smile on his face. His normally strong facial features suddenly looked soft and gentle. "In some ways our relationship is simple; in others, complicated." He grabbed his stick and began poking the embers once again. "Anyone who is influenced by Mattekan's life force, be they leyoen-gifted, kruusta, or Guardian, live exceptionally long lives compared to those of couren. I am one hundred sixty-one years old, but I was a teenager when I first met Kharra's mother.

"After I left my own people, I had no idea what I intended to do or where I planned to go. I wandered about for a while without much of a purpose, getting myself into constant trouble. An odd series of events landed me in front of the Lady Avesa. She had just become the leader of the Zumai and the Queen of Aerous. I, on the other hand, was just a scrawny waif back then, but she seemed to think I had some sort of potential. She took me in, gave me a home, and provided me with an education. We became good friends—family, really. There was a time when I became infatuated with her, but that passed quickly.

"In our third decade of war, I was called to become a Guardian. Though she would be losing her lieutenant, Avesa gave me her blessing, and so I left.

"A Guardian's priority supersedes that of individual people and their kingdoms. Guardians serve Mattekan as a whole, and they are supposed to avoid becoming personally involved with humans. New Guardians go to Xi'ari'asi and remain there for several years while they learn about their new role, abilities, and responsibilities.

So as Aerous fought a slowly losing war, I was sequestered away from the world.

"In my second year of training, I encountered a Guardian named Xeis. He had the ability to glimpse through time, and from him, prophecies came to be. Xeis had a message for me. So I went to him and stepped into his waters. I beheld images I didn't understand at the time. They were of a child."

"Excuse me," said Aria, "what do you mean by 'stepped into his waters'?"

"Oh, sorry, Xeis was a water elemental."

"I don't understand. What's a water elemental?"

"Hmm, you've never heard of an elemental?"

Aria shook her head.

"Interesting. They're pretty rare, but most people have at least heard of them."

"No, sorry," said Aria.

"No worries. Elementals are beings, sentient beings, whose entire body, for lack of a better term, is made up of a specific element."

"So Xeis was a being made up entirely of water?"

Zephyron nodded. "Indeed."

"And he was a Guardian," stated Aria.

"He was. A very old one, in fact. He had the ability to see through time, which to humans like us, seemed like prophecy. When one of us literally stepped into his waters, we were able to communicate with him, and he could show us what he saw."

"That's both bizarre and fascinating at the same time."

Zephyron chuckled. "I've lost perspective on normal or bizarre a long time ago. In any case, a week after I received the visions, something happened that had never happened before in the history of the world. Guardians turned against other Guardians and betrayed Mattekan itself. We call them the Betrayers. One of the first things they did was destroy Xeis, so we wouldn't have any more prophecies."

"Wait, Guardians can do that?" asked Aria. "I thought you all were above that type of thing."

Zephyron frowned. "To be honest, so did I...back then at least. I was still new to the calling and still enamored by the older Guardians."

"But why betray other Guardians?" asked Aria. "Why betray Mattekan? Isn't that who gives them their power?"

"Mattekan calls us, imbues us with a part of its essence, and communicates with us, but becoming a Guardians doesn't magically make us better people. We're still affected by events of the world. We still experience the same types of emotions we felt before our calling."

Zephyron sighed and ran his fingers over the top of his head. "The Betrayers fell back on human desires. They possessed power, and they wanted to exert that power over other people. They didn't want to serve the greater good of the world; they just wanted to serve themselves."

"That's horrible," said Aria, "but not all that different from what's happening here in Tanoria."

Zephyron nodded in agreement. "The war itself continued for sixty-six more years. Everyone with leyoen was either killed or made into a type of slave we call the Vadari. Their abilities are controlled by collars placed around their necks." Zephyron paused, his eyes fixated on the weaving flames.

He took a deep breath and continued. "Their leader was, and still is, a swordsmaster named Xareen. She is from the Toloi tribe, the People of the Dark. She was also my teacher after I'd been called. She wanted me to join her."

"Clearly you didn't."

"No. I tried to talk her away from her path and failed. It still haunts me."

"I'm sorry," said Aria.

"Don't be. That was a long time ago." Zephyron sighed. "The end came eighteen years ago. Avesa, who had fought continuously for one hundred thirteen years, gathered as many of her remaining people as possible and attempted to flee Kelani clutches. She wanted to take the survivors into hiding so her people would not be completely annihilated. Her plan worked, and they escaped."

Aria found herself leaning forward, hanging on each word of his story. "So what happened? What does this have to do with Kharra?" she asked.

"The event I had seen in my vision was coming to pass at that very moment. Avesa's group was ambushed. They had been betrayed by the person who had replaced me as her second-in-command, her nephew Rasic. The ambushers slaughtered the adults and took the children. One child, however, I found before they did. I took her and fled. I took her where no Kelani would be able to find her. We went south across the Serpent Spine Mountains to Marimon, a place with people who had never heard of Guardians, leyoen, Kelani, or Aerous. In some ways, Marimon is similar to Tanoria in its isolation.

"I found Kharra a foster family who would raise her well. I visited as often as my duties allowed me and taught her about her abilities and her heritage. I watched her grow. She has a way of seeing the goodness in the world where I've seen only blood and death."

Wetness dotted Zephyron's cheeks.

"And now?" Aria asked with sadness in her own heart, fearful she already knew the answer.

Zephyron looked up at her with such tender vulnerability Aria's heart ached.

Aria watched him, seeing the blue and white colors swirling. She realized the swirling happened in a predictable pattern and that the pattern had changed since they had started speaking about Kharra. "Did you fall in love with her?" Aria asked softly, fighting to keep the ache she felt from coming out.

Zephyron shrugged. "I'm not sure. I don't know what it is I feel for her. I mean I love her, of course. I'd give my life to protect her. But she's so young, and Guardians aren't supposed to fall in love."

"Why not?"

"Because it could pull our attention away from our responsibilities."

"How is that different from any profession?"

Zephyron scratched his chin. "A Guardian's first duty is to Mattekan. How can we do that if we have loved ones who also must come first?"

"Hmm," said Aria. "I'm sure there is a way to do both."

The Guardian sighed.

"Zephyron, I promise, we'll get her out safely."

"Thank you," he whispered, the pain of worry clear in his eyes.

When they finally lay down for the night, Aria's mind refused to rest. She worried and fretted: two things she had never done much of in the past. She had been resigned to her fate and accepted that she was nearing the end of her days. However, having met Zephyron and Kharra and having learned about the bigger world, she found she no longer had that resignation. She wanted to learn and experience so much more, but she feared she would never get the chance.

18

THE CAPSTONE

Kharra's head stopped spinning. The pain given by the collar left no marks, but the sensation set her skin afire as if it had been stripped from her body and reattached. She had tried to reason with Oracle Lukav. That had only brought additional punishment. Though never showing on his face or in his voice, the man radiated paranoia, and he was more than a bit mad. The insanity was contained though, focused inward, and his subordinates believed his plans and logic to be sound.

Kharra allowed her mind to wander, sensing around for something she might use to free herself. She had done this for many days, and each time she had failed to find what she sought. She growled to herself in frustration and then stopped as a spark of thought took form. Up until now she had been searching the area with mind seeking, but out of habit she had continued to keep her empathy shielded. Having nothing to lose in the effort, Kharra relaxed her mental shield. Her heart raced and her body surged with adrenaline as a torrent of emotions assaulted her. She slammed her shields back into place.

What in the world was that? Kharra thought.

Better prepared, Kharra relaxed her shields once again, a tiny bit at a time. As before the emotions threatened to overwhelm her, but she fought against them to maintain control. With long-practiced discipline, she sorted through the emotions in an effort to locate their source. Sweat beaded on her brow from the exertion. Her weakened state made retaining control more difficult; sheer willpower kept her going.

Kharra succeeded in separating from the mass three sets of emotions, ones that seemed to be closest to her physical location. Her breath caught. She peered at the statues across the room. They were not statues at all but people—people who had been transformed, crystallized. Kharra had no idea if they had been kruustas who had been consumed or just ordinary people trapped in crystalline shells. Though their minds had long since deteriorated, they remained alive, preserved in a perpetual state of heightened emotion—anger, terror, hate; each was different. Unlike the krumetuses, which were bulky with jagged shards protruding from their shoulders and elbows, massive ridged heads, and powerful limbs, these were thin with long, sinuous arms and legs, narrow heads, and smooth exteriors. Their faces were noseless, and solid dark crystalline facets composed their eyes.

As if awakened by her contact, the three statues moved for the first time since she had arrived in this place. They did not walk upright. Instead they collapsed upon their appendages and skittered about with quick, jerky steps one might describe as a creeping crawl—a most unnatural, disturbing motion. The three creepers approached Kharra. She screamed at them to scare them away, but they ignored her.

Oracle Lukav returned, his blue-white robes swishing as he walked. Behind him followed Priest Kilgor, who wore some type of crystalline bracelet on his wrist. The three creatures backed away when the two men entered. Lukav glanced at them and then the priest. "Why are they already active?" Lukav asked.

"I didn't give the command," Kilgor replied, fidgeting with his bracelet.

Lukav unlocked Kharra's shackles, and she slumped to the ground. He peered down his hawklike nose. "I suggest you stand unless you want more pain."

Kharra rubbed her wrists and forced herself to her feet. Her legs quivered so much she thought she might collapse, but they steadied.

"Let's go," Lukav ordered as he grabbed her by the arm and pulled her along through the archway of crystal. "Kilgor, bring them." The bald priest bowed his head. The bracelet on his wrist glowed briefly. The creepers turned and followed behind him. Their awkward movement made Kharra shiver.

"Where are we going?" she asked.

"You'll see soon enough."

Aria scanned the cave entrance, a simple opening. She climbed down along the rocky terrain, picking her footing carefully to avoid slipping. Large plates of rock overlapped, creating a crisscross pattern at the apex of the entrance. Water from the spring rains trickled down from higher on the mountainside and into the mouth of the cave. Water stains and erosion marred the rocks, and moss and lichen clung to them in the shadows of the overhang.

"This fits Pleria's description," Zephyron observed. "And I do sense a vein somewhere within the mountain, but who knows if this will take us to where we need to go. Xi'ari'asi, the home of the Guardians, is located within a cave system as well, but there are thousands of tunnels and caverns within the system. A person might travel for weeks and never actually find the city."

"Let's hope that's not the case here." Aria glanced back at Xierex one final time before moving into the cave. Not knowing how long they would be gone, she had left him untethered. His stomping had been a clear protest over her departure, but he would wait in the area until she returned.

The two companions descended into the cave, following the small stream created by the runoff. The entrance was wider than tall, forcing Zephyron to duck in a number of places to avoid hitting his head on knobby protrusions from the ceiling. Using materials gathered outside, Aria ignited a torch. Zephyron summoned his energy blade, which provided a surprising amount of light. For hours they climbed over rocks, slinked through narrow openings, and crawled into dozens of holes.

Eventually the cave ended, but they located the long, vertical shaft described by Pleria. Using rough-hewn handholds, the Guardian and the kruusta descended deeper into the mountain. The amount of dust collected on the handholds revealed someone had used the passage recently—a good sign. At the bottom of the shaft, the pair squeezed through a narrow crack between two large slabs of stone.

They found the second shaft and descended. A large boulder, once part of the ceiling that had collapsed at some point long ago, blocked the base of the shaft. The boulder had landed upon a V-shaped area of the cave wall, giving them just enough space to move through by crawling on their hands and knees. Beyond the boulder, the pair encountered and passed under a small waterfall, probably from the same stream they had followed up above. The stone was cold and slick but not treacherous. Through a zigzag bend and over a low wall, they finally emerged into an enormous cavern. Aria doused her torch, and Zephyron dismissed his blade.

Pleria had referred to the room as Kargan Cavern. Ambient lighting by an unseen source illuminated the area. The ceiling was pocked full of ridges, reminding Aria of the inside of a person's mouth. Tiered rock shelves meandered back and forth across the floor, with each shelf moving lower than the previous. She and Zephyron had emerged from the side of the cavern, and the shelves from each side met up in the middle. There, a wide man-made stone path snaked along the length of the cavern, disappearing around bends in either direction.

"She said for us to go to the right," whispered Zephyron, pointing at two massive stone columns. The columns were ancient, having long ago joined the bodies of stalactites from the ceiling and stalagmites from the floor.

Aria nodded in agreement. She listened carefully before moving in the direction indicated by Zephyron. She sensed the faint presence of shard beasts as well as the deep resonance of a shard, but she had difficulty pinpointing any specific location.

Zephyron's eyes scanned the ceilings and walls as they advanced up through the cavern, staying near the walls rather than on the path. "We're beneath a large vein," he whispered observantly. "It stretches for several leagues to the north and east."

Aria looked up at the ceiling and nodded, unable to sense what he sensed. According to him, the Guardians' power came to them through their connection to Mattekan. The crystal veins were similar to both a human's nervous and circulatory systems. Like blood vessels the veins pumped life force into Mattekan. Like nerves they served as pathways for transmitted information. The closer a Guardian's proximity to the veins, the stronger their connection to the transmission. Zephyron believed the shards were like a collection of nerve endings with very refined sensors, similar in purpose to a mouth or an eye or an ear, transmitting and receiving information to beings other than Guardians. He had never seen exposed shards such as the ones in Tanoria, so his belief was only a working theory.

Aria and Zephyron followed a series of tunnels upward, all illuminated along well-worn walkways and smooth walls. Aria grew concerned. "Why are there no guards?" she whispered.

"I was wondering that myself," Zephyron answered.

Kharra shuffled along beside Lukav through dozens of tunnels and caverns. At last they emerged onto an overlook within an immense domed cavern, one large enough to house the entire city of Quan'li'ru within its interior. Brightly lit crystal veins snaking across the ceiling and down the walls illuminated the whole area.

The overlook was lavishly furnished with velveteen gold-and-blue sofas, dark-stained carved wooden chairs, plush rugs made up of a type of white animal fur of which Kharra was not familiar, and an assortment of wooden tables of different heights and lengths.

"How do you like the view?" Lukav asked, approaching the edge of the overlook.

Kharra followed. She examined the transparent cover separating the edge of the overlook from the rest of the cavern. Priest Kilgor stood back against the wall with the three creepers. They were motionless once again.

"That is a single piece of crystal," her captor explained. "I encouraged it to grow thin and wide so as to cover the entire frame. It took me a long time to get it right." He ran his fingers down along the glass-looking material. "Years of practice, in fact. They were always too thick, too opaque, or too brittle. My ability to direct a crystal's growth is not as strong as my mother's was. A pain of being a half-breed, I suppose."

Kharra glanced at Lukav from the corner of her eye.

"My mother was Sauru, but my father was Zumai," said Lukav. "Though not forbidden, leyoen-gifted people were generally discouraged from marrying outside their tribe for fear the result of their union would dilute the tribe's specialized gifts. Because I am only half Sauru and half Zumai, my gifts are not nearly as strong as a full-blood of either tribe, but I showed them that using the two halves together could accomplish much greater things than they had ever imagined."

"To be honest," Kharra said, her dry voice cracking, "I don't know a lot about the tribes or how they lived. I was not raised among them. That is just one of the many things I had wished to learn."

Far across the cavern, Kharra spotted dozens of similar overlooks, some the same size and others much larger. Lights illuminated most of them, and she picked out the vague shapes of people moving about within.

What type of place was this? A reflection of light below caught her eye. Looking down, she immediately knew her answer. Several thousand glimmering dots twinkled beneath the cavern lighting. Prism wraiths, krumetuses, shard drakes, glimmer worms, creepers, shen-tahks, voreeks: the spacious cavern floor was filled with every type of shard beast she had ever seen as well as dozens of other types she did not recognize. All of the creatures stood motionless, arranged perfectly in straight lines. One of the creature types in particular grabbed her attention: a behemoth standing as tall as a golden oak tree and just as wide. Jagged shards, larger than a man, protruded from its back. Its arms looked too long in proportion to the rest of its body, with thick-clawed appendages hovering inches off the ground. The legs were thick like the trunk of a tree. The behemoth would not topple easily.

A surge of anxiety welled up within her. Oracle Lukav was build-ing an army, and he had been using the Order of the Shard to help him achieve his goals. A handful of krumetuses or a pack of mutated splinter maws were frightening enough. What type of destruction could a force of this size do?

Lukav stepped away from the vista. He turned to the priest who had been standing off to the side. "It's time. They are making their way up through the south corridor and will arrive at the Atrium shortly. Get your handlers in place."

Priest Kilgor bowed his head and moved toward the door. The bracelet on his wrist glowed white, and the creepers followed.

Lukav turned back to Kharra. "Impressive, no?"

Kharra suddenly felt a faint but familiar presence brush the edge of her senses. Her collar grew cold against her neck. She ignored the sensation with a small smile and a lot of worry.

Zephyron, she sent.

Kharra! he responded. *Aria and I are coming for you. Are you okay? Your sending feels different, muffled.*

I'm fine. Kharra tried to sense his location but found she had diffi-culty pinpointing him. She touched the crystalline band around her throat. *I have a collar similar to the ones Xareen uses, but it's not quite as efficient. It blocks mind moving completely but not my other abilities, though it does dampen them some.*

Zephyron was silent for a few moments and then responded. *Stay put. We'll be there soon.*

No, Zephyron. You two need to turn around. It's a trap.

Silence again. At last he answered, *When has that ever stopped me before?*

A jolt of pain through the collar sent her to her knees, and she grunted.

Lukav strode to the door. "Follow. My capstone arrives."

Aria surveyed the room. Fragments of shattered shard beasts littered the floor. That was the third swarm they had dispatched since reaching this level. Fortunately they had not encountered anything too powerful.

Thick lines of crystal intermixed with the natural cave walls. The farther they moved north, the more prominent the crystal became. Aria stepped forward, entering a low-ceilinged room. A shallow pool of clear water lined either side of the stone path. Blue light shimmered below the water's surface. Hundreds of narrow crystalline stalactites dripped down from the ceiling above the pools. The ceiling resembled wax after someone had gone through with a candle and tried to melt it from beneath.

Not wanting to be trapped in such a small area, Aria moved toward the opening at the end of the path. She wove around three giant crystal protrusions and stopped. The walls of the cavern rose sharply, forming a domed ceiling of dizzying heights. That, however, was not what gave her pause.

Before her, motionless and arranged in perfect lines, stood thousands upon thousands of shard beasts. Aria had never seen so many gathered in a single place. The swarm of prism wraiths in White Bluff did not begin to compare. What in Tanoria was going on here? Zephyron touched her elbow and pointed a short distance away to a series of ledges along the edge of the cavern just above the floor. On four of the ledges were three men and a woman, one per ledge. Their blue robes were unmistakable as priests of the order, and on each of their wrists they wore a glowing white bracelet. She remembered the bracelets from Priest Malechi, the priests in Haan, and some of the priests in Quan'li'ru.

The front row of shard beasts, made up entirely of rhokathedes— long, segmented, mostly transparent creatures with a dozen pairs of legs and deadly pincers—surged forward unexpectedly. Aria and Zephyron both brought up their weapons and backed away, parrying the first attacks as they did. They knew they had a better chance fighting these creatures on the opposite side of the pool room they had just exited, using the narrow tunnel as a bottleneck to funnel the attackers.

Zephyron stopped. "The doorway," he said, "it's gone."

Aria spared a glance behind her. A thick crystalline slab now obstructed the entire wall where the entrance had been. She had never seen such a thing before. Any other time she would have stopped to investigate but not here. Aria focused her attention on the rhokathedes, pushing her way back out through the thick crystal protrusions in order to give their weapons more room to work.

Though quick, the dog-sized shard beasts attacked single-mindedly. She hacked the pincers off the one closest to her and spun toward the next. Beside her, Zephyron's energy blade sliced off the heads of three more.

"In the center!" Zephyron shouted over the roar of their battle. "Kharra is up there."

Aria scanned past the attacking tangle of snapping pincers and over the wall of crystalline figures. Rising in the middle of the cavern, far from their current location, towered a conical pillar of stone, a lonely mountain peak amid a field of snow. About a quarter of the height up the cavern, the pillar tapered off with a wide, round platform following the circumference near the apex. Aria saw movement of some sort on the platform, but the distance was too great for her to discern clear details. She sensed a shard up there as well.

Aria nodded, and the two of them pressed forward. Two new rows of shard beasts surged toward them. Some of them were rhokathedes. Several were glimmer worms, and many were voreeks. Though all minor shard beasts, large numbers of any of them could quickly overwhelm even the most seasoned warriors. One of the voreeks launched itself over the backs of the others, landing in front of Aria with its razor-sharp jaw clapping at her face. Its jaw found her sword as soon as it landed. Greenish liquid oozed from its wound. The other voreeks, savage creatures with cannibalistic tendencies, pounced on their fallen kin. One of the priests on the ledges hollered something, but Aria was too focused on the fight to distinguish what he said.

Aria and Zephyron fought their way through the sea of shard beasts, sometimes facing just one row at a time and other times several rows. The less dangerous ones approached in greater numbers. Aria glanced at the priests, trying to figure out if they were only spectating or planning to engage them as well.

Aria, she heard Kharra's voice speak in her mind, *you need to get away from this place. This is a trap for you. There is an exit tunnel to the east of your location. Please go.*

I made a promise to Zephyron. We've come to get you, she thought in response, hoping Kharra would pick up her message. Kharra's mind remained silent after, so Aria remained uncertain if the message was received.

Time passed. Aria's arms moved in a blur of motion, driven by pure instinct and decades of practiced muscle memory. Beads of sweat dripped along the right side of her face, but the crystalized side remained dry. She no longer gave thought to individual shard beasts. There were just too many. She did whatever she needed to in order to move forward. Her krusword began to sing, and she danced to its song. A glance out of the corner of her eye told her Zephyron was doing the same. Did he hear her song?

It seemed like an eternity since they had started fighting, yet they had barely made any progress toward their goal. A swath of shattered crystal fragments littered the floor for over five hundred paces, evidence of the destruction they had caused. Without it, one might not believe they had destroyed anything at all.

Aria's arms grew heavy, sluggish. A prism wraith nearly clawed her face, but Zephyron's blade flashed in front of her, deflecting the attack. He caught her eyes briefly and held his lips taut. Though she had wanted to avoid drawing on more power, she knew she would not be able to continue fighting at this pace much longer if she did not. Zephyron knew it as well. With caution she pulled deep on the sliver in her hand, drinking in the font of power. She doubted it would be enough to carry her all the way through to the pillar. There were just too many shard beasts between her current location and her destination.

Aria sensed a pulse from the shard up on the platform. It offered itself to her. She had never known of a kruusta capable of drawing power directly from a shard, but she had done it before—several times now, in fact. It would definitely give her the boost she needed, but she knew it would accelerate her condition. She cursed herself for her weakness and accepted its offering.

Sweet, blissful energy rushed through her every fiber like a raging torrent; she let the shard's power fill her. Everything around her suddenly became much clearer. The sizzle and crackling of Zephyron's blade filled her ears, as did the crashing and shattering of dismembered shard beasts. She could now make out Kharra's form up on the platform. On her knees, the woman's face twisted in pain. Aria gritted her teeth and refocused her power on getting through the hordes of shard beasts now assaulting them. Sounds of shattering crystal sang along with the song of her krusword. Faster and faster she spun her blade, the weariness upon her earlier now only a memory.

At some point during the fight, she had called forth a second sword from her left hand, but she'd been so engrossed in the fighting, she could not remember calling it. She had not even known such a thing was possible. Though she had never dual wielded swords before, her body moved as if she had been born to it. She found the circular motions of the style invigorating as the dance became more complex.

Kharra struggled to find her feet again. The pain from the last shock had left her legs shaky and weak, but she needed to witness the events below. Though they were barely a quarter of the way to the platform, her rescuers had no intention of leaving.

Fending off the emotional assault from the anguished shard beasts below, Kharra focused her empathy on Zephyron and Aria. Zephyron, though getting a good workout, had plenty of energy. He had likely tapped into the power from the vein surrounding the entire complex. Aria was another story. At first Kharra felt the kruusta's energy and power sapping at a steady rate. Now, however, Kharra sensed Aria's complete recovery. She knew that meant Aria had resorted to drawing on more of her crystal's power.

Sparks and crystal fragments showered the southern portion of the cavern as the Guardian and the kruusta cleaved their way through swaths of shard beasts. If either had been normal humans, they would have fallen under the onslaught long ago. A good thing for them neither was such. They were close enough now for Kharra to see them clearly. Zephyron's eyes blazed with the same blue energy that ignited his sword, a characteristic Kharra had long since learned to associate with Guardians. Nearly everything that touched his blade shattered before he finished his swing. Aria spun her body about, trying to maximize the damage of her two kruswords. Something about the way Aria fought seemed different.

Kharra studied the kruusta's fighting more closely, and then it dawned on her. She had never seen Aria dual wield before. Her recollection of previous conversations told her that Aria only ever used a single weapon: the massive two-handed krusword. With a cold pit building in the center of her stomach, Kharra realized what she had been unable to identify before. The second sword was not a sword at all but rather an extension of Aria's left arm.

Since the fighting had started, the two combatants had engaged minor or moderately dangerous shard beasts. Now they found themselves faced with much more difficult opponents. From the corner of her eye, Kharra caught Lukav's grin widening. He could have easily crushed both attackers if he had sent in everything at once. Kharra knew that that was not his goal.

Aria and Zephyron clashed with their first krumetus. It came at them by itself. Unlike the other shard beasts they had faced so far, the creature did not shatter when struck by either the energy blade or the krusword. In fact the initial attack only seemed to enrage it. The beast rushed at Zephyron, but the Guardian dived to the side, rolling out of harm's way. Aria leaped at the monster from the opposite side, slashing its shoulder. It attempted to backhand her, but she was quicker and blocked the attack with her second sword. A spray of prismatic dust sparkled under the cavern's light.

Focused on Aria, the beast did not notice Zephyron's leaping strike—a fatal mistake. Zephyron drove his energy blade down into the creature's neck. Though the krumetus had an extremely tough exterior, it still had internal organs and vital points. As Zephyron twisted his weapon, blue-green liquid began spilling out. The Guardian yanked his blade free and leaped off and away. It staggered before finally dropping to its knees. Within moments the creature fell forward and stopped moving.

Their victory was short-lived. As soon as the beast fell to the ground, three more took its place. These three were much quicker and more cunning than the first one. They approached cautiously and spread out, forcing Aria and Zephyron to position themselves shoulder to shoulder with their backs facing each other. All three krumetuses rushed them at the same time. Aria blocked two separate attacks from two of the creatures, one with each sword. Her arms, though still empowered by the shard, strained beneath the force of their blows. She hoped Zephyron was faring better.

Aria spun around and away from the two beasts to give herself better positioning. They sidestepped slowly, forcing her to rotate away from the center platform. Zephyron danced out of the corner of her eye. He was also facing two krumetuses. When had a new one joined in? Swirling in a figure eight to slice through both adversaries, his blade burned afterimages into her eyes.

One of Aria's attackers lunged. At the same time, Kharra's sharp mental yell warned her of another coming from behind. Aria brought up her primary krusword to block the oncoming attack and attempted to twist to avoid the spine hurled at her from behind by a third kru-metus. Her movement was not quick enough, and the spine pierced through her side, just above her right hip. She fell to one knee while still fending off the krumetus that had lunged at her. Between the two of them, Aria and Zephyron now faced five of the beasts.

"We need to run!" Zephyron shouted. "We won't last if we continue to fight."

Aria glanced at the central pillar. They had covered half the distance to it since they had first stepped foot in the cavern. Aria pulled the spine from her body and gave a stiff nod. The warm wetness of the blood spread quickly, but the power of the shard dulled the pain. She would pay a price for that later. She took a quick moment to draw deeper from the shard, savoring the rush of power flooding into her. With her two swords in hand, she rushed toward the two attackers to her left and slid beneath their claws as they attempted to cleave her. She slashed at each of them behind the knee and let her momentum carry her past them before she spun around and sprinted in Kharra's direction. Zephyron performed a similar maneuver and ran along beside her. They wove their way in and out of the still inactive shard beasts toward their destination.

Zephyron reached the pillar first. Without stopping he sprinted up the spiral ramp ascending along the pillar's perimeter. At the top

Aria caught sight of both Kharra and her captor, a lean man of above-average height with blond hair, green eyes, and an aquiline nose. Around Kharra swirled a solid white pulsing light. Around the man, however, wove a web of tainted darkness and chaos represented by dark purple and black. Aria wanted nothing more than to launch the man off the platform, but the krumetuses were right behind her. She and Zephyron spun around at the top of the ramp to engage them, forcing the beasts into a bottleneck.

The krumetuses assaulted them relentlessly, adjusting their attacks to the new arrangement. Aria's vision narrowed as she focused on the enemies in front of her. In her ears, her twin swords began to sing, each harmonizing with the other. In the background, low and steady, the sound of the shard joined in. As she fought the world around her faded away.

When Aria topped the ramp, Kharra gasped as she caught sight of her face. The entire left side of the kruusta's face had crystallized along with her left arm and the sword extending from it. At the moment she still seemed to be in control. Maybe Lukav's plan would backfire.

Watching in tense anticipation, Kharra felt useless. Collared, she had no means of contributing. Lukav showed no concern despite the fact that the two assailants were fighting no more than two dozen paces away from him. In fact he appeared to be enjoying the spectacle. The priests on the cavern ledges had moved farther along. They were now standing on suspended walkways spanning between the walls and the central pillar. The priests were clearly controlling the shard beasts, but they seemed limited as to the number they could control at any given time.

The two fighters held their position for a significant amount of time, felling one of the krumetuses. Suddenly, one of the other beasts that had been unable to engage them launched itself over its companions and came crashing down on Aria. The kruusta screamed as the weight of the beast crushed her right, still human arm. With a solid two-handed grip on his blade, Zephyron twisted toward the creature on Aria and swung upward, connecting under the beast's jaw. It had not anticipated the move and failed to dodge the attack. The monster fell backward, its giant foot grinding Aria's arm further before toppling down to the three krumetuses behind it.

One of the three remaining krumetuses sidestepped the one that fell toward the ramp and took advantage of the disabled fighter. The monster slashed at Aria's face. She brought up her fused left-hand sword to keep its claw at bay. Zephyron attempted to fight off the one on Aria, but a second beast, having regained its footing, backhanded him. The hit connected with Zephyron squarely, sending him flying to the center of the platform. The Guardian's head slammed against the stone pillar. Kharra heard the crack and screamed when he fell limp. She started toward Zephyron but stumbled to the floor as shocks of pain raced down through her neck. She forced herself back to her feet.

Aria found her footing and fought off the beast that had been trying to claw her face. As Kharra watched, she also heard a sound, a deep, resonating sound she felt within her bones. She heard other tones that together sounded like singing. They were sounds no human voice could produce, but they sang pure and strong. Her right arm fine now, Aria brought both swords to bear. The two blades swirled back and forth, a tempest of motion. Aria's movements sped up. Not just her swords, but everything about her moved faster. She moved side to side quicker than the krumetuses could follow. As the moments passed, she quickly chipped away at each of the three remaining creatures. First in front of them, then behind, one side, and then the other. She seemed to be everywhere at once. Kharra had no idea how a person could move so fast.

The first krumetus exploded in a shower of sparkling shards. Aria thrust both of her swords into its body and pulled the beast apart until it could no longer maintain cohesion. The second krumetus toppled as Aria's leaping slash removed its head from its shoulders. Aria drove the final one backward with a rapid succession of strikes until it reached the platform's handrail. With one massive blow from both blades, Aria forced the creature to lose its balance against the railing and fall off the edge. It hit the cavern floor and shattered.

As soon as the last krumetus disappeared, Aria fell to her knees, dropping the krusword in her right hand. The one fused to the left remained. There she sat for several moments, facing the outer edge of the platform.

Kharra moved toward her, half expecting pain from the collar to knock her to the ground again. But the pain did not come.

"Go," Aria said without turning. "Stay away." Her voice sounded harsh, raspy.

Kharra ignored her and continued to approach. She placed her hands on Aria's shoulder, but the kruusta swung her arm backward, flinging Kharra back with such force that it knocked the wind out of her. She landed on her back in the middle of the platform. Aria's motion had turned her slightly, enough for Kharra to behold her face. Even as she watched, the crystalline tendrils crawled along Aria's skin. Several of them radiated outward from the kruusta's right eye. Her right arm was almost completely crystallized as well.

At last Lukav moved toward the kneeling woman. He knelt down beside her and put his hand under her chin. "Don't bother trying to fight it, my dear. You sealed your own fate by coming here, fighting as I knew you would. Though at first I was upset at you for your interference with my plans, it seems I can forgive you in light of your contribution to my cause. With you leading my charge, no military force in all of Tanoria can stand against me."

Through clenched teeth, Aria growled, "I'm…going…to kill you."

Lukav stood and looked down at Aria thoughtfully. "You know, I had almost this exact same conversation with your grandmother over a hundred years ago. That fool half sister of mine had no business sending me away, but she and the others learned what the powers of a half-breed could really do." Aria's hand twitched at the mention of his relationship to her. "Oh, yes, I've known about you all along, but I've had no need for familial attachments. They only held me back."

Aria's fingers flexed. Clawing at the floor, she tilted her head back and screamed, a single wailing note that pierced through Kharra's mental shields and stabbed deep down into her heart, carrying with it a swirl of pain and terror.

"Fight it!" Kharra yelled.

"I...I'm trying...Kharra, I'm trying."

"You can do it. I know you can!" Pain from the collar dropped Kharra to her knees once again.

Lukav glared down his long nose at her. "Keep silent," he said.

Aria's right eye filled with tears as she screamed again. Her face contorted as the crystalline tendrils spread farther.

❧

Aria fought with every ounce of strength she had left to maintain her sanity. Fire seared through her skull as the crystal crawled across the remainder of her skin. She felt Lukav's taint slithering through the crystal. Suddenly, something in her mind snapped, as if a dam had slammed into place between her conscious thoughts and her motor functions.

"Run, Kharra!" she yelled, or tried to yell. Her mouth refused to obey.

❧

As Kharra watched, the crystal consumed the last bit of Aria's skin, and the screaming trailed off. Aria stood slowly. A spectrum of colors reflected off the crystalline exterior that had once been skin. She resembled neither a krumetus nor a creeper. As far as Kharra could tell, Aria's form was unique.

Standing still beneath the illumination of the cavern lights, Aria looked like a perfectly sculpted statue. From either shoulder protruded long, angular crystal shards, resembling the pauldrons of an exotic suit of armor. The line of each arm was muscular but smooth and shiny as if carved by the hands of a master. Each hand held a massive bluish-green, semi-transparent sword with three long, wicked spikes lining each edge. The center of each sword pulsed with a bluish light.

A series of overlapping crystalline plates encased Aria from chest to torso, forming a teardrop shape in the center of her abdomen. In the middle of the teardrop, a blue-green crystal pulsed the same color as her swords. The trousers she had worn were shredded, revealing long legs of pure crystal, sculpted-looking, like her arms. Near her feet were more overlapping plates that gave way to something that resembled the talons of a raptor. They had broken through the new boots she had acquired in Quan'li'ru.

Aria's face, however, drew Kharra's attention the most. Though her eyes and nose were the same shape as they had been with flesh, her eyes had become bright green like sunlit emeralds and faceted like exquisite gems of a king's crown. They seemed to see nothing and everything all at once. Where each of her ears should have been were three slanted shards, giving the appearance of a bird's wings. Her hair was now translucent, shimmering and sparkling beneath the light.

"There we go," said Lukav with an appraising eye as he circled about her. "See, it wasn't that bad. And I must say, I had not expected this. I expected a normal krumetus like the other kruustas became. I thought to have a soldier, and instead I find myself a general. You look just like your grandmother did just before she destroyed Tahrahn Palace." He glanced over at Kharra. "I am sorry that you stumbled into this. You seem like a fine young lady. However, I need to move forward with my plans, and your blood is required to seal her to me.

"Aria, dispose of our guests."

When Aria looked at Kharra, her face held no recognition, no emotion. The green eyes sparkled as she spun each sword once in her hands and strode toward Kharra.

"Aria, no, stop. Please!" Kharra said as she stood up on wobbly legs. Using her mind, she continued, *Aria, this is not you. I know you are stronger than this. Fight it, please!*

𖤓

I'm trying! When there was no response, she tried again, focusing her mind the way Kharra had instructed her weeks before. *Kharra, can you hear me?*

Aria? Is that you?

Yes!

You sound…distant. Aria, stand down.

I can't! Lukav…he's done something. I-I felt him. I'm not in control of my body.

𖤓

Kharra ducked as Aria drew closer and raised her swords to strike. Before the blades fell, however, Kharra felt herself being lifted from the ground.

"No, wait!" shouted Kharra.

Ignoring her shouts, Zephyron held on to her tightly and leaped over the edge of the platform's railing. It was a long way down, and Kharra choked down a shriek as they hurtled through the air. Landing with a grunt, the Guardian continued to hold on to her as he sprinted for the exit in the eastern wall.

"Zephyron, stop! We need to go back for Aria!"

The thud of a heavy crystalline form resounded just a short way behind them. "No, we don't. She's trying to kill us."

Glancing around Zephyron's bobbing shoulder, Kharra caught sight of Aria running in pursuit, closing the distance between them. She was much faster than anything they had previously encountered. Kharra attempted to pull her collar off, but pain seared her fingers as she touched it.

Fight it, Aria! shouted Kharra to the mind of the kruusta, but no response came. Between the collar on her neck and whatever battle Aria was fighting in her own mind, Kharra had no idea if Aria heard her at all.

"But she's still in there! She's just not in control."

A number of blue-robed priests ran toward the ledges above the exit, and several shard beasts in the area began to animate. Kharra caught a glimpse of Lukav's blue-and-white robe mixed in with them. He wanted to make sure his investment was not ruined. Zephyron lowered his head and plowed through the shard beasts in his way. Many of them in this area were of the weaker variety, and the Guardian easily knocked them aside. As Zephyron neared the edge of the cavern, a layer of crystal began to form over the exit. Zephyron roared in defiance as the opening vanished. Zephyron set Kharra down where their escape had been just moments before and turned to face his attackers.

The other shard beasts held back, forming an impassable perimeter as Aria crashed into Zephyron at full force, throwing him heavily against the wall. She flipped backward off him and brought both swords up in front of her. Zephyron summoned his energy blade just in time to block the double slash from Aria's weapons.

"Aria," he said, "get a hold of yourself. I'm not your enemy." Her blades flurried toward his face. It was all he could do to fend them off. "Aria, I don't want to hurt you. Stop this! You're strong."

"She can't hear you," Lukav called out from above, his facial features twisted with a malicious smile that more than hinted at the madness dwelling within. "There is nothing that can match her power, and I now have control of that power."

Please, Aria, try to stop! Kharra shouted toward Aria's mind. There was no response. *I know you're in there. If you can hear me, keep fighting against Luvav. Force him out of your mind!*

It…hurts, finally came a response. *Can't…think.*

"Fight this, Aria!" shouted Zephyron. The kruusta's expression never changed as she continued her assault; her eyes showed no signs of life. A glimmer from tears dotted Zephyron's cheeks. Kharra had only seen him cry once before, and Kharra sensed Zephyron's resolve. Though he closed his eyes, he continued fending off Aria's blindingly fast strikes. When his eyes reopened, they blazed with the Guardian's fire, the essence of his soul, and his blade flared even brighter in response.

"Don't hurt her!" shouted Kharra.

"Kharra," said Zephyron calmly, "my highest priority is to protect you."

At that moment Zephyron began to fight back. Though Aria was extremely fast and amazingly strong from the power the crystal provided her, Zephyron was a Guardian. Blow after blow, Zephyron drove Aria back. Kharra felt the vortex of energy swirling about him before the tempest actually began to form. The wind picked up, circling around his body but never touching him. Clouds formed over his head, small at first and then filling out more as moments passed. They twisted and rotated, crackling with energy. Blue lightning snapped along their edges. The hair on Kharra's arms stood on end as the entire area filled with Zephyron's charge.

Lukav stared up at the clouds, not sure what to make of them. Lightning began striking the ground and the walls. Occasionally it struck at the shard beasts, leaving behind only blackened char. "Aria, quit holding back. Destroy both of them."

Kharra barely saw Aria's blade move, but Zephyron deflected each blow coming from either blade. Lukav yelled orders at the priests around him. The shard beasts closed in on Zephyron once again, but the lightning around him zapped many of those that came near him. A few lunged at him, but he sliced at or dodged them. Several more shard beasts activated, including some of the more powerful ones that had been dormant until now. He was forced to divide his attention between the shard beasts and Aria's continued attack.

Zephyron's fight had taken him farther north, separating him from Kharra. Aria backed off from him suddenly and made a rush toward Kharra. Having no options for cover and no weapon to defend herself,

Kharra attempted to run along the cavern's perimeter. It was no good. Aria intercepted Kharra before she took four steps. Kharra closed her eyes as she anticipated the blow, but it never came. When she opened her eyes, Zephyron stood before her with Aria's krusword protruding from his torso. With those impassive emerald eyes, Aria pulled the blade free and watched Zephyron fall forward onto his knees. Blood ran down the length of her sword as she continued to watch.

Noooo! Zephyron! No, no, no, this can't be happening. Kharra! Help him! Whether Kharra heard her, Aria could not tell.

Kharra screamed at the top of her lungs and rushed to Zephyron's side. A red pool gathered beneath him. He held up a bloody hand to Kharra's face and then toppled forward onto her. She caught him and laid him on the floor. She screamed at him to remain conscious and cried for not having Jayde's ability to heal. Her heart raced. Her throat stiffened. Her stomach roiled, and her body shook. She closed her eyes and held Zephyron's head close to her chest.

"That will do just as well, I suppose," called Lukav from the ledge above.

Wrapped up in her anguish, Kharra did not hear what else he said, and she paid no heed to the shard beasts closing in on her. Kharra continued to shake as she held Zephyron in her arms. From deep within her, the agony over her loss forced her to cross a line she had set long ago. In the distance, someone shrieked.

Aria tried to scream, but her mouth still failed to obey. Zephyron could have easily destroyed her. She knew he had held back. The scene replayed itself over and over in her head. He had taken the strike meant for Kharra, sacrificing himself for the young woman he had sworn to protect. All for what? Aria still had no control of her limbs, and in seconds Kharra would be dead as well. His sacrifice would be for nothing.

Aria's arms and legs moved with her skill but not by her command. A prisoner within her own body, she was forced to watch her hand bring down her sword upon Kharra's head. She tried to turn away, but she could not. Just before the sword cleaved Kharra's skull, the collar around the other woman's neck fell free. Kharra's hand came up and caught the blade, stopping it without as much as a cut. Aria would have gasped if she could.

Kharra lifted her head and met Aria's eyes. Within them a wild fury raged unlike anything Aria had ever seen. Suddenly an unseen force struck Aria, throwing her off her feet and flinging her a dozen paces away. Hundreds of shard beasts around her exploded into thousands of tiny shards and colorful spray. The priests up on the ledges screamed as the bracelets on their wrists turned bright white and shattered. Lukav fell to his knees and clasped his hands to his head.

Lukav pulled himself up and growled, "Aria, destroy that filth!"

Aria put everything she had into resisting his command, but pain seared through her mind as the crystal tendrils he controlled dug deeper into her consciousness. With each minute he gained more and more control. Pretty soon, even her inner thoughts would be his. Aria felt her hands push herself up from the ground. Before she regained her footing, Kharra came into view.

Run, Kharra! Please, I can't bear to lose you too! she screamed with her mind.

Before she realized what was happening, Kharra had placed both of her hands on either side of Aria's face. Aria stared up at Kharra, wanting to appear pleading but knowing she could not. Tears streamed down Kharra's face, making the wild-eyed look even more menacing.

Do it, she thought at Kharra with all of her remaining will, praying to the spirits that she would be heard. She knew that if Kharra hit her point-blank with the blast she had felt earlier, it would rip her apart. She would gladly pay that price for what she had done to Zephyron and to save Kharra's life. Aria looked deep into Kharra's eyes, and in them she saw the woman's emotional struggle. Sanity and reason hung on a tenuous thread, threatening to snap and tumble over a bottomless abyss.

No, Kharra responded at last.

In that instant the mighty dam in Aria's mind broke loose, and an overwhelming deluge of emotions assaulted her. She faltered and teetered back, but Kharra held her in place. Aria tried to pull away, but the petite woman somehow prevented her from moving. The colors returned. They had disappeared at some point during the fighting, but now they were back. Around Kharra, she saw a brilliant white radiance, pulsing slowly, steadily. Nearly blinding, it was the most beautiful thing Aria had ever seen. She thought to shield her eyes, the light was so bright, but she forced herself to keep looking. Tears cascaded down her own cheeks.

Her eyes grew wide as she glanced at her hands. The crystal encasing her body was receding. Her swords reabsorbed into the single crystal shard that remained in her hand. Aria looked back at Kharra. The light that had enveloped her dulled, but it still pulsed. The woman appeared haggard, and she staggered forward. Aria caught her and said, "I got you. I'm so sorry."

Kharra smiled weakly. "You are free."

"Aria!" Lukav shouted from above.

Aria looked up at the disheveled oracle. "Your plan failed," she said as she held Kharra steady on her feet.

"H-how…" he stammered. "No matter, I'm done playing games here." As soon as the words left his mouth, the entire cavern filled with a series of high-pitched tones. People from the overlooks high above the cavern floor poured out from their protective areas. Priests, all of them, had been watching the entertainment. Glowing bracelets now lit up on each of their wrists. Aria sensed the rumbling of awakening from every other shard beast within the cavern.

A momentary panic washed over Aria. "We need to escape. I promised Zephyron we would get you out of here."

Kharra glanced at Zephyron's lifeless body and nodded sadly.

"Do you know another way out?" Aria asked.

"We don't need another way," Kharra responded. She gestured to the wall and it exploded, revealing the passage that had been blocked.

The shard beasts, including all of the remaining krumetuses and several of the other much larger types, thundered toward them. Aria pushed Kharra along into the tunnel and the two of them ran. Their pursuers closed in on them rapidly. Aria felt slow and weak now without the crystal's influence. She feared to even call forth her sword.

"Don't fear the crystals," Kharra said in between breaths. She must have picked up on Aria's thoughts. "They weren't the enemy." The young woman looked drained and likely would not be able to run much farther.

"I may lose control again."

"You won't. I found and removed the taint and what Lukav used to control you. The problem was never the crystal itself."

Aria watched Kharra out of the corner of her eye as they ran, considering her words. Do not fear the crystals. Zephyron had said something similar. A pang of guilt washed over her, but she pushed it aside. With a deep breath, Aria searched within herself for the power of her crystal. Her crystal sang to her heart immediately. If it had arms, Aria would say it embraced her with childlike fervor. Beneath her crystal's song was the song of the shard within the complex. The problem had never been the crystal. Aria opened herself up to the shard, allowing its sweet warmth to flow into her.

Though Aria's speed increased tenfold, Kharra's did not. Aria called forth her sword and turned to fight. Not only did the krus-word manifest, but both her crystalline armor and the second sword reemerged. In seconds she was encased once again. Aria struggled with momentary panic.

You're okay, said Kharra with both mind seeking and empathy. The mental reassurance filled Aria with confidence.

Forcing down her panic, Aria realized she was in complete control this time. She stared down her pursuers, swords ready. Anything daring to move within range shattered against her blades. Kharra, now free from the collar, attacked with her mind moving, throwing shard beasts into one another.

Pull them back, Kharra projected to her mind as she scooted backward through the next room and into the tunnel beyond.

Aria edged her way back, her whirling blades not allowing any of the creatures within more than an arm's length. The krumetuses launched a series of deadly spines. What Aria did not deflect, Kharra redirected, in some cases, right back at the creature that had launched it. A couple spines managed to find a hole. One of them struck Aria's crystalline right arm. She smiled when it bounced off harmlessly.

Aria caught sight of the priests moving in behind the shard beasts, each of their bracelets glowing. Their control over the shard beasts had limits, both in the quantity of beasts and the distance at which they could manipulate them.

Hold here, said Kharra.

Aria spun her two blades about in tight circles, not giving the beasts any room to attack. Crystal fragments piled up at her feet, and shimmering dust filled the air. The ground beneath Aria's feet rumbled.

Aria glanced at Kharra. The woman's brow wrinkled in concentration, and her breathing was labored. Her lips parted in a snarl of strain. Her nostrils flared. The entire tunnel shook violently. Aria put a hand against a wall to keep from falling over. Moments later crystalline stalactites and large chunks of rock fell from the ceiling. The priests screamed. Shard beasts hissed and growled. The ones that were not crushed turned on those of other species.

Aria finished off the few that had been at the mouth of the tunnel with her and Kharra. "Let's get out of here," she said.

19

AN ANCIENT OATH

I t was the early hours of morning, the sun only beginning to light the sky, when Aria and Kharra finally escaped the mountain complex and located Xierex. The zegu stomped, snorted, and bobbed his head at their approach. They were both exhausted, but neither wanted to risk resting so close to such a dangerous place. Rested and ready, Xierex carried them throughout the day and well into the night before they stopped. Kharra said not a single word.

Aria recognized the terrain and directed Xierex toward a small cove tucked away in a mountainside; it was a site she had used in the past. Rocks and boulders surrounded the area, providing concealment and protection from the elements and predators alike. The moons hung high in the sky, bathing the world in silvery light.

Aria started a fire and set up their bedrolls. Shadows began to dance against the rocks surrounding them. Still, Kharra said nothing. She just sat on her bedroll and stared at the bobbing flames, her expression unreadable.

Unable to stand the silence any longer, Aria approached the younger woman and began, "Kharra…" Her words faltered. She had never been skilled at expressing emotion verbally. "I-I am so sorry. Zephyron was a good friend…"

At last, Kharra whispered, "'Good friend' does not even begin to describe what he meant not just to me but to the world. He has sacrificed and fought for over a century so people like you and me could live free."

Aria swallowed, struggling to maintain her composure. "He loved you more than life itself," she found herself saying.

Kharra glanced at her through watery eyes. The white around her began to wane, slowly being replaced by slashes of red. "I warned both of you to stay away, that it was a trap for you." Her voice was controlled, but the red Aria saw told of Kharra's anger. "You disregarded my warning, and now he is dead. And for what? We had a single but vitally important mission to fulfill. Not only did we not achieve our mission, but we got pulled into some local, petty political struggle for power."

Aria looked down at her hands. "You should have killed me back in the cavern."

Kharra closed her eyes, sighed, and shook her head. "That would have done nothing but cause more grief." She opened her eyes. They were so full of anguish Aria's heart immediately began to ache.

"Kharra, I can't bring him back, but I owe you a debt for bringing me back."

Kharra pulled her knees to her chest and began to cry. Aria moved to sit beside her. Inexperienced though she was with regard to emotional support, she did what only seemed natural. She wrapped Kharra in her arms and rocked her gently.

Then a thought occurred to Aria. "Let me in," she whispered.

At first there was no acknowledgment of the request. Maybe Kharra had not heard her or maybe she did not understand. Just before she asked again, a rush of emotions washed over her: anger, grief, sorrow, loss, despair, words left unsaid, potentials unreached, moments unshared, and a void unfilled.

Unsure if it would work, Aria reciprocated the sharing of emotions. She wanted Kharra to know the truth of her undying gratitude for the friendship she had gained from her and Zephyron. She wanted Kharra to know the depth of her sorrow for his loss. She wanted Kharra to know the seriousness of the debt she owed for having her life restored. She wanted Kharra to know how sorry she was to have been the cause of the entire situation. The red swirling about Kharra disappeared, and the white once again became the only color evident.

Aria pulled herself away from Kharra. Before she realized what she was doing, she called forth both of her swords. She planted the tips of either sword in the ground beside her and knelt before Kharra. With her head down, she whispered hoarsely, "Be loyal of word and deed, and serve Mattekan as best you may. Seek those of kindred spirit whose hearts are good and purpose true. I pledge to protect and guard the spirit of Mattekan—the Zumai, the People of the Spirit.

"Kharra il Marquin, I bond my swords and my life to you. I swear to you that I will do you no harm. I swear to you that I will promote the well-being of Mattekan. I swear to you that I will strike down those who seek to destroy it so that your hands know no blood. My swords sing with the resonance of the crystal and the heartbeat of this world."

Aria opened her eyes slowly. Kharra was standing, her mouth hanging open. She stared at Aria with a look of disbelief.

"Aria," she said in hushed tones, "how do you know my full name? And what you said, that was the oath of the Sauru swordsaints. How did you…" At a loss for words, Kharra's voice trailed off.

"Zephyron told me a little bit about your mother, including her name and your family's history. He told me of that oath as well."

Kharra nodded. She placed her hand on Aria's head. A tingling sensation rippled throughout Aria's body. This was the first time her body had reacted to Kharra's touch. "Aria Moonblade, or should I say, Aria du Tronalt?" Aria looked up at the use of her real name, something she was certain she had never mentioned to either Kharra or Zephyron. Kharra winked at her. "I have seen the nature of your heart, and I have witnessed you in battle. Responding to the wishes of Mattekan, I, Kharra il Marquin, am minded to accept the offer of your bond. From this day forward, you are known as Aria du Tronalt j'il Marquin."

Kharra removed her hand from Aria's forehead. "Zephyron taught me those words long ago as part of my history lessons. I never thought I would ever recite them."

Recalling her swords, Aria climbed to her feet. Even without physical contact, she continued to sense Kharra's presence within her mind. When she first spoke, she thought the bond was merely the words of an oath, pledged and obeyed, but she now understood that the bond linked them on a much deeper level. Aria sensed Kharra's continued pain, so intense that Aria wondered how the woman remained standing.

"Kharra, I know you can't forgive what I've done—" Aria began.

"I already have."

Aria blinked at her. Within their bond Aria sensed the truth. Despite all the pain, sorrow, and grief weighing heavily on Kharra's heart, she still maintained the capacity to both forgive and love. Aria was not certain she could have been so strong.

Kharra studied her for a moment. "A kruusta you are no longer. In fact I don't think you ever were one of them, not really. You were raised by the order, and you carry the shard and talents of their profession, but you are Sauru. That is why Zephyron taught you the oath. You already had within you the ability to call upon the crystal's power. You were just blocked, though I do not know how or why.

"The Order of the Shard, in an odd sort of way, serves the greater good of Mattekan. However, their ranks have been corrupted by the machinations of Oracle Lukav, and the shards are being drained and destroyed for reasons we still do not fully understand. I still have my mission to complete, but I also can't ignore what's being done here. I'm going to need your help with both, particularly in dealing with the order."

Aria agreed, and as the night wore on, the two women shared their thoughts of how to proceed. At last exhaustion from their physical and emotional ordeal took its toll, and they both retired for the evening. Aria stared up at the sky. Aery was the only moon still visible, the other two having set. Aria took comfort in its silvery-white light. So much had happened in the past few weeks, it was difficult to absorb. She had wanted to live and be free of the curse that had loomed over her head for so many years. Her wish had been answered, but it had come with a heavy price.

"Aria?" came a quiet voice.

"Yes?" she answered, still lost in her own thoughts.

"You were wrong about one thing in your line of thinking."

Aria propped herself up on her elbows. "What's that?" she asked.

"You feared Zephyron was in love with me. It's true we shared a deep bond, but it was not me he loved. It was you. He fell in love with you. It entered his heart the very first moment you two touched."

"But he said he loved you—"

"He loved me, surely, but while his love for me was great, it was the love that one has for a sister."

Stunned by the revelation, Aria did not breathe for several moments. Someone had actually loved her...and she had killed him. Aria wept quietly for the next few hours. At last her emotions settled, and her mind began to wander.

As her mind wandered, Aria sensed a distant call in the night. It was not a sound on the wind but a feeling, a sensation of knowledge whispering into her thoughts. It came from deep within the earth and from all directions at once. Aria frowned, not understanding the meaning of what she had absorbed. "Kharra?" she said softly.

"Yes?" came Kharra's sleepy voice.

"You understand powers of the mind, right?"

"I do, yes."

"I think I have been given a message. I think it is from the shards, but I'm uncertain of the meaning."

"What is it?" Kharra asked.

"It doesn't have words exactly, but it left an impression. It implied that something is sleeping."

Kharra sat bolt upright in her bedroll. "What did you say?" she asked eagerly.

"Something is sleeping? Do you know what that means?"

Though the dying embers gave off no light, Aery's moonlight gave off enough for Aria to see new tears forming in Kharra's eyes. For the first time since their escape, a truly happy smile sprang across her lips. Through their bond Aria sensed...hope.

EPILOGUE

Yron listened for danger and heard nothing for the moment. He was in a strange place deep within a mountain. His stomach hurt, but he had licked the wound enough to stop the bleeding. He sensed Earth Mother's call strongly in this place. She was upset and sad, both of which bothered him. He became upset as well. Soul Brother had fallen silent some time ago. That also made him upset. They had been companions for so long the silence pained him. How one could go for an entire life with such silence and isolation was beyond him.

More of those unnatural creatures paraded through the tunnels in front of him. They had been created by bringing pain to Earth Mother, by maiming and damaging her. Yron resisted the urge to rush out to them and tear their fragile limbs apart. They would shatter beneath his claws and teeth, but there were too many for him to handle alone. Soul Brother needed to be moved to safety, and a fight would risk Yron's ability to do that. Even with Earth Mother's help, Soul Brother barely hung to this side of life. It took a lot of his concentration to keep hold of Soul Brother.

Yron growled lowly as a small creature wandered away from its pack and over toward his location. With a powerful swat of his claw, the corruption crumbled and shattered. No others deviated from their group. Yron skirted up the tunnel, moving in the opposite direction of the vile corruptions.

Yron looked about, noticing how much of these caverns and tunnels resembled earth-home, though much smaller. The walls were made of rock in some places, but Earth Mother's lifeblood in others. Solidified shards of lifeblood hung from the ceiling and jutted out from the ground. This place was nothing like earth-home, he thought. Though Earth Mother's presence was just as powerful here as elsewhere, she seemed weaker, as if stricken by some sort of illness. He did not think it was possible for Earth Mother to become ill, but that was the sensation he felt.

Yron pressed on. One of the caverns had collapsed, and he paused to observe it. Several humans, the type who had no ability to sense Earth Mother, were working to dig away stone and debris. Were they responsible for her pain? They would crumble even faster than the vile corruptions stalking the tunnels if he chose to attack. No, he must get Soul Brother to safety. Yron dismissed the humans, doubled back, and searched for another exit.

Yron recalled how much he disliked being underground. He revered Earth Mother, but tunnels were not the best environment for his massive frame. He much preferred the openness of the forest and the expanse of the sky above. Confinement caused him to bristle.

A long time passed before Yron finally caught the scent of fresh air. He paused and sniffed several times to be sure. Moving faster but still cautiously, Yron followed the scent. At last he saw light ahead. He picked up his pace even more, wanting nothing more than to be free of this tainted place. Finally he emerged from the tunnel entrance, a place bordered with statues of skyguards and framed by lines so straight that they must have been cut by the hands of men. Odd that men such as these would know anything about skyguards. Brilliant light from the sun nearly blinded him. He blinked several times before the spots in his eyes cleared.

Man voices shouted out to him from above. Apparently this location was guarded. Yron wasted no time and sprinted away, down the mountainside and into the woods. Men, even those who commanded horses, would not be able to catch him. Still, he needed to put distance between him and them before he could stop. So Yron ran, elated at the sensation of being free from the caverns. He worried for Soul Brother's well-being, but he would find Spirit Sister. She would be able to make Soul Brother well again.

Distracted by his worry, Yron failed to recognize the signs of the trap in time to stop. He struggled unsuccessfully to grab hold of the edge of the pit before falling headlong into it. Fortunately the pit trap had no spikes. Still, Yron understood the workings of men. He had been captured once, long before he had encountered Soul Brother, and he had been forced to kill many men before breaking free. With him holding on to Soul Brother's life, he would not be able to fight as he had then.

The scent of the men arrived long before they did, and the snapping twigs above announced their arrival. Several faces peered down into the pit. The men wore earthen colors, greens and browns. Each wore a bow around his back and a long knife at his side. Yron growled at them.

"What in Tanoria is that?" one of the men asked.

"I don't know," another responded. "I've never seen anything like it."

A third man stared down at Yron, his eyes wide with disbelief. "I think it's a tigron," he whispered. The other two men looked at him, confusion clear on their faces. "It is a mythical creature, something I learned about as a child. I never thought they were real, but according to the myth, they are more powerful and more intelligent than any other animal. More powerful than a zegu even. It will kill us if we get near."

"Then let's make sure we don't get near," said the first man. The man held a long tube to his lips and shot something at Yron. The thing struck Yron's neck. The tigron roared at the man. The other two men held up tubes as well and copied the man's actions. Each man repeated the procedure two more times. At the end of the third time, Yron staggered and fell over. His only thought before the darkness overcame him was to hold on to Soul Brother as tightly as possible.

ACKNOWLEDGMENTS

Thank you, Lisa Krebs, for spending many selfless hours double-checking both my writing and my sanity as I pushed deep into Aria's world. You were quick to call shenanigans if something didn't feel quite right.

Katie, I truly appreciate you venturing into Tanoria and facing off against shard beasts.

Shaun, you dove into the deep end and came out the other side. Your sharp eye and keen insights proved invaluable.

Finally, to my husband, Darrin, and my daughter, Freya. These past couple of years have been difficult ones, but we've been able to face them together as a family. Thank you for allowing me to spend the extra time I needed to share this story with the world.

www.ingramcontent.com/pod-product-compliance
Lightning Source LLC
Chambersburg PA
CBHW020236180626
46810CB00006B/2219